IN THE

COMPANY

OF THE

COURTESAN

IN THE

COMPANY

OF THE

Courtesan

A Novel

SARAH
DUNANT

Random House
New York

Copyright © 2006 by Sarah Dunant

Published in the United States by Random House,
an imprint of The Random House Publishing Group,
a division of Random House, Inc., New York.

RANDOM HOUSE and colophon are registered
trademarks of Random House, Inc.

Map credit: Grande Pianta Prospettica—Venice, c. 1500
(engraving), Barbari, Jacopo de' (1440/50-1515)/Museo Correr,
Venice, Italy;/Bridgeman Art Library

ISBN: 978-0-7394-7189-0

A HISTORICAL NOTE

The history of Europe in the first half of the sixteenth century is one of political and religious upheaval. A corrupt Catholic Church, centered in Rome, found itself challenged by the emergence of Protestantism, which grew out of Martin Luther's rebellion in 1517 and spread rapidly through Germany and across northern Europe.

Italy was still a set of city-states, vulnerable to attack from within and threatened from without by foreign invasion, most notably by France and Spain, the latter under the rule of the Holy Roman Emperor Charles V.

The most powerful Italian cities were Rome and Venice. With Florence in decline, the art and culture of the High Renaissance had moved to Rome, under the patronage of the popes. Meanwhile Venice, situated on the mouth of the Adriatic, was still at the height of her success. A republic run by a large group of noble families, she enjoyed remarkable domestic political stability, a cosmopolitan population, control of the western Mediterranean, and a dazzlingly rich economy, built on foreign trade and commerce; Venice was a honeypot for merchants, travelers, and adventurers.

The story you are about to read begins in Rome in 1527.

PART I

CHAPTER ONE

Rome, 1527

My lady, Fiammetta Bianchini, was plucking her eyebrows and biting color into her lips when the unthinkable happened and the Holy Roman Emperor's army blew a hole in the wall of God's eternal city, letting in a flood of half-starved, half-crazed troops bent on pillage and punishment.

Italy was a living chessboard for the ambitions of half of Europe in those days. The threat of war was as regular as the harvest, alliances made in winter were broken by spring, and there were places where women bore another child by a different invading father every other year. In the great and glorious city of Rome, we had grown soft living under God's protection, but such was the instability of the times that even the holiest of fathers made unholy alliances, and a pope with Medici blood in his veins was always more prone to politics than to prayer.

In the last few days before the horror struck, Rome still couldn't bring herself to believe that her destruction was nigh. Rumors crept like bad smells through the streets. The stonemasons shoring up the city walls told of a mighty army of Spaniards, their savagery honed on the barbarians of the New World, swelled with cohorts of German Lutherans fueled on the juices of the nuns they had raped on their journey south. Yet when the Roman defense led by the nobleman Renzo de Ceri marched through the town touting for volunteers for the barricades, these same bloodthirsty giants became half-dead men marching on their knees, their assholes close to the ground to dispel all the rotting food and bad wine they had guzzled on the way. In this version, the enemy was so pathetic that even were the soldiers to find the strength to lift their guns, they had no artillery to help them, and with enough stalwart Romans on the battlements, we could drown them in our piss and mockery as they tried to scale their way upward. The joys of war always talk better than they play; still, the prospect of a battle won by urine and bravura was enticing enough to attract a few adventurers with nothing to lose, including our stable boy, who left the next afternoon.

Two days later, the army arrived at the gates and my lady sent me to get him back.

On the evening streets, our louche, loud city had closed up like a clam. Those with enough money had already bought their own private armies, leaving the rest to make do with locked doors and badly boarded windows. While my gait is small and bandied, I have always had a homing pigeon's sense of direction, and for all its twists and turns, Rome had long been mapped inside my head. My lady entertained a client once, a merchant captain who mistook my deformity for a sign of God's special grace and who promised me a fortune if I could find him a way to the Indies across the open sea. But I was born with a recurring nightmare of a great bird picking me up in its claws and dropping me into an empty ocean, and for that, and other reasons, I have always been afraid of water.

As the walls came into sight, I could see neither lookouts nor sentries. Until now we had never had need of such things, our rambling fortifications being more for the delight of antiquarians than for generals. I clambered up by way of one of the side towers, my thighs thrumming from the deep tread of the steps, and stood for a moment catching my breath. Along the stone corridor of the battlement, two figures were slouched down against the wall. Above me, above them, I could make out a low wave of moaning, like the murmur of a congregation at litany in church. In that moment my need to know became greater than my terror of finding out, and I hauled myself up over uneven and broken stones as best I could until I had a glimpse above the top.

Below me, as far as the eye could see, a great plain of darkness stretched out, spiked by hundreds of flickering candles. The moaning rolled like a slow wind through the night, the sound of an army joined in prayer or talking to itself in its sleep. Until then I think even I had colluded in the myth of our invincibility. Now I knew how the Trojans must have felt as they looked down from their walls and saw the Greeks camped before them, the promise of revenge glinting off their polished shields in the moonlight. Fear spiked my gut as I scrambled back down onto the battlement, and in a fury I went to kick the sleeping sentries awake. Close to, their hoods became cowls, and I made out two young monks, barely old enough to tie their own tassels, their faces pasty and drawn. I drew myself to my full height and squared up to the first, pushing my face into his. He opened his eyes and yelled, thinking that the enemy had sent a fatheaded, smiling devil out of Hell for him early. His panic roused his companion. I put my fingers to my lips and grinned again. This time they both squealed. I've had my fair share of pleasure from scaring clerics, but at that moment I wished that they had more courage to resist me. A hungry Lutheran would have had them split on his bayonet before they might say *Dominus vobiscum*. They crossed themselves frantically and, when I questioned them, waved me on toward the gate at San Spirito, where, they said, the defense was stronger. The only strategy I have perfected in life is one to keep my belly full, but even I knew that San Spirito was where the city was at its most vulnerable, with Cardinal Armellini's vineyards reaching to the battlements and a farmhouse built up and into the very stones of the wall itself.

Our army, such as it was when I found it, was huddled in clumps around the building. A couple of makeshift sentries tried to stop me, but I told them I was there to join the fight, and they laughed so hard they let me through, one of them aiding me along with a kick that missed my rear by a mile. In the camp, half the men were stupid with terror, the other half stupid with drink. I never did find the stable boy, but what I saw instead convinced me that a single breach here and Rome would open up as easily as a wife's legs to her handsome neighbor.

Back home, I found my mistress awake in her bedroom, and I told her all I had seen. She listened carefully, as she always did. We talked for a while, and then, as the night folded around us, we fell silent, our minds slipping away from our present life, filled with the warmth of wealth and security, toward the horrors of a future that we could barely imagine.

By the time the attack came, at first light, we were already at work. I had roused the servants before dawn, and my lady had instructed them to lay the great table in the gold room, giving orders to the cook to slaughter the fattest of the pigs and start preparing a banquet the likes of which were usually reserved for cardinals or bankers. While there were mutterings of dissent, such was her authority—or possibly their desperation—that any plan seemed comforting at the moment, even one that appeared to make no sense.

The house had already been stripped of its more ostentatious wealth: the great agate vases, the silver plates, the majolica dishes, the gilded crystal Murano drinking glasses, and the best linens had all been stowed away three or four days before, wrapped first inside the embroidered silk hangings, then the heavy Flemish tapestries, and packed into two chests. The smaller one was so ornate with gilt and wood marquetry that it had to be covered again with burlap to save it from the damp. It had taken the cook, the stable boy, and both of the twins to drag the chests into the yard, where a great hole had been dug under the flagstones close to the servants' latrines. When they were buried and covered with a blanket of fresh feces (fear is an excellent loosener of the bowels), we let out the five pigs, bought at a greatly inflated price a few days earlier, and they rolled and kicked their way around, grunting their delight as only pigs can do in shit.

With all trace of the valuables gone, my lady had taken her great necklace—the one she had worn to the party at the

Strozzi house, where the rooms had been lit by skeletons with candles in their ribs and the wine, many swore afterward, had been as rich and thick as blood—and to every servant she had given two fat pearls. The remaining ones she told them were theirs for the dividing if the chests were found unopened when the worst was over. Loyalty is a commodity that grows more expensive when times get bloody, and as an employer Fiammetta Bianchini was as much loved as she was feared, and in this way she cleverly pitted each man as much against himself as against her. As to where she had hidden the rest of her jewelry, well, that she did not reveal.

What remained after this was done was a modest house of modest wealth with a smattering of ornaments, two lutes, a pious Madonna in the bedroom, and a wood panel of fleshy nymphs in the salon, decoration sufficient to the fact of her dubious profession but without the stench of excess many of our neighbors' palazzi emitted. Indeed, a few hours later, as a great cry went up and the church bells began to chime, each one coming fast on the other, telling us that our defenses had been penetrated, the only aroma from our house was that of slow-roasting pig, growing succulent in its own juices.

Those who lived to tell the tale spoke with a kind of awe of that first breach of the walls; of how, as the fighting got fiercer with the day, a fog had crept up from the marshes behind the enemy lines, thick and gloomy as broth, enveloping the massing attackers below so that our defense force couldn't fire down on them accurately until, like an army of ghosts roaring out of the mist, they were already upon us. After that, whatever courage we might have found was no match for the numbers they could launch. To lessen our shame, we did take one prize off them, when a shot from an arquebus blew a hole the size of the Eucharist in the chest of their leader, the great Charles de Bourbon. Later, the goldsmith Benvenuto Cellini boasted to anyone who would listen of his miraculous aim. But then, Cellini boasted of everything. To hear him speak—as he never stopped doing, from the houses of nobles to the taverns in the slums—you would have thought the defense of the city was down to him alone. In which case it is him we should blame, for with no leader, the enemy now had nothing to stop their madness. From that first opening, they flowed up and over into the city like a great wave of cockroaches. Had the bridges across the Tiber been destroyed, as the head of the defense force, de Ceri, had advised, we might have trapped them in the Trastevere and held them off for long enough to regroup into some kind of fighting force. But Rome had chosen comfort over common sense, and with the Ponte Sisto taken early, there was nothing to stop them.

And thus, on the sixth day of the month of May in the year of our Lord 1527, did the second sack of Rome begin.

What couldn't be ransomed or carried was slaughtered or destroyed. It is commonly said now that it was the Lutheran *lansquenets* troops who did the worst. While the Holy Roman Emperor, Charles V, might be God's sworn defender, he wasn't above using the swords of heretics to swell his army and terrify his enemies. For them Rome was sweet pickings, the very home of the Antichrist, and as mercenaries whom the emperor had conveniently forgotten to pay, they were as much in a frenzy to line their pockets as they were to shine their souls. Every church was a cesspool of corruption, every nunnery the repository for whores of Christ, every orphan skewered on a bayonet (their bodies too small to waste their shot on) a soul saved from heresy. But while all that may be true, I should say that I also heard as many Spanish as German oaths mixed in with the screaming, and I wager that when the carts and the mules finally rode out of Rome, laden with gold plate and tapestries, as much of it was heading for Spain as for Germany.

Had they moved faster and stolen less in that first attack, they might have captured the greatest prize of all: the Holy Father himself. But by the time they reached the Vatican palace, Pope Clement VII had lifted up his skirts (to find, no doubt, a brace of cardinals squeezed beneath his fat stomach) and, along with a dozen sacks hastily stuffed with jewels and holy relics, run as if he had the Devil on his heels to the Castel Sant' Angelo, the drawbridge rising up after him with the invaders in sight and a dozen priests and courtiers still hanging from its chains, until they had to shake them off and watch them drown in the moat below.

With death so close, those still living fell into a panic over the state of their souls. Some clerics, seeing the hour of their own judgment before them, gave confessions and indulgences for free, but there were others who made small fortunes selling forgiveness at exorbitant rates. Perhaps God was watching as they worked: certainly when the Lutherans found them, huddled like rats in the darkest corners of the churches, their bulging robes clutched around them, the wrath visited upon them was all the more righteous, as they were disemboweled, first for their wealth and then for their guts.

Meanwhile, in our house, as the clamor of violence grew in the distance, we were busy polishing the forks and wiping clean the second-best glasses. In her bedroom, my lady, who had been scrupulous as ever in the business of her beauty, put the finishing touches to her toilette, and came downstairs. The view from her bedroom window now showed the occasional figure skidding and hurtling through the streets, his head twisting backward as he ran, as if fearful of the wave that was to overwhelm him. It would not be long before the screams got close enough for us to distinguish individual agonies. It was time to rally our own defense force.

I had called the servants together in the dining room as she entered. How she looked I shall save for later: they were all familiar enough with the power of her appearance and at that moment were more interested in saving their own skins than in standing in awe of hers. She took in the scene with a single glance. To her left Adriana, her maid, was crouching, her arms wrapped around herself so tightly it looked as if she could no longer breathe. Baldesar, the cook, was in the doorway, his face and upper arms shining with sweat and grease from the spit, while at the end of the newly laid table, the slender twin house-boys were standing, each with a glass goblet in his right hand, the only discernible difference in their appearance being the level of trembling.

"If you cannot hold it properly, put the goblet down, Zac-cano." My lady's voice was strong and low. "Our visitors will not thank you for finding their places over shards of glass."

Zaccano gave a moan as his fingers loosened around the stem, letting the glass fall into the open left hand of Giacomo, who, as always, seemed to know what his brother would do be-fore he did it.

"Bravo, Giacomo. You will be the one to serve the wine."

"My lady—"

"Baldesar?" she said, barely turning to look at him.

"There are three guns in the cellars. And the kitchen has a drawer full of knives." He wiped his hands on his trousers. "If we take one each—"

"If you take one each, tell me, please—how will you carve the pig?" And now she turned and looked him in the eye.

He held her gaze. "If you'll excuse me, madam, this is mad-ness. Don't you hear what's happening out there? We're the pigs now. They're skewering us like so many cuts of meat."

"I daresay they are. But despite their gross lack of manners, I doubt even they have the temerity to assuage their hunger by roasting and eating us after they have killed us."

To her side, Adriana let out a long wail and sank to the floor. I made a move toward her, but Fiammetta stopped me with a glance.

"Get up, Adriana," she said sharply. "It is well known that when a woman is on the ground, it is a good deal easier to lift her skirts. So get up. *Now.*"

Adriana rose, the whimpering caught in her throat. The room vibrated with her anxiety.

Fiammetta turned on her heel, and I watched the fury col-lide with the fear. "What is wrong with you all?" She slapped her hands on the table, hard enough to make the cutlery rattle. "Think about it. They cannot massacre every single one of us.

Those who live will save their skins by cunning as much as by any set of blunt kitchen knives—for which, you should know, I excuse you, Baldesar, because your sauces make up for the butchery of your cuts.

"When they get here, I daresay there will be those who are still hungry for cunt and bloodshed, but there will also be others who have had enough. Hell roasts even its own devils, and it can make you sick as well as mad, this killing frenzy. So we are going to save them from themselves. We are going to open our house to them; to offer them comfort and hospitality, an art in which we are well practiced. And in return, though they will take—indeed, we will offer them—the cutlery, the glasses, the rugs, the trinkets, and anything else they can rip from the walls, if we are lucky, they will leave us our lives. Not least because when you have been on the road for years, a house to come home to can be a great solace as well as a safe place to store your booty, and the only thing better than a good whore is a good cook. And this house, I would remind you, has both."

In the silence that followed, I could almost hear the applause of another audience: one of clerics, bankers, or scholars, powerful men who, having eaten and drunk their fill, revel in the art of debate with a beautiful woman, especially when the elegant is spiced with the crude—a talent in which my lady excelled. But there was no one applauding now. Did they believe her? She had sounded convincing enough to me. It didn't matter. As long as they stayed. Still no one moved.

She took a breath. "So—for those who want it—there is the door."

She waited.

Finally the cook turned, growling. "I'm on my own in there. If you want good cooking, I need the girl to help."

"She's not ready. You'll have to do with one of the boys. Zaccano. Don't fret. You will not be separated for long. Giacomo, you get the tapers ready. I want the candles in all the holders for when dusk comes. You, Adriana, get to avail yourself of the finest cloth. Take the blue dress with the high neck from my chest and a pair of satin slippers to match. Use a little rouge on your face—but only a little. You are aiming for sweetness, not seduction. And don't take all day about it."

The girl, caught now between joy and terror, made for the stairs. As the room cleared, Fiammetta sat down at the head of the table. Now, with the light on her face, I could see a fine sweat on her skin.

"It was well done," I said quietly. "No one will leave now."

She shrugged and closed her eyes. "Then they will probably die here."

We sat for a moment listening. The noise level outside was rising. Soon those few lost souls would be a rush of madmen.

The doubt was there anyway. I simply gave it voice. "Can we do this?"

She shook her head. "Who knows? If they are as starved and weary as the rumors say, then maybe we stand a chance. Let's pray for Spaniards. I've never yet met one who didn't savor the juices of life over the piety of death. If it's the Lutherans, then we would do better to hold on to our rosaries and hope for martyrdom. But I'll take a stomach full of jewels with me first."

"Then what? Shit them out in Hell and bribe the guards?"

Her laughter flared up like a small flame of hope. "You forget I am a cardinal's courtesan, Bucino. I've got enough indulgences to see me at least as far as Purgatory."

"And where does that leave the cardinal's courtesan's dwarf?"

"Small enough to be concealed under a penitent's shirt," she said, and as she did so a single voice rose up from the clamor for an instant with a few mangled but recognizable words: "*Casas de la gente nobile . . . Estamos aquí.*"

The enemy, it seemed, had arrived. If grace belongs to God, there are those who say that luck belongs to the Devil and that he looks after his own. All I know is Rome was a playground for destiny that day, and when they came to pile the bodies into the pits, there were as many innocent souls slaughtered as there were guilty ones who survived. About our status, I leave it to others to make up their minds.

My lady stood up and smoothed her skirts, a finely dressed woman rising to meet her guests. "Let's hope their captain isn't far behind. I wouldn't like to waste my best gold brocade on a rabble of soldiers. You'd better check Adriana. If she looks like someone's daughter, she might survive longer than a servant. Though too obvious a virgin will undo us also."

I moved toward the stairs.

"Bucino."

I turned.

"Can you still remember how to juggle?"

"You learn something early enough, you never forget it," I said. "What would you have me play with?"

She smiled. "How about our lives?"

It took longer than we thought for them to get to us. But then rape and pillage is a time-consuming business, and there were so many and so much to get through. It was almost dusk when I stood up on the roof watching them flood into the street below. They took the corner howling, nine or ten of them in front, their swords out and their clothes half off them, mouths open like black pits, bodies jerky and wild, as if they were puppets strung up by the Devil and dancing to his tune. Behind them came a dozen or so more, dragging a cart piled high, and some way behind them there was a man on horseback, though if he was their captain, he was clearly no longer leading from the front.

As they reached our piazza, they stopped for a moment. The city was filled with rich houses, all with locked doors and shuttered windows. A couple of the men were swaying on their feet. Rome had better wine than the sad countryside they had ravaged, and they must have downed barrels of it by now. A big man from behind let out a roar and grabbed an ax off the cart, lifting his arms high in the air and staggering a little as he ran before smashing the ax down on the window frame of the spice merchant's house on the corner. You could hear the crack echo through the building and then the fluttering screams it evoked from inside. The sound drew the rest like moths to a flame. It took maybe a dozen of them ten minutes to smash their way in.

Behind them, others were eyeing the rest of the square. The officer was almost off his horse as I moved from the roof to call down to my lady. But the courtyard below was already empty, and I got back to the edge in time to hear the main doors unlock beneath me and watch her move out into the twilight of the square.

What did they see as the doors swung open to reveal her? By this time in her life, Fiammetta Bianchini had received more than her fair share of compliments, many of them substantial enough to be buried away in grand chests under a heap of dung. But for now we will keep it simple, like the men she faced. She stood tall, in the way only rich women can do, used as they are to riding with their heads above the crowd, and she was beautiful. Her skin was smooth and pale as alabaster, and her breasts pushed up from her gold-threaded bodice in a way that revealed as much as it concealed: the perfect modest seduction in a city of rich celibates who needed to pretend virtue even when they walked the streets with their cocks up like flagpoles underneath their clerics' robes.

Her eyes were green as new growth, her lips full and red, and her cheeks had a dusting of peach blush to them. But it was her hair that set her apart. Because my lady had hair like a golden river in spring flood, its hues as rich as the rush of the waters; streams of white gold and sunflower mixed with honey and red chestnut, so strange and yet so natural that it was clearly God's gift rather than that of any apothecary's bottles. And because she had no ring on her finger or husband in her house, when she entertained she wore it long and rippling free, so that on an evening when the mood took her and she flung back her head in laughter or pretended pique, this rich curtain of hair flew with her, and if you were close by, you might swear that the sun had come out for you alone.

So, yes, those club-limbed peasants reeking of death and booze were stopped in their tracks when she appeared. Rome was a city filled with lovely women then, many grown lovelier on its easy virtue, and each and any one of them would have been like a cool draft to men dying of thirst. But few had my lady's wit, which was sharper than a toothpick, or her cunning when presented with a fight.

"Good evening, soldiers of Spain. You have come a long way, and you are welcome to our great city." Her voice was strong and her vocabulary honed on a generous handful of Spanish merchants and itinerant clerics. A good courtesan can seduce in many languages, and Rome had trained the best of them. "Where is your captain?"

The man on horseback across the square was turning, but there were others nearer. Now that her voice had broken the spell, they started to move toward her, one ahead of the others, grinning and holding out his arms in jubilant supplication, the knife an added attraction to his charms.

"I am the captain," he said in a thick voice, while behind him the men whooped and snorted. "And you must be the pope's whore."

He was almost upon her now. She didn't move, simply drew herself up a little higher, until she had maybe two inches on him. "The whores, sir, you have already had. This is the house of Fiammetta Bianchini. It offers food and lodging for men who have not yet tasted true Roman hospitality."

He grunted, staring at her, as if the words befuddled him. Behind him three more moved forward, smelling the kill. The captain was off his horse now, pushing his way through the knot of men who had gathered. Next to me on the roof, Zaccano's hands were starting to shake so much that I began to worry about the gun in his grasp. You would be hard-pressed to find two brothers in Rome more beautiful, but such was the synchronicity of Giacomo's and Zaccano's twinned characters that it was always a danger to separate them. Without the stable boy, though, we had no choice.

Another soldier, his face black from the soot of spent shot, shoved his companion aside and marched up to my lady, closer this time. His hand moved toward her body. She stood stock-still until it came within an inch of her breast, then, with the speed of an evening swallow, she swooped her right hand up and cracked his aside. His yelp was as much of indignation as of pain.

"I am sorry, sir," she said, and quick as an ink stain, her left hand had pulled out a silk embroidered handkerchief, which she held out to him. "Your hands are dirty. After you have washed, I will be happy to make your acquaintance. Please—keep the cloth."

He took it, and after he had briefly wiped himself, he turned on her again. But whether to give it back or to add something to it I never found out, because that was the moment when my hand slipped and Zaccano misread my panicky nudge as the sign for action. The shot rang out mercifully far above their heads. Their eyes swiveled upward. Along the line of the roof, three guns and half a dozen broomstick handles fashioned crudely to resemble gun barrels sat trained down onto the street. With the smoke of the shot still in the air, the house might even have looked defended. We have since disagreed about that moment, she and I. I say that while she had not yet lost the game, the shot gave them good pause for thought. She is of the opinion that she could have won them over without it. As it was, the hesitation lasted long enough for the captain to get himself to the front.

He was as tall as she but skinny; even his face was more bone than flesh, and though, after he cleaned up, he lost ten years off his age, the look in the eyes never got any softer. Killing is a grown-up business, even when the young do it. A crude city map was pushed into his belt. To judge from the size of the cart, it had made them better treasure seekers than those working on blind frenzy. He and his men already had more than enough booty to make them rich, but his status and his strategies would give him the pick of the most precious things. And one of those was now standing in front of him.

"My lord," she said, smiling. "Please forgive my servants. They are overzealous in the protection of their mistress. I am the lady Fiammetta Bianchini, and it is my pleasure to invite you and your men to a feast in my house. Bucino!" And while her voice lifted up to me, her eyes never strayed from the captain's face. "You hear me? We are among friends and have no need of weapons now. Throw them down from the roof and get yourselves back to the kitchen."

We did as we were told. Three old guns and six broomsticks hit the stone below, the soldiers yelping in delight at our pathetic subterfuge.

"Gentlemen. We can offer you suckling pig with truffle sauce, roast capon, salted pike, and the choice of finest salamis—you would not believe their size. . . ."

Their laughter turned to whoops of delight, and my lady laughed with them, though not enough to take her concentration off the prey in front of her. "Followed by marzipan, milk puddings, and sugared fruits, along with the best of our cellar. We have the highest-quality beeswax candles with scented oils, entertainment with sweet lute music such as the Holy Father himself delights in, and once you have eaten and drunk your fill, you can fall asleep on clean linen over fresh straw in the rooms and stables below. While for you, Captain"—and here she paused for just a second—"there is a carved bed and a goose-feather mattress soft as a cloud. Our house is yours for as long as you care to stay. When you leave, you may take your pick of whatever riches it possesses. All we ask is that you give us your protection from those who may follow."

I daresay that if he was well born, he might have come across her like before. Or maybe he had lived on dreams till then. Well, she was real enough now. Each and every one of the men was watching him. While it is possible he might have done less killing than some of them—the ones who give the orders also yield something of the risk—he was clever enough to have earned their attention. And for now, at least, their obedience. Though that might have had as much to do with the smell of roasting pig flesh, which was rolling in waves through the open doors out into the square. I swear, even from the roof I could spot the drool on their lips.

He nodded, then glanced around him and grinned. "Roman hospitality! What did I tell you about it?" He yelled, and the roar rose up around him. "Put the cart into the courtyard and sheath your weapons. Tonight we sleep on soft beds with the lady Bianchini as our host. Let's show her how Spanish manners can match Roman wealth."

Then he turned back to her and held out his hand. And,

though it was no less bloody and stained than that of the man before, she laid her own gently within it and bowed.

As for me, well, I went back to juggling. In lieu of balls, after our guests had stuffed themselves stupid, I took half a dozen of my lady's pricked copper pomades and spun them through the air in the candlelight, though their musk perfume offered scant relief against so many gaping mouths belching bad breath. Drunken men can be a dwarf's worst enemies, for their curiosity turns easily to violence, but these had had their fill of blood, for a while at least, and wanted only to be entertained. So they yelled and applauded my skills and grinned at my devil faces and guffawed as I waddled around the room with a napkin the shape of the papal crown on my head, blessing everyone who approached to touch my robes, each of them by now too drunk and raucous to know what else he might be missing. So it was that Adriana kept her virginity, the cook his kitchen knives, and our mistress her pearl necklace and her best Murano glasses. For that evening at least.

Not everyone survived, though. Before the night was out, the bloodlust returned and two men had skewered each other over the dining table. Ours was a house that had seen cardinals and diplomats gamble away the tribute of a small town over which of them should share my lady's bed that night, but no one before had died from pique over who should drink from the wineglass and who from the silver goblet. Within seconds one had his fingers around the other's throat, while his adversary was flailing at him with a knife. By the time the captain got down from the bedchamber, his clothes half on and his sword unsheathed, it was already over and both of them were on the floor pumping blood into puddles of red wine. They were so drunk that if it had been sleep rather than death, I daresay neither of them would have remembered it in the morning. We rolled them up in old sheets and bumped them down the stairs to the coolest part of the cellar. Above, the party continued unabated.

Eventually, excess exhausted them. In the yard, even the pigs slept, their great carcasses rolling and snorting over our hidden riches. The smell in the house was much the same. The place reeked of belches and urine, each room filled with heaving, snoring men, some in blankets, some on straw, some lying where they had fallen. At least they were loyal enemies now. Our doors were locked and bolted, with the posted sentries semicomatose, empty flagons by their sides. In the kitchen, the cook was asleep under the sink, while Adriana and the twins were inside the larder, the temptation of their various beauties locked out of harm's way for the night, and I was sitting on the table, picking scraps off pig bones and teaching Spanish swear-words to my lady's parrot, whom, though he would never thank me for it, I had saved from roasting earlier that evening. Outside, the sounds of the city were a ragged chorus from Hell: distant blasts of gunshot mixed in with staccato yelps and howls.

Somewhere in the dead of the night, the horror got closer when a man in one of the neighboring houses started screaming: a single, protracted screech of agony followed by moaning and shouting, then another scream, and another, as if someone was chopping off his limbs one by one. Those who keep their houses locked have something to save apart from their skins. Where does a rich merchant hide his coins or his wife her jewels? How many cuts do you have to suffer before you tell them where to look? What point to jeweled rings when you have no fingers left to wear them on?

The banging came at the side door at the same instant.

"Bucino? Adriana? Open up! For God's sake . . ." A rasping voice, then a more rasping cough.

One of the guards growled, then snored on. I opened the door, and Ascanio fell into my arms, his chest catching for breath and his face shiny with sweat. I helped him to the bench, and he gulped down some watered wine, the liquid slopping out of the cup with his trembling. "My God, Bucino," he said, taking in the chaos of the kitchen. "What happened here?"

"We are occupied," I said lightly, cutting him off a bit of left-over meat. "And have been entertaining the enemy."

"Fiammetta?"

"Is upstairs with a captain of the Spanish guard. She used her charms to buy his protection."

Ascanio laughed, but it rolled back into his lungs, and for a moment he couldn't speak for coughing. "Do you think when Death comes she'll offer to fuck it first?" Like every man in Rome, Ascanio had a longing for my mistress. He was assistant to the city's greatest printer-engraver, Marcantonio Raimondi, a man of stature enough to be an occasional visitor to my lady's soirees, and like his master, Ascanio knew the ways of the world. How many evenings had the two of us sat together while the powerful went to bed with the beautiful and we drank their leftovers, talking scandal and politics long into the night? While Rome was now being punished for its worldliness and deca-dence, it had also been a place of wonder and vibrancy to those with the talent or the wit to join. Though not anymore . . .

"How far have you come?"

"From Gianbattista Rosa's studio. The Lutheran devils have taken everything. I barely got out alive. I've been running all the way with my belly close to the ground. I know how you see the world now."

He started to cough again. I refilled his glass and held it up to him. He had come from the country originally, with a fast brain and deft fingers for setting the letters into the press, and like me, his dexterity had got him further in life than he could have expected. His master's books were in the libraries of Rome's greatest scholars, and the workshop engraved the art of men whom the pope himself employed to beautify his sacred ceilings and walls. But the same press also inked satire and gos-sip sheets for Pasquino's statue in Piazza Navona, and a few years before, a certain set of engravings had proved too carnal even for His Unholiness's steady gaze, and Ascanio and his master had tasted the hospitality of a Roman jail, which had left them both with weak chests. There was a joke that they now mixed the ink for the paler washes with their own phlegm. But it was meant well enough. In the end they earned their living by spreading the news rather than by making it, and thus they were neither wealthy nor powerful enough to be anybody's enemies for long.

"Sweet Jesus, have you seen what's happening out there? It's a charnel house. The city is blazing halfway to the walls. Bloody barbarians. They took everything Gianbattista had, and then they set fire to his paintings. The last I saw him he was being whipped on like a mule to carry his own riches onto their carts. Ah! God damn it!" Under the draining board, the cook gave a grunt and knocked a wooden spoon across the floor, and Ascanio jumped like a fish out of water. "I tell you, Bucino, we're all going to die. You know what they're saying on the streets?"

"That this is God's judgment upon us for our sins?"

He nodded. "Those stinking German heretics are reciting the fall of Sodom and Gomorrah as they smash the altars and ransack the churches. I tell you, I keep seeing that madman hanging off the statue of St. Paul and ranting about the pope."

" 'Behold the bastard of Sodom. For your sins will Rome be destroyed,' " I said, rolling my voice down into my chest. It had been the talk of the season: how the wild man with flaming red hair and a naked, stringy body had come out of the country, climbed up onto St. Paul's stone shoulders with a skull in one hand and a crucifix in the other, damning the pope for his evil ways and foretelling the sack of the city within fourteen days. Prophecy may be a divine art, but it is an imprecise one: two months later he was still in prison. "What? You really think that if Rome had changed her ways, this wouldn't be happening? You should read more of your own gossip sheets, Ascanio. This place has been rank for decades. Pope Clement's sins are no worse than those of a dozen holy embezzlers who came before him. This isn't bad faith we're suffering from but bad politics. This emperor doesn't brook challenge from anyone, and any pope who took him on—especially a Medici one—always risked getting his balls squeezed."

He sniggered at my words and took another gulp of wine. The screaming began once more. The merchant again? Or maybe the banker this time? Or the fat notary, whose house was even bigger than his paunch and who earned his living creaming off cuts from the bribes he processed into the papal coffers. On the street, he had a voice like a gelded goat, but when it comes to agony, one man's screams sound much like another's.

Ascanio shivered. "What do you have that's so precious you wouldn't give it up, Bucino?"

"Nothing but my balls," I said, and I tossed two of my lady's pomades high into the air.

"Always the smart answer, eh? No wonder she loves you. You may be an ugly little sot, but I know a dozen men in Rome who'd swap their fortunes for yours, even now. You're a lucky fellow."

"The luck of the damned," I said. Strange how, now we were so close to death, the truth seemed to tumble out so easily. "Ever since my mother first looked at me and fainted in horror." And I grinned.

He stared at me for a moment, then shook his head. "I don't know what to make of you, Bucino. For all your twisted limbs and fat head, you're an arrogant little bastard. Do you know what Aretino used to say about you? That your very existence was a challenge to Rome, because your ugliness was more true than all of its beauty. I wonder what he'd make of all this, eh? He knew it would happen too, you know. He said as much when he blasted the pope in his last *prognostico*."

"Just as well he isn't here then. Or both sides would have set fire to his pen by now."

Ascanio didn't say anything, just slid his head down on the table as if it was all too much for him. There was a time when you would have found him hunched over the machines late into the night, running off newly printed gossip sheets to keep the city informed of its own bowel movements. He had liked being on the edge of it all then; I daresay it made him feel like he owned a slice of it. But the rankness of a prison cell had drained his spirit and pumped bitterness into his veins. He gave a groan and started up. "I have to go." But he was still trembling.

"You could stay here, for a while at least."

"No, no, I can't. . . . I—I have to get out."

"You going back to the press?"

"I—I don't know." He was up and moving around now, the energy of nerves, twitchy and jumpy, eyes everywhere at once. Outside, our neighbor's screams had turned to wild, sporadic moaning. "You know what I'm going to do as soon as this is over? Get my stinking carcass out of here. Set up somewhere on my own. Taste the good life for myself."

But the good life was seeping away all around us. His eyes darted around the room again. "You should come with me, Bucino. You can do accounting in your head, and those juggler's fingers would be good with the typesetting. Think about it. Even if you make it through this, the best whores last only a few years. This way I could see us both right. I've got money, and with your knowledge of the backstreets, I bet you could find us a way out of here safely tonight."

There came a sound from inside the house. Someone was up and moving. Ascanio was at the door before I could answer. He was sweating again, and his breathing was rough. I went with him to the main entrance, and, because he had been a friend of sorts, I told him a back way through to near the gate of San Spirito, where yesterday there had been a city wall but now there would be a gaping hole. If he made it that far, he might stand a chance.

Outside, in the darkness, the square was empty. "Good luck," I said.

He kept close to the wall, head down, and as he turned the corner, it struck me that I would never see him again.

As I came back into the kitchen, I noticed something lying on the floor under the table, something that must have fallen from beneath his jacket as he got up to leave. I slithered down and retrieved a fabric purse. Out of it slipped a small, scarlet, leather-bound book: Petrarch's sonnets, its perfect skin tooled with gold lettering and fixed with silver corners and an elaborate silver barrel lock with a set of numbers running across it. It was the stuff of a scholar's library and the kind of object that would have made any printer's reputation in a new city. I might have gone after him if I hadn't heard footsteps on the flagstones outside. As it was, I slipped the volume underneath my doublet the second before my lady arrived in the doorway.

She had a silk robe pulled around her, her hair tangled fiercely down her back and the skin around her mouth red and puffy from the scrape of the captain's stubble. But her eyes were bright enough. It is one of her great talents, to make it look as if her glass empties at the same rate as those around her, and so to remain clearheaded long after their lust has blended into the alcohol.

"I heard voices." She took in the debris of the kitchen. "Who was here?"

"Ascanio. On his way back from Gianbattista's studio. The painter is taken and his work destroyed."

"Oh! And Marcantonio and the press? What news of them?"

I shook my head.

"Ah me . . ." She moved to the table, sitting in his place and putting her hands palm-down on the table. She moved her head slowly to one side and the other, stretching her neck as if coming back to life after a long sleep. It is a gesture I know well, and there are times when the work is challenging or the night long and she likes me to climb up on the bench behind her and massage her shoulders. But not tonight. "Where's Adriana?"

I pointed to the cupboard. "Curled up with the twins. *Virgo intacta*, all of them. Though I can't guarantee for how long. How is our captain?"

"Sleeping in fits and starts, thrashing around as if he were still at war." She paused. I did not ask. I never do. Which is why, I think, she often tells me. "You should have seen him, Bucino—he was a Spaniard to his loins. So concerned with his reputation that his anxiety undermined him. Maybe he is grown sick of his own power. I think he was almost glad to have someone else taking charge after so long." She smiled a little, but there was no wit in it. The screams would have penetrated the shutters of the bedroom as easily as they had the kitchen. "But he is young underneath the grime, and I doubt we can trust to his protection for long. We must contact the cardinal. It's our only hope. Others will be fair-weather friends, but if he is still alive—and Charles's troops would have reason enough to be good to him, given how he has supported the emperor's cause in the Curia—I am sure he will help us."

We looked at each other over the table, both of us no doubt weighing our chances.

"In which case, I should go now," I said, because we both knew there was no one else. "If I move quickly, I might get back before the house is awake."

She looked away as if it was still a matter for debate, then slipped her hand beneath her robe and put her fist down on the table in front of me. Underneath her grasp lay half a dozen rubies and emeralds, their edges a little chipped from where she had prized them out of their settings.

"For the journey. Take them. They can be your own set of pearls."

The square was silent now, our neighbors either dead or more effectively gagged. Around me, Rome was caught between fire and dawn, part of the city glowing like hot coals in the dark while clouds of smoke billowed east toward a gauzy gray sky ripe with the promise of another perfect day for killing. I moved like Ascanio, close to the ground and the edges of the walls, before breaking into the main street. I passed a few corpses in the gutter, and once a voice yelled after me, but it was wayward and might have been a cry out of someone's nightmare. Farther down the street, a single figure came rolling toward me out of the gloom, moving as if in a daze and seeming not to see me. As he passed, I saw him clutching his shirt, with a bloodied mess of what might have been his own innards in his hand.

The cardinal's palazzo was off the Via Papalis, where the city gathers to gape at and applaud great church processions that pass through to the Vatican. The streets here are so fine you need to dress up even to walk along them. But the more the wealth, the greater the devastation and the heavier the stench of death. In the dawn light, there were bodies everywhere, some broken and still, others twitching or moaning quietly. A small knot of men were moving methodically through the carnage, poking around for leftover wealth like crows plucking out the eyes and the livers. They were too intent on their business to notice me. If Rome had been Rome and not a battlefield, I would have had to be more careful on the street. While I may be the size of a child, people still spot my rolling walk from a distance, and until they see the gold trim of my cloth—and even then, sometimes—they can tend to all kinds of cruel mischief. But that morning, in the chaos of war, I would have looked simply small, and therefore neither a promise nor a threat. Though I think that is not enough to explain why I didn't die. Because I saw enough children skewered and split into pieces as I went. And it was not because I had my wits about me either, for I stepped over the remains of all kinds of men, some of whom, from their clothing—or what was left of it—had had more status or wealth than I ever would, though little good it would do them now.

Later, when the stories from the night screamers who survived told of a hundred ways in which an enemy can squeeze gold out of seared and punctured flesh, it became clear that those who were butchered in that first attack were the lucky ones. But at the time it didn't feel like that. For every dead soul I passed, there was another barely living one, propped up against the wall staring at the stumps of his own legs or trying to push his guts back into his stomach.

Yet, strangely, it was not all awful. Or perhaps it was not all awful precisely because it was so strange. In places there was almost a sense of wild pageant to it. In the area closest to the Vatican, where the Germans now ruled, the streets were full of fancy dress. It was a wonder the invaders knew whom to fight anymore, so many of them were wearing their victims' clothes. I saw small men swamped by velvet and fur, their gun barrels high in the air laced with jeweled bracelets. But it was their wives and children who made the show. The women who follow mercenary armies are legendary, living as they do like cats in heat around the edges of the campfire. But these women were different. They were Lutherans, harpy heretics driven as much by God as by war, their children conceived and suckled on the road, thin and hard as their parents, their features blunt as woodcuts. On their stick bodies, the pearled gowns and velvet skirts fell like tents, the jeweled combs clung to limp hair, and swathes of priceless silk trains turned black in the blood and mud behind them. It was like watching an army of wraiths dancing their way out of Hell.

For the men, the church costumes were the greatest prize. I saw more than one "cardinal" rolling through the streets in fire-red robes, their hats on backward and great jugs of wine in their hands—though no one bothered dressing up in priests' robes, for even in chaos hierarchy rules and their cloth wasn't rich enough. Heretics may read the Devil in decoration, but they're as greedy as the next man when the gaudiness comes from real gold. There were no rich chalices or jeweled *monstranci* stamped into the mud that morning. Instead the sewers were clogged with smashed ceramics and wood: enough dismembered Madonnas and Jesus statues to keep the sculptors' guild at work for the next half century. Then there were the relics. Without belief, Saint Anthony's rib or Saint Catherine's finger is just another yellowed old bone, and that morning there were bits of saints littering the streets that pilgrims would have walked five hundred miles to kiss or pray to the day before. If they performed any miracles in the gutter, I never heard about it, though the Church would use that word soon enough to describe their recovery and the shrines would reopen as fast as any shops, so fast I swear that the next wave of gullible pilgrims would be shelling out their scudi to see what could as well have been a fishmonger's thighbone or a prostitute's digit.

Our cardinal's house was one of Rome's finest. My lady had been his favorite for years by this time, and he was as faithful to her as any marrying man might have been to his own wife. He was a clever man, an honored member of the pope's inner circle, as much a politician as a prelate, and right up until the last he had played his hand both ways, supporting the pope in his power games but also arguing the case of the emperor. His evenhandedness was well known, and in theory it should have saved his life. In theory . . .

There were two men with guns outside the entrance to his palazzo. I danced up to them, grinning and prancing like a man whose brain was as squashed as his body. One of them stared at me, poking me with a bayonet. I squealed in a way that always seems to delight men with weapons, and then I opened my mouth wide, stuck in two fingers, and brought out a small, glittering ruby, letting it lie in the palm of my hand. Then I asked if I could see the cardinal. First in pidgin German, then in Spanish. One of them answered in a vomit of words, then grabbed at me and forced my jaw open again, but what he saw there made him let me go fast enough. I repeated the exercise until there was another jewel sitting next to the first. Then I asked again. They took one each and let me inside.

From the main hall I could see deep into the courtyard beyond. A great pile of His Eminence's possessions were stacked up ready to go, though not all of them were deemed worthy. He was a cultured man, my lady's cardinal, with a gallery of precious artifacts whose value was their age as much as the weight of any precious metal. As I moved inside, I heard a cry from above and watched as a muscled, marble Hercules came hurtling down over the balustrade, his head and left arm undergoing instant amputation as he crashed onto the flagstones below. Halfway down the corridor, a man in a dirty shirt facing away from me was scrubbing the floor. He sat back, his gaze fixed on the decapitated head. The sentry went over and kicked him so that he fell onto his side. So much for His Eminence's allegiances: when an army hasn't been paid for as long as this one, clearly it makes no difference whether the booty comes from friend or from foe.

I watched him get up and turn toward me. He moved as if his legs were as bandied as mine, but then, being on his knees for so long would have been novel for a man of his high clerical stature. He recognized me right away, and his face lit up for a second hoping—what? That I was come leading an army of the great Roman soldiers, the likes of which probably last existed in the antiquity of which he was so fond? But the hope dissolved soon enough. As one of Rome's more erudite pleasure seekers, he had always had a certain nobility to his looks. Not now, though. His thinning hair was stuck to his head like tufts of grass clinging to hard ground, and his skin was almost yellow; his health, wealth, and worldly confidence had all drained away. There seemed little point in asking him for help. He wouldn't be alive that long. But while his world was collapsing, his brain was fast enough.

"Your mistress should know that there are no protectors or patrons left," he said urgently. "The pope himself is besieged. St. Peter's is made a stable for the imperial cavalry, and with the Bourbon prince dead, there is no leader to stop the slaughter. The only hope is that the troops will turn on one another, and in the turmoil we may flee with our lives as they fight over the spoils. Tell her that she would do better to pretend piety or find another city where her beauty and her wit will be more appreciated. This Rome . . . our Rome . . . is gone forever." He glanced back nervously toward the devastation of his life. "Tell her that I dream of her still as Mary Magdalene and intercede with God for her forgiveness along with my own."

Though I moved as fast as I could, the journey back took longer. It may have been my despair, for with no champion to defend us, we now faced the prospect of being squeezed and squeezed until we burst. The world was collapsing, but the day was rosy bright and the pillage had begun in earnest again. I passed through streets where the cardinal's prophecy was already coming true and where the two armies were vying for the next kill. I moved fast, dodging in and out of backstreets until my legs grew numb from the effort and I had to stop to get the feeling back. Between his house and ours, a large troop of Lutherans was following in the footsteps of the Spanish, the violence all the greater because there was so little left to steal. I took the longer way to avoid them, skirting to the east and passing close enough to Marcantonio's press and workshop to see that the whole area was invaded or alight, its inhabitants either hostages or dead. By the time I reached our own quarter, the sun was overhead, its heat spicing the bloodlust. Our invaders had become defenders now, with Spanish and German soldiers howling and brawling with one another. This time I ran through my exhaustion, so that, when I reached our square, I was trembling as much from the numbing throb in my legs as from mounting fear. At our gate the sentries were gone, and the courtyard doors were thrown open to anyone who had the weaponry to walk in.

In the yard the pigs were squealing as they were herded against the walls, and a group of men, including the cook, were deep in shit and flagstones digging up the chests. In the frenzy for treasure, no one noticed a crumpled dwarf moving inside.

The kitchen was empty. I found Giacomo and Zaccano in the dining room, both sitting propped against a wall, smashed glass and pottery all around. As I approached, Giacomo looked up, but Zaccano remained with his head on his chest, a hole darker than the red velvet of his jacket under his left breast, but neat, so that it seemed neither cruel nor deep enough to have let out his soul. I stood myself directly in front of Giacomo so that our eyes were at the same level and asked him what had happened. He looked back at me and opened his mouth, but only a slow trickle of blood came out. Of Adriana there was no sign.

I moved to the staircase. On the bottom step, a figure was hunched over, trembling. Underneath the filth and the stink of him, I recognized our stable boy. There was a gash on his cheek and he looked scared out of his wits, but all of his limbs were intact, and in his fingers he was playing nervously with a single grubby pearl. No doubt he had deluded himself into believing that by betraying his mistress and her wealth, he would earn the rest of the necklace.

"Where is she?"

He shrugged.

I spat into his face and went up the stairs like a dog, for I can move more quickly that way when I am tired.

I still say we were blessed compared with many. If the city

had survived the onslaught, ours would have been one of the many houses to throw a great celebration. Not least because Fiammetta Bianchini was due to celebrate her twenty-first birthday. She was now in her prime. In the six years since her mother had brought her as a virgin to Rome, she had slept with a generous list of the city's richest and best-educated men. And she had learned things from them that would surely aid her now. For while a wife is her husband's possession and must know and cleave to only one man, and a common whore belongs to and is used by everyone, my mistress had been lucky, for she had been able to choose some of her suitors and in that way had kept something of herself. This, mixed with her wit, training, and palpable beauty, had given her a certain confidence in matters of the flesh that is denied to most women. So now, if fortune and circumstances moved against her, surely the talents of her profession would help her to survive the ordeal. Or that was how I comforted myself as I reached the landing.

From behind the door, I could hear murmuring, almost like the rhythm of a chant. I turned the handle, expecting it to be locked. Instead it opened.

My lady was kneeling by the bed in her slip, her head down and covered so that I could not see her face, a Bible in front of her with pages torn out and blood splattered across them. Next to her stood a rake-thin woman with a face like pig's hide, her lips moving in constant prayer, while behind, another one, much bigger, had her fist around a pair of cook's carving scissors. Lutheran harpies—as much at home with the knife as with the word of God. They turned as I entered, and in the moment of mutual shock between us I saw the floor ankle deep in ropes of golden hair.

The fat woman with the blades moved toward me, yelling. I slammed the door and skidded around her. My lady cried out, the shawl falling off her head. I saw her face streaked with blood, her scalp like the stubble of a cornfield, scarred black in places where the fire had eaten into the roots. Her hair, that great river of beauty and wealth, was all gone.

"Oh, no! Please! You must not hurt him," she cried, waving

her arms around like a woman demented. "This is Bucino, of whom I spoke: the sweet, sad Bucino, whose body carries a terrible stigma but whose mind has always been simple and would gain such comfort from God's love."

The woman halted for a second, staring at me. I grinned at her, pulling my lips away from my teeth and jabbering slightly, and she took a step back, transfixed by my hideousness.

"Oh, Bucino, come kneel with us and listen to what I have to say." My lady reached out her hands to me, and now her voice had changed and she spoke slowly and carefully, as if to a half-wit. "I have been in thrall to the whore of Babylon, but these good women have shown me the way of the true Christ. Our riches, our clothes, our hidden wealth, all are given to God. So also is my soul. I have been taken from the evil of my profession to be born again through God's infinite mercy. To which end I have swallowed every last jewel of my pride. And when you have done the same, we may pray together, and then, with Christ's great grace, we may commence our journey to a better life."

I clasped my hands first to my jerkin, then to my mouth, and, working up as much saliva as I could, swallowed the rest of the rubies and emeralds as I sank to my knees, half-choking and repeating the name of the Lord and thanking him for our salvation.

So it was, that same night, when the dark was at its thickest and our Protestant victors were sleeping the sleep of the just and the well-stuffed on goose-feather mattresses, that we, the hypocrites and the damned, slipped out from the stable where we had been quartered with what was left of the pigs. With our guts grinding stones, we moved silently through the wreckage of Rome until at last we reached the breached wall at San Spirito, where the frenzy of that first attack had left gaping holes in the masonry, too many to police in the darkness.

Where they swarmed in, we now crept out, a deformity and a shaved whore, bowed in defeat. We walked all through the

night, and as the darkness bled away into dawn, we found ourselves merging into a slow train of refugees, some already desti-
tute, others carrying whatever was left of their lives on their
backs. But their good fortune was short-lived, for with first light
the vultures came wheeling in: stragglers from the army who
had yet to make it into the city and instead were taking booty
where they could. Had my lady been raped but left with her
hair and her looks, I swear she would have found herself on her
back soon enough again and I, no doubt, beside her to be used
as bayonet practice. As it was, her bloodied head and the perfumes of the pigpen kept them at safe distance. We had nothing
worth stealing anyway, save for a small volume of Petrarch. Like
good Christians, we carried all our riches on the inside.

We stayed pure for as long as we could (those who don't eat
don't shit for longer; that was the sum total of the wisdom I
gained during these momentous days), and then on the third
evening, when we could wait no longer, we broke off from the
road into the forest and found ourselves a stream beside which
we could squat until the loosing of our bowels made us, if not
wealthy, at least solvent again. And while it was little enough
triumph given all that we had lost, it was better than death, and
we kept each other's spirits high on its sweetness. That night we
feasted on berries and fresh spring water—upstream from our
ablutions—and counted our blessings, which amounted to
twelve fat pearls, five emeralds, and six rubies, the largest of
which my lady had had to smear with her face oil to get down
her gullet. My God, how must it have been, choking down one's
future as the harpies hammered on the door? It was a throatful
to be proud of, and I told her so as we sat huddled together in
the gloom, trying to keep the forest sounds benign in our city
dwellers' imaginations.

"Indeed it was. A much more valiant act than you swallowing your paltry emeralds. And"—she stopped me before I could
answer—"I want no Bucino-style jokes on how well trained I
am in such things either."

And while it was not that funny, I was so bone-weary, so
worn down by trying not to show my fear, that once I started

laughing, I couldn't stop. Once it had bitten me, it jumped like a flea onto her, so that despite our constant shushing of each other, we were soon doubled over and helpless with it, as if by our mirth we could mock Fate and ensure our survival.

When it was over, we lay back against the trees and stared into space, exhausted by our commitment to being alive.

"So," she said at last. "What happens now, Bucino?"

What happens now? "Well, you would make a ravishing enough nun for a while," I said. "Though they might question the madness of your ardor when they see how violently you shaved your own head." But despite our earlier laughter, it was not a thing to joke of, and I felt a shudder go through her. In the gloom it was hard to see her face, though the terror in her eye was sharp enough and the blood gash on her forehead vivid against her white skin. I took a breath. "Or we could bide our time and lick our wounds, and once you are healed we could start over again. The city won't be occupied forever, and there will always be men with taste who will want what you have to offer."

"Not in Rome," she said, her voice fierce with anger as much as fear. "I won't go back there. Not ever. Not for anything."

Which, when I considered it, was just as well, since most men, especially those with something to forget, like their women sweet as spring lambs, and by the time there would be anything worth going back to, we would both have grown too old to reap its rewards. Not Rome then.

I shrugged, keeping my voice light. "So where?"

We both knew the answer, of course. With war wiping its bloody fingers all over the land, there was only one place to go. To a city of wealth and stability ruled by men who had the money and manners to pay for what soldiers take at the end of bayonets. An independent state with an eye for beauty and a talent for trade, where clever exiles with enough imagination could make their fortunes. There are some who think it the greatest place on earth, the most prosperous and the most peaceful. Except, for all the tales of magic and wonder, I had never wanted to go there.

But this was not my choice. In these last days, she had risked and lost more than I ever had, and she deserved, if that was what she needed, to think of going home.

"It will be all right, Bucino," she said quietly. "I know your fear, but if we can get ourselves there, I believe we could make it work. We'll be partners now, you and I; split everything, expenses and profit, take care of each other. Together, I swear, we can do it."

I stared at her. My very bones ached from running. My stomach was shriveled and starved. I wanted to sleep in a bed again, to eat pig rather than smell like it, to spend time again with men who had brains as well as bloodlust and who measured wealth by more than raw booty. But more than all of that, I didn't want to walk the world alone anymore. Because it had been a much warmer place since we had found each other.

"All right," I said. "Just so long as I don't get my feet wet."

She smiled and slipped her hand over mine. "Don't worry. I will not let the water consume you."

They arrived at night by rowing boat from the mainland.

On the jetty at Mestre, the squat, misshapen one began the bargaining. It was clear from the state of their clothes and meager baggage that the pair had traveled far, and his thick Roman accent, along with his insistence on traveling under cover of darkness to avoid the plague patrols, gave the boatman an excuse to charge them triple what the journey was worth. At which point the woman intervened. She was tall and thin, wrapped up like a Turk so that one could see nothing of her face, but she spoke the dialect so perfectly and haggled so fiercely that the boatman became almost the loser, agreeing to be paid only once he had delivered them to the exact house in the city.

The water was black and choppy under thick cloud. Almost as soon as they had left the land, the dark enveloped them, the only sound the slapping of the waves against the wood, so that it felt for a while as if they were heading into open sea and that this city in the water that people spoke of with such awe was simply an idea, a fantasy built out of our need for miracles. But just as the blackness was at its most complete, it was broken by a glow of flickering lights on the horizon ahead, like the iridescence of mermaid hair caught by moonlight on the water's surface. The boatman pulled with strong, even strokes, and the lights grew and expanded until eventually the first buildings took shape, hovering on the water like lines of pale tombstones. A passageway of colored wooden markers came into view, guiding them from open sea into what looked like a widemouthed canal, where shacks and warehouses rose up on either side, their jetties crammed with stone and mounds of timber, thick barges lining the moorings. This canal curved lazily in upon itself for a few hundred yards, until it met a much broader band of water.

The boatman steered the craft to the left, and now the vista began to change. They passed dwellings and a church, its stern brick frontage stretching up into the sky, its forecourt flat and empty. Then, as a sly half-moon slipped out from the clouds, larger houses started to appear on either side of them, their inlaid and gilded façades seeming to shoot up directly out of water. The woman, who had taken the open crossing in her stride, as if it was a journey she might make every day, now sat transfixed. The misshapen one, by contrast, was clutching the side of the boat, his squat little body tense like that of an animal, his big head darting from side to side, as much afraid of what he might see as of what he might miss. The boatman, who had grown old watching other people's wonder, slackened his speed in the hope that the view might earn him a tip. The canal was wide and black here, like a great polished corridor in an even greater mansion. Despite the late hour, there were a few other boats abroad, particular in their appearance, sleek and thin, with small cabins at their centers and solitary figures standing in their sterns maneuvering by means of a single long oar so that they moved effortlessly through the dark water.

In the waxy, pale light, the buildings on either side grew grander, like ghost palaces, three or four stories tall, their entrances low, a few stone steps all that separated them from the slapping sea. In some, the great doors stood open onto cavernous halls with rows of the slim-hipped boats tied up outside, their silvery prows glinting under an occasional lamp. The woman was animated now, her eyes drawn to the upper stories, where, under rows of pointed-arched windows, their fretted stone shone like lacework in the moonlight. Many of them were dark, for the night was at its deepest now, but in a few, the sparkle of hanging chandeliers, the numbers of candles bearing witness to extraordinary wealth, lit large, echoing spaces so that you could make out silhouettes of moving figures and the singsong of voices tossed and swallowed by the water.

Every fifty or hundred yards there came a gap in the houses and the stone gave way to other waterways, narrow as fingers and black as Hell, flowing into the main one. After they had been traveling for perhaps twenty minutes, the woman motioned to the boatman and he changed his stroke, turning the craft in to one of these channels. The world became dark again, the sides of the houses shooting up like canyon walls, obscuring the moonlight. Their progress became sluggish. A little way farther on, a stone pavement opened up, running alongside the water. The air was muggier here, the day's heat still clinging to the stone, and there were smells now: rot and the sharp tang of urine, the perfumes of poverty. Even the sound was different, the slip-slap of the water more hollow, almost angry, as it bounced and echoed off the narrow walls. They passed under bridges low enough to run their hands along the undersides. The boatman had to work harder, his eyes like a cat's glinting into the darkness ahead. These alleyways of water merged into one another at different angles, in some cases so suddenly that he had to bring the boat to a virtual stop before he turned, and as he did so he would cry out to warn anyone who might be heading toward him on the other side. Or someone might call first out of the darkness, a voice twisting and falling in the night. The etiquette of the water seemed to demand that whoever called first would be the one to move, while the other boat waited. Some had candles in glass jars on deck so they appeared out of the darkness like dancing fireflies, but there were others that remained black, the thick sigh of the water the only evidence of their passing.

They rowed slowly through this maze until they hit a broader canal, where the houses grew wealthier again. Ahead, one of the sleek, black boats glided toward them, lit up this time by a hanging red lamp. The woman was instantly alert, moving to the end of the boat to get a better view. The figure in the

stern ahead seemed to merge into the dark, his skin and his cos-
tume the same hue as the night, but the cabin was more colorful, decorated with gold curtains and tassels, and as the two
vessels moved closer, it was possible to catch a glimpse of a
young woman in fine clothes, her rising breasts and neck the
color of moonlight, and a shadow of a man next to her, his fingers in her hair. As the two boats slid by each other, a ringed
hand slipped out and pulled the curtain across to hide them
from view, and in the still night air, the movement sent a rush
of lavender and musk across the water. In the rowing boat, the
woman closed her eyes, her head tilted up like a hunter's toward
the scent, and long after the boats had passed each other, she
stayed that way, lost in the moment, breathing deeply. Across
the length of the boat, the dwarf watched her closely.

The silence was broken by the boatman's voice. "How far?"
he muttered, his arms aching at the prospect of the journey
back. "You said it was in Cannaregio."

"We are nearly there," she said; then almost to herself, "It has
been a long time." A few moments later, she motioned him into
a smaller stretch of water. The channel led to a dead end, where,
to one side, a three-story house loomed up in front of them, a
rickety wooden bridge close by. "Here. Here. We are here." And
her voice was excited now. "You can bring the boat in to the
steps. The mooring is to the left on the side."

He pulled up and secured the boat. The building looked
forbidding, plasterwork peeling, broken shutters closed. The
tide had risen during the journey, and the water was slurping
over the top step. He dumped their bags on the wet stones and
demanded his money roughly, and though the dwarf tried to
persuade him to wait until the doors were open, he would have
none of it, and by the time they started banging, he had already
disappeared into the slick dark.

The sound of their fists on the wood jumped into the air
around. "Open up," she called. "It is Fiammetta come home.
Open the doors, Mother."

They waited. She called again. This time a light flickered on
the first floor and a face appeared at the window.

"Meragosa?"

A woman's voice grunted.

"Open the door. It's me." Above, the figure seemed to hesitate, then pulled the shutter closed, and they heard movements
as someone came down the stairs. Eventually the great wooden
door swung open and an old woman was revealed, thick as a
cart and wheezing with the effort, a single shaded candle in her
hand.

"Meragosa!" The woman, subdued for so long, was excited.
"It's me, Fiammetta."

"Fi-Fiammetta. Maria Madonna! I didn't recognize you.
What happened to you? I thought . . . well . . . We heard about
Rome. . . . Everyone's talking about it. . . . I thought you were
dead."

"We might as well be, for the shape of us. For God's sake,
help us in."

The woman shifted a little, but not quite enough to make
way.

"Where is my mother? Is she asleep?"

Meragosa gave a small moaning noise, as if someone had
struck her. "Your mother . . . I . . . God help us, I thought you
knew."

"Knew what?"

"Your mother . . . is dead."

"What? When? How? How could I know?"

"Half a year ago. We . . . I sent a message to you. In Rome."

In the gloom it was impossible now to see either of the
women's eyes.

"A message. And what did it say?"

The answer was almost a mumble again. "Only that . . . well,
that she had passed away."

There was a small silence. The younger woman dropped her
eyes, and for a moment she seemed to hesitate, as if she did not
know quite how to feel. The dwarf moved closer to her, his eyes
fixed on her face. She took a breath. "In which case, Meragosa, it
would seem you are now living in my house."

"No . . . I mean . . ." The old woman stammered. "Your

mother . . . she fell sick suddenly, and on her deathbed she told me I could stay on . . . for all that I've done for her."

"Oh, *carina*." Her voice was sleeker now, like a long caress on cat's fur. "All these years of practice and you still lie as badly as an old whore. The rent on this house is paid for out of my loins, and we have come to take possession of it. Bucino, take our bags inside. Our room is on the first floor above the entrance—"

"No." The woman's bulk blocked the way. "You can't stay. I—I've taken lodgers. I—I needed the money—to keep the place going."

"Then they can sleep on the landing till they leave in the morning. Bucino."

The dwarf moved quickly by the old woman's legs, and she screamed as he brushed past her, a word spitting from her lips.

"What did you call him? A water rat? You should be careful, Meragosa. From where I stand, you're the only vermin I see in this house."

There was a silence. Neither of them moved. Then, suddenly, the old woman gave ground, growling and standing aside to let her in.

And so the young woman and the dwarf walked into the darkness, the water lapping greedily at the steps behind them.

CHAPTER TWO

Venice, 1527

My God, this city stinks. Not everywhere—along the southern wharves where the ships dock, the air is heady with leftover spices, and on the Grand Canal money buys fresh breezes along with luxury—but everywhere we are, where crumbling houses rise out of rank water and a dozen families live stacked one on top of another like rotting vegetables, the decay and filth burn the insides of your nostrils. Living as I do, with my nose closer to the ground, there are times when I find it hard to breathe.

The old man who measures the level of the well in our *campo* every morning says that the smell is worse because of the summer drought and that if the water falls any lower, they will have to start bringing the freshwater barges in, and then only those who have money will be able to drink. Imagine that: a city built on water dying of thirst. According to him, this summer is so bad because war has brought in a flood of refugees and with them the threat of the plague. Those travelers who arrive from the sea with the contagion, he said, are found out because the city sends officers aboard every merchant ship looking for fever or boils, and if they discover symptoms, they cart the suspects off to one of the outer islands for quarantine. That's why there's no leprosy in Venice anymore, just a few remaining mad souls watching their limbs rot away in an old hospital fenced in by water. But they can't stop everyone, and these days the mainland holds as many dangers as the open sea. He stares fixedly at me as he says all this, because he suspects that's how we got here. Gossip travels faster than smell. Across the thin canals, women cackle and squawk at one another like so many hungry seagulls, and the arrival of a dwarf brings out nosiness in the most taciturn of souls. I have been gaped at by every trader for miles around, and across from our house, a squint-eyed old bat with no teeth sits at the window, day in, day out, eyes going in both directions at once, so that if my lady and I speak of anything that is not the weather, we must close the windows, for there are no such things as secrets when words dance so freely across water.

But whatever the rumors, the old man still talks to me, no doubt because he is lonely and because age has bent him as double as I am small, so my mouth comes close to his deaf ears and he can hear me better than he can others. He has lived in the same quarter of the city for eighty-one years, and he remembers everything, from the great fire in the shipyards started by the spark from a horse hoof to the great Battle of Agnadello, almost twenty years ago, when Venice was defeated by an alliance of Italian states and the government was so ashamed, he says, that it prosecuted its own generals and all you could hear for days was the sound of people wailing in the streets and on the water.

Venice, as he never ceases to tell anyone willing to listen, was the greatest city in the world then, but now prostitutes threaten to outnumber the nuns, and there is only blasphemy, ridicule, and sin. While it would give me the greatest pleasure to believe him—the city he describes would surely make our fortune—impotence often makes grumblers of old men, for as death gets closer, it is more comforting to imagine that they are leaving Hell for Heaven rather than the other way around.

Still, in those first months, when my lady was housebound and I was negotiating my way between the canals, his gossip was sweet to my ears and made him both my historian and my first guide.

To begin with, though, there was only sleep, a great, deep well of it, our bodies greedy for the oblivion that comes with safety. In the room above the canal, my lady lay upon her mother's bed like a dead woman. I took a pallet by her door, my body acting as a lock against the old woman's malevolent curiosity. I think sometimes now about that sleep, for I have never experienced anything like it before or after: it had such a sweetness that I might be tempted to trade Paradise for the promise of such profound forgetfulness. But we were not ready to die, and on the morning of the third day, I woke to spears of light through broken shutters and a stabbing hunger in my gut. I thought of our kitchen in Rome; of roasted fish, its skin crisp and bubbling from the oven, the thick taste of capon stuffed with rosemary and garlic, and the way the warm honey oozed from Baldesar's almond cakes, so that you almost had to eat the tips of your fingers to be satisfied; my hand went out to the bulge above my groin the size of a small volume of Petrarch and a purse of emeralds, rubies, and pearls, a shape more reassuring to me now than any stirrings of desire.

My lady was still sleeping, her face half buried in the mattress, the filthy turban clasped to her head. Downstairs, in the dank kitchen, Meragosa greeted my arrival with the scream of a stuck parrot, as if the Devil's incubus itself had come into the room. In a pan over the fire, there was a steaming liquid that may once have held the richness of animal bones, though there was little to show for it now. When I asked what else there was in the house, she flapped and yelped again, spitting insults through her panic. While there are many cruel things in life, there is nothing quite as mean as an old whore, for as their bodies go slack their appetites stay sharp, tormenting them with memories of full bellies and rich clothes, which they know they will never have again. So when I asked her directions to a good pawnbroker, the battle between suspicion and greed was writ large on her face.

"Why? What is it you have to sell?" she said, her eyes moving cunningly over my body.

"Enough to put meat in your gruel."

"The only lending here is done by Jews," she said flatly, then gave me a sly glance. "But everybody knows that they cheat foreigners. You had best let me do the deal."

"I'll take my chances. Where do I find them?"

"Where? Oh, here in Venice they have their own ghetto. It is easy." She grinned. "If you know your way around." And she turned her back on me, giving her attention to the stove.

Of the labyrinth that is this city I will tell more later. It is its own legend anyway, made up from stories of rich visitors too mean to hire guides on their arrival, only to be found later floating in back canals with their throats cut along with their purses. I went on foot. Our back door opened onto a street barely wide enough for two people to pass each other. This in turn led to another and over a bridge to another, which finally gave onto a small square, or *campo*, as they call it. It was here I came across my old man next to his beloved well, and while his accent was coarse, his gestures were simple enough. Later, when I faltered, the streets were busy with people on their way to and from church, and the merchants I asked gave exact instructions, for as I soon learned, it is not uncommon for the Venetians to go straight from God to the Jews to raise money, the sacrament of commerce being in its own way holy for a state founded on trade.

The Ghetto, when I found it, was like a small town within a town, cordoned off by walls and great wooden gates; inside, houses and shops huddled and scrambled together. The pawn-brokers' shops were marked by blue awnings over their fronts flapping like sails in the wind. The one I picked was run by a young man with soft, black eyes and a long face made longer by straggling curls. He took me into a back room, where he studied our last two emeralds long and hard under a special lens, Venice being a city of the most expert glass, for both magnifying and faking. Then he explained the terms of the bond as laid down by the state, gave me the document to sign, and counted out my coins. Through all of this transaction, he treated me with admirable care, exhibiting no surprise at my stature (his attention was more on the jewels than on me), though as to whether he cheated me or not, well, how would I have known,

except by the feeling in my gut, which in this case was too confused by hunger?

Outside, in the heat, the smell of my own unwashed body
became as pungent as the city around me. From a secondhand
shop on the edge of the Ghetto, I bought a jacket and trousers
that I could butcher to fit me and some fresh slips for my lady.
For food I chose things easy to digest: whitefish broiled in its
own juices, stewed vegetables, and soft bread, egg custards with
vanilla, and half a dozen honey cakes, less moist than Baldesar's
but enough to make me drool as they sat in my hand. I ate one
on the streets, and by the time I found my way back, my head
was spinning with the sweetness. Through the darkness of the
stairwell, I called out for Meragosa, but there was no answer. I
left a portion of the food on the table and carried the rest with
a bottle and chipped glasses of watered wine to the chamber.

Upstairs, my lady was awake and sitting up in the bed. She
glanced at me as I came in but turned her head away swiftly.
The shutters and the windows were open, and her body was
free from its wrappings, with the light behind her. It was the
first time in many weeks that she had felt safe enough to dis-
robe, and her silhouette now showed clearly the ravages of the
journey. Where her flesh had once been pillow plump, her col-
larbones now stuck out like planks of wood, while her ribs were
the skeleton of a ship's hull pressing hard against her thin slip.
But it was her head that was the worst: with her turban unrav-
eled, one's eyes were drawn instantly to the scabby, cropped
mess that was her hair and the jagged scar that began on her
upper forehead and zigzagged its way into her hairline.

For months we had been too focused on survival to give
much thought to the future. That early optimism of the night
in the forest had dissolved fast enough as we got back onto the
road. With the army dropping away, the refugees had become as
eager to rob one another as to save themselves, and by the time
we reached the port to take a ship for Venice, most of the boats
had already been commandeered by soldiers with Roman
booty. In the sweltering weeks that followed, my lady had been
felled by a fever, and while I had done the best for her wounds

with whatever salves I could find, it was clear now, in the crueler light of our security, that it had not been enough.

From the look in her eyes, I knew that she knew it too. God knows, she was still not ugly: the cut glass of those green eyes alone would have caught the attention of any man on a street. But great cities are full of women who can earn their next meal by raising their skirts. It is the ones who keep you in thrall to more than their snatches who command the houses and the gowns to go with them. And for that they have first to love themselves.

I busied myself with the food, laying out the fish, vegetables, and wine, though I could find only a blunt knife and a broken fork, which I laid with careful ceremony on her knees, and next to it a clean gown. From this close, I could smell that the hangings around the bed held the odor of her mother's last sickness in their folds. The morning contained more than the loss of her looks.

"It is Sunday," I said cheerfully. "And we have slept for three days. The sun shines, and the pawn merchants here are Jews who give fair prices for fine gems." I pushed the plate nearer to her fingers. "The flesh is tender, though the flavor a little weak. Take it slow to start with."

She did not move, her eyes still fixed intently on the window.

"You don't like it? There is custard and honey cake if you would prefer."

"I am not hungry," she said, and that voice, usually so expert at melody, was flat and dead.

She told me once, not long after we met, how at confession she was often hard-pressed to decide which sins to admit to first; for while vanity, along with fornication, made up a necessary part of her profession, it was gluttony that she saw as her greatest weakness, because ever since she was a child she had loved her food. "That is because your stomach has shrunk. The juices will ease it open once you start," I urged.

I clambered onto the end of the bed with my own plate and started eating, cramming my mouth with fish flesh, licking the

sauce off my fingers, concentrating on the food but always keeping her hands in sight so I could see if they moved. For a few
moments the only sound was that of me chewing. One more
mouthful and I would try again.

"You should have told me." And now there was sharpness in
the voice.

I swallowed. "Told you what?"

She clicked her tongue. "How many jewels have we left?"

"Four pearls, five rubies, and the one great one from your
necklace." I waited. "More than enough."

"Enough for what? A miracle?"

"Fiammetta—"

"Tell me—why is it you find it so hard to look at me, Bucino?"

"I am looking at you," I said, pulling my head up and staring
directly at her. "You are the one who is looking away."

Now she turned to me, her eyes as green and cold as the two
emeralds I had just pawned to keep us fed. "And? What do you
see?"

"I see a beautiful woman with the luck of the Devil in need
of food and a good bath."

"Liar. Look again. Or maybe you need help."

Her hand slid under the grimy sheet, and she pulled out a
small, ivory-backed mirror. Time was in Rome when she could
barely go an hour without scrutinizing her beauty, but with the
Devil at your heels, you move too fast for vanity, and looking
glasses are few and far between in the hull of a cargo ship. She
twirled the stem of the mirror in her fingers, the sun catching
the surface and sending prisms of light around the room. "It
seems Meragosa sold everything that she could rip out of the
floor, but what she didn't know about she couldn't steal. It was
in between the slats of the bed. When I was young, that was my
mother's safe place for the money she earned."

She handed it to me. It was heavy, but the glass was still fine
enough to do its work. I caught a glimpse of a face under a great
misshapen dome of a forehead, and just for an instant I was surprised by myself again, for, unlike the rest of the world, I do not

register my ugliness daily. Compared with me, my lady is a newly risen Venus. But then my looks do not earn our living.

"I have been looking at myself in that mirror ever since I was a child, Bucino. Studying my reflection was part of my training. The glass was a gift to my mother from a man who ran a shop in the Merceria. It used to be mounted on the wall next to the bed and covered by a little curtain to keep the sun off the silver. There was a shelf underneath, where she kept pots of oils and perfume, and she would pick me up every day to see myself—"

"Hunger distorts the world as badly as tarnished glass," I interrupted. "Eat something, and then we'll talk."

She shook her head impatiently. "—and each and every time I looked she would say, 'I don't do this for you to become vain, Fiammetta, but because beauty is your gift from God and it should be used and not squandered. Study this face as if it were a map of the ocean, your own trade route to the Indies. For it will bring you its own fortune. But always believe what the glass tells you. Because while others will try to flatter you, it has no reason to lie.' "

She stopped. I said nothing.

"So, Bucino, is it lying now? If so, you had better tell me, because we are the only sailors left together in this enterprise."

I took a breath. If I had had wit enough, I suppose I might have embroidered the truth a little, since she had lived her whole life on the rich cream of compliment, and without it her spirit would become as enervated as her body. If I had had wit enough . . .

"You are ill," I said. "And thin as a street whore. Hardship has eaten your flesh away. But it is only flesh, and food will make you plump again."

"Well-picked words, Bucino." She took the mirror from me and held it briefly up in front of her. "Now," she said. "Tell me about my face."

"Your skin is dull. Your scalp is scabby, you have too little hair, and there is a cut that rises into your hairline. But your glow will come back, and if you fashion it right, your hair, once it grows again, will easily disguise the flaw that remains."

"Once it grows again! Look at me, Bucino. I am bald." And her voice was like a child's wail.

"You are cropped."

"No. Bald." She put her head down toward me, her fingers moving across her scalp. "Look, feel! Here. And here. And here. There is no hair, or none that will grow again. My scalp is like ridges of earth after a drought. Feel it. Look at it. I am bald. Oh, sweet Jesus . . . this is what comes from the spite of skinny German cows. I should just have lifted my skirts in the hall and let the men at me. The pricks of two dozen Protestants would have been easier to bear than this."

"You think so? And how would it have been once they turned their lust into your sin and butchered us all to assuage their guilt?"

"Hah! At least we would have died more quickly. Now we shall starve slowly from my ugliness. Look at me. What price my talents in bed now? I am bald, God damn it, Bucino. And we are lost."

"No," I said, my voice as fierce as hers. "I am not lost, though you may be. You are certainly half starved and infected with melancholy and melodrama."

"Oh. And when did I give you permission to insult me?"

"When you started insulting yourself. We are partners now, remember? It was you who promised that if I could haul my carcass here, then together we could make this work. What is this bog of self-pity? Your mother didn't teach you this. We could be breeding maggots now, like half the rest of Rome. With the right salves on your wounds and a fire in your stomach, we might be eating off silver plates before next summer comes around. But if they shaved your spirit when they shaved your head, then you'd better tell me now, because I didn't come to this cesspit of a city, where sewers run like open veins and where I am indeed scarcely bigger than the rats, for you to give up on us now."

I pulled myself off the bed. There are those who say that it is funny to watch squat men posture indignation, that when dwarves stamp their feet, kings and nobles only laugh. But my mistress was not laughing now. "I'll come back when there is more in your stomach than bile."

I moved toward the door and stood there for a long moment. When I looked back, she was sitting, staring at the plate, jaw set, and though she would not admit it later, there were tears sliding down her cheeks.

I waited. She put out her hand and took a scoop of fish flesh. I watched the flakes go into her mouth, saw the threads of saliva forming at the edges of her lips as she chewed doggedly. She sniffed and took a sip from the glass. I stayed where I was. She took another mouthful, and then another slurp of wine.

"When she left Rome, she had enough to live well here," she said in a fierce whisper. "It was what she wanted. To come back to this house and live like a lady. Yet all that's left is filth and sickness. I don't know what happened here."

I have few enough memories of my own mother. She died when I was still young. Some people said it was the burden of having given birth to such a monstrosity, but I do not believe that, for in the hazy tumble of the past, there is a woman's face smiling down at me, holding me, running her fingers over the top of my head as if it was a thing of wonder rather than a thing of shame. My lady's mother I had known for the best part of two years, when my employment overlapped with her increasing homesickness in Rome and her decision to leave. No doubt she had been a beauty once, for she still held herself more like a lady than like a whore, but her face had grown sharp counting purses. For the first six months, she spied on me as a falcon spies on a mouse in the grass, waiting for it to break cover enough to pounce, and she would have had my liver for dog meat if she had spotted as much as a missing button from the household accounts. There are those who would say that she sold her only daughter into prostitution to provide for her own old age. But all the moralists I have met either live off the Church or have purses of their own to nourish their sanctimony, and where I come from, anyone with a profitable trade would be a fool not to pass the tricks of it on to their children. All I know is that Madame Bianchini was a woman with a stout head on her and a fist as tight as an asshole when it came to money. When she was in her right mind, it would have taken more than Meragosa to swindle anything out of her. Though my lady had missed her when she had left, she was well trained by then and not one to dwell on what she couldn't have. That, too, was something she had been taught. There are times, how-ever, even in the best learners, when despair cuts sharper than the will.

I walked back to the bed and clambered up close to her. She rubbed her eyes fiercely with the back of her hand. "Remember what they say, Bucino?" she said at last. "How if you sleep in a bed where someone has died, you too are doomed unless it's been blessed with holy water?"

"Yes, and the same people also say that God doesn't let any-one die on the same day they go to Mass. Yet the ground gob-bles gangs of pious widows and nuns every day. What? You never heard that one?"

"No," she said, and her smile ignited the spark of her spirit just for that instant. She held out her glass, and I refilled it. She took a longer draft this time. "You don't think it was the pox, do you? I saw no sign of it on her, and surely she would have told me if it had been. But everyone knows that this city has it even more than Rome. Boats and boils—they go together. That's what she used to tell me." She looked up at me. "Have you really decided against it so soon, Bucino? I warned you that it would smell worse in summer."

I shook my head and lied with my eyes. At another time she would have noticed.

"There was a girl, when we lived here," she said. "She was young, maybe only a few years older than I. . . . Her name was Elena something, but we used to call her La Draga. She had something wrong with her that made her walk strangely, and her eyes were bad, but she was clever and knew about plants and healing. My mother would get potions from her. There was a liquid. The Courtesans' Cordial we used to call it. Holy water and pulped mare's kidney. I swear that's what my mother said it was. It would bring on bleeding if you were late. La Draga could make all kinds of stuff. She cured me once of a coughing fever when everyone else thought I was going to die." She ran her fingers over the edge of the cut on her forehead into her stubbly hair. "If we could get in touch with her, I think she might know what to do with this."

"If she's in Venice, I'll find her."

"What price did you get for the emeralds?"

I told her, and she nodded quietly. "I don't think he swindled me."

She laughed. "If he did, he would be the first."

Outside, a fat gull swooped past, screeching at the sun. She glanced out the window. "You know the air is better on the big canals. Many of the bigger houses have gardens, with frangipani and lavender and bowers of wild jasmine. When my mother was at her most successful, she was invited sometimes to such places. She would come back in the mornings afterward and wake me; get into my bed and tell me of the rich guests, the food and the clothes. Sometimes she'd have a blossom or some petals she had hidden in her dress, though to me they smelled as much of the men as of the garden. She would try to find the right words to make me imagine it all. 'As sweet as Arcadia' was the nearest she could get."

She looked back at me, and I knew the danger was past.

"As sweet as Arcadia. Now that would be something to aim for, wouldn't you say, Bucino?"

CHAPTER THREE

Downstairs, the kitchen is still empty and the food untouched. In the closeness of the room, with my stomach sated, my own smell rises up to clog my nostrils. I wedge a broken chair against the door, mix a pail of stove water with a few cups from the well bucket, and pull off my sweat-caked clothes. In Rome we used to wash with imported Venetian soap, so scented and fat that it looked almost good enough to eat, but here there is only a sliver of hard cake, which, when I pump fast enough, makes a thin lather sufficient to drown a few lice, though I doubt it does much to sweeten my smell.

The road has taken its toll on me also, eating into the roundness of my trunk and thinning my thighs so that the skin on them is flabby. I suds my balls as best I can and hold them in my hand for a moment, my prick shriveled like a salted slug. It has been some time since it has been as gainfully employed as my wits. While there is nothing to be earned from my squashed stature (if you discount the oohs and aahs of a bored crowd watching a dwarf juggling fire and then prancing around as if it had burned him), my body and I have lived together now for some thirty years, and I have grown fond of its strangeness— which, after all, is not that strange to me. Hunchbacks. Cripples. Dwarves. Children whose mouths are joined to their noses. Women with no slits for babies. Men with breasts as well as balls. The world is full of tales of the Devil in deformity, yet the truth is that ugliness is a good deal more common than beauty, and in better times I have usually been able to find pleasure enough when I needed it. Just as men are ruled by their pricks, so women, I have found, are more curious, even mischievous animals, and while they may mope and pine after perfect flesh, they also have a hankering for novelty, are susceptible to humor in flattery, and may come to enjoy acquired tastes even if they do not like to admit it in public. And so it has been for me.

Still, even in the most adventurous of houses, filth and poverty do not rank as natural aphrodisiacs.

I am rinsed and pulling on my new old clothes when the chair rattles against the wood and Meragosa pushes her way into the kitchen. On the table my purse is near the plate of food. My fist covers it fast, though not so fast that her narrow eyes don't take it in.

"Whoa . . . sweet Jesus!" She shivers theatrically in disgust. "The rat has got itself wet at last. You found the Jews then?"

"Yes. That's yours." I motion to the plate. "If you want it."

She pokes a finger into the fish flesh. "How much'd it cost you?"

I tell her.

"You was cheated. You give me the money next time, and I'll sort it for you." But she is sitting and eating it quickly enough. I stand watching for a while, then pull the broken chair closer to her. She yanks away quickly. "You keep your distance. You may be washed, but you still smell like a sewer."

In the battle between her need to keep the purse strings open and the gut swell of her loathing, she is having trouble getting the balance right. I lean carefully back in the chair, keeping my eyes on her as she eats. Her skin is like an old leather purse, and there are barely any teeth in her mouth. She looks as if she has been ugly forever. From the pulpit, her hideousness would be proof of her sins, but there would have been a time when even she was peachy ripe, when her clients saw sweetness rather than decay. How many hours have I spent watching old men with chicken-gizzard necks trying not to salivate over my mistress's flesh as they swap Platonic platitudes about how her beauty is an echo of God's perfection? The word *sin* never slipped their lips. One of them even sent her love sonnets in which the rhymes careered between the carnal and the divine. We would read them aloud together and mock him. Seduction is amusing enough when one is not deceived by it.

"Do you know a woman called La Draga?" I say after a bit. "Her real name is Elena something."

"Elena Crusichi?" She looks up briefly. "Maybe I do. Maybe I don't. What d'you want her for?"

"My lady needs to see her."

"My lady, eh? Needs to see La Draga? Well, what a surprise. What's she going to do for her? Weave her a wig?"

"What she does for her is none of your business, Meragosa. And if you want to keep your belly full, you should be careful what you say now."

"Why? Because of the size of your purse? Or maybe because I've got a famous Roman courtesan upstairs? I've seen her, re-member. I went up there and had a good look while you were out. She's not going to be making anybody's fortune anymore. Oh, she used to have it, all right. She was the most luscious lit-tle virgin in Venice for a while. Trained to have a man's tongue hanging out of his mouth at a hundred paces. But it's gone now. Her snatch is stretched and her head is burned stubble. She's a freak with no future. Just like you, rat man."

The more she rants, the quieter I am beginning to feel. Sometimes that's how it works with me. "What happened to my lady's mother, Meragosa?"

"I told you. She died. You want to know how? She rotted away with diseases given to her by a hundred different men, that's how." She stabs at the remains of the fish, snorting. "And I had to stand by and smell the stink."

Now, for the first time, I understand why my lady's mother had left Rome when she did, for she always seemed to me a woman driven more by business than by homesickness. But no man yearns for fresh young flesh when it is managed by a body with the pox. She must have known it was coming even then. Better to die in private and leave your daughter the spoils.

I wait until she gets the mouthful in.

"Actually, Meragosa, you're wrong," I say quietly. And I lift the purse in my hand so that the coins rattle a little against themselves and the rubies. "That's not how it happened at all."

"What d'you mean?"

"I mean my lady's mother was quite well when she got here. In fact she spent her last years happily, well tended and well looked after. Then, six months ago, she caught a fever. You nursed her and made her last days as comfortable as you could, given how loyal you were to her, and she died quickly and without pain. A sad but not such an awful end. Can you remember all that?"

Her mouth is open now, half-masticated bits of fish stuck to her teeth. I rattle the purse again. But she is getting the point. You can see her adding up the coins, offer and counteroffer.

"Because when my lady asks you how it was, that is what you're going to tell her."

She snorts out a gob of food, which hits the table close to my hand. I ignore it, slipping my hand into the purse and pulling out a single gold ducat, which I lay on the table between us.

"If you say this, if you tell it to my mistress in a way that she believes, then I guarantee you that as well as this coin now there will be meat in the kitchen every day of the year and a new gown for you by All Saints'. And that until you die you will be looked after and cared for, rather than thrown on the scrap heap like the old hag you are."

She makes a clumsy move toward the money.

"However—"

And because a juggler, even an out-of-practice one, can move monkey-fast when he needs to, I am up and over the table with my face shoved into hers even before she has time to scream. "However, if you don't"—and while she yelps, she also listens, because my mouth is too close to her ear for her not to hear every word—"then I promise you that you'll die much sooner, wishing that I really was only a rat. Only by then you will have lost so many tops of your fingers and gobbets of your flesh that they will wonder what devil has been sucking on your teats as you slept." And as I say it, I open my mouth wide, so that even as she squirms backward, she can't fail to see the two filed and pointed side teeth, which hold pride of place in the roof of my mouth.

"So," I say, pulling myself off her and sliding the bright coin across the table, "let's talk about La Draga."

She is away so long I wonder if she might not have taken the ducat and fled. But even the threat of my rat fangs would not persuade her to let me accompany her. This healer, it seems, will come only by means of a message and even then only to people she has met or knows about. It is nearly dusk when they finally arrive. By which time my lady is asleep again, so they come first to me in the kitchen.

I have spent most of my life watching people's reactions to me as I walk into a room. I have grown so familiar with them that I can tell fear from disgust, or even assumed pity, before the expressions have fully settled on their faces. So it is a novelty for me now to find myself the viewer rather than the viewed.

At first glance she seems so small that she might almost be a child, though it is clear soon enough that this is partly the fault of her spine, which is twisted to the left so that she has to bend to compensate, keeping one shoulder higher than the other. As for her age, well, it is hard to tell, for incessant pain does more damage to a person than wild pleasure, particularly the young. In her case, the impact is more on her body. In fact, the very sight of her face, caught as it is between beauty and horror, almost stops your heart. The skin is ghostly pale and smooth, rising full and high enough over the bones to make the shape almost lovely. Until she looks up at you. For she has eyes that are pulled from the grave: pits of white death, wide, fierce, open, with a coating of milky blindness.

Even I, who am familiarized with the shock of ugliness, feel myself assaulted by the madness I fear inside the stare. Unlike me, however, La Draga does not have to suffer the sight of the world gaping back at her deformity. Indeed, it does not appear to bother her. Certainly if she senses anything, she does not show it. I rise to greet her and offer her the chair, but she declines. "I have come for the lady Fiammetta. Where is she?" And she stands stock-still in front of me, tense and alert to the room around her as if she can see it anyway.

"She—she is upstairs."

She nods sharply. "Then I will go to her right away. You are . . . her servant, yes?"

"Well, er . . . yes."

And now her head tilts, as if to catch my voice better, and her forehead puckers slightly. "How small are you?"

"How small am I?" And I am so taken aback by the directness that I react before I think. "Why—how blind are you?"

In the doorway, I see Meragosa smirking. Damn it. Of course.

"I already know you're a dwarf, sir." She seems to smile now, though it looks crooked on her face. "But even if I did not, it is easy enough to work out. The chair moved as you stood up, but your voice still comes from here." And she puts out her hand, palm down, its height exactly measuring my own.

Despite my pique, I am impressed. "Then you already know how small I am."

"But it is your limbs that are small, yes? Your body is a man's size."

"Yes."

"And your head is big in the front? As if the round of an eggplant is pushing out from it?"

An eggplant? In my prouder moments I like to think of it more as the dome of a warrior's helmet. However, I daresay eggplant would describe it well enough. "Excuse me. I am not the patient," I say crossly, for I will not give Meragosa the pleasure of a list of my deformities.

"Bucino?" My lady's voice comes down the stairs. "Is that her? Is she arrived?"

She tilts her head again, more sharply this time, as if to locate the sound exactly, and for that second she looks like a bird latching on to a song nearby. As she turns, I am already forgotten.

Upstairs, I watch from the door as the two of them greet each other with an almost childish glee, my lady clambering off the bed and putting out her hands toward the healer. While La Draga may be older, they would still have been girls when they last met. My God, what events would have taken place between then and now. Whatever my lady hears she will no doubt tell me later. As for La Draga, well, her fingers are her eyes, as she moves her hands over my lady's body and face and then up onto her scalp, playing along the scarred ridges and scabs, immediately finding the line of the ill-healed wound that runs from inside the stubble onto the forehead. It lasts a long time, this examination, and the atmosphere in the room changes with it. We are all silent now; even Meragosa is tense by my side, waiting for what La Draga might say.

Eventually, she drops her hands. "You should have come to me sooner."

Her voice is quiet, and I see the fear spark in my lady's eyes.

"We would have, only we were busy saving our lives," I say firmly. "Does that mean you can't help us?"

"No," she says, turning toward me with that sharp little move of the head that I already recognize. "What it means is that the remedies will take longer."

From that night on, my lady sleeps in clean sheets, warmed by Meragosa's lies (told with the same gusto with which she delivered me the truth) and tended by a crippled, blind sparrow of a woman whose unctions and pastes smell so rancid that every time she arrives I can hardly wait to get out into the sour air of the city.

And thus do we come to live in Venice.

PART 2

CHAPTER FOUR

As my lady's health and hair grow, so does my knowledge of the city.

I begin with what I know: the alleyways that lead from our house; the first to the second, the second over a bridge, the third into the *campo*. Its huddled buildings, its small stone well, its church, the baker's oven, from where the smell of fresh bread draws a small crowd every morning; all this feels more like a village than a great city. But every city has to start somewhere, and my old man tells me that when Venice was born out of the lagoon, at first there were only dozens and dozens of tiny islands formed from clumps of houses sunk randomly into marsh water and that everyone moved everywhere by boat. But as each community grew bigger, with its own church and *campo* and freshwater well, gradually they joined together as best they could by way of more buildings and bridges, until there was a city where the main thoroughfares were liquid and the meaning of life was the sea.

Whether this is his fancy or fact I do not know, but it suits me well, for now I see Venice as a series of bigger and smaller circles, coalescing and overlapping, each one a filigree of land and water, like the lace pieces that the nuns produce as presents for their relatives. Each day I trace a new one until I have most of the great north island mapped in my head. Like a modern-day Theseus, I spin out threads of memory to help me: the façade of a certain house with a gold mosaic, the shrine with a decapitated Madonna on a corner, the broken ramp of an old wooden bridge, the arch of a new stone one, the particular smells that come from an alleyway that leads only to dank water. In this way I can move from the Jewish Ghetto in the west, around the market streets of the Merceria, across the piazza of San Marco, above the convent of San Zaccaria, and over a dozen small canals as far as the great walls of the Arsenale shipyard, without getting my feet wet—though it's a fragile enough confidence, for there are still parts of the city in which even a compass would become confused, where the alleys are as bent as used nails and the canals as gnarled as the veins in an old woman's hand.

My senses are acclimatizing too. I understand my old man's Venetian tongue better, for my vocabulary is as foreign as his now and I can make my own mouth go crooked so that my accent makes sense to others. As for the smell? Well, either it has cauterized my nostrils or the arrival of colder weather with storms and rains has washed the city cleaner. In the summer I ran to stay ahead of the stink, now I run to keep myself from the cold.

Meanwhile, La Draga's seeing fingers are healing my lady's scalp, and her company is massaging her spirit. The inside of our house, while it is as poor as ever, is colored now by laughter, the kind that only women's voices can bring, so that even Meragosa has lost her sour edge. My lady's hair is the length of a rebel nun's, the new growth thick and with sufficient sun and honey in its color to form a wild gold halo around her sweetening face, while what was once the forked lightning of a wound is now the palest ghost of a scar. A diet of good food has filled her body, so her breasts push against the lacing of her bodice, and though the dresses she wears still carry the scent of other women, she is fiercely critical of their bad stitching and failings of style. Indeed, her wit has returned sharp enough to have her fretting at her inactivity, so that last week, after our black-eyed Jew changed another ruby, I bought her a lute, an inferior thing of pine and sandalwood, but strung with five courses and enough tone to get her fingers and voice working again.

Maybe she can smell opportunity in the air. For in recent weeks the city has gone mad with business as the first ships have arrived from the Levant, brought in early by good winds.

While I have tried not to show it in her presence, these last months I have suffered heartache for Rome, its solidity as well as its familiar corruption. But even I am excited now. From above the great bridge down to the wharves on the southern island, everywhere is a chaos of trade. The Rialto drawbridge opens for so many tall-masted ships that it is almost impossible for people to cross, while other boats are so crammed together in the canal that they form their own bridges, an army of seamen and laborers forming human chains to move the bales and crates onto land. There are no beggars now; even the most professional cripples can find enough agility to earn a day's wage. You could furnish a life from the contents of these ships: silk, wool, fur, wood, ivory, spices, sugars, dyes, raw metals, precious stones. You feel rich looking at it. Whereas Rome made her money selling forgiveness for sins, Venice grows fat on feeding them. Gluttony, vanity, envy, avarice—the raw material for all of them is here, and for each and every box or bale that moves into or out of the city, there is a duty to be paid to the government.

You would think the rulers of this state must be the richest men in Christendom. Of course, there is no king or the tyranny of a single family to squander the profits. The doge, who looks regal enough when they wheel him out in his white-and-gold plumage, is a figure more of ceremony than of power, picked by means of a series of secret ballots so convoluted that even my old man cannot properly explain the process. When he dies— as this one will soon enough, I think, for he looks as wizened as an old bat already—his family will be excluded from the next ballot. In this way Venice prides herself on being a true republic. A fact that everyone knows because she never stops talking about it. In Rome, when Venetian visitors would begin extolling the virtues and wonders of their city, most people would fall asleep under the weight of the hyperbole. While other cities are wealthy, Venice is priceless . . . while other states are secure, Venice is impenetrable. Venice: the greatest, the loveliest, the oldest, the most just, the most peaceful. Venice—La Serenissima.

Given such monstrous pride, I had expected more ostentation. Yet the truth is that the men who run this state look more like priests than like rulers. You see them everywhere, in the great Piazza of San Marco and all over the Rialto, in their uniform of long, dark coats, cloths like togas thrown over one shoulder, and the simplest of black caps on their heads. Gathered together every Saturday morning, when the Great Council meets, they resemble nothing so much as a great flock of well-kept crows. My lady can decode subtle gradations of power in the trim of ermine over sable or fox fur and the varying shades of darker velvets, but to understand the rules fully, you have to have been born into them, your name at birth, marriage, and death entered into a golden book held in the Doge's Palace and checked by officials to ensure the bloodline is not corrupted by commoners.

The modesty of the men, however, is nothing compared with the invisibility of the women. And here my wanderings have taken on a keener edge, for if we are to make our living, it is my job to smell out the competition. By the end of the first month, I was in despair. While there isn't a city in Christendom without laws to keep the modest and wealthy whores, as well as the richest ones, off the streets, in Venice they actually seem to work. On market days, you might catch sight of the occasional matron in full regalia tottering on high shoes from one side of a *campo* to the other, her hands paddling jewels and attended by twittering servants and yapping dogs. But for the most part, rich women travel by water in covered boats or stay sequestered in their houses. The young do what they can to get attention, the girls preening themselves noisily at the windows, but you'd have to be twice my size to gain anything more than a crick in your neck, and when youngbloods in tunics and multicolored tights throw longing sighs upward (if the adults are crows, the young are gaudy parrots, all strut and plumage), the girls become instantly silly, flapping their arms and giggling, pulled hurriedly out of sight by some lurking protector.

However, every man needs to scratch the itch sometimes, and wherever there is public virtue, there is always private vice. The main brothel is near the market and the great residential hotel where the German merchants live. With the ships in, business is roaring, but the whores work strict hours, their day dictated like that of every other Venetian by the tolling of the Marangona bell, and to keep the peace on the streets, they are locked in for the night. If a man needs relief after closing time, he has to risk the labyrinth.

My old well man pretended to be shocked when I first asked him where to go, but he gave the answer fast enough. Once inside the alleys, vice grows like fungus, and if he wasn't so concerned with the state of his soul, I might show him the latest variety: the street of the tits, where the women perch on the sills of the upper-story windows, like some gross parody of the rich, stripped to the waist and dangling their feet for all to see under their skirts. Even here, though, there is strategy in vulgarity; for, as Meragosa tells it through her gappy grin, it's the government's own idea, because the state is in rising panic over the numbers of young men to be found in dark alleyways pleasing one another rather than sinning in the way God intended.

But Venice has more than sodomites to challenge her purity. During those dark, long nights when we were holed up outside Rome, my lady would lift my spirits by painting pictures of the wealth to be made from her native city, and I learned then that the city offers the right kind of women rich pickings when it comes to nobility. It is a simple case of mathematics over morality. If the rulers in the golden book are to keep their wealth intact, they have to limit marriages. Too many daughters with fat dowries and too many sons with slices of the family fortune spell disaster. So, to keep the lineages intact, the nunneries of Venice are bursting with wellborn women, and the family palazzi are home to a host of bachelors, men born into fine living in search of women with equally fine taste, but suitably compromised morals, to keep them serviced and entertained.

Enter the courtesan.

And in this, Venice being the most successful commercial

city in Christendom, supply and demand are powerfully tuned. Just as the Doge's Palace holds the Golden Book of Lineage, there is another book—a rather more scurrilous one—that gives details of another set of citizens. A book so infamous that even I, who was ignorant of Venice—save for the fact that it is a great republic sunk into water that had fought the Turks to rule the eastern sea—had heard of it before we came. This is the Register of Courtesans: a list of the names of the city's most beautiful, most cultured, and most desirable women, with a space next to every entry where clients can write or read descriptions, prices, even assessments of value for money.

The only question is how to gain an entry. How does a courtesan eager to make her mark announce herself in a city where public ostentation is seen as a sign of vulgarity rather than success? The answer is simple. Since no trader worth his salt buys sight unseen, there are public places where sellers can go to advertise their wares. And in this, for all her protestations of purity, Venice turns out to be no more virtuous or more imaginative than the Holy City itself.

For courtesans, like everyone else, go to church.

CHAPTER FIVE

We have taken our places—separately—in the middle, where it is crowded and where, while we can see those in front, they cannot see us. For we are not here to be seen. On the contrary, until we have better cloth and a house furnished for hospitality, we must keep to the shadows. I would not have her here at all if I had my way. I am noticeable enough on my own, and if spotted together in public, we will be remembered. At least her head and face are well covered, though thanks to the ministrations of La Draga, my lady is nearly enough restored to her former self to hold the gaze of any man she might choose to look upon, and because she knows it now, she will find it harder to resist the challenge. I am done arguing with her, though. There is a limit to how long she can sit in a room with the rancid smell of magic in her hair, and as her confidence has returned, she has become more impatient with my secondhand reports.

"You are the nearest thing to a woman I have found in a man, Bucino, but you cannot judge the competition as well as I can. Anyway, you are too small to see properly over the pews and will therefore certainly miss some of the theater. It is time for me to be there now. When you go next, we go together."

The church we have picked is Santi Giovanni e Paolo, which the Venetians call San Zanipolo—they have more names for their buildings than old women have endearments for their lapdogs. It has less gold and fewer relics than San Marco, and its interior cannot make your heart soar in the same way as the great vaulted nave of Santa Maria dei Frari, but it is big—one of the biggest in the city—and powerful, with the tombs of more than a dozen doges, and it brings the great and the wealthy flocking to Mass, not least because it has a fine and spacious *campo* outside, where after worship the faithful can mingle, showing off the cut of their new cloth along with their piety.

It is a feast day, and the mood on the streets is high. We arrive early so we can watch the congregation gather. The stone floor is alive with the rustle of silk skirts and tapping wooden heels. Of course, not all the women are professionals: in a city where rich women are sequestered, a great church is also a marketplace for pursuing possible marriage contacts, and to this end even respectable girls are allowed to try a little harder with their wardrobes to get themselves noticed. Still, any man with eyes in his head would be able to tell the difference soon enough.

According to my lady, the first trick is the entrance: "You can tell a successful courtesan from the moment she walks in. A good church will have four, maybe five hundred men gathered for Sunday Mass, and I warrant at least sixty or seventy of them will be as interested in the women as in the prayers, though some may not even know it yet. That's why the best courtesans dress for the space as much as for the watchers. You have to give the men time to study you as you come in, so they will know where to find you again during the rest of the Mass."

There are at least four women in San Zanipolo today who know how to make an entrance, two dark, two fair. All of them I have seen before, and they come with their heads high, their dresses so full that in effect they carry their own stages around them, which means they can walk as slowly as they like, their skirts held delicately high over raised shoes and ankles as they pick their way across the flagstones.

They settle in the seats of their choice and spread their skirts, arranging their shawls carelessly, carefully, to show a glimpse of skin, though no breast—too much flesh too fast in church and a man can be reminded of Hell as easily as Heaven.

One of the fair ones, with her hair in a golden net, soars above the crowd, for her stilt clogs are even higher than the rest. I would need a ladder to get even as far as her waist, but fashion makes perfect silliness of sense, and there are already a few tongues hanging out at the sight of her.

The Mass begins, and I glance across to where my lady sits, eagle-eyed, reading their posture as carefully as she has studied their wardrobe. I hear her voice in my head.

The trick now is to keep the men's attention on you even while you do nothing. So you follow the prayers, head erect, voice sweet but not too loud, eyes on the altar, but always aware of what others are seeing. The side or back of your head is as important as your face. While you dare not wear your hair loose, as the virgins do, you can tease a few curled strands down here and there, and weave or braid the rest into gilded or jeweled veils in ways that make it as interesting to study as any altarpiece. And if you've washed and dried it that morning with the right oils—the best courtesans take longer to get ready for Mass than any priest—then its scent can rival the incense. Though you should also have your own perfume, mixed especially, and when no one is looking you should waft it around a bit with your hands. In this way the front pews as well as the back will know you're there. But all this is just preening and preparation for the real test—which is the sermon.

The way my lady tells it, for this moment to work you first need to know your church, because, though it might be filled with the wealthiest men in the city, if the priest is a hellfire preacher who delivers his threats blunt and fast, then any whore worth her salt might as well give up and go home. But get a scholar who's never heard of an hourglass, and every courtesan in the church is already in Heaven.

As we are now; for though the preacher in San Zanipolo is a Dominican who avows purity, he is particularly fond of his own voice, which is a grave mistake, since it is a thin and reedy instrument that stupefies more souls than it saves. By ten minutes in, the older heads are going down onto their chests. As the snoring starts, the rich virgins come to life, slipping their veils aside and sending out glances like coy cupid darts while their mothers wrestle with the weight of a dozen biblical quotations.

All this fluttering makes for a perfect screen for more serious business. While my lady is hawkeyed for the women, I am also interested in the men and what is going on in their heads. I try to imagine myself in their place.

I pick out one figure—I noticed him when he came in. He is tall (as I would be in another life), substantial in girth, maybe forty years of age, and by his dress one of the ruling Crow families, the sleeves on his black coat lined with sable and his wife as rich and square as a four-poster bed. I sit myself in his seat. One of the dark-haired courtesans is in front to the left of me. Zanipolo is my regular church. If things go well, I am hoping to endow a small altar and intend to be buried here. I go to confession every month and am forgiven my sins. I thank God regularly for my good fortune and give him back his share of it, for which, in turn, he helps bring home my investments safely. This morning I have meditated on my Savior's wounds on the cross before praying that the price of silver will stay high enough for me to fund a share in another vessel to leave for Tunis in the spring. In this way I will raise a good dowry for my second daughter, who is ripening fast and must be protected from contamination, because young men do so lust for the crevices in young women's bodies. As, indeed, do older men at times, for there is great and comforting sweetness to be found there . . .

(Ah—see! So it happens: inch by inch, thought by thought, the slip-slide from the spirit to the flesh.) The air is grown stuffy now, and the priest's voice drones on. I shift a little to give myself more space, and as I do so I spot her, five or six rows away, upright amid a sea of slumped shoulders, her fine head high in the air. Of course, I knew she was there—I mean, I had noticed her before, when she first came in, how could I not?— only I had promised myself that today I would not . . . Well, never mind. We have sorted things out, God and I, and a man deserves a little pleasure now and then. I give myself time to really look at her, and she is indeed lovely: ruby dark hair—how lush it would be cascading down her back—golden skin, full lips, and the glimmer of flesh as she adjusts her shawl where it has slipped a little over her breast. Oh, she is so lovely that you

might think God himself has put her here so I could appreciate the sublime perfection of his creation.

And now—oh my, and now—she moves her head in my direction, though she is not looking at me directly. I see the hint
of a smile and then, then, the slow flick of her tongue moving
to moisten her lips. She must be thinking of something, something pleasant no doubt. Something very pleasant. And before I
know it, I am hard as a rock under my coat, and the line between redemption and temptation is already behind me, though
I cannot for the life of me remember when I crossed it. Just as I
don't really think about the fact that those moistened lips and
that secretive smile are not for me only but also for the banker
on my left, who has already enjoyed more than her looks and is
eager to see her roll her tongue for him, not to mention the
young admiral's son five rows behind, who is recently parted
from a lady and is on the lookout again.

And so, as my lady would put it, "Without a word being
said, the fish swim into the net."

Mass ends, and the church is filled with busyness as the crowd
starts to push out. We move fast and, once outside, place ourselves on the small stone bridge overlooking the *campo*, from
where we can watch the final act of the performance. It is cold
and the sky threatens rain, but that does not deter the crowd.

The space is so perfect for courtship that you might think
the women had designed the *campo* themselves. To the right of
the church as you leave, the shining new façade of the Scuola of
San Marco is an excuse for all kinds of dalliance, since to appreciate the cleverness of its marble reliefs, you have to loiter in certain places, moving your body a little to the left or the right,
tilting your head until you get the exact effect. You'd be amazed
how many young, sweet things are suddenly aflame for the
wonder of art. Farther into the center, other knots form around
the great horse statue. The rider was some old Venetian general
who left his fortune to the state on condition they immortalize
him and his horse. He asked for San Marco, but they gave him

Zanipolo instead. He sits up here now, all bellicose and bronze, boastful, oblivious of the action underneath him as young men and women exchange looks while pretending to study the straining muscles in the horse's metal thighs. I like the animal better than the man, but then Venice is a town that favors mules as much as horses, and while I'm safer on the streets these days, I still miss the stomping, snorting power of the great Roman breeds.

My lady's metaphor of the fish is an apt one, for now the whole congregation is out, with small shoals gathering around the more exotic species. Some of the men swim straight in; others hover at the edge, as if they have not yet decided in which direction they are headed. At the center the women turn and float, keeping track of all around them. They carry handkerchiefs or fans or rosary beads, which sometimes slip from their fingers to fall at the feet of a particular man. They smile and pout, tilting their heads as conversations start, covering coral lips with white, manicured hands when a certain compliment or comment causes a spurt of laughter in them and those around them. But while their mouths may be closed, their eyes are talking loudly.

At my lady's instruction, I move off the bridge into the square to observe them better. It's a mark of the excitement that the only people who notice me are a few elder statesmen and their warty wives, who cannot decide whether to stare at me or to shiver with distaste. Though I am not the only dwarf in the city (I've seen one in a troupe of acrobats who perform in the piazza sometimes), I am unusual enough to be a spectacle, which is another reason why it is better we are not seen together, or at least not until we are in business again, when my ugly exoticism can become part of her attraction.

I concentrate on the women in the crowd I know from other visits: the dark-haired beauty with the flashy yellow skirts and snapping fan, and the pale, willowy one with the skin of a marble Madonna and what looks like a net of stars in her frizzy hair. For these I have already discovered names and gossip. The rest I am still studying. If I were not so squat and ugly, I might try to play the acolyte to a few of them now, along with the rest of the suitors. But their game is too tall and quick for me, with glances and smiles darting to and fro as the women divide their time between the converted and the still tempted.

And so the attracted meet the attractive, and in this way is the trade begun.

I am about to turn back to my lady when something catches my eye. Maybe it is the way he holds his arm, for the story was that the attack left him maimed in the right hand. He is behind two other men now, and my view is blocked by their girth. He appears for an instant close to the woman in yellow, then disappears again. He is bearded, and I catch his face only in half profile, so I still cannot be sure. The last I heard of him he had fled Rome for the safety of Mantua and a patron whose wit was as crude as his own. Venice would be too stern for him, surely. But there is a certainty that comes more from the gut than from the brain. And I feel it now. He has his back to me, and I watch him and another man making their way toward the woman with the stars in her hair. Of course. He would like her. She would remind him of someone, and in the book there would no doubt be some entry about her wit and cleverness.

I turn back to the bridge, but while my lady has the eyes of a falcon, her view would be obstructed by the plinth of the statue.

I take a last look, but he is nowhere to be seen now.

It cannot be him. Fate would not do this to us.

CHAPTER SIX

"No flattery now, right, Bucino? This is not the time."

We are sitting together near a thick seawall. The water of the lagoon in front of us is as flat as the surface of a table. With the crowd dispersed, we have made our way across the arched bridge by the Scuola of San Marco, then north along the waterway that cuts upward from the Grand Canal to the shore until we are at the very top of the north island. The sky has cleared, and while it is too cold to loiter, the air is clear and bright, so that we can see past the island of San Michele as far as Murano, where a hundred glass foundries belch thin columns of smoke into the pale air.

"So. Let's start with the one in yellow, the one who couldn't keep her head still, even in church. She is either famous or desperate to become so."

"Her name's Teresa Salvanagola. And you're right, it's fame that's making her brazen. She has a house near the Scuola of San Rocco—"

"—and a list of clients as big as her tits, I have no doubt. Who are her keepers?"

"There's a silk merchant and one of the Council of Forty, although she also entertains outside. Most recently she has taken up with a young bachelor from the Corner family—"

"—at whom she was making eyes during the raising of the host. She needn't have bothered, he is well enough hooked. She is lovely, though the plasterwork on her face probably means she's starting to show her age. All right, who's next? The young, sweet one, in the deep purple silk bodice and crimson lace. Delicate, with a face like one of Raphael's Madonnas."

"The rumor is she is from out of town. There's not much I could find out about her. She is new."

"Yes, and very fresh. And still finding it all great sport, I suspect, as if she can't believe her luck. Was it her mother next to her? Oh, it doesn't matter. For now let's assume it was. She can't be doing it alone so young, and as they came out, I thought there was a certain similarity around the mouth. But did you see her then? Oh, there was spice in that innocence. Like honey to the bees, buzz buzz . . . Who else? There was one I couldn't see properly in the square because the statue was in the way. Fair, frizzy hair and shoulders like bed pillows."

"Julia Lombardino," I say, and I see again his limp and the glimpse of a beard as he moved through the crowd.

She waits. "And? Even I could find out her name, Bucino. You are not to be congratulated yet. What else?"

Not now. There would be no point unless I was sure. "She is native Venetian. Clever, known for her education."

"Outside the bedroom as well as in, I presume."

"She writes verses."

"Oh, God, save us from whore poetesses! They are more boring than their clients. Still, from the flock she had gathered around her, it appears she must flatter as well as she rhymes. Was there anyone else there I should know about?"

And because I cannot be sure it was him, I say nothing. "No one serious, not today. There are others, but they all operate in different parishes."

"So let me hear about them."

I talk for a few moments. She listens carefully, asking only the occasional question. When I am finished, she shakes her head. "If they are all successful, then there are more than I expected. Rome was not so full."

I shrug. "It's a sign of the times. There were more beggars too when we came. War breeds chaos."

She slips a finger up to her forehead. The scar is almost invisible to the eye now, but I daresay she can still feel it. "Is there any news, Bucino? Do you know what's happening there?"

We do not talk about the past, she and I. It has seemed better for us to be looking forward rather than back. So I have to think before I speak, because it is hard to know what to tell and what to leave out.

"The pope is fled to Orvieto, where he struggles to raise his ransom and where his cardinals are forced to ride on mules as if they were the first Christians again. Rome is still run by soldiers, and bad water and rotting flesh have brought pestilence and cholera."

"What of our people? Adriana, Baldesar?"

I shake my head.

"If you knew, you would tell me, yes?" she says, and does not let me look away.

I take a breath. "I would tell you." Though I do not tell the stories I have heard of the pits dug near the city walls where a hundred corpses a day were pushed into quicklime; no names, no tombstones.

"What about the others? Did Gianbattista Rosa get out?"

"I don't know. Parmigianino, it seems, is safe, as is August Valdo, though his library is lost. The Germans used it to light their stoves with."

"Oh, my Lord. What of Ascanio?"

I watch him again, darting into the mayhem, his fancy little book left behind him. "No news."

"And his master, Marcantonio?"

I shake my head.

"Then he must be dead. If he had survived, he would have made it to Venice by now. The best printing presses in the world are here." She pauses. "And our cardinal? He is dead too, yes," she says, and there is no question in her voice. I say nothing. "You know, Bucino, sometimes I think about that night when you came back from the walls. If we had known how it was going to be, I wonder if we wouldn't have given up then and there."

"No," I say quietly. "If we had known, we would have done exactly what we did."

"Ah, Bucino, sometimes you sound like my mother. 'Regret is a rich woman's luxury, Fiammetta. Time is short, and you must run with it rather than against it. Always remember that the man yet to come could be richer than the one before.' " She shakes her head. "Just think, Bucino. Some mothers teach their children prayers to go with the rosary beads; by my first confession, I already knew things I couldn't tell any priest. Ha! Well, it's as well she can't see us now."

Behind us the hulls of the boats crack against the stone quays. Though the sun is out, the wind is sharp. I can feel it ringing in my ears, and I lift my shoulders to protect them. When I was young, I would sometimes suffer from pains that would worm deep inside my head, and I fear the winter might bring them on again. In Rome you hear horror stories of the North: how sometimes people's fingers freeze at night so that they have to crack them back into life in the morning. But my lady is almost recovered now and will soon be making heat in all kinds of places.

"So." And her voice is different, as if it too has changed with the weather. "This is how it seems to me. If we substitute the bachelors for the clergy and add all the businessmen and foreign merchants and ambassadors, then there is as good a market here as in Rome. And if the others are all as they were today, then in the right clothes I could take on any one of them."

As she says the words, she stares straight at me to read any shadow of doubt she might see there. Her hood is pushed back and her hair secured into a wide band woven with fake flowers, so that it is impossible to tell its real length. While the decoration is secondhand, the face is her own. In Rome, toward the end of her reign, she had been known to let young painters measure the distances between her chin, her nose, and her forehead in their search to verify the dimensions of perfect symmetry. But what made their hands tremble was the way those fierce green eyes looked directly into theirs and the stories of how, when she was naked, she could cloak herself in her hair alone. Her hair. That is my only question.

"I know, I think about it constantly. But La Draga has a source. There are certain convents where she heals sick nuns and where there is a market for novitiates' locks. And she knows a woman who can weave new hair into old using golden threads so that the join leaves barely a mark. I think we must try it. If we wait for mine to grow back long enough, I'll be using as much chalk on my cheeks as the Salvanagola woman. We have enough money for it, yes? How many rubies do we have left?"

I take a breath. "After this last one I changed, two, including the great one. And a few good pearls."

"We have spent four rubies in six months? How is that possible?"

I shrug. "We feed a household now. Your hair grows again and your face is lovely."

"Still, La Draga's prices are not so expensive, surely?"

"No, but neither is she cheap. We gambled you would recover quickly, and so you have. No one doubts her skill, but she charges witches' rates and it's a sellers' market."

"Oh, Bucino . . . La Draga is no witch."

"That's not what the gossip says. She does a good enough imitation. Her eyes are turned inside out, and she walks like a spider with half its legs cut off."

"Ha! You are a dwarf who waddles with a grin like an imp from Hell, yet you'd be the first to skewer anyone who read the Devil into your deformity. And since when do you listen to gossip as if it were fact?" She stares at me. "You know, Bucino, I do believe you're cross with her because she spends more time with me than you do. You should join us. Her wit can be as ripe as yours, and she sees well enough into people without using her eyes."

I shrug. "I'm too busy for women's talk."

It's true that while my lady's recovery is as much in my interest as in hers, the endless business of women's beauty can crush a man with boredom. But it is more than that. My crossness, as Fiammetta calls it, is real enough. For all her magic fingers, La Draga still sends shudders through me. I came upon them together once at the end of the day, in a fit of laughter over some tale my lady was telling about the wonder and richness of life in Rome. They did not notice me right away, and though no one can read greed into a blind woman's eyes, I swear in that moment I could feel longing like a fast fever in her, and I wondered how wise my lady was to trust her so.

For her part, La Draga is as wary of me as I am of her. I get none of her laughter or wit; instead we meet only briefly at the end of each week, when she comes for her money. She stays standing at the kitchen door, twisted inside her cloak, her eyes milk-thick so that she seems to be looking backward into her own skull. Which suits me well enough, for I don't want her looking any further into mine. She asked me a few weeks ago if my ears hurt with the cold and said that if they did, she could give me something to help with the pain. I hate the fact that she knows so much about my body, as if she feels herself superior to me, she with her twisted spine and mad blindness. Her eyes and the stink of her remedies make me think of drowning in scummy water. At first, when I was more homesick than I would let myself admit, she summed up all that I loathed most about the city. Now, even if I am wrong about her, it is hard to break the habit of crossing swords.

"Well, all I know is she can cure more than wounds, and despite her bent body, she feels sorry for no one, least of all herself. Which is a quality you share with her. I think you would like her if you gave her a chance. Still . . . we have more important things to do than argue about La Draga. If we put the pearls and the great ruby together, do we have enough to set ourselves up?"

"It depends on what we're buying," I say, relieved to be back to business. "For clothes, it's better than Rome. The Jews running the secondhand market are sharp, and they sell tomorrow's fashions before today's are old. Yes"—I put up my hand to stem her objection—"I know how much you hate it, but new clothes are a rich whore's luxury, and for now it will have to do."

"Then I do the choosing. That goes for the jewelry too. Your eye is good, but Venetians can spot a fake long before the foreigner can. I'll need my own perfume too. And shoes—and they cannot be secondhand." I bow my head to hide my smile: the pleasure is as much in the edge of her hunger as in the rush of her knowledge. "What about furniture? How much must we buy?"

"Less than in Rome. Hangings and tapestries can be hired. So can seats, chests, plates, linen, ornaments, glasses . . ."

"Oh, Bucino." She claps her hands in delight. "You and Venice were made for each other. I had forgotten how much it is the city of the secondhand."

"That's only because so many fortunes are broken as well as made here. And," I say, because she needs to remember that I am as good at my job as she is at hers, "to that end, if we have to hire a house, we will start in debt, and we have no security to buy us credit."

She stops and thinks for a moment. "Is there any other way to begin?"

"Like what?"

"We take a house but hold it only until we have snared the right prey."

I shrug. "God knows, you have grown lovely again, but even with new hair, it will take time to build up a trade."

"Not if we were offering something special. Something—immediate." And she rolls the word in her mouth. "So imagine this. A lovely young woman comes to town and takes a house in a place where the world walks by. She is new, fresh. She sits at the open window with a copy of Petrarch in her hands—my God, we even have the right book already—and smiles at those who pass. Word gets around, and some young—and not so young—men come and look at her. She doesn't move away as modesty demands she should but instead lets them gaze more, and when she does notice them, she is coy and flirtatious at the same time. After a while a few of them knock on the door to find out who she is and where she comes from." And there is mischief in her eyes as she tells it now. "You didn't know me then, Bucino, but I played this once to perfection. Mother took a house near the Sisto bridge for a week when we first came to Rome. She had had me practice every smile and gesture for

weeks before. We had twelve bids within the first two days—
twelve!—most of them from men of substance. We were set up
in a small house on the Via Magdalena two weeks later. I know,
I know, it is a risk. But I was never seen here—my mother made
sure of that—and I am not so old that I couldn't pass for
younger. As far as they are concerned, I could be fresh merchan-
dise."

"Until they get you between the sheets."

"Ah, that's where La Draga comes in. She has a trick"—she
is laughing now, so I don't know if this is sport or not—"for
women who need to fool their husbands on their wedding night.
A plug made with gum alum, turpentine, and pigs' blood. Imagine that! Instant virginity. See—I told you you would like her.
It's a shame you aren't taller with less stubble. We could dress
you to play my mother." But we are both laughing now. "As it is,
they'd have to go through Meragosa, and I'd lose the highest
bidder before they even got halfway up the stairs. . . . Oh, Bucino, you should have seen the look in your eyes. I do believe
that I took you in for a moment. Though I am not saying I
couldn't do it, you understand. . . . Oh, it is an age since I have
fooled you so well."

There were times in Rome—when the money was flowing
and when the wit in our house was such that it was the best
place to spend an evening even if you didn't end up sleeping
with the hostess—when we had laughed until the tears rolled
down our faces. For all its corruption and hypocrisy, the city
was a magnet for clever, ambitious men: writers who could use
words to charm their way under women's skirts or to launch
satires as deadly as a hail of arrows into their enemy's reputation, artists with the talent to turn empty ceilings into visions of
Heaven, with Madonnas as beautiful as any whores rising out
of the clouds. I have never known such excitement as when I
was around them, and though we are alive when so many of
them are dead, I still miss it dreadfully.

"What are you thinking?"

"Nothing . . . Of the past."

"You still don't like it here, do you?"

I shake my head. But I keep my eyes somewhere else.

"It doesn't smell so bad now."

"No."

"And with the ships in and my looks back, we can make things work for us."

"Yes."

"There are people who think Venice is the most wonderful city on earth."

"I know," I say. "I've met them."

"No you haven't. You've met the ones who boast about it because it makes them rich. But they don't really understand its beauty." She looks out over the sea for a moment, her eyes squinting in the sunlight. "You know what is wrong with you, Bucino? You live with your eyes too close to the ground."

"It's because I'm a dwarf," I say, with an irritation that surprises me. "And it stops me from getting my feet wet."

"Ah. Water again."

I shrug. "You don't like men with big bellies, I don't like water."

"Yes, but when they come with purses the same size as their paunches, I get over it quickly enough. I can't make the water go away, Bucino. It *is* the city."

"I know that."

"So perhaps you have to learn to look at it differently."

I shake my head.

She pushes herself against me playfully. "Try it now. Look at it. There—in front of you."

I look. A wind has come up under the sun and is cutting the surface into fitful waves. If I were a fisherman and saw a man walking toward me over it now, I would surely lay down my net and go with him. Even if his Church did end up selling pardons to the rich and damning the poor.

"See how the light and the wind move over it, so that the whole surface shimmers? Now, think about the city. Imagine all those rich houses with their inlays and frescoes, or the great mosaics on San Marco. Every one of them is made from a thousand tiny fragments of colored glass, though of course you don't notice that when you first see them because your eye makes the picture whole.

"Now look back at the water again. Squeeze your eyes, tight. See? It's the same, yes? A surface made up of millions of fragments of water lit by the sun. And it's not only the sea. Think of the canals, the way the houses are reflected in them, still, perfect, like images in a mirror; only, when the wind blows or a boat goes by, the image breaks and trembles. I don't know when I first saw it—I must have been a child, because I was allowed to walk out with my mother or Meragosa sometimes—but I can still remember the thrill of it. Suddenly Venice wasn't solid at all, just made up of pieces, fragments of glass, water, and light.

"My mother thought there was something wrong with my eyes, because I kept squinting as we walked. I tried to explain it, but she didn't understand. Her eyes were always focused on what was in front of her. She had no time for frills or fancies. For years I thought I was the only one who could see it. As if it was my secret. Then, when I was thirteen and started to bleed, she put me into the convent to learn decorum and protect my precious gum alum, and suddenly it was all taken away from me. No water, no sunlight. Instead, everywhere I looked there was only stone and brick and high walls. For the longest time I felt as if I'd been buried alive." She pauses. "I felt the same thing when we first went to Rome."

I stare out over the sea. We used to talk together about all manner of things, she and I: the price of pearls, the rise or fall of a rival, the wages of sin, the judgment of God, and the wonder of how two paupers like us came to find themselves invited to the feast. If I had been born full-size with a purse as big as my prick, it would have been her brain as much as her body that ensnared me. But, as she often tells me, I am more a woman than a man in some things.

A small fleet of boats are making their way across from Murano to the north shore, their hulls splashes of solid black in a multicolored sea. She is right, of course: once you look hard enough, the surface is its own mosaic, each and every fragment a sparkling mix of water and light.

But that still doesn't mean you can't drown in it. "How long did it take you to get used to it?" I ask grimly.

She laughs and shakes her head. "From what I remember, I don't think I began to feel better until the money started flowing in."

CHAPTER SEVEN

The world becomes busier as we move back into town. We pass noisy knots of men, some laborers, some youngbloods in embroidered jackets with legs as colorful as the striped mooring poles in the Grand Canal. My lady keeps her body covered and her head well down, but neither of us can miss a rising excitement in the air. For a city known for its sense of order, Venice also understands the need for release. There have been so many feast days since we got here that I am beginning to lose count of the saints we have celebrated. By nightfall the Piazza San Marco will be heaving. Though it is too early for street mayhem yet.

As we turn in to the Campo Santa Maria Nova, I hear the rush of the feet too late, and they hit us head-on. The impact hurls me against the wall, knocking my breath out at the same instant as I see her lose her balance and sprawl onto the cobblestones. The men are so intent on their destination they don't even pause to register the damage. But halfway across the *campo*, a Turk in turban and flowing green robes has watched it happening, and before I can recover myself, he is at her side, solicitous for her welfare.

Her cloak is half off, her hood has fallen from her head, and as he raises her from the ground, I watch their eyes meet and I know that she will not be able to resist the challenge.

If there were not so many rules to hinder them, I think that men would look at women all the time. Once there is food enough in one's stomach, what else is there to do in life? You see it every day with women in the market or on the streets: the way men's eyes fix on them, like iron snapping onto a magnet, scooping their breasts out of their bodices, lifting petticoats and parting shifts, savoring thighs and bellies, burrowing into the beard that hides the moist little pleat beneath. Whatever the priests may tell you about the Devil, for most men it is so natural that it is like a second language, chattering away under the surface of life, louder than prayer, louder even than the promise of salvation. And while I may be small, I am as fluent in its vocabulary as any man twice my size.

So I also understand something of the thrill a man might feel if such a moment were to be reversed and a woman were to look at a man in the same way. In all my years, the only women I have ever seen do it with conviction are either drunk or professional. And while most men, if they were honest, would not refuse either, if they had the choice they would surely take the second, for it is only women like my lady who make the idea of desire as much a thing of joy and mischief as of sin and desperation.

Or such has been my observation of Christian men. As to the effect of her talent on a heathen—well, I have never seen it until now, though the gossip on the street is that the Turks are so jealous of their women that they do not even allow their painters to put their likenesses onto canvas in case their beauty should inflame other men. Which, if you think about it, would suggest that they are as susceptible to temptation as any men, regardless of creed.

By the time I get my breath back, it is over. They are standing, facing each other: she smiling, sweet now rather than coquettish, her hand on her breast, protecting and exposing the paleness of her skin underneath, while he, dark eyes in a dark face, is still looking, his attention as fierce as a bright ray of sunlight. Her skills work, it seems, with heathens too.

"Are you hurt, my lady?" I say loudly, shouldering my way into the magic circle and kicking her in the shin somewhat more sharply than I had intended.

"Ah! Oh, no, I am quite fine. This courteous gentleman—er . . . ?" She stops.

"Abdullah Pashna. From Istanbul, or Constantinople, as you still call it." And while there are no doubt as many Pashnas in Constantinople as you might find Corners or Loredans in Venice, the name comes laden with mystery. "At your service, Madam . . . ?"

"Fiammetta Bia—"

"If you are well, then we are late," I interrupt rudely. I look up at him. "Sorry, Magnifice Pashna, but my lady is due at the convent." And I hit the word hard. "To visit her sisters."

To my disgust, his look is more amused than aggrieved. "Then I will accompany you both to the door. Your fellow Venetians are fighting one another on a bridge in the Cannaregio, and the city has gone mad to see the show."

"Thanks. But we prefer to go alone."

"Is that your opinion too, my lady Bia—?"

"Bianchini." She enunciates carefully. "Oh, you're very kind, sir," she goes on, her voice like a feather over skin. "But it is probably better that I travel with my servant."

He stares at us both, then turns and gives her a little bow, holding out his hand. The wild scent of ambergris from his glove rises up to torment us with its price tag. I feel her waver, and if there were not a risk of crippling her, I might kick her again. But she holds firm.

"Then I will let you go alone." He drops his hand. "Though for a man as homesick as I am, a woman of such beauty and a dwarf of such . . . perfect proportion and passion bring rare warmth to my heart. I have a house off the Grand Canal, near Campo San Polo. Perhaps on another occasion, when you do not have your 'sisters' to visit, you might—"

"Thank you, but—" I break in.

"We might indeed," she adds sweetly.

I pull her away, and we walk carefully across the square, his eyes on our backs until we move around the corner into another alley. Once we are far enough away, I turn on her.

"How could—"

"Ah, Bucino, don't lecture me. You smelled those gloves. That was no ordinary Turkish merchant."

"And you are no ordinary whore, to pick up men on the streets. What would you have done? Taken him back to your bedroom and had me creep in and steal his jewelry? . . . That would have been the end of it then and there."

"Oh, it was safe enough sport. He was as eager to get to the fight as the rest of them. I wouldn't have done it if he hadn't been. But you have to admit, we had him, Bucino. With no hair and someone else's dress on, we still had him."

"Yes," I say. "We had him."

The house sleeps early tonight. In the kitchen, Meragosa is wedged into the broken chair by the stove, a grumbling snore coming from her open mouth—a pose to which she is becoming accustomed as her stomach grows rounder on our savings. While I cannot swear to it, I suspect that these last few weeks she has been creaming off a few scudi from each shopping purse, but I have had better things to do than watch her every move, and until we are ready to fend for ourselves, the devil we know is the one we have to live with.

Upstairs, my lady lies buried beneath the coverlet. She often sleeps this way now, her head and face covered as if, even in sleep, she is protecting herself against attack. But while I am tired enough, my spirit is jumpy with the excitement of the day, and from the window there is a glow to the south, where the city is celebrating. I slip a few coins from the purse between the slats of the bed and head to the streets toward San Marco.

Though I would not admit it freely, the city still sends shivers into my soul at night. By daylight I have trained myself to walk the narrowest of the canal *fondamenta* without fear of falling in. But after sunset, the city shifts closer to nightmare. In Hell the boiling oil at least has smoke rising off it, but on nights with no moon and few lamps, there is little here to tell black water from black stone, and in the darkness sound moves differently, so that voices which start by moving toward you end up surprising you at your back. Since many of the bridge parapets are higher than my nose and most windows start above my head, any journey after dark is like running through swerving tunnels, and there are moments when the water comes loud on all sides and my heartbeat interferes with my sense of direction. I move fast, keeping tight to the walls, where my companions are rats, who scurry head to tail like links in a chain. The only consolation is that, while they look fierce enough, I know them to be as scared of me as I am of them.

Tonight, at least, I am not alone on the streets, and by the time I reach the Merceria, I am merged into a stream of figures pulled like moths toward the lights of the great piazza.

In general I am not much prone to wonder. I leave that to those who have the time and the stature. Heaven is too far above my head for me to be able to detect even a shadow of it, and what others see as great architecture usually gives me a crick in my neck. In fact, there were times before I realized how easy it was to die when the great Basilica of San Marco would have been an opportunity more for crime than for wonder, since any crowd of pilgrims busy gaping upward would have offered instant pickings for a dwarf with fast hands. But I am a respectable citizen now, and I value my lumpy flesh too much to risk having bits of it strung up between the Pillars of Justice, and while the Roman in me still finds the basilica's fat domes and Byzantine gaudiness too rich for my classical stomach, I have seen how its splendor puts the fear of God—and of the power of the Venetian empire—into all those who come to wonder at it.

As for me? Well, I am fonder of the more humble stone carvings around the columns of the Doge's Palace in the *piazzetta* nearby. Not only are they low enough for me to see but the stories they tell are more about real life: bowls of fruit so lifelike that the fig skins look about to burst open; a dog with startled eyes crunching on a mouthful of honeycomb with the bees still buzzing in it; and my favorite, the story of a man courting a woman, goes all the way around the column, even—after marriage—into bed, where they lie wrapped together under a stone sheet, her hair cascading in hard, frizzy waves across the pillow. When I was young, my father, who was so shocked by my shape that for some years he assumed I was an imbecile, once gave me a piece of wood and a small whittling knife in the hope that God might have put talent in my thumb. I daresay he was thinking of the stories of the great Florentine artists who were discovered in the countryside chipping Madonnas out of road stones. All I did was gouge a piece out of my finger. But I could remember the Latin name of the salve the doctor gave us to stanch the wound, and by the end of the day I ended up in my father's study with a pile of books in front of me. I would probably be there still if he hadn't died six years later.

But there is no room for maudlin thoughts, not tonight; the place I walk toward now is filled with pleasure, bursting with people and noise, and lit by so many firebrands and candle lamps that the basilica's high old mosaics glow fiercely in the firelight.

I cut in from the northeast. I have a healthy fear of crowds (we dwarves are as vulnerable as children in mobs and are more likely to die underfoot than in our own beds), but I know this one will be worth it, and I thrust my way quickly through until I am near a stage built in front of the basilica. A group of half-naked, blackened devils are prancing around, yelling obscenities and poking pitchforks at one another and into the crowd, until every now and then a spout of flame leaps up from a hole in the floor and one of them is pulled screaming and shouting down through a trapdoor nearby, only to clamber back onto the stage a few minutes later to boost the throng. Behind them under the north loggia, a choir of smooth-faced castrati is singing like a host of angels, only someone has built their platform too close to the dogfighting pen, and their voices are half drowned by the frenzied howling of the animals waiting for their turn to die. Meanwhile, on the other side, in a built-up pit of sand, a man and two large women are wrestling as a crowd cheers them on and occasionally joins in.

From every window around the piazza, there are tapestries and banners of arms unfurled and hanging, and the open spaces are crammed with young noblewomen, dressed as if they were going to their own weddings, so that when you look up it feels as if the whole city has let down its hair and is showing off to the crowd. Gangs of bright-stockinged young men are gathered underneath, yelling up to them, while an old man parades back and forth through the crowd, a wooden prick the size of a club poking out from his velvet cloak, gleefully showing off his wares to anyone who cares to look.

I skirt around the edge of the crowd and buy some sugared fruits from a stall in the *piazzetta* near my beloved columns, where the butchers and salami makers have their stalls during the day. The great wharf at the end is filled with long ships, their masts all dotted with hanging lamps so that it looks as if the very sea is lit up. Everywhere you look there are flags of the great lion of Saint Mark, and in front of the two Pillars of Justice, a troupe of acrobats is forming a human pyramid four stories high to be finished off with a dwarf on its top. They have set poles with firebrands all around so the spectacle is well lit, and the first three tiers are already complete. I worm my way forward, and the spectators, taking me to be one of the performers, push and manhandle me gleefully to the front. The final two men are scaling their way up now, cautious, like young cats, while at the side the dwarf is perched on the shoulders of another single acrobat, waiting for his turn.

When the top tier is secure, the two of them move over to the pyramid, the dwarf waving to the crowd and swaying dramatically as if he is already about to fall. He is dressed in silver and red, and if anything he is even smaller than I, though his head is better proportioned, which makes him less ugly, and he has a wicked grin. He hooks himself onto the back of the existing second story. In the torchlight, you can see the sweat on their bodies and the twitching of the muscles as they strain to hold the geometry in shape against his extra weight. He stills himself for a moment before starting to clamber higher. While the street is full of performances that are made to look harder than they are, this is not one of them. A fit dwarf may be able to do all kinds of things that another man cannot, like squatting on his heels for hours or getting up from sitting on the ground without using his hands (you would be surprised how people delight in watching me repeat this simplest of movements), but once we are standing, our leg bones are too short to allow much flexibility. Because of this, we make bad acrobats but excellent clowns, and for that reason we are more fun to watch.

He is up as far as the third story now, and the pyramid is shaking a little with his clumsiness. One of the men at the bottom lets out a savage yell, and the dwarf grimaces and flaps, so the crowd thinks he is really in trouble, which allows them to laugh at him even more. But he knows what he's doing, and when he finally gets to the top and secures himself, out of his doublet he pulls a piece of colored silk on a small stick like a flag and gives a triumphant wave. Then he sticks it on his back and bends himself over until he is crouched like a dog, his hands and feet balanced on each of their shoulders, so the flag now flies like a standard above him.

It takes the crowd a moment to grasp the impact: to see how, in the light of the firebrands, his pose is a mirror image of the great stone winged lion at the top of the Pillar of Justice above him, its wing standing up like its own flag from the ridge of its back.

Despite myself, I, like everyone else, am applauding madly, because it is magnificent and because, of course, I wish that I could have done it myself.

"I would not even consider it, Bucino. There are a dozen better uses for your talents."

The voice is strong and low, like that of a singer who has been taught to hold the note longer than the chorus, and I would have known it anywhere. I turn, and even though all I can think of is the trouble he will cause, I am pleased to see him.

"Look at this, my friends! The ugliest man in Rome has come to Venice to show up its beauty. Bucino!" he yells, and grabs me around the middle, raising me till my eyes are level with his. "God's wounds, man, you are a sight to behold. A dozen chin hairs don't make a beard. And what's this pauper's shit you are wearing? How are you, my little hero?" And he shakes me a little to emphasize his point.

Around him, a group of youngbloods and noblemen, encouraged by his insults, laugh louder at the sight of me. "Don't laugh," he booms. "This man may look like a jester, but he suffers from the cruelest joke God can play. He was born with the body of a dwarf and the mind of a philosopher. Isn't that right, my squat friend?" He is grinning as he sets me down, though his face is a little flushed from the weight of me.

The truth is he is no painting himself, but then he was growing plump on patronage even before the attack maimed his hand and sliced a zigzag into his neck.

"Whereas you, Aretino, have the body of a king and the mind of a sewer."

"A sewer? And why not? Man spends as much time excreting as eating, even if the poets would have us believe otherwise."

And the young men behind him whoop their delight.

"I see you've found like-minded souls to befriend you in this strange city."

"Oh, indeed. Look at them. The cream of the Venetian crop. All dedicated to my advancement. Aren't you, boys?"

They laugh again. But for the last interchange we have slipped into Roman dialect, and they have probably caught only half of what we were saying. He takes me by the shoulder and pulls me off to the side, leaving them a little way behind.

"So." And he is still beaming. "You are safe."

I bow my head. "As you see."

"Which means she is too."

"Who?"

"Ah, the woman you would never have left Rome without, that's who. God, I have been frantic these last months for news of you both, but I could find no one who knew anything. How did you get out?"

"I ran between their legs."

"I would expect no less! You know the bastards broke into Marcantonio's workshop. Destroyed all his plates and machines, beat him to within an inch of his life, and then ransomed him. Twice. Ascanio abandoned him, did you know that? At the first gunshot. Stole the best books from his library and ran, the scum."

"And what of Marcantonio now?"

"Friends raised the ransom and got him as far as Bologna. But he'll never engrave again. His spirit was broken along with his body. My God, what a circus of infamy. You didn't read what I wrote about it? My letter to the pope? It had even the sharpest of Roman critics crying in shame and horror."

"In which case, I'm sure your words were more real than my experience," I say evenly, and brace myself for his guffaw and the hearty slap on the back. Like my lady, he was never one to hide his talents from the world.

"Oh, thank God for the fact of your deformity, Bucino. Or I would have to count you as my rival. So—tell me. Seriously. She is safe, yes? Thank God. How was it?"

How was it? "It was a huge party of death," I say. "Though you would have approved of parts of it. Along with ordinary Romans, the Curia and the nuns took much of the worst."

"Ah, no. There you do me an injustice. I flayed them with words, but even I wouldn't wish the stories I have heard upon them."

"What are you doing here, Pietro?"

"Me? Where else would I be?" He raises his voice now with a gesture to the men behind him. "Venice. The greatest city on earth."

"I thought you said that about Rome."

"I did. And so it was. Once."

"And Mantua?"

"Ah, no. Mantua's full of numbskulls."

"Does that mean the duke no longer finds your poems flattering?"

"The duke! He is the greatest numbskull of them all. He has no sense of humor."

"And Venice does?"

"Ah—Venice has everything. The jewel of the Orient, the

proud republic, mistress of the eastern seas. Her ships are the womb of the world's treasures, her palaces are stone and sugar icing, her women are pearl drops on a necklace of beauty, and—"

"—and her patrons don't know how to close their purses."

"Not quite yet, my little gargoyle. Though they are all noble merchants in this city, with taste and appetite. And money. And they are eager to turn Venice into the new Rome. They never liked the pope, and now that he's melting down his medals for his own ransom, they can get their hands on all of his favorite artists. Jacopo is here. You know? Jacopo Sansovino. The architect."

"Fancy that," I say. "Maybe he'll get a few decent commissions at last."

"Now, now. There is already work for him. Those lead camel humps on their gold monstrosity—sorry, the great basilica—are falling down, and there is no one here who has a clue how to hold them up. You don't understand, my little friend. We are great men here. And we will soon be wielding even greater influence. So—where do you say she is?"

I shake my head.

"Oh, come. She's not still angry with me? When one has looked death in the face, what is a little slander? It made her famous anyway."

"She was famous enough without it," I said. And the memory of his betrayal hardens me against his charm. I move away from him. "I have to go."

He puts his hand on my arm to hold me back. "There is no quarrel between you and me. And never has been. Come. Why don't you take me to her? This city has wealth enough for all of us."

I stand still and say nothing. He drops his hand. "You know I could have you followed. God's teeth, I could have you murdered in the street. Assassins here have a higher success rate than in Rome. No doubt something to do with all that dark water. Which I seem to remember is not to your taste at all. God, Bucino, you must truly worship her to have followed her to this dank world."

"I thought you said it was the greatest city on earth."

"And so it is." He gestures back to the boys, raising his voice. "The greatest city on earth." Then, dropping it again, "I could help her, you know."

"She doesn't need your help."

"Oh, I think she does. If she didn't, I would know of her already. Why don't you ask her anyway?"

The group comes up and surrounds him again. He wraps his good hand around one of their shoulders, and they move off together into the crowd, though not before he has thrown a final look at me. Seeing them closer now, I realize they are not quite so well dressed that they own the streets. Though you would not tell that from the way they walk them.

One thing is for sure. Even with La Draga's gum alum and pigs' blood, we will not be pretending virginity now. Damn him.

The house is dark when I let myself in, but as I climb the stairs I hear music coming from the upstairs room.

I open the door quietly. She is too intent on her playing to notice me. She is sitting on the edge of the bed facing the window, one leg crossed high over the other under her skirts, the better to support the body of the lute, and the light from a cheap candle at her feet is throwing flickering shadows around her face. Her left hand is on the fret board while the fingers of her right are cupped and moving high like spiders' legs over the strings. The sound makes me shiver, not just for the beauty of it—her mother, who was scrupulous about developing her talents, would have had her learning when she was barely able to walk—but because it speaks of the possibilities of our life to come. I have not heard her perform since we were thrown out of Eden almost a year ago, and when her voice comes, while it is not quite the siren song that pulled Odysseus toward the rocks, it is still sweet enough that were there babies awake in their cradles nearby, it would soothe them into sleep. The notes rise and fall as the song weaves a story of fresh beauty and lost love. It never fails to amaze me how a woman whose job it is to suck the seed from a dozen wrinkled pricks has a voice pure enough to rival that of a virgin nun. Which only goes to prove that while God may hate sinners, he sometimes saves his greatest gifts for them. We will need all of them now. Her fingers stay high over the strings as the sound dies away.

I clap my hands slowly from my place by the door. And she smiles slightly as she turns, for she is always good at sensing an audience, and gives a gracious bow with the nod of her head. "Thank you."

"I've only ever seen you play for men," I say. "Is it different playing alone?"

"Different?" She plucks at a string, and the note vibrates in the air. "I don't know. I was always playing for an audience, even when it wasn't there." She shrugs, and I wonder, as I do from time to time, how strange it must be to be bred expressly to pleasure others. As much a vocation surely as that of any nun in thrall to God. She is, however, mercifully unsentimental about such things. That too, I daresay, is her training.

"Though this instrument is rubbish, Bucino. The wood is warped, the strings are too tightly strung, and the pegs too stuck for me to alter."

"Well, you still make it sing well enough for my ears."

She laughs. "Which were always made of cloth when it comes to music."

"As you will. But until you have a bed full of lovers, you will have to make do with the compliments I give."

But she is not one for false modesty, my lady, and I know that she is still pleased.

"So. How was it? Did you go to the piazza?"

"I did." I hear again the voices of the castrati in chorus with the howling of the dogs and see the dwarf's flag and the lion's wing in silhouette together against the burnished night sky. "And—it was very fine."

"Good. She always dresses well for her pageants, Venice. It is one of her great talents. Maybe you will grow to like the city after all."

"Fiammetta," I say softly, and she turns, for I do not use her name often. "There is something I must tell you."

And knowing, as she does, that it must be serious, she

smiles. "Let me see. You found yourself in conversation with a noble merchant who has a house on the Grand Canal and has been looking all his life for a woman with green eyes and shorn fair hair."

"Not quite. Aretino is here."

CHAPTER EIGHT

It is a shame that they ended up as enemies, for they had much in common. They were both strangers to Rome, both from humble beginnings but with enough of an education to be unafraid of those more powerful yet more stupid than themselves. They each had a sharp wit and an even sharper hunger for the wealth it could bring them, and they seemed not to recognize the meaning of failure. If she was younger and more beautiful, then that was only fair, since women make their fortunes from their looks, not their pens. And if he had a crueler mouth, well, that was because, for all her experience of the flesh, he was as much a whore as she was, though he made his living by selling his wit rather than his body.

By the time they met, they were each established in their different ways. Aretino had wormed his way into the outer circle of Leo X, where his tart reporting on the scandals of the day brought him to the attention of one Cardinal Giuliano d'Medici, who became his patron as much to deflect the vitriol from himself as to target it toward other people. When Leo died and the papal crown was there for the taking, Aretino did such a good job of insulting all of Giuliano's rivals that when one of them became pope instead, it was safer for him to disappear for a while. He came back two years later for the next papal election, where his horse finally won the race. Enter Clement VII.

By then my lady was herself a force to be reckoned with. In

those days Rome was the natural home of courtesans. Indeed, it had been their birthplace. A city full of sophisticated clerics, too secular to be saints, especially when it came to matters of the flesh, had soon enough created its own court, with women as refined out of bed as they were wayward in it. Such was the appetite for beauty that any girl with a wit and intelligence to match her looks and a mother willing to procure for her could make a small fortune while her looks lasted. Those twelve offers for my lady's virginity had resulted first in a house paid for by the French ambassador, a man who, as she tells it now, had a liking for young girls but a passion for boys, and so she mastered early the attractions of male clothing and sodomy. While they are worthy talents for a successful courtesan, they are limiting for a young woman with her potential, and my lady's mother was soon wheeling and dealing to find her other keepers. One of those was a cardinal in the new pope's circle, and because he had a fondness for conversation as well as copulation, my lady's house became a place for pleasures of the mind as well as the body. In this way she came to the attention of Pietro Aretino.

In another life they might indeed have become lovers (he was pretty then, and you had only to spend an hour in the company of either of them to understand how that mutual wit and energy might spark a flame). But my lady's mother was a dragon at the gates, and she was smart enough about the business to know that when rich men keep women in the style to which they themselves are accustomed, they don't want to find some sewer satirist pushing his nose into their pots of nectar. As to what exactly took place, I have no idea, for I was new to the household then and still confined to the abacus and the kitchen, but I do remember the morning when we woke to find my lady's name, in a series of Aretino's satires on the Pasquino statue, being used as a byword for the licentiousness of Rome. While such publicity was as much advertisement as it was insult for a good courtesan, his behavior was ungentlemanly to say the least, and for a time both parties went out of their way to demean each other whenever they got the chance.

Yet that is not the whole story either. For it has to be said

that a few years later, when Aretino wrote a set of obscene sonnets to support the disgraced engraver Marcantonio Raimondi,
he chose not to use my lady's name as one of the Roman whores
he exposed there. And later, when the papal censor, the sour-
faced Bishop Giberti, hired an assassin to knife him down on
the streets, my lady, when she received news of his injuries, did
not choose to celebrate as so many did but instead kept her
thoughts to herself.

She has moved to the window, so I cannot see her face. Like
most good courtesans, she is adept at living with two sets of
feelings: the ones she has and the ones she pretends to have to
humor her clients. In this way she is often interested when she
is bored, sweet when she is peeved, funny when she is sad, and
always ready to pull back the sheets to play when what she
would most like to do is sleep alone in them.

"My lady?"

She turns on me, and to my surprise there is laughter in her
eyes. "Oh, Bucino—don't sound so worried. Of course he would
end up in Venice. We should have guessed. Where else could he
go? He's offended most of the rest of Italy by now. And scum always collects on the top of the water. What? Why are you looking at me like that? You didn't believe those stories people told
about us, did you? It was all lies. Roman gossip, nothing more. I
couldn't care less about him."

"Unfortunately, it is not as simple as that," I say, a little
piqued that she finds it necessary to dissemble to me of all people, though I suspect it is as much to herself. "While he may be
scum, from what I saw he is indeed floating close to the top
here. And he knows that we are in trouble."

"Why? How does he know that? What did you say to him
about me?" And now she is angry at the very thought. "Jesu, Bucino, you know better than to tell anybody our business, especially a poisonous windbag. While I have been rotting in this
room, it was your job to find out the lay of the city. How did
you miss a toad as big as Aretino?"

"Possibly because he doesn't wear a dress," I say evenly. "Don't let your anger steal your wits. I told him nothing. I didn't need to. Even if his boasts of influence are only half true, the fact that you are not known here is its own testimony to our misfortune."

"Oh! To have survived the massacre of Rome only to be trashed by a gutter poet. We do not deserve this."

"It's not as bad as you think. He spoke fondly of you. I think he was afraid you had died in the rubble of Rome. He says he can help us."

She lets out a long sigh and shakes her head. In the end she always looks a thing straight in the eye. Believe me, not all women arrive so quickly at where they need to be. "I don't know. You have to be careful with Aretino. He is smart, and he flatters your wit so you think he is your friend. But cross him and he has a tongue like a viper. And his pen always goes where the money is. Our 'disagreement' was a long time ago, but I would not choose to be beholden to him for anything."

She pauses. "Still, you're right, Bucino. His presence makes our decision for us. Now that he knows we're here, we had better get on with it, or his gossip will run before us. The only reason Venice has not heard of me is because I am not yet announced. But I am ready. We both know that. And while this house may not be on the Grand Canal, with some nuns' hair and the right tapestries and furnishings, we can give that snoop across the water something to confess to at her next confession."

Women are weak vessels, their humors too cold and their hearts too afflicted by irrational emotion to stand as tall as men. So says every philosopher from Saint Paul to the old man who measures the well. What I say is they have not met my lady. "You have the resilience of a great whore," I say, grinning. "And you play the lute like an angel."

"And you flatter like a bucket of slops. I should have left you dropping the balls next to that banker's table. If—"

"I know, I know. If he had had a monkey instead of a dwarf, you would have bought the monkey. Though I doubt it would have taken to the water any better than I have."

It is so late now that it is early. The morning light is making stripes on the floor through the shutters, and it is so long since I have slept I can no longer tell if I am tired.

"Oh, God." She yawns, stretching back against the bed. "You know what I miss most of all, Bucino? The food. I am so hungry for taste every day that if I were still intact, I would sell my virginity for a good dish of sardines fried in orange and sugar. Or veal with morello cherry sauce and squash baked with nutmeg and cinnamon and—"

"No. Not veal, wild boar. With honey and juniper. And a salad of endives, herbs, and caper flowers. And anchovies, fresh and salted. . . . And for dessert—"

"—ricotta tart with quinces and apple."

"Peaches in grappa."

"Marzipan cakes."

"Ending with sugared fruits."

"Oh . . . oh." And we are laughing now. "Help me. Oh, I am drooling here."

I pull a grimy paper from my pocket and uncover the remains of the sugared pears I bought in the piazza.

"Here. Try this," I say. And I lift it up to her. "Here's to the best whore and the best cook under the same roof again."

CHAPTER NINE

Next morning La Draga and I meet in the kitchen to negotiate the price of my lady's new head of hair. Mindful of Fiammetta's comments, I make a greater effort to be pleasant. I offer her some refreshment, but by now we are equally suspicious of each other, and she refuses, keeping to her place in the doorway while she calculates the sums of materials and the labor. Her addition is as fast as mine, and when I have checked it, it comes to more than I expected, though what do I know of the price of nuns' locks? Still, I am loath to question her outright.

"Hmm. It makes a tidy profit for the convent then, this trade in hair?"

I watch her head tilt again. Her eyes are closed today, and her mouth stays slightly open, so there is almost a quality of the simpleton about her. "The money does not go to the convent. It goes to the nuns."

"So what? The novices are not yet properly acquainted with the custom of charity?"

"I think it's you who are not acquainted with the customs of Venice," she says quietly, and the notion of the simpleton dissolves fast enough. "The best hair comes from the richest girls. They need the money to dress up their habits and keep their cells in good fashion."

"In good fashion? And you can tell what is good and bad fashion, can you?" Damn it. For it comes out both faster and, I swear, crueler than I intended.

The little breath she takes in is sharper than before, but the voice remains cool. "I can tell when I'm in a room with no furniture, bare flagstones, and the smell of sweat and cooking grease, yes. And how that's different from lavender pomades and the sound of voices against soft woven carpets and tapestries. Perhaps you're one of those people who're used to seeing only with their eyes. When you next go to the Merceria, look for the rug merchant whose blind wife grades the quality of the weave. He runs a wealthy business." She pauses. "I am asked for at the convent this afternoon. Do I buy the hair or not?"

I think of my carved dog with the honeycomb of bees in his mouth. God damn it. It is like being in the room with a swarm of them. I have lived too long with women like my lady, who are trained to charm men, always sweetening their sting with flattery. Perhaps, if she had eyes and could see the impact of her tongue, she might be more sparing with its acidity. Still, her business with me is not courtship. And neither is mine with her.

"Here."

I open my purse for her and hold out the requisite number of coins. She registers the clink with a tilt of her head, but as she moves toward me, her body catches the leg of the chair. As I knew it would. She stumbles but holds her balance. I see a shadow move over her face. On the street the rumor is that she can fold curses in with the mix of her herbs and ointments, and for that reason it is best not to cross her. But she will not curse us. We give her too much money. I go to her and press the cold metal of the ducats into her hand, and she pulls away as if my touch burns, though the coins are already safe in her fist. Is it my imagination, or do I see her smile ripen a fraction? Every middleman I have ever known takes a slice out of the profits, and here in Venice each and every one of them is an expert. What did Meragosa tell me about her only the other day? That for all her manners, she was born poor as a whore, and that she would kill her grandmother for the right amount of gold. Of course, it is Meragosa's way to demean everyone, but the fact is, in a profession such as ours, there are always hungry ticks looking for a fat body to draw blood from, and we are too lean and weak as yet to risk such blood loss, and need to be careful.

Well, if our strategy works, we will not need her ministrations for much longer.

Meragosa, by contrast, is like some grotesque, skittish lamb, all eager and excited by the idea of our venture. Over the next few days she even starts filling buckets of water to begin scrubbing a decade of filth from the walls and paintwork, ready for our new life. Our house has ticks everywhere.

With my purse open now, the Jewish secondhand traders are lining up to serve us. Such is the quality of their stock that even those who curse them behind their backs are eager to do business with them face-to-face. I have some sympathy for them, for while there may be places in the world where dwarves make up the government and Jews own their own land, in Venice, as in the rest of Christendom, they do only the dirtier jobs, like lending money or buying what is already used, though they have become so good at it that many people resent them for it. That and the fact that they killed our Lord, which in the eyes of many makes them more fearful than the Devil himself. Until we came to Venice, the only Jews I had met were men who seemed to scuttle in the shadows, and for that reason it was easy to fear them. But this city is so full of strangers with strange religions that the Jews feel more familiar than most, and while they might be confined to the Ghetto at night, they walk the streets in daylight like any other men. Indeed, my sallow-skinned young pawnbroker has such a solemnity behind his dark eyes that I sometimes yearn to set aside the business of money and talk to him of life for a while.

It is his uncle who runs the clothes business that we pick, for everyone knows the other here. He arrives from the Ghetto with his two assistants carrying huge bundles on their backs, and when they undo them, my lady's room is transformed into a market stall of cloth: rainbows of velvet, brocades, and silks; dresses with clouds of white lawn breaking out from their tight-cut sleeves and low bodices fringed with temptations of lace; yards of petticoats; swirls of cloaks and shawls; filigree-veined gold and silver veils; and high-laced clogs, some as tall as a hod of bricks to raise a beautiful woman out of the threat of high tides and lift her head into the heavens. During the years when such luxury had been commonplace to us, I had become fluent in the language of women's clothes, understanding how a certain color or cut might suit my lady better than another. While it is not a talent most men would boast of, since their purpose in life is more to remove such garments than to put them on, I have found honesty in this matter more effective than flattery when it comes to winning the trust of a beautiful woman. Or at least the one I have grown to know best.

My lady, though, does not waste time indulging herself but becomes instantly as sharp a trader as the man in front of her, not least because inside this riot of secondhand cloth there is always a selection of cut-price new garments. (In this the Jews are like everyone else in Venice: while they obey the laws in the spirit, they are not averse to a little commercial enterprise if both sides gain and neither is found out.) She moves through the piles, plucking one thing up and throwing down another, pointing out flaws, asking prices, tutting and moaning over what isn't there, balancing quality against price, and even smell—"This one you should give to the dogs, it has the smell of the pox about it"—though careful to praise and drool over enough pieces, usually ones she does not want to buy, to keep their spirits up.

Just as she has her job, now I have mine. I have become again the majordomo, the capo, the accountant, and the keeper of the purse. I sit with paper and pen in front of me watching the cloth fly. The buying pile grows higher, and as fast as they do their sums, I do mine, so when the time comes to pay, it is I who do the talking, while my lady sits pretending fits of the vapors over the ferocity of the haggling and the price. And in this way we all acquit ourselves with enough deceit for the transaction to be honorable and for them to leave as content with what they have not sold as we are with what we have had to spend.

That night we eat spiced rabbit stew in new old clothes, she in green brocade that sets off perfectly the color of her eyes and I in an outfit of new hose and velvet doublet, with specially altered sleeves so that at least it fits me—for no dwarf can serve a woman of substance in a suit whose slits are more of wear than of style. Meragosa is pleased with her gown too, for though it has more of the kitchen than of the salon about it, it is in addition to the one I promised and have already delivered to her, and that evening she goes out of her way to feed us well, so all three of us share a sense of high spirits at the thought of what is to come.

Next morning La Draga arrives early, carrying shining falls of golden hair, accompanied by a young woman whose eyes are as alive as our healer's fingers. The day before, my lady had bought a second shawl from the Jews (her idea, not mine), and as she puts it into La Draga's hands now, the healer's pale face lights up like a candle. Yet almost immediately she becomes unsure of herself, caught between pleasure and embarrassment by the compliment my lady pays her. As for me, I am polite but get out as soon as I can, for I will not risk another encounter. Today I am more interested in business than in beauty anyway. I have already retrieved our purse from between the slats of the bed and am off to meet my dark-eyed Jew to exchange the last of our jewels.

As do the proprietors of every other business, the pawnbrokers open their shutters with the Marangona bell. It is raining, and I am not the first to arrive. A man in a cloak and hat is already waiting with a bag held inside the folds of his garment, trying to look as if he is not really here. I have come across his like before. In a city where trade is glory, the difference between a ship that docks with a fortune in its hold and one that falls prey to piracy or bad management is bankruptcy for the merchant who financed the trip with money he didn't have. Those who belong to the ruling Crow families have the advantage of their birth and breeding, for even the poorest of them can sell their votes to richer, more ambitious nobles looking for a step up into one of the smaller governing councils or senates that make up the pyramid of this celebrated state. (It is a mark of the sophistication of Venice that, while every ballot at every level of government is secret, every appointment can nevertheless in some way be rigged. It makes Rome's more obvious corruption feel almost honest in comparison.) But for the citizen traders, there is no such safety net, and the move from grace to disgrace can be dizzyingly fast. When we come to pick our rugs and chests and dinner service, we would do better not to speculate on whose failed lives we will be buying secondhand.

The pawnbroker lets us both in, and I wait in the shop front while the two of them conduct their business in the back. The man leaves about a half hour later with his head down and his bag empty.

Inside the sanctum, I clamber onto the stool, take out my purse, and empty the jewels onto the table between us. He goes straight for the great ruby, and I am pleased to see his eyes flicker at its size. As he turns it over in his hand, I try to imagine the price. It must indeed have choked her to swallow, but it will be worth it now. Depending on its quality, it might be as much as three hundred ducats. Which, along with the others, might give us almost four hundred. The memory of my lady captivating the Turk and the sight of her in finer clothes again had brought back some of the lost confidence of Rome, so that now even I can imagine us renting a house near the Grand Canal for a few weeks. Rich bait to catch richer fish.

Across the table, the pawnbroker is studying the gem through his special lens, the muscles in the right side of his face creased up to keep the glass in place. What age is he? Twenty-five? More? Would he be married? Is his wife lovely? Is he ever tempted by others? Maybe the Jews have their own prostitutes inside the Ghetto, because I cannot remember seeing any Jewesses on the streets. He takes the glass from his eye and puts the stone down.

"I will be back in a moment," he murmurs, and the creases in his forehead are deeper.

"Is there something wrong?"

He gives a shrug and stands up. "Please, wait. I leave the stone here, yes?"

He goes out of the room, and I pick up the gem. It is perfect.

Not a flaw in it. It came from a necklace given to my lady by a banker's son who developed such a passion for her that he became a little deranged, and in the end his father offered her money to let him go. He was later sent away on business and died in Brussels of the fever. I daresay his ruby came closer to her heart on its journey through her insides than he himself had ever done in real life, though she was never cruel to those who pined for her. It was—and, I hope, will be again—one of the hazards of the profession. She will—

The thought is stopped by the opening of the door. My doe-eyed Jew ushers in an old man, with a shock of silver hair and cap, who moves slowly to the table, his eyes on the floor. When he is seated, he pulls the stone toward him and fixes the eyeglass.

"He is my father," the pawnbroker says, acknowledging his lack of grace with a small smile. "He knows a great deal about jewels."

The old man takes his time. The air is beginning to feel stiff—though I can't tell whether it is from the smallness of the room or my growing anxiety—when the old man says: "Yes . . . it is very good, this one."

I let out a sigh, but it sticks in my throat when I see the younger man's face. He mutters something in his own language, and the father looks up and replies sharply. There are more curt, angry exchanges between them, and the old man pushes the ruby back across the table to me.

"What?"

The young man shakes his head. "I am sorry. The jewel is a fake."

"What?"

"Your ruby. She is made of glass."

"But . . . but that's impossible. They all came from the same place. You saw the others. You bought them. You told me yourself they were high quality."

"And they were. I still have two of them here. I can show you the difference."

I stare into its heart. "But—it's flawless."

"Yes. Which is why I was not sure. That along with the cut. You heard my father. It is good, this fake. In Venice there are many who are very clever with glass. But once you see it . . ."

But I am no longer listening. I am in the room, feeling my hands under the mattress for the purse, thinking, sifting through a thousand images and memories. It doesn't make sense. The gems left the room only when we did. And when my lady slept, I slept too. Or was that true? Of course there had been times when she was there alone. But she would never have left them, surely. And for whom? Meragosa? La Draga?

"I don't believe you. I saw your face. You weren't sure. And he"—I poke my hand toward the old man, furious that he still will not look at me—"he can't even see his hand in front of his face. How can he tell anything?"

"My father has been dealing in gems his whole life," the pawnbroker says gently. "I ask him only when there is a doubt. He has never been wrong. I am sorry."

I shake my head. "Then I'll take it elsewhere," I say, squirming my way off the chair and gathering the stones back into the purse. "You're not the—"

Now the old man's voice rises to join mine, his tone as angry as my own. And this time he looks at me. His eyes are filmy and half blind, like those of the mad La Draga, and it turns my stomach to see it. "What does he say?" I yell furiously.

His son hesitates.

"Tell me what he said."

"He says that this city is full of conspiracies against us."

"What—Jews, you mean?"

He nods slightly.

"And he thinks what? That I came here for the last six months trading good gems with you to pass you off a fake now? Is that it?"

He makes a gesture with his hand as if to show that this is only an old man's opinion.

"You tell him that when I lived in Rome, our house was so rich we played dice with better stones than he'll ever see in this hovel."

"Please . . . please, we can still do business." And I realize as he says it that I am shaking. "Please, sit down again."

I sit.

He says something in a firm voice to the old man, who scowls and gets up, shuffling his way toward the door. It slams behind him.

"I am sorry. My father is anxious about many things. You are a foreigner, so I think you don't know, but the Great Council has voted to close the Ghetto and send us out of Venice again, even though we have a contract with them to stay. It is about money, of course, and if we pay again, then no doubt we can change it, but my father is an elder of the community, and it makes him angry. For this reason he is sometimes suspicious of the wrong people."

"I would say so, yes. I didn't come to cheat you."

"I do not think you did."

"But someone *has* cheated me."

"Yes. And it has been done with some cunning. But then Venice, she is a cunning place."

"But how? I mean, how does . . . one make such a fake?" And I can hear the tremble in my voice as I say it. Five minutes before I was planning our rich future, now I am spinning through black space. Oh, my God. Oh, my God . . . How could we have been so stupid?

"You would be surprised how easy it is. There are men who work in the glass foundries on Murano who can make stones so fine that even the doge's wife would not know she was wearing them. If they have the original, they make a not so good copy fast for a quick substitute, then a better one in a little more time. You hear stories—"

"But I check the purse every day."

"And did you study each and every stone?"

"I, er . . . No—just enough to see that they were there."

He shrugs.

"So, what are you telling me? That it's worth nothing?"

"In terms of money, no. It would have cost maybe ten, twenty ducats to make . . . which is not so cheap for a fake. But it is a good one. Good enough to wear as a jewel. Your mistress, because—I think you are selling for somebody else, yes?"

I nod.

"Well, she might wear it around her neck, and most people will not know. But if you want to pawn it now, here, to me, then it is worth nothing. I have no need for such things, and for me it is better if they are not on the market."

"And the others?"

"Oh, the others are real enough. And I will buy them."

"How much will you give me?"

He stares down at them on the table, moving them around with his finger. "For the little ruby—twenty ducats." He looks up at me. "This is a good price."

I nod. "I know. And the pearls?"

"Another twenty."

Forty ducats. It might rent some tapestries for one room, and maybe buy a set of glasses to drink from. Though the wine in them would be vinegar. No noble worth his salt would come near us, or those who came once would certainly not return. Nevertheless. "I will take it."

He pulls down the papers to make out the bond. I look around me. I have grown to like this room. With its books and ledgers and pens, it speaks of ordered management and perseverance. But all I can feel now is panic like bat wings smashing around my head. He dusts the ink and pushes the paper over to me. He watches me as I sign my name.

"You are from Rome, yes?"

"Yes."

"So, what? You came here with the troubles?"

"Yes."

"It was a bad business, I think. Many Jews died there too. I never saw that city, though I hear it was very rich. But I know Urbino. And Modena. And this is better than both of them. Even with our great argument with the state, Venice is a safe city for us Jews. I think perhaps it is because here there are already so many people who are different from one another, yes?"

"Perhaps," I say. "I . . . er . . . I am sorry for your misfortune."

He nods. "And I for yours. If you have anything else to sell, please, I will look at it for you."

We have, it seems, after all, talked about life.

Outside, the sky is as gray as the buildings, and the cobbles are streaming under the rain so that the whole city is like a great mirror, its surface speckled and cracked in a million places. I run like a dog, head down, close to the walls, my legs splashed to my knees and my new velvet doublet sodden within minutes. The sudden exertion hurts my legs, but I go on regardless. At least it stops the thoughts for a moment. There is nowhere to go but home, but perhaps because I dread it so, somewhere on the way I take a wrong bridge or alley and find myself at the edge of the Rialto, where the streets are thick with market crowds and there are dozens of taverns and wineshops in which you could crush memory and drink yourself toward oblivion. I might even have gone in if I had found the right one, but the next turn I take brings me to an alley I don't recognize, and from there I emerge at the water's edge at right angles to the Rialto Bridge. The Grand Canal here is so crammed with barges and boats serving the great fish market that even the rain smells of the fish flesh and the sea.

On the other side, the morning crowd is pouring out from the covered walkway of the bridge when a woman starts screaming "Thief! Thief!" at the top of her lungs. At the same instant a figure breaks free and smashes and skids his way along the canal edge. He tries to push inland, where the alleyways will swallow him, but the throng is too thick, and instead he jumps onto one of the barges and starts clambering across the great canal by way of the fishing boats lashed together for unloading. The crowd is going mad now, flapping and squealing as he slips and slides across wet planks. He is more than halfway across, close enough for me to be able to see the fear in his face, when he hits a mess of fish guts and comes crashing down between the hulls of two boats, so hard I can almost hear his ribs crack as he hits the wood.

A roar of triumph goes up from the other side, and within minutes two great fishermen are hauling him up, he howling with pain, and dragging him back over the boats toward the bank. Tomorrow, if he isn't dead by then, he'll be strung up in front of the magistrate's office next to the bridge with the skin off his back and his thieving hand hanging from his neck. And for what? A purse with a couple of ducats or a grabbed ring or bracelet, of which, for all he knew, the stones would only be worth the glass they were made of.

I stand in the deluge listening to his screams with the water cascading down my face and my nose running with a mixture of snot and rain and the terror of poverty like great stones grinding together in my gut. And when I can no longer see or hear him, I turn and make my way back to the main streets and home.

CHAPTER TEN

The worst of the downpour has slackened by the time I get to the house, and my wits, if not my spirit, are somewhat restored. Only my lady and I had known where I had gone that morning. So the thief, whoever she is, would not necessarily be aware that her deception had been found out.

The kitchen is empty and Meragosa's cloak is gone, but this is the time when she is always at the market, and while she is lazy in many ways, she enjoys the power and the gossip that come with a purse enough to brave the rain.

I move silently up the stairs until I am on the landing and can see into the room ahead. Fiammetta is sitting next to the window, her eyes covered by what looks like a mask of wet leaves and her head a storm of golden hair, the new tresses falling from under a silk band woven halfway up her head. Were it any other moment, I would be transfixed by the change. But there is someone else in the room who takes my attention first. The young woman is gone, but in the middle of the bed sits La Draga, all twisted up, her sightless, egg-white eyes staring into the distance as her hands move swiftly over pots and packages and a small dish into which she is mixing some kind of ointment.

But though she is blind as a newborn ewe, she knows I am there long before I appear in the doorway. As I walk in, I see, clear as daylight, a shadow cross her features, and she shifts her hands back quickly from the bed into her lap. And I have it then and there, in that look. What was it Meragosa said about her? That she would sell her grandmother for the right amount of gold. Amid all that laughter and gossip, I daresay there had also been the story of our escape from Rome. La Draga would have no need of sight to find a purse under a mattress or to feel the size of a jewel, for as she is only too eager to tell me she sees the world through other senses, and she is smart enough to know what sells to whom and at what price. I know who has stolen from us. And she knows that I know it, because I see the fear mounting in her body even before I have accused her. God's wounds, no wonder I have been so suspicious of her.

"Are you comfortable there?" I say as I walk toward her. "You don't feel the need to slide your fingers down the slats to help you balance at all?"

"Bucino?" My lady slips the leaves from her eyes and turns, careful of both the glory and the weight of her new hair. "What is it? My God, what has happened to you? You look awful."

On the bed La Draga has brought both her arms up to protect herself. But she needn't have bothered. Nothing in the world would persuade me to touch her. The very thought makes me sick.

"Nothing's happened," I yelp. "Except this witch here has made fools of both of us."

"What are you talking about?"

"I'm talking about theft and forgery, that's what. Our great ruby is a fake, lifted by clever fingers and replaced by a piece of glass. It's worthless. As are we. So maybe," I say, jabbing my finger at her, "maybe when *she* comes to give us her next bill, she might offer you a small discount for making her so rich. Eh?" And I take a step closer to the creature on the bed so that she will feel the wind from my breath on her face because, yes, for all her clever words, I want to see her scared.

"Oh, sweet Jesus!" My lady has her hand clutched to her mouth.

On the bed, La Draga still doesn't move. I am near enough now to see how pale and milky her skin is, to catch the dark circles under the eyes and watch her lips tremble. I bring my mouth close to her ear. And she is frightened enough now for she senses my closeness: I can feel it, like an animal, her body febrile and startled, frozen in the moment of tension before the jump or the run.

"Eh? Eh?" I say, and this time I shout.

Now at last she moves, snapping her head around and giving out a violent hiss through her teeth, like the sound some snakes make before the kill. And though I could crack her head in my hands, I jump back, for there is such wildness in her defense.

"Oh, my God. No. Leave her alone." And my lady is pulling me away now. "Leave her, do you hear? It isn't her. She didn't do it. It's Meragosa."

"What?"

"It's Meragosa. It has to be. Oh, God, I knew it. I knew there was something wrong this morning when I saw her. Maybe even last night. Didn't you feel it? She wasn't interested in the dress. Couldn't have cared less. But then when we ate she was— I don't know—almost too happy about it all."

I think back, but I can remember nothing except her sour little smile and the taste of her rabbit gravy. God save me from my own complacency.

"After you'd left this morning, she asked where you'd gone. I didn't think to—I mean . . . I said you went to the Jew. She left straight after. I thought she was at the market—"

But I don't hear the rest of the sentence because I am already halfway down the stairs.

Since our arrival, Meragosa had moved her carcass into a room off the kitchen. It had little enough in it to start with, but now it has even less. The old wooden chest that held her clothes is open and empty. The crucifix from the hook above the bed is gone, and even the coverings have been stripped off the mattress.

How? When? Anytime, that is the answer. Anytime when I was out and my lady was sleeping or careless. It had been too dangerous to keep the purse with me always on the streets. Dwarves make fair game for those intent on mischief, and one with precious stones in his crotch would have ended up with no gems and no balls either. But the real fault had been in my judgment. I thought that between my fangs and the promise of wealth I had subdued her: that she would see a richer future in loyalty than in theft. And so it had seemed all these months. But she had just been biding her time. Waiting for the right moment to fleece us even as she slid the blame onto someone else. God damn it—I, whose job it is to be clever, have let myself be shafted by a vicious old slut.

It takes me longer to climb back up to the room. When I get there, my face tells the story that my voice can't manage.

My lady drops her head. "Ah—the poxy hag. I swear I never left her in here on her own. . . . I had her in my sights the whole time. . . . Oh, Jesu, how stupid could we be? How much have we lost?"

I glance quickly at the woman on the bed.

"Oh, you can say it. We have nothing left to hide now."

"Three hundred ducats."

Her eyes close, and the moan is low and long. "Oh, Bucino."

I watch her face as the meaning of the loss seeps like a black stain into the colors of our future. I want to go up to her, to touch her skirt or take her hand, something, anything, to reduce the pain of the moment, but now, with all my fury spent, my legs feel like slabs of marble, and a deep, familiar ache is starting to pump itself up from my thighs along the cord of my spine. God damn my stupid, stunted body. Had I been tall and fat with a set of butcher's hands, Meragosa would never have dared to cheat us. How she must have been laughing at us. Even the thought of it makes me murderous.

The silence is heavy around us. On the bed, La Draga sits completely motionless again, her head tilted into the air, her face like wax, as if she is absorbing the drama and pain around her through the pores of her skin. God damn her, too. But I have spent enough time being stupid, and among the many ways in which the world is turned upside down is that she is now a confidante in our disgrace, and without the ruby's ducats we will be among her creditors soon enough.

I take a step toward her. "Look," I say quietly, and from the way she shifts her head, it is clear that she knows the word is meant for her. "I—I am sorry . . . I—I thought—"

She starts to move her lips in silence. Praying or talking to herself? I glance at my lady, but she is too locked in the misery of our misfortune to pay me any heed.

"I was wrong. I got it wrong," I repeat hopelessly.

Her lips continue to move, as if she is almost reciting or incanting something. I have never given credence to the power of curses: I have been cursed enough by my birth not to be afraid of being further hammered by words, but even so it chills me to watch her.

"Are—are you all right?" I say eventually.

She shakes her head slightly, as if my words are disturbing her. "You have been running, yes? Are your legs aching?"

Her voice is harsher than before, concentrated, almost as if she is talking to someone else, someone inside herself.

"Yes," I say quietly. "My legs are aching."

She nods. "Your back will be starting to throb too. That is because your leg bones are not strong enough to carry your trunk. So it presses down like a great stone at the bottom of your spine."

And as she says it I feel it, pain like a fat pulse near my fat ass.

"What about your ears? Has the cold got in yet?"

"A little." I glance at my lady, who is recovered enough at least to be listening now. "But not like before."

"No? Well, you must be careful with that, for when pain flares inside the head, it is the worst of all."

Yes, there it is already, in my memory: the taste of my own tears as the red-hot skewers twist into my skull.

She frowns slightly. Her face is tilted upright now, the eyes half closed, so I see only the smooth paleness of her skin.

"It seems there is a great deal wrong with you, Bucino. So what, I wonder, is right about you?"

It is the first time that she has ever used my name, and coming so close on my humiliation, it takes me aback, so that I flounder for a moment. "What is 'right' about me? I . . . er . . ."

I look to my lady, and I feel sympathy there now, but she says nothing. "Well, I—I am not stupid. Ha—not usually. I am determined. And I am loyal and . . . while I shout, I do not bite. Or not to any effect, it would seem."

She is quiet for a moment. Then she sighs. "It was not your fault. Meragosa hated everyone," she says, and her voice is soft again. "It came off her like a bad smell. I am sure you are not the first or the last that she has destroyed with her greed."

She starts to gather her pots together, feeling for their lids, slipping them on, pulling her bag toward her. "I will come back to finish the hairline another day."

I make a move toward the bed, I suppose to offer help if she needs it. But she stops me in my tracks. "Keep away from me."

She is still packing when the noise rises from below. What do I think? That Meragosa has had a change of heart and come back to apologize?

By the time I reach him, he is already on the turn of the stairs. He is dressed for visiting, in a fine cloak with a fresh velvet cap on his head, dry enough to have come by cover of boat, although for him to know the way to our house someone else would have had to nose it out before him. God damn it. Is there any end to my carelessness?

There is no point in trying to stop him now. I move back into the room quickly, mouthing his name to Fiammetta. She pulls herself upright, and as she turns to greet him, she lets the new fire of her hair slide around her face so that it masks the panic I see there just before the smile comes.

Secondhand dress, secondhand hair, still first-class beauty. No doubt about that. I read it in the shine of his eyes.

"Well, well . . . Fiammetta Bianchini," he says, moving the words around his mouth as if he can taste her in them. "What a totally expected pleasure it is to see you again."

"Yes, I imagine it is," she replies softly, and you would think from the ease of her tone that she has been waiting this whole morning for him to walk through the door. It is a marvel to me still: how even when the world is crumbling around her, the kind of challenge that would have most people pissing in fear seems only to make her more relaxed, more vibrant. "It is a big place, Venice. How did you manage to find us here, Pietro?"

"Ah . . . I am sorry," he says with a grin, and throws a fast glance at me. "I did not mean to break my word, Bucino. But you are such a visible addition to any city. As soon as one knows you are here, it is not difficult at all to find out where you have been and where you return to."

Secondhand clothes merchants and pawnbrokers. He is right. It can't have taken much. Whoever followed me home, I hope they are coughing their guts out from a fever caught in the rain.

He turns back to her, and the look between them holds. "It has been a long time."

"A long time, yes."

"I must say, you are as . . . radiant—yes, radiant—as I remember."

"Thank you. You, on the other hand, seem to have spread a little. Though I daresay you are rich enough to go with it."

"Ah, ah." His laugh is too spontaneous to be anything but pleasure. "There is nothing in the world so sharp and sweet as the tongue of a Roman courtesan. Bucino told me you escaped, but I am glad your wit is as unscathed as your body, for I have heard the most terrible stories. You know I predicted it would happen, of course. My *prognostico* written in Mantua last year said as much."

"I am sure it did. And therefore you must have been delighted to hear how the army flooded in reciting your very words on the degradation and corruption of the Holy See."

"I . . . No, no. I didn't know that. . . . Is that true? Did they? My God, you did not tell me that, Bucino."

He glances at me, and I try to keep my face neutral. But he is too sharp not to read it.

"Ah. My lady Fiammetta. How cruel to play upon a poet's sensitivities. But I forgive you, for the barb was . . . excellent." He shakes his head. "I must say, I do believe I have missed you."

She opens her mouth to throw back a witticism, but there is something in his tone that makes her stop. I watch her falter.

"And I you, sir . . . in my fashion. You survived Giberti well enough?"

He shrugs and lifts up his hands, one of which he holds folded in on itself. "God is generous. He gave me two hands. With a little practice, the left can tell as much truth as the right."

"More, I would hope," she says a little tartly.

He laughs. "Oh, you don't still hold a few lines of poetry against me?"

"Not the poetry. Only the lies. You were never in my bed, Pietro, and it was sly of you to pretend that you were."

He glances at me and for the first time seems to notice La Draga, who is curled rock still and silent.

"Well . . ." He is, I think, just a little embarrassed. "I daresay my recommendation did you no harm. But, *cara*, I have not come to open old wounds. God knows I have enough of those. No. I am here to offer you my services."

She says nothing. I need her to look at me now, for there is a conversation to be had between us, but her eyes stay fixed on him.

"I am a fortunate visitor in Venice. I have the use of a house. On the Grand Canal. And it is my way to entertain sometimes: the literati, a few of the great merchants, some of the more artistic nobility of this extraordinary city. In this endeavor I am joined by a number of charming women. . . ."

I see her eyes spark with fury.

"Of course, no one of your caliber, but successful enough in their way. If you would like to join us all one evening . . . I am sure . . ."

He leaves it hanging in the air. Ah, the precise art of insult. Even though our very future is at stake, I cannot help but enjoy myself, for it has been a long time since I have watched my lady with so worthy an opponent.

The room has grown cold under her stare. She gives a small laugh and moves her new hair prettily around her shoulders. Thank God for greedy nuns.

"Tell me, do I look in need of charity, Pietro?"

And the risk takes my breath away. "Ah, no. Well, not in person, never. But . . ." And he waves his good arm around the room.

"Oh!" And my lady's laugh is like the sound of silver tapped against glass. "Oh, of course. You were following Bucino, and so you think . . . Oh, I am so sorry. This is not our home."

And as my eyes grow wide at the audacity of the lie, she turns to La Draga. "May I present to you Elena Crusichi. A gentlewoman of this parish and a kind and good soul to whom, as you can see, God has given a different kind of sight so that she may be blind to the ills of the world and closer to his truths. Bucino and I visit her often, for she is in need of comfort and conversation as well as clothes and vitals. Elena?"

As smooth as the pile on the richest of velvets, La Draga lifts herself up and turns to him with a dreamy smile on her lips and her eyes more open than I have ever seen them, so that a man could not help but fall into the depths of their milk blindness.

"Have no fear, my lord." My lady's voice is soft as silk. "Her grace is not contagious."

But though her blindness has taken him aback, he is not afraid. Instead he too starts to laugh. "Oh, madam. How could a man have made such an elementary mistake? To follow a dwarf bringing secondhand clothes to a secondhand house and think it could be connected with your good self." He pauses while he studies, rather obviously, her not quite new enough dress. "And to you, Madam Crusichi, I can only say I am honored to be in your sightless presence. It will be my pleasure to have a basket of food delivered to you later so that you might intercede with the Lord on my worthless behalf also."

He turns to my lady. "So, *carissima*. Is the charade between us complete now?"

She does not reply, and for the first time I fear for her. The silence grows. We have almost no money, and no way of getting more. And the man who might help us at the price of our pride is about to walk out the door.

But it is now, as he turns to go, that something truly marvelous happens. From the bed a voice sings out clear and deep, like the bell that calls nuns to prayer in the middle of the still night. "Signor Aretino."

He turns.

She is smiling in his direction, her lips slightly open as if they were already in conversation, and the smile is so sweet, so pure under the fathomless cloud of her eyes, and it lights up her face with such joy, that for that moment it is as if the grace of God himself is shining through her skin. Though whether or not I believe it . . . "Please. Come to me. Here."

He looks confused, as do we all. But he does as he is asked. As he reaches the edge of the bed, she draws herself up on her knees and puts her hands onto his upper chest, moving her fingers to his neck, to where his scarf has slipped a little so that the top of the scar is visible. She finds it with her finger. I glance at my lady, but her eyes are fixed on them.

"This wound has healed better than your hand," La Draga says quietly. "You were lucky. But"—her fingers slide down across the doublet—"there is something not right here, a weakness within." And she puts her palm close to the place where his heart is. "You must be careful of this. For it will fell you someday if you do not take notice."

It is so serious, the way she says it, that while he laughs, he also glances nervously away from her. For my part, I cannot take my eyes off either of them: for if this is neither God nor witchcraft, then all I can say is she is the best trickster I have ever come across in my life.

CHAPTER ELEVEN

For the first few days, we mask our despair with bickering. We, who have faced Spanish pikes and Lutheran furies, have been tricked by a fat, old slut who even now is pushing silver across a table in payment for roasted boar and good wine. The pain of her triumph turns us as sour on the inside as the world now feels bitter around us, so that we disagree not only about the past but also the future.

"I've told you, I won't do it."

"Let's talk about it at least. We cannot just sit here and do nothing. You say yourself you can match any woman in the city. The fact is that whatever the humiliation of Aretino's house, we know the rewards will be big enough."

"Not necessarily. It will be a catfight. You know his taste. It is the ink in which he dips his pen. He revels in watching women purr and scratch for men's attentions. I have never performed for him, and I won't start now."

"You have never been this unemployed, Fiammetta. If we don't start somewhere, we are doomed."

"I would rather be on the streets."

"If you stay this stubborn, that's where we will end up."

"Oh, really? It seems this loss is down to both of us, but only I am called upon to right it."

"And what would you have me do? Become a juggler while you become a street whore? Together we'd make barely enough to buy the bread we need to keep on opening our legs and lifting our hands. I didn't steal from you and you didn't steal from me, Fiammetta. But unless we are going to face this together, we might as well give up now."

"Together? You think we should face it together. As partners. Is that what you mean?"

"Yes, partners. For good and bad. Wasn't that what we agreed?"

"Which means what? Two people who tell each other the truth, however difficult it is."

"Yes."

But she keeps on looking at me.

"So why don't we talk about Meragosa, Bucino? The woman who cheated us out of a small fortune. Except it wasn't just us, was it? Because she cut her thieving teeth on someone else. Before us she cheated my mother, too. Didn't she?" And her voice is steady and cool.

"I . . . What do you mean?"

"I mean you told me that Meragosa looked after her. That she cared for her in her last illness. And because I believed you, I believed her when she told me the same thing. But it wasn't true, was it? She didn't help her. She just watched her die and bled her dry. La Draga told me yesterday before she left. She said the rumor on the streets was that my mother died of the pox. And that she had never once been called to visit her. Yet she is the best healer there is. Maybe she couldn't have cured her, but she would have helped. But Meragosa didn't ask her. She left my mother to rot." She holds my gaze. "Are you telling me you didn't know that, Bucino? Was I really the only one who was so fooled?"

I open my mouth to let out the lie, but it gets caught in my teeth. She is right. If we cannot tell the truth to each other, we are lost, and, my God, we need each other now.

"Look . . . I . . . at the time I didn't think it would help you to know."

"No? You don't think if you had told me that I might have suspected her more, watched her more closely? And in that way we might not be here today."

Ah, but this is a swamp in which we will both drown. I take

a breath. "Actually, you know what I think, Fiammetta? I think you did know. Somewhere. Only you preferred to believe what she told you because it hurt less."

"In which case you have nothing to blame yourself for. Do you?" And the words come out roasted in scorn as she turns away.

If I am the more guilty, then my penance takes a cruel form: thrumming legs and howling backache as I cross the length and breadth of the city trying to find her. Day after day I trudge the markets to see if I might spot her lumpen figure gloating over new fabrics or fingering cakes of sweet scented soaps with which to clean her foul crevices. But if she is buying, it isn't in any shop or stall I ever find. I try to see the world through her eyes. Where would I go now, what riches would I covet or what rock would I find to crawl under? Three hundred ducats. You could live like a noble for months or a rat for years. For all her greed, I think she is too shrewd to squander it all.

After the markets I go to the rat runs, places near the Arsenale where the ship workers live, where strangers can disappear into streets of one-room slums and a woman can spend a lifetime sewing sails or braiding strands of ropes together in a hall so big that those who have seen it say you could launch a ship in it. A person who wanted to could get lost easily enough here. Once I think I see her crossing a wooden bridge near the walls of the shipyard itself, and I run till my thighs are singing to catch up with her, but when I reach her, she turns into another ugly, old crone wearing a cloak that is too rich for her, and her screams send me reeling. I walk slum streets and knock on doors, but I have no money to loosen tongues, and while the abuse I take suits my mood, even humiliation becomes tedious after a while.

Eventually, I end up in some foul part of town where my nose is assaulted by the stink coming from a drained canal, now a quicksand of mud into which a dwarf would sink as fast as a fat pebble. Running from its stench, I find a drinking hole where I spend the night turning my stomach on *teriaca*, a tipple that would be poison in any state except one where the government earns revenue from brewing it. That doesn't keep me from drinking more of it. For a man scared of drowning, I am lost in liquid now, but then punishment can be a sweet pain sometimes. I forfeit another day and night throwing my guts up and finally wake on the edge of a canal with the stark comfort that there is no farther to fall.

It is three days since I left the house. I have never been away without my lady's knowledge for so long. It is time to leave Meragosa to her devils and come home to face our own.

By the time I drag myself back, it is early afternoon. I arrive at the house by way of the bridge, where the sun plays so bright on the water that it hurts my eyes to look. My God, one day Venice will be beautiful and I will be ready to appreciate it. But not today. I see her before she sees me. She is standing at the window staring out through half-open shutters, a robe pulled around her, her hair crumpled over her shoulders, as if she is waiting for someone. I am about to call to her, for I know she will be worried, when something in her gaze stops me. On the other side, the leathery old bat is at her station, mouth silently muttering into the empty air. They seem to be staring at each other. What do they see? The journey from the dream to the nightmare? For when it comes down to it, what is it that separates the two of them but a slice of water and a fat span of years?

When I study women on the street (for it is my business, remember, as well as my pleasure), I think sometimes of how their bodies remind me of fruit: budding, firming, ripening, and softening, before they fall into blowsiness and decay. It is the decay that scares most, tending as it does to either the wet or the dry: flesh blowing up like a pig's bladder, fat, pasty, as if it might split open—pulp for worms—or the slow attrition of desiccation and shriveling. Is that how it will be for my lady? Will there come a time when those pillow cheeks are loose parchment and those lips, so full that men's tongues itch to press inside, wither to the thinness of a closed mussel? Is that what she is thinking now? Staring across at her own decay? With fewer than forty ducats in our purse and the rent due within the week, it is time for both of us to stop crying and start working. I climb the stairs with renewed determination.

She turns as I open the door, and for that split second I don't know what to look at first: the way her arm is cradled to her side or the body on the bed. The flash in her eyes decides me. He is half dressed, his shirt open on a thick barrel chest, his naked legs sticking out from under the sheet, long and hairy like a spider's. His breath is so heavy and snorting that it is hard to tell if this is the stupor of sexual satisfaction or the sledge-hammer of booze, since the smell coming off him is easily rivaled by my own.

I look at her again. He has done something to her arm. God damn it. What is the first rule of good whoring? Never be alone with a man without backup behind the door.

"What—"

"It's all right. I'm not hurt." And she is firm and focused now: whatever reverie she had fallen into is fast dissolved. "I didn't realize he was so drunk till I got him up here. He was sober enough on the piazza."

"How long has he been out?"

"Not long."

"You got his purse?"

She nods.

"Anything else?"

"He had a medallion, but it's not worth much."

"What about the ring?" I say, both of us staring at the thick band of gold embedded in a sausage finger.

"Too tight."

"Well, we had better get him out of here." I glance around the room, thinking as fast as my gut will let me. The lute, with its fat wooden base, sits by the door.

"No," she says quickly. "Not that. We need it. He has a dagger. We can use that instead."

I find it as she pulls the shutters closed. The sound of their clacking rouses him a little, and he heaves and flops over on one side. So now his face is at the edge of the bed. I give her the knife, throw his clothes near the door, and position myself in front of him so that my face is staring straight into his. I am in good shape for this: my breath is fouler than his and I warrant I have the look of a man for whom Hell holds no horrors anymore. I glance at her, and she nods. My God, I swear it is almost excitement I feel as I yell into his face, my mouth stretched open wide to show my fangs.

He is so befuddled and so shaken by the roar and the sight of me that he is half out of the bed before it occurs to him to question my size. And when he does, he is greeted by the glint of the blade held low—and not without intention—in her hands. In my experience, it is always harder for men to be brave with their balls flapping between their legs. He yells a bit as he moves toward the door, but it is more for the sake of his vanity. By the time he finds his manhood again, he will probably be halfway home and worrying about the pox. In this way does our chastisement bring sinners a little closer to God. Until the next erection undermines all our good work.

Our reward, which is the exhilaration that comes from action, fades faster.

"I tell you, I could have dealt with him. I was on my way to reintroduce myself to the Turk when I met him in the piazza. His cloak was new, and while I could barely understand his accent, he had the look of a successful merchant, and he said he was leaving in two days' time. I thought he was richer than he was."

"I don't care if his prick was gold plated. The rule is you don't bring them home alone. What if he had turned on you?"

"He didn't."

"So what is wrong with your arm?"

"Just a bruise. He was too drunk to notice what he was doing."

"Hmm. Your choice was never so flawed before."

"My choice was never so limited before. Sweet Jesus, Bucino, you were the one who wanted me working again."

"Not like this."

"Well, it wouldn't have been like this if you'd been here, would it?"

She looks away from me, and I see her at the window again, staring at an empty future.

"You should have waited," I say quietly.

"So where were you?"

"You know where I was. Looking for Meragosa."

"For three days and two nights? It must have been an absorbing search, Bucino."

"Well . . . I—I fell into some hole and started drinking."

"Good. Because for a moment I thought the stink on you might have come from finding her. That she'd made you a better offer and you had taken it."

"Oh, don't be ridiculous. You know I would never leave you."

"Do I? Do I really?" She stops herself angrily, then shakes her head. "Three days, Bucino. With no word. This city throws up corpses with every tide. How did I know where you were?"

There is a silence as the flame of our newfound energy fades. If she were not so angry, I think there might be tears.

Through the slit of the shutters, the old woman is shouting out loud now, a stream of abuse about our nosiness and our dubious morals. I go to the window and throw the broken shutters open. I swear, if I had an arquebus, I would let off a shot now and blow her to kingdom come, for I am sick of her beady eyes and muttering drivel. I look down at the water with its flashes of sunlight, and suddenly I am back in a wood outside Rome, with a river in front of me, the sparkle of a newly washed ruby in my palm, and the promise of a future planned between us. God damn this poxy city. I never wanted to come here anyway. She is right. It swallows paupers faster than a carp swallows minnows. It would not take much for us both to die here, facedown in a sewer canal.

"I am sorry," I say. "I didn't mean to frighten you."

She shakes her head. "Or I to send you away." She stops, and her fingers play with the mark on her arm. "It does not do for us to argue."

How scared was she of his violence? I wonder. She would not admit it if she was, even, I doubt, to herself. Of all the courtesans I have met—and I brushed against the skirts of a fair many in Rome—she has always resisted the vulnerability that comes with feeling with the most vibrancy.

"I—I have been thinking about what you said. About Aretino's offer. I should have listened to you."

I let out a breath, for now it feels less a victory than a further hurdle.

"Look, I would not suggest it if I didn't think he still held some feeling for you. I know he crossed you in Rome and you are angry with him for it. But his job was to offend people then, yet there were still those who spoke of him as having a generous heart, and I think he has mellowed here."

"Mellowed! Aretino?"

"I know it sounds unlikely, but I think it's true."

The fact is I have not been so completely consumed that I have failed to keep my ears and eyes open, and it does seem he is changed. Whereas in Rome he was a self-proclaimed public figure, vomiting out his views to any who would pay for them, here he is a more private citizen. No political satire, no lampoons, no civic vivisection to keep the city honest. While there are rumors of letters written to the pope and the emperor to bring the two back together (his arrogance is not quite dead), when it comes to his views on Venice, there is only a river of praise for this earthly paradise of a state, rich in liberty, prosperity, and piety. Personally, I liked him better as a lion than as a house cat, but his pen has made him enemies all over Italy now, and he too is in need of a safe home and new patrons to flatter and fawn over. For now he nuzzles close to those who are already feted: Jacopo Sansovino from Rome, who, it seems, is indeed employed to stop the San Marco's domes from falling down—there are shipments of lead piling up in the piazza now, ready for work to begin—and Tiziano Vecellio, who some say is as good a painter as any that Rome or Florence has produced (I am a dolt when it comes to such things, though I like the way his scarlet Madonna amazes all the men beneath her as she swirls up to Heaven above the altar of Santa Maria dei Frari). With friends such as these, Aretino can afford to wait for the right patrons.

Which means, for now at least, his soirees would be worth attending.

"Well, since we have no other option, you had better go to him and tell him I will come."

And I believe I would indeed have done that had it not been for our visitors two nights later.

CHAPTER TWELVE

"Come on! Open your doors, you great whore."

"Wooh, yes! Get 'em open. We're here for the renowned courtesan of Rome."

We are awake and by the shutters within seconds. It is blackest night, and from the sound of them they have been drinking for hours. A lesser boatman might already have lost a few of them to the water, but even through the slats it's clear it is a fancy craft with lamps on either end. And from the looks of them they are an even fancier flock—nobles, maybe six or seven of them, all young enough still to be wearing colored stockings and rich enough not to care who else they disturb while they are disturbing us.

"Fiam-met-ta Bian-chi-ni."

They slap their oars on the water with each syllable, their voices about as melodious as artillery fire.

"Sweet, white *Bianchini*."

"Little flame, *Fiammetta*."

"Sweet, white, little flame."

"Hot tart without shame."

And a great guffaw goes up at their own excruciating poetry. There will be no house for half a mile around that has not been woken by their cacophony. Young men with the poisons of booze and privilege flowing through their veins. The truth is they break more laws and split open more women's bodies than those who live in poverty. But how often do you find them strung up with half their backs peeling off as examples to others? My God, I despise them, even when they're paying proper rates for it—and I doubt that's what they have in mind tonight.

There is only one way in which men of their status could have learned who and where we are. While I think Aretino is not a cruel man, he is an inveterate gossip, and whatever he has told them about her, they have taken it as a sign that she is available. I can feel her fury in the dark beside me. I make a move to open the window, but her hand snaps out to stop me. At the same instant, there come the creak and bang of shutters nearby and then a stream of foul insults moving to and fro. She is right. If they were to see us now, it would only make it worse. The pantomime grows louder in the night.

"And you can close your poxy legs, lady. We're not here for scrawny hags."

"Not when your neighbor has had cardinals and popes inside her. Aaagh."

But they have met their match here, and from the howl that goes up I daresay the liquid that hits them is richer than water. We stay behind closed doors as the screaming and swearing go on for a while, until finally the youngbloods tire of the game and the boat slaps off noisily into the night. We wait until their voices are swallowed up by the silence, then turn from the window and try to go back to sleep. But their drunken insults echo through my brain, and I am still awake when the first light comes.

I slip out early to fetch the bread. The line is long, and I can hear people muttering around me. Across the *campo*, a group of old women hiss at me as I move back into our street, and when I arrive at my door I find myself staring at a crude drawing of a prick and balls scrawled large in burned charcoal on our outside wall. God damn it, even our neighbors are our enemies now. I climb the stairs with my heart heavy, bracing myself for more fury or despair.

To my astonishment, what I find instead is excitement.

I can hear their animated chatter through the door. Inside, my lady is up and dressed, while opposite her on the bed sits La Draga.

"Oh, Bucino. Look. See what Elena has brought me—cream for my skin. To help its whiteness."

"How kind of her," I say dryly.

La Draga turns toward my voice, and we face each other. Though it is only I, of course, who do the seeing. Her eyes are wide open today, pits of dense white cloud that suck you in even as you look at them. Barely two weeks ago she and I were clawing at each other over this bed, yet now she walks back into the lion's den. She has courage, that much I grant her, and she has made my lady smile when there is nothing to smile about, which is no small thing.

"She is come to offer help if we need it."

"Then I only wish we had the money to employ her . . . you," I say, stumbling over the words, for she still makes me nervous.

"Oh, she doesn't want payment. It is an offer of friendship after our loss, isn't that right, Elena?"

My lady grins at her and takes her hand, and I'd wager that even a blind woman could feel the warmth of her smile through the squeeze.

"But then, then as we were talking and I was telling her what happened last night, I had such a wonderful idea. Oh, Bucino, you will love it. It is perfect. How much money do we have left now? Forty ducats—that was what you said, yes?"

"I . . ." But while we may all be best friends now, I will not share the true depth of our humiliation with anyone but ourselves. "I . . . don't know."

La Draga has read my voice as fast as any look and is on her feet already, withdrawing her hand from my lady's and pulling her shawl—the same shawl that we gave her when our star was in the ascendant—across her body. "I must go now. I—I am called across the city to see a woman whose baby has not turned." She bows to my lady, then turns to me. "If you need me, Signor Bucino, then send a message and I will come."

My lady is so excited she can barely wait for her to get out the door.

"So! Forty ducats. Right?"

"Yes," I say. "Forty, but—"

"Plus the nine ducats from the merchant's purse. The medallion is cheap, I am sure, and his dagger the Jew won't touch. And what about our book? The Petrarch that Ascanio left behind, with its fancy lock? We'd get something for that, surely? Lord knows we've carried it for long enough, and even though it is worn, the gold tooling and silver clasps are the best of Roman printing. The Jew would take that, yes?"

"I've no idea," I say. "We can't even open it."

"We could break the lock."

"But that would ruin part of its value. What are you—"

"Still, it must be fine enough, yes, if Ascanio was going to build his fortune on it. Even if we got, say, fifteen for it. That would give us sixty-four. I am sure we could do it for sixty-four."

"Do what? Fiammetta—what are you talking about?"

"A boat. I'm talking about a boat of our own. A floating bedroom. Sweet Madonna, I don't know why I didn't think about it before. It wasn't until this morning, when I was telling Elena about the thugs on *their* boat. Don't you remember—that woman on the first night?"

The first woman? Of course. How could I forget? The gold curtains, the lazy fingers in her hair, the rush of scent and sex across the water. Even in the exhaustion and fear of our arrival, its exoticism had captured me.

"It's a risk, but I swear we could make it work. Those aren't street whores on those boats. They are special to Venice. My mother always told me that visiting merchants love the romance of them. Only here could a man have such an encounter. And for that reason the best women can charge accordingly. As long as they and their boats are fancy enough."

And, my God, some of them are: black-and-gold-trimmed gondolas with dancing red lights and cabins made out like miniature bedchambers, all satins and silks and damask curtains, with their own shiny, dark Saracen boatmen to maneuver them through the night and, no doubt, look the other way when it is called for. Of course I have wondered about them. Who are they? How much, for how long?

"What about the weather?" I say. "I doubt there's much romance for a prick caught in a sharp wind on the Grand Canal at this time of year."

"I know. The timing is not perfect. But it is getting warmer and there are places where a boat can be sheltered. This way we could get a regular income without destroying our independence. La Draga will help us, and if we're lucky we might even find ourselves a patron. I know, I know, it is not the kind of business that you and I are used to. But it is not nothing, and you are right. We have to start somewhere. My mother knew women who made good livings with the right clientele. Well?"

And because I have lived for years with the set of her jaw, and because her new energy is a thousand times more beguiling than her anger or our despair, I know better than to waste my breath on arguments I will not win.

"Very well. I'll take the sonnets to the Jew."

CHAPTER THIRTEEN

I've forgotten how much an object of beauty it is. All those months on the road crushed inside my jacket have battered and stained its cover somewhat, but the dye of the leather is still a deep, ripe red, its tooled gold lines and lettering of the finest quality, and its edges saved by their silver filigree bindings and clasps. My lady is right. It is the best that Rome could offer, and in the house of a thriving courtesan it would make for fine entertainment: both for the sport of the lock and for the beauty of the Petrarch sonnets inside it. At least if it goes to the pawnbroker, we can buy the time to earn it back.

He seems pleased enough to see me again. In the back room on the shelf, there is water and a plate of small, hard biscuits, which I daresay act as his supper, and he offers me one of them. Aware of the privilege, I accept, though it is tasteless and dry and I have trouble swallowing it.

The book sits on the table between us. He looks but does not touch.

"It is not the Bible," I say. "It is a book by Petrarch."

"And who is he?"

"He is—was—a poet and a philosopher."

"But a Christian?"

"Yes."

"So the book talks of religion?"

"Yes. No. Not really. I think it talks more of life and love."

"I am sorry. I cannot take it. The law is clear: there is no pawning of Christian objects allowed."

"What—my jewels were heathen?"

He smiles. "The ban is against words. Books. And certain artifacts. Things from churches. Or weapons."

"You mean if my rubies had come encrusted in a dagger, you would not have taken them?"

"No, I would not. I could not. This is not only the law of Venice; it is also the ruling of the rabbinate."

"So, what? You would be defiled by such things?"

"The defilement, I think, is on both sides."

"In which case maybe you could take it just for its leather and its silver, for its content will not trouble you. It is locked, and I cannot open it."

God knows, I had tried often enough, playing the numbers like throws of the dice, to penetrate its sequence. There were times on the journey, while I was curled inside my bunk in the bowels of the ship, my imagination useless in thickening the wood walls between me and the water, when, if I had had the tools, I would have smashed the lock open just to have another world to enter to take my mind off the one I was in.

Once my father had taught me how to read, I know he gained much solace from the voraciousness of my appetite. He had wooed my mother with the love sonnets of Petrarch. And because, as a teacher, he thought that what one knew was as important as what one owned, his love of words poured out from him into me. If I had not been still young when he died, I do believe my life might have been different. But while he would be as ashamed of my profession as of my body now, I like to think he might be impressed by how I am able to recite so many philosophical arguments at the more erudite of our carnal gatherings.

"And what does he say, this Patract?"

"He talks of beauty and love."

"What does he say about them?"

"Well, they are sonnets, poems about love. But," I add quickly, thinking I see a frown pass across his face, "he is a philosopher as well as a poet, and he warns of how carnal love between men and women can become a disease, rotting the will and pulling them into madness toward Hell, while love of God transcends the body and frees the soul to start its journey into Heaven."

"And Christians agree with this?"

"Yes." And I think of my father again, for whom Petrarch was near to a saint. "Though it is more honored in the breach than in the observance."

"Which means?"

"That it is easy to say but hard to do."

He sits for a moment with the thought. "But I think God's laws are not meant to be easy. That is the burden and the challenge. For all of us."

I like his seriousness. It feels as if there is curiosity as well as certainty to him. I think how strange it must be to be him. To live in a city and yet not live in it. To be heathen and yet to feel as if you have heathens all around you. To see yourself as chosen while others see you as the Devil's missionaries, your existence so poisonous that you must be locked inside a ghetto at sunset and even pay the wages of the soldiers who guard your gates. What do they do in there all night? Do they spend their time worshiping? Or do they dance and laugh and tell stories and put their pricks into their wives' warm holes like everyone else? They might as well have come from the Indies the little I know about them. And maybe they of us . . .

He puts out his hand, and his fingers touch the silver edge of the book, then the round, engraved barrel of the lock. After a moment, he pulls it toward him.

"You say it is as richly made on the inside as well?"

"The man who did it was Rome's greatest printer and engraver. The quality of his work was famous all over the city."

"And the lock?"

"Was the idea of his assistant, I think."

"A man who worked with metals and cogs."

"Yes."

"I have seen such things before. There is a mechanism in

here, a way that each of these little numbered cogs, if they line up correctly, will snap open."

"That much I guessed. But I have never been able to bring them together in the right order."

He moves the lamp nearer to him and, fixing his lens to his eye, studies the lock.

"What do you see?"

"Small things made bigger, gaps where there was no space before."

"Is that the way you tell a fake?"

"No. With gems it is how the light moves through the stone. There is no fire at the heart of a stone that isn't true." He puts down the lens. "You would be surprised at how many ways a thing looks different when your eye can get inside it."

"Do you think you could open it?"

"Perhaps. I will try."

"Thank you." I watch his face as he concentrates on the lock. "Can I ask you a question?"

He doesn't reply, but I take the little shrug as a form of assent.

"What would you do if you didn't have to do this?"

"This?" He stops. "If I didn't have to do this?" He gestures around the room as if to remind himself where he is. He shakes his head. "If I didn't have to do this . . . I would take a ship and go to the place where the greatest stones are found and I would look inside the earth to see where they came from and how they were made."

"And would you then dig them up and sell them?"

"I don't know." I can see the question surprises him. "I will tell you when I get there."

"How long will you need to open the book?"

"I close with the second to last bell. Come back then."

I maneuver my way off the stool. "If you open the lock, will you look at what's inside?"

"I don't know," he says, his hand reaching for the lens. "I will tell you when I get there."

◆ ◆ ◆

Outside, the city is changing. While we have been talking of God's laws and secrets of the earth, a cold fog has come rolling off the sea, pushing through the alleys, sliding over the water, rubbing up against the cold stone. As I walk, the street falls away behind me, the shop's blue awning lost within seconds. People move like ghosts, their voices disconnected from their bodies; as fast as they loom up, they disappear again. The fog is so dense that, by the time I have crossed toward the Merceria, I can barely see the ground under my feet or tell if the gloom is weather or the beginning of dusk. I weave through streets I know well enough without my eyes until I come to the Campo dei Miracoli.

While it is a small enough *campo* it feels now like entering open sea, nothingness all around and the horizon dense and empty as far as the Indies. I have heard about Venice's fogs from my old man at the well, dark stories of how the mist descends as thick as doubt, so that men can no longer tell where the land ends and the water begins. The next morning, he says, you can always find one or two fellows with bad consciences floating facedown in a canal barely a hundred yards from their homes. Maybe I have lived with a bad conscience for so long now that it is simply a part of me, because, despite my hatred of water, my nerves are more of excitement than of fear, for there is something almost exhilarating in the wildness of it all, as if each step one takes is its own adventure.

The gray-green marble façade of Santa Maria dei Miracoli emerges from the gloom like some great ice statue, the fog swirling so that it seems almost as if I am still and it is the building that is moving. In the middle, its doors are open, the glow of candlelight warm in the cold haze, and I find myself moving toward them.

For a moment, as I cross the threshold, it is as if I am still in the mist. Around me the floor and walls are marble too, and the gray-purple light filtering through high windows is cool and hazy. Though I pass this church almost every day on my way to the markets or beyond, I have never been inside. It's a well-known axiom among pilgrims to Venice that you can die before you visit every church in this city, and I am always too busy to be curious, especially about chapels too small for professional considerations. But now, with the world stopped around me, I have time to stare.

There is a newness to this building, you can feel it. Not just the cleanness but the way everything about it feels simple, with none of the incrustations of time that mark so many of the others: no tombs, no scrambling for status with a dozen rival family altars. On the vaulted barrel ceiling, the medallion portraits are so bright that you can almost smell the paint, and on the altar at the end—on which a portrait of Our Lady of the Miracles sits awaiting worship—the marble screen is carved and intricate, like a piece of lace altar cloth. The half statues of saints and the Virgin gaze peacefully down onto the dozen or more people sitting in the pews. Perhaps they too have come out of the gray sea in search of some solidity to hold on to, but the gauzy air and the silence make it feel, if anything, more dislocated, as if this is neither earth nor water but somewhere in between.

I sit in the back and watch as the church fills up in readiness for evensong, the congregation quiet and somber as if in awe of the weather. Above me, in the balcony built over the doors, I hear the footsteps of the cloistered nuns as they file in from the convent nearby, entering the church unseen by way of an elevated corridor that joins the two buildings. If you listen hard, you can make out sporadic chatter among some of the younger voices, though, as always, they will remain invisible for the service.

La Draga had not needed to be so tart with me about convent matters, for I am not that ignorant. Even in Rome the nuns of Venice are famous. While every Christian city gives girls to God rather than to husbands to avoid the bankruptcy of too many dowries, Venice's boast is that she has as many brides of Christ as she has brides of nobles. In this way the state looks pure and the governing families stay rich. However, it is hardly a secret that conscripted armies show less enthusiasm for their work than do volunteers or mercenaries. In Rome, my lady paid various local nuns to embroider her linen, and I passed many an entertaining hour in convent parlors being poked and prodded under my doublet by giggling young nuns in fashionable dress eager to see if the rumors about small men are true while my lady sat exchanging the latest gossip with the rest of them.

While the government of Venice may be more outwardly committed to virtue, the minds of young women anywhere are not that different when it comes to the boredom of involuntary incarceration. Of this I am certain because it is my business, understanding the ways in which desire overwhelms God's rules, and though men may be the more inveterate offenders, women are not immune, not even those indentured to God. Indeed, given what I know about the power of the human itch, I would go so far as to say that if I were a poor man in Germany with Luther as my preacher, I might have heard his railings against the failed celibacy of the church as common sense rather than heresy. Which in turn makes me think again of Petrarch and how his exhortations away from the carnal to the spiritual came more easily to his older self than to the besotted young poet writing his burning love sonnets to a woman called Laura, who, if you believe his descriptions of her, had the same dazzling beauty as my lady. Though with greater modesty.

I wait till the service is about to begin, then slip away. I cannot hear the Marangona bell here, and it will take me time to get back to the Ghetto in the fog.

The temperature has dropped with the weather, and I walk as fast as I can to keep my spirits and my blood up. It is like moving through a blanket now, and I can feel the anxiety gnawing at me. If he has been successful and the book is as fine inside as it is out, then I will surely be able to find a collector who will pay, if not a ruby's worth, at least enough to buy a boatman for a few days. Without it . . . well, without it is not something I will think about now.

He is standing at the door of the shop, peering out into the gloom as if he has been waiting. "I am sorry," I say. "The fog is thick. It takes time to find your way."

I thought he might let me in, but he doesn't move, and his face looks as gray as the mist.

"I am late. I have to close immediately."

"Did you open it?"

He stares at me, but I still can't see his eyes. From a table inside, he picks up a parcel wrapped in cloth. "I have written the numbers of the lock on a piece of paper inside," he says, thrusting it at me, looking around as if he doesn't want anyone to see us together.

"Thank you. How much? I mean, what—"

"You cannot come here again." And now his voice is angry. "Do you understand?"

"Why? What happened?"

"It is the law that we do not handle the books of Christians."

"I know," I say. "But—"

"You do not come here again. I will not do business with you." He is already closing the door. I try to put out a hand to stop him, but he is stronger than I. "This place is closed to you now."

The door slams in my face.

I stand there, my face hot from the exchange. I slam my hand hard against the wood. Damned Jew. What makes him think he has the right to tell me what not to do? But the truth is, his anger has shaken me. I fumble at the wrapping on the book. As the cloth unwinds, a piece of paper flutters out and down into the gutter. I grab at it frantically, peering at it in the gloom. On it are written four numbers. 1-5-2-6? Yes, 1526. 1526. I have them in my head now. I crumple up the paper and stuff it in my doublet. But there is no way I can open the book here, now.

In this wild weather, it will take me time to get home. I move out of the Ghetto before the gates close and retrace my steps to the edge of the nearest *campo*. To the left is a small bridge, newly restored in stone. I still can't see it, but I know it is there. There is a lamp on a corner, a new one put up to go with the new bridge, which is the pride of the commune, and it is lit every evening regularly at dusk. During normal weather it illuminates the *fondamenta* to either side. I am halfway across before I make out its weak glow, but if I stand underneath it I can at least see enough to arrange the numbers correctly. My fingers are stiff with the cold, and their stubbiness makes it hard to hold the barrel with enough precision to maneuver the cogs. 1. 5. 2. 6.

I hear something click, and as the lock snaps open I am thinking that if you read the numbers together they not only show a pattern but they also make a date, and I wonder what happened in that year that would have made Ascanio pick it as the key.

In the same instant as I pull off the lock and open the book, I know what it was.

CHAPTER FOURTEEN

Of course I have seen them before. There weren't many in our profession who hadn't at least glimpsed them, though we never owned a copy, for they changed hands immediately at rich men's prices, and when the law came down, they disappeared fast as cockroaches under a rock. The pope's censor, Cardinal Giberti, and his men did a good job. There were rumors that he had built a fire in the courtyard of the Vatican and burned them, as Savonarola had burned the vanities of Florence a generation before. As little as a year after, it was impossible to find a single edition in the city. Or at least I heard of none.

Later, some crude woodcut copies were made, which so blurred the lines of Giulio's original pen and muddied his shading that it was hard to see what exactly was taking place. But the original engravings were as clear as the morning light, for Marcantonio Raimondi was known to have the steadiest hand in Rome when it came to incising steel lines into copper. If he was the city's best engraver, then Giulio Romano was certainly her best draftsman, for though he lacked the easy charm of his master, Raphael, he understood the human body as if he had investigated each and every muscle under its skin, and the positions into which he put his figures were a testament both to our appetite for pictorial drama and to his joyful ability to contort and explore the human form.

It is worth remembering that, before these engravings, Romans were by no means innocents in matters of artistic lust. In the richer houses, you could see any number of fleshy nymphs chased by satyrs or swooning Ledas transfixed by the great beating wings of Zeus's swan, and rumor had it that in the Chigi Palace there was even a Roman statue of a satyr in a state of advanced priapic agitation for a young boy. As for women, well, anyone with an appetite for such things could find naked Venuses by the handful, coyly studying their perfect reflections in hand mirrors or lying staring out into the distance, unaware they are being so watched by so many sets of eyes. Yet though the desire they pricked may have been modern, the subject matter was mostly classical, their nakedness clothed in at least a semblance of mythology, to be appreciated only by those with an educated taste. And, however carnal the suggestion, there was always something left to the imagination. Conclusion, climax, coitus, was missing.

Until Giulio Romano.

My poor, sad-eyed Jew. How long did it take him to realize? Had the book fallen open halfway through, or had he been careful and started with the frontispiece? No trace of Petrarch here, though he might not have known it from the first page. A short title, just two words: *The Positions*. I suppose he might still have imagined philosophy, or even theological discussion. And the curiosity grown from our conversation would surely have made him turn the page. But what about the next one? And the one after that?

The Positions: sixteen images of sixteen couples, showing sixteen positions of fornication. In the fog of the bridge, it is hard to make out all the details, but as I flip the pages, my memory adds what my eyes can't. That had been the power of those prints. Once seen, you couldn't forget them. Each image was explicit, exuberant, and even acrobatic. Set amid a smattering of classical allusions—the odd pillar and some flowing drapery—these very modern bodies were busy at the work of love. In some the couples lay twisted together on beds; in one a woman was propped up on cushions on the floor, her buttocks high in the air, in another lowering herself onto a man as if she were arranging herself on a seat, in another balancing on one leg as she guided him inside her; in yet another a man whirling the woman around the room skewered on his prick. Figures with the physiques of gods and goddesses and the imaginations of whores, the men strutting and rippling, the women with an abundance of soft, open flesh. And all of them enamored, enslaved by lust.

I feel again the Jew's agitated fury toward me. What had I read in his eyes? Disgust poisoned by excitement? The outrage of arousal. He wouldn't be alone. Most men, once they had started looking, couldn't stop, though I have come across a few more fragile souls who, when they had finished, were hardpressed to tell their lust from their self-loathing.

Those who knew Giulio Romano's work could hardly have claimed complete surprise. His appetite for both the act and the re-creation of it was common knowledge. Not least to Pope Clement VII, who was one of his biggest patrons. As a Medici, Clement came from a noble lineage of the erotic: his uncle, Lorenzo the Magnificent, had written an infamous sonnet extolling the virtues of sodomy within marriage, and the pope himself enjoyed the stimulation of art as much as the next prelate. He also paid well for it. Though the rumor, which spread like fire through Rome after the engravings first appeared, was that Giulio had first drawn the couples straight onto the Vatican walls in protest for not being paid for already finished work.

Still, while Clement may have been more or less displeased to discover such blatant eroticism decorating his salon, he certainly did not expect to wake up one morning to find Marcantonio's engravings of it circulating—at a pretty price—through Roman society. Which, of course, included the most prestigious members of the Curia. For months, no one could talk of anything else. They did wonders for our profession. My lady was beside herself with excitement, trying to recognize her fellow courtesans from a telltale bracelet left on a wrist or the Medusa curls of a certain hairstyle. Clients arrived with copies under their cloaks: louche men who liked the idea of imagining it just before they did it, timid men who had long desired things they hadn't been able to name. The same images that inflamed young man's fancies were used to improve the performances of old men's tools. For a while it seemed as if most of Roman society, secular and sacred, was busy in bed.

But even when the scandal was at its hottest, there were some, like myself, who followed politics as much as pleasure and who knew we were flying close to the sun. To be fair to the pope's sour-faced censor, Giberti, these were dangerous times. Half of Germany was alight with rebellion and heresy, and their printing presses were working day and night, spewing out their own images of Rome, showing our Holy Father as the Antichrist and the Devil's whore presiding over the city of Sodom. This was not the moment for His Holiness to be seen as producing propaganda to rival theirs.

And so, through Giberti, the papal fist closed. And squeezed. Giulio beat a quick retreat to Mantua, where he had a patron with more money and less guilt, while Marcantonio and his assistant found themselves incarcerated in the Vatican jail, with all existing copies of the engravings confiscated and the original copper plates destroyed.

Or so we all believed.

But now as I stand here on the edge of the bridge in the fog, with the book open in my hands, I am no longer sure. Of course, there might always have been a single last copy concealed somewhere in the studio, cleverly disguised under the innocence of Petrarch. While it felt too devious for the down-to-earth commercial spirit of Marcantonio, it was the kind of cunning one might expect of an assistant, especially one who might already have been planning a future without his master.

But even that does not totally explain the wonder of the book that is now in my hands.

Because this edition of *The Positions* is more than just a set of images.

This edition has words as well.

The verses—"The Licentious Sonnets," as they were known—are not new either. Our very own scourge Pietro Aretino had written them after the scandal, in support of his old friend Marcantonio and to thumb his nose at his even older enemy Giberti. Putting his playwriting muscles together with his talent for the vernacular, Aretino had composed each sonnet as a conversation between each couple, a dialogue of lust for every position, written in a jubilant language of pricks and snatches, cocks and asses; mouthfuls of rich, fat words to complement the rich, fat flesh on its journey away from God into an ecstasy of sin. Celebration, damnation, and defiance. Aretino at his worst and best. It was all here.

It didn't take long for some inferior printer to produce a set of inferior woodblock illustrations to go with them, and for these to be chased around town onto the nearest fire. As for Aretino, well, Giberti slipped his avenging sword to someone else to use. After another public battle of words, the poet found himself knifed in a dark alley, ostensibly by the jilted lover of one of his conquests, but a man who everyone knew was in need of the money he got for the job. With his neck decorated with blood and his writing hand maimed, Aretino left Rome for good. A few copies of the offending book remained hidden away or smuggled out of the city, but they were so crudely produced that they did a disservice to both the images and the words.

But the real triumvirate of Rome's erotic imagination— Giulio's exuberance etched by Marcantonio's pen and brought to life by Aretino's scurrilous tongue—this had never been captured for posterity.

Except that is exactly what I am now holding in my hands; a delicious transgression put together by the clever hands of Ascanio with the engravings on one page and their accompanying sonnets, printed in a flowery, flowing script, on the other. A volume to set the world aflame, locked away inside the gentle leather binding of Petrarch's sonnets.

CHAPTER FIFTEEN

"Oh, Bucino! Our ship is come home from the Indies. You are a Marco Polo among dwarves! Venice should raise a statue to you. Look at this, will you? Every line is so clean, so perfect. See—you can make out a single braid in Lorenzina's hair. Though at that angle, her thighs look as big as a bull's. But then Giulio always made our flesh fatter than the men's. Even when I was eating all the time, I was never large enough for his taste. It is as well there are so few positions where the woman is on top. For there might have been injury otherwise."

Her eyes are as bright as newly polished emeralds, and you can feel the joy and the laughter bubbling up underneath. I don't think my lady could be more pleased if the doge himself had offered to become her patron then and there.

"Oh, oh—my Lord, remember this one? 'I am not Mars, I am Ercole Rangone, and I am screwing you, Angela Grega, and if I had my lute here, I would play you, while fucking you, a song.' Dear God, that's more poetry than ever came out of his mouth when he was upright. And this is supposed to be Lorenzina speaking. . . . Listen: 'Give me your tongue and prop your feet on the wall, squeeze my thighs and hold me tight. . . . One day I'll take your prick up my ass, and I assure you it will come out still in one piece.' Imagine Lorenzina delivering that! Remember that coy little look she used to specialize in when you met her in the streets? Maybe she had teeth down there after all.

Though I doubt it. He is such a liar, Aretino. Really. He boasts of how he gives the women voices, but then he lets us say only the words that men want to hear. He is always going on about how *real* it is when he writes, but I tell you, there's as much fantasy in here as there is in any courtly love poem."

"What—you mean courtesans actually talk like wives when they're in bed?" I say. "What a disappointment. I must stop saving my wages."

"Ah, Bucino! Don't be so modest. I bet you could get a wife talking at least a little dirty. I remember how those Roman matrons used to look at you in the market. So-o-o curious they were. What? You think I didn't see? It's my job to notice such things. . . . Difference. Novelty. The pleasure of the new. Getting abroad what you can't have at home. That's what we are all about. You know that as well as I do. Look at these. No wonder most people couldn't get enough of them. I doubt anyone outside the Church had ever seen this much sodomy. Ha! Poor Giberti. We did put the fear of the Devil in him for a while there, didn't we?"

And, my God, she is right. For that brief moment when the images seemed to rule Rome, what others called sin we sinners called an honest trade. Giving people what they want at a fair price. We certainly made a fair enough profit out of it.

"So tell me, Bucino, how do we go about selling this treasure? Should we be trying to find a Venetian cardinal? I know my own dear Roman one would have given most of his antiquities to have this in his collection."

"A cardinal? I don't think so," I say. "Most of them are Crows before they are cardinals and nowhere near as rancid here as they were in Rome."

In which case, who *are* we going to sell it to?

I have been asking myself the same question since the moment I opened that first page on the bridge in the fog. Because while there is no doubt that its sale is rich with promise, it is also fraught with danger. As soon as a book like this arrives on the market, its seller will become as infamous as its owner— not to mention those responsible for the original work.

"Are you sure that we really want to let it go?" I ask quietly.

"Of course! . . . I mean, if we were established now, I would keep it under my pillow, for with this in my bedroom, I would soon be the most sought after whore in Christendom." She laughs. "But we are not established, Bucino, and with the right bidder this will bring us a small fortune."

"And once it is gone from our hands, what then? News of it will spread like a fire through rafters. Even without the original plates, there are so many printers in this city that there'll be bad copies burning off the presses within days, just as in Rome. It will get back to us eventually. Such things always do, and while there is money in fame, there is danger in notoriety."

"Indeed. But at this moment, I would take it over obscurity."

"Maybe, but what about the others? Giulio is safe in Mantua, and Marcantonio is already half dead in Bologna, but Aretino is a faux Venetian now and eager to win his way into the government's good books. To have his name brazenly displayed next to the world's most obscene sonnets at this tender moment will not endear him to those who make the laws and hand out the patronage."

She shrugs. "But everyone knows he wrote them. He is a libertine already. He is famed for it."

"Maybe. But even he doesn't shit in the drawing rooms of his patrons. Think about it, Fiammetta. Venice boasts a good deal more piety than Rome. There are more codes here, the convents are stricter, and the doge is so upright that he sends his own daughter home when she wears a dress too rich for the law. Once this gets out, Aretino might argue that it was aimed only at the corruption of Rome, but the truth is it will harden men's pricks whichever city they live in. In no time at all most of the government will be sporting their own erections, and they will be forced to suppress the book in the name of public good. And Aretino's hopes of patronage could go down along with it."

She is silent for a moment. "We don't owe him anything. You know as well as I do it was he who sent that boatload of thugs to us."

"Yes," I say. "Though I don't think his aim was to destroy you. More to try and bring you to him."

"That's because he likes to win. He always did."

"And what? Now you want to see him lose?"

"I . . . Yes . . . No . . ." She sighs theatrically. "Oh . . . I don't know." I have watched her act the smart whore for so long, I forget sometimes that in years she is a young woman still. She frowns and sighs again. "He treated me badly, Bucino. Haven't you ever felt angry toward someone who hurt you?"

"Incandescent," I say, seeing a certain man's smug face as he introduces me to a sad young girl. My God, I have not thought of him for a long time. And I will not now. "But if that same person came to me with a fat enough purse, I wouldn't let that get in the way. All I am saying is that at this moment, with his sphere of influence, we have more reasons to keep him as a friend than to make him our enemy."

She smiles wryly at my use of what was once her own advice. "Oh, I know . . . a courtesan should always put business above her heart! Ah, how many times did my mother hammer those words into me? I tell you, Bucino, I could write my own book about this profession. The cost as well as the profit. For sometimes it is as hard as anything you would ask a man to do."

"I know," I say. "I have watched you for long enough to understand that."

"However . . ." And now her voice is strong, as if she is suddenly declaiming to the world. "It is still better than anything else you or I would have been offered in this life. So! Where does that leave us? We cannot afford to make an enemy of Aretino. Which means we cannot afford to sell the book. Which means we are now in possession of a priceless object that we cannot afford to keep because we are still as poor as Dominican nuns—well, the few of them who obey the rules, anyway. It seems I must become a gondola whore after all."

I look at her and think how lovely she is when her spirit is alight, and how it is the way people deal with hardship, rather than success, that sets them apart. I swear I would live with her poor rather than anyone else rich. Though I would still prefer not to have to make the choice.

"How would it be if we didn't make an enemy of Aretino,

kept the book, forgot about the boat, but still made our fortune?"

She looks at me sharply. "Tell me."

In the end I go alone. She takes some persuading, for we both know that she could play it well, but she will get her own performance soon enough if it works, and if there is to be bad blood, then it is better that it remain between him and me.

I choose my moment carefully, dressing up for it, washing with lavender water, and wearing my new doublet and hose so that I look more an equal than a supplicant. I make sure that I eat so my stomach does not rumble, and I hire a boat, which I pay to wait so that if he looks out of his window, he will not see this as a strategy of despair and because, though the water makes me nervous, it is better than arriving with trembling legs, which is always a risk after I have walked too fast or too long.

It is sunny this morning, a tender spring sun that makes the Grand Canal shimmer and lights up the ultramarine and gold of the Ca' d'Oro as if it were an entrance to Heaven, which you could almost believe it is from the number of visitors and pilgrims who rock to and fro on crowded little boats in the middle of the canal gaping at it. Aretino's house, which I already know to be rented from one Bishop Bollani, stands on the same side of the canal to the east, closer to the mayhem of the Rialto. It is a grand enough address—and one my lady would have given another virginity for—but there are no people gaping here: the water is too busy with boats of yelling tradesmen maneuvering their way to shore laden with vegetables and meat for the markets.

The house itself, for all its size, is dingy, its decorations nibbled by salt water and wind and its doorway off the canal so forbidding that it looks more like a way into prison than like a home.

The boatman works his way to its landing bay, trading insults with those who block his passage or scrape his paintwork. The water is so choppy with activity that there is a widening gap between the edge of the boat and the jetty, and my legs are too short to make it over without him giving me a hefty push, which sends me flying onto the wood headfirst and causes a riot of laughter from anyone within fifty yards of us. As I pick myself up, I glance at the balcony window, but there is no one above to witness my humiliation. I imagine myself standing up there: my God, what a view that would be—Venice spread at your feet as if you had been given shares in the wonder of the city.

I pick myself up and move inside. The stone stairway off the entrance is equally crumbling, and I recognize the smell of urine along with water rot; even rich men, it seems, roll home drunk and careless.

The view improves as I turn the corner to the level above and a pretty, young woman with plump cheeks and plumper breasts appears on a sunlit landing to welcome me. I watch her eyes grow round with astonishment as she registers my shape and size. Rising up from the darkness, I probably resemble an incubus come to suck the youth and virtue out of her nipples. Ah, listen to me! A first hint of good living and I am already prey to temptation. Given Aretino's reputation, while I might still get a taste of youth, any virtue would already be long gone.

"My dear lady," I say, bowing—which always makes them laugh, for my legs are too small for it. "Please don't be alarmed. I am one of God's smaller creatures but full of his grace and, as you can see, perfectly formed. Well, almost. And I am here to see your master."

It takes her a while to get over her giggles. "Oh! Who shall I tell him you are?"

"A Roman courtesan's dwarf."

She giggles again before disappearing down the corridor. I watch her go. A domestic treasure certainly but probably food more for comfort than for inspiration.

He comes out himself to greet me. He is dressed for the house, with his shirt half out and his beard and hair untidy and ink stains on his left hand. Now that he is without a jacket, for the first time I can more clearly see his right one, which falls awkwardly by his side.

"My splendid monkey friend!" He punches me loosely in the

chest. We are men's men, he and I—or at least we pretend as much to each other. "What a great pleasure. I am busy at my scribbling, but I will break off for you. Especially if you have brought news of your tart-tongued lady. Come."

I follow him into the *portego*, the great room that is also the broad central corridor of the *piano nobile* floor of all Venice's grand houses and stretches from the back of the house to the front, overlooking the canal. In my life I have learned well enough to curb envy, for it is the most unrewarding of all sins except perhaps for sloth, but now it comes gushing like bile into my mouth, so that it makes me almost sick to swallow it back. It is not that the room is rich. It isn't. The decoration is modest: a couple of threadbare tapestries, coats of arms and weapons, some chests and seats, and two rusty hanging candelabras; old taste, bygone fashions. No. It is not the wealth, but the light. The room is alive with it, great, golden waves rolling through the windows off the canal, bathing the walls and gilded ceiling and shining off a terrazzo floor that is its own mosaic, made up of a thousand tiny chips of polished stone. We have been living in an underworld of dark stone and dank water for so long that I feel like a sewer rat exposed to the sun. I take a deep breath and fill my lungs with the wonder of it. Oh, if we could find ourselves somewhere like this, I swear I'd never complain again.

"You like it? Puts Rome to shame, eh? Only God's natural ingredients—space, sunlight, and stone. With a little help from the ingenuity of man. Venice, my friend. Heaven on earth. How did we ever live anywhere else? I'm afraid it is too early to eat, though I have the promise of a good fish for later. But I can offer you fruit and wine. Anfrosina!" he yells, though he doesn't bother to wait till she answers. "Bring in that basket of winter-berries that Count Manfredo sent us from the country. With a bottle of Signor Girolamo's wine"—she pops up at the door, her eyes still full of me—"and proper crystal glasses, mind. For my guest is—as Plato said of Socrates—a short, ugly, but very wise man."

Anfrosina, who knows as little of Socrates and Plato as she does of me, simply giggles again and flees.

"Your timing is excellent, Bucino. There is a great demand

on the mainland for a proper work on the Catastrophe of Rome. With a big enough audience, it could shame the emperor into better behavior and the pope into more piety, for they are each as stubborn as the other. To which end I am gathering stories that I will weave into a tapestry of grief: my aim is to bring to life the huge party of death, in which, along with the ordinary Romans, the Curia, the priests, and the nuns suffered the worst." He grins as he recalls my words. "See? Next time people say that Pietro Aretino doesn't tell the truth, you remind them that he does not change a single word. So—let me pull out more threads of memory from that great fat head of yours. What, for example, was Fiammetta's place in this? For I could tell from her face that her story must have been extraordinary."

A courtesan who welcomed the invaders and then lost her hair and part of her spirit to a group of harpy heretics—such a tale he might indeed have made up, though in his words it would no doubt become even more foul.

"The story isn't mine to tell. If you want it, you must ask her."

"Oh! She will not talk to me. She is angry with me still. Ah! A woman's rage: molten rock from a volcano, never to be stopped and taking forever to be cooled. You should counsel her, Bucino. She would listen to you. She would do better to settle this feud. We are all in exile together now, and while Venice has its fair share of beautiful women, few have her flair or her wit. And, believe me, this is a place ripe for rich living, liberty, honor, prosperity—"

"So you are saying all over town, I hear. I hope you are making a fine salary out of all this civic toadying."

"Ha! Not yet, though I have great hopes that the doge will smile on me. He is very eager to hear his city praised in print."

The lovely Anfrosina appears with the fruit and the wine, making a meal of setting it on the table and being rewarded with a careless pat on her rump as she leaves. It strikes me that one would probably tire of her after a while. Though it would be fine enough to be given the chance. I put her out of my mind, for it is as well not to mix business with pleasure.

He offers me first pick. "See how well my friends treat me?

Baskets of fresh produce from the country. The best wines. I am more loved than I deserve."

"Maybe you are more feared."

"No. From now on Aretino is a man of peace, piety, and praise. Or for a while at least." And he grins.

I take a breath. "So there will be no poems of pricks and snatches and prelates sodomizing courtesans in Venice then. No more screwing until we die of it, in celebration of poor Adam and Eve, who brought the sin of shame upon us."

He stares at me. "Bucino! You have a better memory than I do. I did not know you were so fond of my work that you could quote it so eloquently."

"Well, it is my work too, in a manner of speaking."

"Indeed, it is. And as you know, I have the highest opinion of it, and I am sure I will return to it someday. For the time being, though, I am a reformed pen, giving my attention to more civic and spiritual concerns."

"Of course. So you wouldn't know anything about a boat-load of drunken louts outside our windows two nights ago."

He stops for a second. "Hmm. Has your lady been receiving admirers?"

I say nothing.

"Well, it is true that I sang her praises to a few who appreciate real beauty. But only because I miss her."

I keep my silence.

"She is all right, though? I mean, there was no trouble? That's not why you're here, I hope. I wish her no ill, Bucino. You of all people know that."

And his posturing makes me feel better about what is to follow. "Actually," I say, "I am here because I have a business proposal to discuss with you."

"Business. Ah." And he reaches for the bottle and pours me some wine. It is pale gold, and the sunlight in the room plays through its bubbles. "I am listening."

"Something has come into my hands. A work of art, of considerable worth. It is a copy of Giulio's *Positions*." I pause again. "In the original engravings . . ."

"The original! Marcantonio's?"

"Yes." I am enjoying myself now. "And with 'The Licentious Sonnets' attached."

"But how? It's not possible. Marcantonio's plates were destroyed long before I put pen to paper."

"I cannot tell you how," I say, "because, to be honest, I do not know. All I know is that I have them."

"Where did you get them?"

I pick up a few more berries. They are a little sharp in my mouth, but it is early in the year, and the sun has not had time to sweeten them. "Let us say they came to me in the madness of the last days of Rome. When many people were on the run."

"Ascanio," he mutters. "Of course, the little shit."

"If it is any consolation, he left Rome without the one volume that would have made his fortune."

He glances at me. "Where is it? Can I see it?"

"Oh, I didn't bring it with me. Its carnal sentiments would stain the streets of this pure city."

He grunts. "I see. What do you want from me, Bucino?"

"I thought we might enter into a publishing venture together. With your connections, we could get them well copied and sell them around town. They would make our fortune."

"Yes," he murmurs. "Your fortune and, at this moment, my disgrace."

"Ah. In which case, perhaps it would be better for me to sell them to a single collector. Someone of taste and influence. We are a little pressed for funds at the moment, and I think it possible we might get a few bids."

"Ooh—blackmail!" He takes a swig from his glass and watches me as he swallows. "I must say, I am disappointed. I had thought more highly of you."

I bow my head. "I learned everything I know from a man more talented than myself. A great writer who has earned his living spreading scandal. Or being paid not to."

And this time he laughs. "God's blood, I do like you, Bucino. Bring the prints and your mistress here to live with me. Together we will rule Venice."

Again I stay silent.

He sighs. "Alas, I could not support her anyway. For I have no money. That is the real problem with your plan, you see. This, all of this"—he moves his hand around the table and the room—"is as yet just the charity of friends."

"I don't want money," I say.

"No? Then what do you want?"

I take a breath. "I want you to find her a patron. A man with position and wealth. Someone who appreciates beauty and wit, and who will treat her well."

He sits back in his chair. "You know, I think it was for the best that she and I fell out all those years ago. For we would have found ourselves rivals otherwise, and I would have lost her in another way. Poor Fiammetta. Has it really been that hard?"

"You have no idea," I say.

"Oh, I would not be so sure of that. There was a moment in an alley in Rome when I thought I heard death's rider in the steps of the assassin who butchered my writing hand. And I have stood by and watched a man with a bigger soul than either of us beat his head against the wall to stop the agony of an amputated leg dragging him into death. I cried like a baby after he went, for he was one of my greatest friends." He shakes his head. "I have no appetite for suffering, Bucino. I like pleasure too much. Sometimes I think I must have something of the woman in me. Which is why I love their company so. It will be my undoing. But I will make life run before it stops me. So, the demand is that I find her a good patron. Anything else?"

"That you get her name into the Register of Courtesans. I will write the entry, and you will find one of your noble friends to put it in."

"No," he says firmly. "That I will not do."

For a second I am not sure what to do. I squirm my way off the chair. "Then I will take the book elsewhere."

"Ah! Wait! If you claim to have learned from the master, then do not be so hasty. For men to make a bargain, there must be give and take on both sides. Sit down."

I sit.

"The entry in the book I will find a way to do." He makes me wait. "But the words will not be yours. They will be mine."

I stare at him. "And how do I know you will not cheat her?"

"Because," he says. "Because, because, because, Bucino, even when I exaggerate, I tell the truth. Especially about women. As you know only too well."

I stand up again.

"And how do I know that you will keep to your end of the deal, and once she is settled and rich, I won't wake up the next day to find copies of *The Positions* all around Venice with my name attached?"

"Because, if you are loyal to her, then I will be loyal to you. As you know only too well."

CHAPTER SIXTEEN

Across the canal, our old bat is at her window, transfixed. The day is cooler now, and the same drafts that rattle our frames will be rattling hers too, but still she does not budge. Her face is set like thunder, and if she could manage to focus her roving eyes for long enough, I daresay we would feel the hammer of her disapproval, but we have our own witch to protect us and are too busy with the business of decorating young beauty to give much credence to soured age.

La Draga and my mistress have been together since the early afternoon. I have not been allowed in until they are finished, and my job is to be impressed by what I see. As it happens, my capacity for dishonesty is barely stretched at all. She is so high in her clogs that I have to stand on the bed to get the full impression. She is wearing the best of the secondhand dresses. It is made of a wild scarlet silk. Its sleeves are pale cream, gathered tight at the wrists before exploding into clouds of red at the elbows; its bodice is trimmed with gold to draw attention to the swooping neckline, and its skirts fall wide and billowing from a jeweled band under her breasts. It contains such a luxury of material that one might hope Aretino's guests do not include the doge himself, for he has been known to send women home from gatherings when the lengths of cloth were so obviously excessive that it wouldn't take a measuring tape to define them as outside the law.

But no one would send my lady home. For the dress is just the wrapping. As for the woman inside, well, after this many years in her service, my compliments are threadbare with over-use. But I will offer a few words about her hair, some of which is not her own and therefore worthy of criticism, and which has been coaxed and teased into a dozen feathery curls at her brow and a few flying ringlets around her cheeks, with the rest of it falling in slow, rolling waves from what looks like a braided band of her own tresses set halfway back on her head. I close my eyes to see the imprint of her on the backs of my lids, and the air is filled with the smell of musk roses and the promise of summer.

"Well?" I open my eyes onto her question. "You could at least say something. We've been at this all day. A few lines of Petrarch perhaps? Or that other man you are so fond of quoting. What is his name? Something about the way my lady eclipses sunlight and joy?"

But she is so confident that I will not please her without some fun first. I keep my gaze as empty as I can manage. "You smell nice," I say flatly. "If the dress and the hair don't work, we could always ask them to close their eyes."

"Bucino!" She throws a redundant hair comb at me, and I glance in La Draga's direction in time to see what could almost be a smile passing over her ghostly face as she gathers up her pots and picks up her shawl, ready to leave. I watch the concentration in her face as she walks to the door, each step already marked out in her head.

She and I have not discussed money since the theft of the jewel. Though she has offered my lady help, the fact is we still owe her, not just for the hair but also for various new potions that have moved between them over the last few days, things that pertain to the secret places in a woman's body, no doubt, and, I suspect, a few tricks to increase a man's appetite for love, of which my lady knows I disapprove and of which therefore I will be told nothing. While my lady tells me she is content to wait for payment until our fortunes are more recovered, I would prefer to settle with her now. I do not like to be in anyone's debt, and since my lady's conquest and the boatload of raucous young-bloods set tongues wagging, La Draga's continued presence in our house has done nothing to improve our reputation in the neighborhood.

While many of our neighbors now move to the other side of the *campo* when they see me coming, my old well man still talks to me, if only to swamp me with "good advice." His views about La Draga are clear enough. She is, he says, a witch of the womb, and he crosses himself as he uses the words, for anything to do with the fertile, bloody parts of women fills men with suspicion and dread. He says she was born on one of the islands but came to the city when she was young, though it seems her parents died soon after. He tells a story of how, when she was small and still had some sight, she went missing from her home and was found in the *piazzetta*, near the Pillars of Justice, her hands filled with earth gathered from the cooled pyre on which a sodomite had been burned to death the day before. When she got back, she made a paste from it, along with various herbs and plants, and that very day cured a local woman of the most terrible fits. It is the kind of tale that has already changed hands many times and thus may or may not be true, but it is potent enough that, once known, it cannot be refuted. After that, he said, any women who fell sick in her district didn't bother with the doctor but always went to her. As much as anything, no doubt, out of fear that those she did not cure she might take to hammering with curses instead. The way he tells it, the more she healed, the more crippled she became, and the clearer her second sight, the blinder her eyes.

While I am less susceptible than many to the panic that surrounds witches (anyone who has suffered terrible pain will take help wherever he can get it), I have never known a healer who doesn't pretend more wisdom than she has, and in particular I have seen too many courtesans develop an appetite for love spells to bind men and help them in their work, which—since it creates a dependence in them as well as the men—is in the

end no help at all. While it might be churlish to attribute La
Draga's generosity toward us solely to business, the fact is, her
kind of help we can live without—certainly if I have anything
to do with it.

She has made her way downstairs and is already out the
door and moving steadily down the street by the time I reach
her. In a race across the city, I would not pit myself against her,
because, while her sight may have gone, she has taught herself
to see well enough by the use of her ears. So she knows it is my
flat feet following her long before she turns, and I sense the
wariness in her face.

"Bucino?"

"Yes."

She relaxes slightly. "Did I forget something?"

"I . . . You left without payment."

She gives a little shrug, but her eyes stay fixed on the
ground. "I told you before, it can wait." And she turns again.
Even before I attacked her that day, she was as uncomfortable
talking to me as I was to her.

"No," I say more loudly now. "I would prefer to settle with
you now. You have been most kind, but my lady is healed, and
we will have no need of you for a while."

She puts her head to one side, like a bird listening to a mate's
call. "I think she and I are not finished yet," she says, her voice
like a rustle of wind and a silly little smile on her face.

"How? How are you not finished? My lady is healed now," I
repeat, and I hear an edge in me. "And we have no need for love
spells in this house."

"I see." The smile shifts, and her mouth contorts a little.
Close to her now, I am amazed by how much movement there
is in her face. But then, she will not know its impact on others.
I only learned the power of my full grin from reading it in the
mirrors of other people's faces.

"Tell me what it is that you have around your neck, Bucino?"
Her hand darts out toward me, but even she cannot judge my
height in her darkness, and it flaps above my head like a bird in
caged panic.

"How do you know I have anything there?" I snap back, and emboldened by her mistake, I move closer until we are almost touching, so that I look up straight into her eyes, straight into the foul fog of her blindness, and she must feel my breath on her face, because she stiffens, but she still holds her ground.

"I know because you swore upon it the other day."

I remember I did and am angry with myself that I hadn't realized it. "It is a tooth."

"A tooth?"

"Yes. From one of my father's dogs. He gave it to me when it died."

"And why did he give it to you? As a memory? A decoration? A charm against misfortune?"

"I . . . Yes . . . and why not?"

"Why not indeed?"

And she smiles now, that same dreamy smile she used on Aretino, the one that takes over her whole face and makes her skin shine. In the same way that she does not know when her expression is forbidding, she is unaware now when it becomes luminous. While I spend my life holding my fists up against her, there is a peculiar sweetness to her sometimes that threatens to undermine me.

"Yes, the lady Bianchini is healed in her body. But it has been a long time since she was out in the world. She is nervous. You are busy running all around the town, and so you miss what's in front of your eyes. What I give her is something to take away the fear. That's all. If she believes in it, it works. Like your dog's tooth. You understand? That is what my 'love spells' are about. And for this I do not charge anyway. So you can put away your purse."

There is nothing to say. I know that she is right and I am wrong. And, though I have been stupid, I am not so stupid that I do not recognize it now.

A boy is moving toward us on the other side of the street. I recognize him as one of the baker's assistants who helps with the bread in the early morning on the square. As he draws up to us, he stops, his eyes out on stalks, because, of course, together we are probably the strangest thing that he has ever seen in his life. I offer my largest openmouthed grin to get rid of him, and he pulls away as if I had spat at him. It will be around the commune within minutes: how the witch and the midget were cavorting together in broad daylight. In the telling, it will probably take on the shadow of carnality, for the sins of sex are never far away in idle imaginations, especially when there is deformity involved, and everyone would know that we both work for the whore whose smell pulls boats of panting young men to her doorway in the middle of the night.

She waits, and when I am still silent, she says, "Tell me, why is it that you don't like me, Bucino?"

"What?"

"We are both servants to her. We care for her. And she for us. Yet we always fight, you and I."

"I don't . . . not like you. I mean—"

"Perhaps you still think that I swindled her somehow, that her hair would have grown without me. Or that I am a witch, because people gossip about me as much as they do you. Is that it? Or is it that you don't like looking at me? Am I really so much uglier than you?"

Of course I do not know what to say. I, who have an answer for everything, have no answer to this. I feel almost sick, like a child caught out in a lie. Her face is still, and for the moment I'm not sure what she will do. Now, when her hands come out, they do not miss. She touches the great pate of my forehead and it is my turn to freeze. I am amazed by how cool her hands are. She moves her fingers slowly across my face, feeling her way over and into my eye sockets, then over my nose, my mouth, my chin, reading me with her touch. I feel myself shiver, not least because she says nothing but, once she is finished, simply drops her hands and after a few seconds turns and walks away.

I watch her until she is across the little bridge and has disappeared into the next alley. I see it all: her limp, the stones under her feet, the deep blue of her gifted woven shawl. Clear as daylight, all of it. But I have no idea what I feel inside. Though I know why I do not like her. It is because in some way she makes me feel smaller than I am.

♦ ♦ ♦

"Oh, it is come, Bucino. It is come. Quick . . ."

When I reach the room, my lady is up and gathering her cloak excitedly. "The gondola is here. It is waiting outside."

I look down from the window. Now that we are rich with promise, we can feel easier about the money spent on one night's transport. It is a stately craft. Not as sumptuous as the one we might have hired to earn our living, but graceful enough, its polished silver rudder glinting in the fading light, its black-skinned boatman clad like a courtier in red and gold velvet, standing tall in the stern, his single oar resting in its socket. It would have been a long time since this house had welcomed such ostentation, and across the canal, our cockeyed spy is now bent so far out of her window that at any minute she might risk drowning in her own curiosity. Only this time she is not alone. Farther along there are faces appearing from houses every-where, and by the time we get ourselves downstairs and open the gates onto the canal entrance, the nearby bridge has become a viewing platform, with the baker's boy and five or six others gathered to gape. I think of my old man, who prides himself on knowing everything, and I almost wish I had warned him in ad-vance so that he, too, could watch us go.

I brace myself for the taunts. The young Saracen takes my lady's hand and helps her into the boat. The sun is low across the bridge, and its rosy light sets fire to her scarlet skirts, which sweep around her. She looks up, taking in the audience in a sin-gle glance before moving into the cabin and arranging herself on the cushions. I perch myself on the wooden bench as the boat-man slides his oar down into the water and maneuvers us away from the dock and out to the main channel.

"Water whore!"

"Witchy woman!"

"Show us what you're selling."

They are boys' voices still, not yet fully broken, and you can hear the longing welling up through the insults. The boat turns away from them, and as it slides under the window of the old woman, she leans out and hawks up a great gob of spit as if from a slingshot, and it splats onto the wood close to me. I look up and am about to thumb my nose at her toothless face when, with one clean, clear pull of the oar, we are gone, slipping through the water like tailors' scissors through silk, leaving it all behind us.

The Saracen knows his water as well as I do the land. He stands, his left foot placed almost on the edge of the boat, his body turning like that of a dancer as he slips us around corners and glides us like a long sigh under a tunnel of low-arched bridges. The daylight is dying fast now, and the gondola sits low in the water, so at first I brace myself to be fearful. But I am too busy in my head for fear. This is the reverse of the journey that we made many months before, now out through the labyrinth of small canals toward the wider water. It all feels so long ago: the summer darkness and the clammy heat, the woman with her smell of musk and her hand pulling the curtain across the cabin as the man reached out for her. My lady sits now where she did, tall and still, head up, neck long, her hands folded into her billowing skirts, aware of her own grace as clearly as if she were staring at herself in a mirror. I want to ask how she feels, to tell her that her beauty has no need of love spells, but mindful of La Draga's words on how the confidence lies in the belief as much as the draft, I keep my mouth shut. There is a transformation going on between us now anyway: after so long as companions in adversity, we are become professionals again, and a little distance is necessary between the courtesan and her exotic plaything.

We move out into the Grand Canal as it enters its long, lazy curve toward the Rialto, and a spectacle opens up in front of us. The hubbub of the markets is over now, and the traffic is more sophisticated; small fleets of decorated gondolas with cabins, some open, some closed, carrying people to a hundred different evening rendezvous. To our left, two young women sit wrapped like expensive parcels in veils and shawls, but they duck their heads out of the cabin soon enough to study my lady's exposed skin and hair. We pass a boatload of distinguished Crows in full regalia, each set of eyes swiveling as they catch sight of her. Behind us the sky is the color of an overripe apricot. On wooden terraces, perched like four-poster beds on the tops of the roofs, young women are pulling in carpets and hangings from the day's airing and collecting flagpoles of washing, while around them the city's mass of chimney pots rise up like great pottery wine goblets laid along the table of the skyline, dinner settings for the gods. In the grand houses to either side of the canal, they are lighting up the *piano nobile* rooms now. Through the open loggias, you can spot servants moving with tapers to wall-mounted candles or round chandeliers, which, once lit, they winch slowly into the air. During our poverty, we have had to make do with the spitting stink of tallow, and I cannot wait to see the world through the flame of beeswax again, for as any courtesan worth her price will tell you, its light flatters even poxy skin into swan softness. Which, I daresay, is why so many of the greatest conquests are planned and conducted at night.

Aretino's house is lit already, and there are four richly decorated gondolas moored in the water yard below. The boatman brings us skillfully to dock, and together we lift her skirts to avoid the wet stone and the filth of the entrance hall while he calls up to tell the house we are arrived.

As we mount the stairs, we can hear voices and laughter coming from above. On the higher landing, Aretino is waiting. My lady rises like a great ship under sail, and he puts out his hand to greet her as I dump great armfuls of silk train behind her. And though he has reason enough to resent us, it is clear that he is pleased to see her, for he has always liked beautiful objects and was never afraid of the smell of adventure. It was one of the things that pulled them together.

"My dear Fiammetta," he says loudly, waving his hand like the courtier he will never be. "Your stature is greater than that of the queen of Carthage, and your beauty puts the Venetian sunset to shame. My house is honored to welcome you."

"On the contrary, sir, it is my honor to be here," she declares with equal volume, then sinks to meet his height, for he was never tall, and in her clogs she towers above most men. "Your insults were always more original than your compliments, Pietro." Her voice is now low and sweet.

"That's because you're not paying for them. I keep the best for retail. So—your dwarf drives a hard bargain, and it seems we are in business together. Though given your nobility of spirit, I trust you won't mind sharing a little of it with me. There are three men in my house tonight who in their varying ways have enough money to feather both of our nests. It's not a problem for you if we work on them together, is it?"

"Not in the least," she says, her eyes clear for business. "Tell me."

"The first is Mario Treviso, one of Venice's sweetest-smelling merchants, since his fortune comes from soap. He spends his days checking his warehouses and writing atrocious verses, for which he's in search of a muse, as his wife is spread so fat from a dozen children that the last time she tried to leave the house, they had to winch her down into the boat."

"Where does he stand? Is he nobility or citizen?"

"Citizen, though if money bought nobility, he'd long ago have bribed his way into one of the state's councils, for he has more cash than many with the right names. Things have changed since you left. Some of the great families are too lazy to go to sea anymore, and their blood runs richer than their coffers. Still, if you don't mind wealth over breeding, Treviso is an excellent catch. He is as rich as Croesus, and he has an eye for beauty, though he's deaf as a post when it comes to poetry. He kept a courtesan called Bianca Gravello for a time, but her loveliness was surpassed only by her stupidity, and her greed made her crude, so that now he is in need of more delicate handling. He is a dull dog at heart, and I doubt he will cause you any trouble, though you may want for excitement."

She smiles. "I have had enough excitement lately to welcome boredom. He sounds perfect. Perhaps I should take him home with me right away."

"Oh, no. I have planned a party here, and you will have to work for your living. So. Next is Guy de Ramellet, an emissary from the French court. The French star is waning here, and he comes to makes friends and buy influence. He sees himself as a scholar and a thinker. He is in fact a buffoon, and it is possible that he is infected with the pox—I offer you this tidbit in the spirit of friendship, for he will be eager to get into your bed. However, his king owes me for verses in his favor, and the more pleasure this oaf associates with me, the more he is likely to remind His Majesty of it. Though you do not have to act as my debt collector."

"Or you as my pimp," she says, for they are equals again and enjoying the game. "Though if your wit ever fails you, I daresay Bucino might take you as an apprentice. And the third?"

"Ah, the third is a strange bird. An infidel, though with a refined palate. It is his manner to observe rather than join in. He is the sultan's chief merchant here, and his work is to buy whatever luxuries he thinks will entertain his master and ship them back to Suleiman's court. I've made it clear to him that you are not for export."

"So what good is he to you? Or do you sell your pen to both sides now to hedge your bets?"

"Oh, if only I could. They may be heathen, but I tell you, they are better soldiers than most that Christendom produces these days. The latest news on the Rialto is that the sultan's army is halfway to Hungary and that he has his eye on Vienna. No. I don't look for his patronage, though I do have other plans for him. Well, if you are ready . . ."

"I think you have overlooked someone."

"How?"

"I counted four boats at the dock."

"Ah, yes, of course. The fourth is not for you. He is my personal guest: a man of infinite talent with a wife he is valiantly faithful to, though his brush itches to trace the pearl sheen on the skin of every lovely woman he meets. He is here on a friend's wager that a Roman courtesan has more beauty and charm than any he could find in Venice."

"What do you stand to win?"

"A portrait of myself with my new beard and belly."

"And if you lose?"

"Oh, I have not offered anything in exchange."

She smiled. There was a small silence. "I am grateful to you, Pietro."

"Hmm. I like to think I would have done it without coercion. I know, I know . . . Fiammetta Bianchini does not ask and Aretino once offended. But he did not come out unscathed either; you should perhaps remember that."

He leans over and kisses her hand. It is dark where I stand behind them on the stairs. Small men often hear secrets that were not meant for their ears. But it seems to me that, whatever the past, these two were cut from the same cloth, bred for business as much as for sentiment, and they will fare better as friends than as almost lovers.

"Ah. Let's face it, Fiammetta," he says as he straightens up, and I can hear the smile in his voice. "Your independence was always as irritating as it was interesting. Still, you'll have your own establishment soon enough again, if you play your hand right tonight. For now, we are both in debt to the cunning of your dwarf. Come on, come out from beneath her skirts, Bucino; it does not suit you to sniff around a woman's backside, even if you are the right height. My goodness, you have changed your clothes for the evening. We are honored. I presume your wit is as smooth as your velvet. What are your plans for the night? Are you loitering in the kitchen with the lovely Anfrosina or playing the cultivated monkey entertainer here with us?"

I, of course, would give anything to be there, and my lady would gain from my presence, if only for their astonishment at the contrast between her beauty and my ugliness. But her look tells me quickly it is not to be. La Draga was right. She is more nervous than I realized. I close one eye and wink at her solemnly as I turn to him. "I'll avail myself of the facilities in the kitchen."

"Perhaps it is just as well. We wouldn't want the Turk to fold you into his robes and steal you away. I hear they have a great fondness for squashed men in the sultan's court. Though you are a rogue, I would not like to lose you."

And so the door pushes open, and my lady goes in.

CHAPTER SEVENTEEN

I have been thinking recently about confession. (These introductory evenings are slower and more formal than one might
suspect, and I know better than most the frustration of wasting
one's imagination on events one cannot influence. For all her
nerves, my lady has years of experience behind her, and if she
needs help, she will ask for it. For now I have time to dawdle.)
When I say I have been thinking about confession, I am not
talking about my own soul: by and large I am comfortable
enough with the weight of sin I carry, which is more than some
but less than many. No. It is more than that. Having worked for
so many years in the business of fornication, I am curious to
know what takes place when all these great and good merchants, nobles, and scholars, usually husbands, who pass
through our hands find themselves in the confessional seeking
forgiveness for the devils that seem to rise so regularly out of
their loins. What a job it must be to hear their stories: all those
details; the nature of each impure thought; the choreography of
every unclean act. It would take a holy man indeed to keep his
mind always on the sinner and not let it stray sometimes to the
sin itself. In Aretino's world, of course, there is no such thing as
an honest priest. Instead they are all opening their confession-
als to offer personal absolution to the sinful parts of violated
young women, or to help soothe the inflammations of misguided young men. But then Aretino has long been famous for

his crusade against the cloth and has been known to read an erection into a stiff fold of a monk's robes.

For my part, I am sure there must be some good men among them who try their best to keep us within the sight of God. Yet even for them, the gradations of sin within fornication are legion and not without theological confusion. In Rome, before we left, young confessional priests were being given written instructions as to the correct sexual behavior within marriage. I know this for a fact because at the same time as Ascanio was checking the ink line on Giulio Romano's illicit couples, the press was also busy rolling off sets of confessional manuals. Indeed, it was only from studying a few such sheets held back because of printing errors that we ourselves for the first time realized quite the crushing numbers of sins to which men and women are prone within the marriage bed.

Some are obvious enough. No couple, however eager for novelty or fearful of another pregnancy, must ever allow themselves to mistake the orifice necessary for procreation. While sodomy will send a man to the stake faster than it will a woman, in the eyes of the Church, it is a grievous sin for both. And while I hear there are a few scholars and medical doctors now who argue the case for pleasure within marriage as an aid to the begetting of healthy children (my lady's own cardinal had been one of a group of emerging thinkers who were eager to defeat heresy by reforming the mother Church), the pleasure must still come in straight lines. The wife lies down, and the husband lies on top of her. Any excess of copulation, any standing, sitting, lying to one side, or, God forbid, any woman climbing on top of the man—all these would require a visit to the confessional to cleanse the soul. The drama of Giulio's lusty illustrations and the papal censor's wrath he incurred was less about the blatancy of the act than about the fact that every single one of his sixteen positions was banned by the Church. As he well knew. We never did such business as in the weeks after they circulated through Rome. But let's face it—men are more drawn to such things than women are. Indeed, with such a raft of rules and regulations, it is not surprising that a man plagued by such carnal temptations, rather than leading his wife into damnation, should take his sins out of the marital home to the bed of a woman better able to contain them.

In this way Fiammetta Bianchini, by sinning herself, is actually acting as the savior of others. To which end her cardinal once quoted Saint Augustine to me on the subject: that public women are like the bilge of a good ship, since without them the sewer level would rise and rise until it overwhelms the crew and passengers and sinks the whole vessel. As with a seaworthy ship, so with a virtuous state. After that, when men came to us from their wives' beds, I didn't feel so bad if I charged them for a bottle or two more than they had drunk or a whole night when they left before dawn, for in many ways we were sacrificing ourselves for the good of the fleet.

As for my lady, well, in Rome she had been much comforted by finding the right confessor: a young Dominican priest who did not drool or probe but instead gave a fair penance in return for a fair offering to the poor box. As for our life here in Venice: well, first the sin, then the money, and then the confession.

From the noises coming from the *portego*, it seems that the sin at least may be close at hand. The laughter is growing louder, and I can hear voices raised in mock argument and once even in a snippet of song. There is nothing now to keep me in the kitchen. The fire has died down, and Anfrosina (an impure thought that never got as far as an unclean act, though I should admit to the pleasure of a little kissing and fondling) is asleep on the pallet at the side of the room. I am thinking of ways in which to infiltrate myself into the entertainment when Aretino comes to get me.

"Bucino! You look so melancholy. Don't tell me Anfrosina has deserted you." I gesture to the pallet, and he moves over and stands beside her. "Ah! Look at that. It makes your bones melt. I used to sleep with the dogs sometimes when I was a child. I think that was where my appetite for women's bodies first came from. All those warm bits of fur. I am surprised you didn't avail yourself of some of it."

"I am working," I say stiffly.

"Indeed you are, now. Your lady wants you—"

And I am up and scrambling off the bench before he can finish.

"Whoa! Not so fast." He laughs, placing himself between me and the door. "You are wanted—but not yet. No one is to know that you have been called. You are to wait outside the door until she gives you the signal."

"What are they doing?"

"Playing a game about art and the senses it engages. No doubt you have seen it before, though it feels fresh as new grass to this audience. Ah, the pleasure of watching a good courtesan work for her living. I will leave the door ajar so you can judge how it goes for yourself. You will know the plan better than I."

I wait till he is gone, then make my way quietly up the narrow back stairs and along the great corridor to the doors of the *portego*. I am careful not to stand too close, but I needn't worry: no one is looking at me anyway.

Through the gap I see Aretino sitting to one side, then two other men and my mistress. She is standing in front of them with her arms outstretched and her torso half twisted as if she is in flight from some insistent pursuer. Her expression is one of open-eyed wonder, half fear, half expectation, and the pose is so still—even her eyes are unblinking—that she looks as if she has been frozen into a statue, albeit one whose firm marble breasts cannot help but rise and fall with her breathing, a movement caught prettily enough by strategic candlelight.

There is a hushed silence for a second, and then a florid-faced stick of a man jumps into view, gesticulating around her.

"Oh, feast your eyes on this, my friends. The goddess wins my argument for me. Behold the power of sculpture: the representation of nature in all of her finest truth. I tell you, Monsignore Vecellio, even in your hands the painter could not capture this." And he puts out his hand toward the soft curve of her naked shoulder.

"Uh-uh. *Ne touche pas.*" And the room explodes with laughter as the statue moves its lips to address him without altering a muscle of the pose. "The discussion in question, Monsieur

Ramellet, is sight versus hearing. Touching is a baser sense alto-
gether, however pleasant."

"But I have to touch you." He moans. "That is the power of
sculpture. Why did you think the artist took his Pygmalion to
bed after he had made her?"

"Ramellet is right." Aretino's voice comes in loudly. "Although he destroys his argument with it. Think of those ancient semen stains on the great Cnidian statue of Aphrodite.
Sculpture has long been in the business of arousing through the
eye."

"Yes! Yes. And why is that? Because more than any other art
form it captures the essence of nature and life. Just look at her."

"Of course it's life," roars one of the men in front of her.
"That's because she is alive, you dolt. She's flesh, not marble. You
want a real contest of art forms, let me paint her. Then we
would have something to compare nature with."

"Ah, but how would you paint me, Maestro Vecellio?" she
says sweetly, still holding the pose. "With or without my clothes
on?"

He tuts and shrugs. "That would depend on who's paying
for it."

And a clamor of voices goes up, urging him on.

My lady laughs and uses the moment to break the pose,
stretching her head and shoulders gracefully and tossing back
her hair so she can throw a glance toward the door to check that
I am in place.

"I am flattered, gentlemen, that you should be so generous
about my beauty. But I am afraid you have played into the
hands of my argument. Or rather our argument, because I
think, Signor Treviso, that is what you were saying a little while
ago"—and she turns her attention on the soap merchant, who
is next to the painter and up to that moment has been rather
silent—"that though the eye has the capacity to move us toward
God, it can sometimes be deceived. Because, while it responds
naturally to beauty, beauty is not always truth."

"What? Are you mounting a full-scale attack on Ficino's philosophy or simply warning us against yourself?" shouts Aretino,

whose job it is tonight to let others make the running but who cannot keep himself out of the fray.

"Oh, sir, I would not dream of pitting my wits against such a great scholar. As for the truth of my beauty, well, you would have to experience it to find out." And she laughs with adeptly false modesty. "No, I am talking about the power of the eye in all its forms."

As they sit there waiting on her next—and every—word, I recognize where she is going and what my part will be, and I smooth my doublet down and get myself prepared.

"I want you to think about love, gentlemen. That cruelest and sweetest of all perturbations of the blood. The disease of which no man wants to be cured. How does love enter a body if not through the eye? A man looks at a woman. Or a woman looks at a man." As she speaks, she turns now to each one of them, holding his gaze for a moment in earnest conversation. "And in that golden look something is transmitted. You may call it spirit, you may call it animal spark, you may call it a damned infection—even the most learned disagree among themselves—but whatever it is, it moves between the lover and the beloved, and once it is received it is unstoppable, traveling down into the entrails and from there flowing everywhere into the bloodstream. Do you not agree, my lord Treviso?"

Her eye stays on him as he murmurs his agreement. My God, he will have to be very rich to be so dull.

"How about you, sir?" she says, looking straight at Aretino.

"Oh, absolutely," he replies, grinning. "That which leads us into temptation cannot deliver us from evil. Though I tell you, men suffer this disease far worse than women."

"You think so? You don't believe it is mutual?" She smiles, looking around for support.

The Frenchman shakes his head vigorously. "Oh, no, no, but he is right. I myself have known this illness many times. I cannot sleep, I cannot eat, I am beset by joy and pain in the same moment. It is a kind of madness"—he laughs—"from which I never want to be well."

I must say, from where I stand he doesn't look healthy either. Aretino is right. Were she to take him to bed, she would need more than La Draga to purge her passages.

Her eye passes over the one figure my view cannot locate, who I know must be the Turk, and I hear a voice murmur something that I can see interests her, but I cannot catch his words.

She turns back to the soap merchant, who is agreeing more vociferously now, in return for which he is rewarded with her most radiant smile. "Ah, be well assured, sir. When next time this sweet disease afflicts you, come to me with it, for I have studied it long and hard and consider myself an expert in curing it. Indeed, I have been known to sacrifice my own purity to help others regain theirs."

The company laughs again. Dear God, what overgrown children men become in order to get themselves under a woman's skirts. The sin of Eve. Sometimes I do not know whether to pray for her soul or celebrate her appetite, for without her, my lady and I would be sewing sails and braiding ropes in the Arsenale for eight soldi a day.

"So, gentlemen. Enough of this carnal banter. Our task, you will remember, is to find the sense and the art form that bring us most profoundly to God's inner beauty. Since we now have good reason to suspect the eye for its proclivity toward temptation, let us move on to the ear instead. To which end, if you are willing, I have another experiment for you."

I straighten up and swallow hard, for I have a tendency to burp when I am nervous, and I would not want to give the game away.

"My lord Aretino. May I prevail upon you to furnish me with a lute?"

He brings it over, and I note that while it is better than ours, it is not that special, and I hope she will be able to squeeze some beauty from it. She settles herself into the glow of candlelight, arranging her skirts and her curtain of hair with a quiet concentration that the observer might mistake for a love of music rather than for the perfection of the picture she is painting of herself. She tests the strings for a moment, then bows her head, lifts her fingers, and starts to play. While I am for that second nervous that her fingers will betray us, the notes spill out like a shower of gold into the air. I watch their faces. What more could one want from a woman? Beauty, wit, ripe flesh, a smile like the sun, and celestial fingers. All you have to do is pay the price.

She plays first a short piece, long enough to entrance, brief enough not to bore, for while they are cultured men, they are here for entertainment and, like me, they can sense a climax coming. She lets the closing notes linger in the air, and when they call for more, the loudest voice belongs to Treviso. The look has done its work, and the infection of desire is moving through his blood to his entrails.

"So, gentlemen. If you are ready? We will test the power of the ear to recognize true beauty. I want you now all to close your eyes."

She looks around as they do. "Abdullah Pashna, I am learning that your silence is golden, but I must tell you that right now I think you may be cheating." There is a ripple of laughter. "Thank you."

When she is satisfied that she has them, she puts her fingers back on the strings and starts to play again, and then, after a moment, beckons me in with her eyes.

I push open the door as quietly as I can—she has chosen a full-throated tune to cover my tracks—and pad over to stand beside her. My palms are damp with nerves. In our time we have wooed and won half of Rome with our games, but I have been as long out of practice as she has. I stare at them seated around her: eyes obediently closed, half-smiles on their faces. How men love to be seduced. She has picked well; the piece has passages of light and sweetness to it, making the moment more prone to magic. She comes to the end of a phrase and hesitates.

"Gentlemen. No, no, don't move. . . . I want to warn you that in a moment I will be finishing, but as the last notes die away, I would like you to rest with your eyes closed for a moment, the better to digest the experience."

As she speaks, she rises silently to her feet and is already handing me the instrument. I squirm my way gently onto the stool, hoisting my leg to take the lute, which, I must tell you, is a test for a man of my stature, and settle myself so that as soon as her words end I am ready to play the closing phrases. Of course they are familiar to me, and I also have the kind of temperament that likes to rise to a challenge. My rendering may not set the world alight, but there is delicacy and feeling to it, and enough of an ending flourish to keep their attention acute.

In the silence that follows the last notes, we risk a smile between us.

Her voice, when it comes, is like a caress. "Gentlemen, open your eyes and behold the beauty that produces great music."

And five sets of eyes duly pop open to see an incubus with a mad grin and a lute clutched to his breast. The exoticism of ugliness and the beauty. Our specialty.

Whatever they have been expecting, it is not this, and I think they may actually be shocked, because for a long moment the room remains frozen. I stumble off the stool and take a clumsy bow as she moves toward me, raising her hands to greet me and them.

"Gentlemen. I give you the power of sound and the talent of my faithful and 'truly' ugly dwarf, Bucino Teodoldi."

And now, suddenly, everybody laughs, and claps and claps again—for what else can they do?—and Aretino whoops and slaps me on the back and calls for more wine, and my lady sits and fans herself and sips at her glass and receives the stream of compliments for which she has worked so effortlessly hard.

The drink and the wit flow awhile longer, until a few candles start to splutter out. My lady lavishes her praise upon our host, who uses the moment to pluck the poxy Frenchman to his desk to show him a new letter he is writing for his great king, while our painter drowns the sorrows of fidelity in another bottle. At this point our Turk, Abdullah Pashna—for it is indeed the same man who aided us in the *campo* a few weeks before— gathers his cloak and starts to say his good-byes; there is an unspoken protocol to such introductory events, and it is clear to everyone by now that the flow of the night has gone the way of the soap fortune.

I must say, it does not seem to worry the Turk much. In fact, ever since my appearance, he has expressed as much interest in me as in my lady, and now, as he leaves, he comes to where I am sitting again and lays a purse of ducats in my lap.

"For the silence of your feet and the skill of your fingers. It was a fine show, my friend."

I glance at my lady, for I do not take tips without her permission, and as I haven't witnessed the evening, I have no way of knowing what might already have passed between them. Her look lets me know it is fine, and I accept happily, for I, too, still have the excitement of the performance running through my veins.

"I am a better juggler than I am a musician."

"Then you must come and juggle for me sometime. I have a keen appetite for such talents."

"Did you go to the bridge fight that day?" I ask, because he may be a heathen, but I have liked him from the moment I met him on the street. Though that, perhaps, is because I know he likes me too.

"The fight? Most certainly. The ship workers won a great victory, took the bridge from the fishermen within an hour. I have never seen so many people, either in combat or watching. When I go home, I shall petition my sultan to build bridges all over our magnificent city so we may train our own fighters. And you? Do you follow this sport?"

"I would love to, but I have never seen it. I hear the crush would be deadly for someone of my size."

"Then we will find you a boat of your own to watch it from."

And I must say, I think that he will keep his word.

He leaves as the dawn starts to break. Now my lady becomes more focused. She and Treviso sit close to each other on a settle, and she is quiet, almost demure, so that when he puts his hand on the skin of her shoulder, she shivers a little, and the look she gives him is as much one of wonder as one of encouragement.

"Signor Aretino tells me that you are planning to live in Venice now and that you are in need of a house of your own."

"Oh, yes indeed. My home in Rome, which was a place of such merriment and grace, is only a sad memory now."

"I would be honored to help find you another."

"Oh, sir . . ."

She takes his hand and turns it over in her own, as if to study his goodness through his palm lines. Then she bends her lips to it and, I daresay, gives him a promise of things to come with her tongue. And after that they sit a little longer, and then she yawns, putting her hand so sweetly up to her mouth, and says: "I do so love the dawn, though I have never seen it from the water before. Do you think it will be too cold to watch it this morning?"

And before you can say "Forgive me, Father, for I have sinned," they are up and wrapped in cloaks, our boatman is roused, and they are heading for a mutual sunrise.

The Frenchman is dispatched, somewhat miffed but placated by the promise of another evening, and I find myself alone with Aretino and his blessed painter: a situation that feels familiar enough to them if not to me. I help myself to the remains of the food—cold fish pie and sweet berry sauces—while they sit and drink and gossip for a while together, dilatory stuff about people I don't know, business that isn't mine. Then they drink some more and move on to the pleasure of the evening and the talents of my lady.

"So? How do we settle our bet then, eh, Tiziano? I have bought a red velvet jacket with brocade so complex it'll have your brush shaking with excitement to capture its texture. Though I wouldn't want it to detract from my face. What do you think my expression should be? One of sober triumph, yes?"

The painter shakes his head. "I'm drowning in convent commissions. It'll have to wait."

"Ah! You're too scared of the mother superiors, that's your trouble. They exploit your Christian charity to pay you less. Forget altarpieces for a while. You'd get a damned sight more for copying the sultan's face off a medal and sending it home to him via the infidel. You heard him yourself—he was very set on the idea tonight. But as to our wager—you have to admit— I won fair and square. She has the rhetoric of the Greek courtesan Aspasia and the beauty of Phrynê. My God, those Greeks understood the powers of women. A veritable Venus, wouldn't you say? The perfect fusion of modesty and lust."

"Hmm. I got more of her modesty than her lust."

"That is because you weren't bidding."

"Where is she anyway?" And he makes an effort to raise himself. They have become maudlin now, in the way men do when the women have left and they are thinking of bed but cannot be bothered to get up to go there. "Where did she go?"

"To put her mark on the contract."

"With whom? Treviso? Venus and a soap merchant! God's teeth, she is wasted on him."

"Oh, don't mope. Only hungry men need to eat away from home. You know Cecilia would scourge you, and you would regret it soon enough. Fiammetta will probably take off her clothes for you in the name of art if you ask nicely enough. Anything else would be too expensive anyway. I'm right, aren't I, Bucino? How much does she charge these days?"

I shrug, for now that the deal is done, the wine and the thought of a future are warming my stomach too. "We have a lot of expenses to make up these last months. What can I say? She isn't cheap."

"Though between us men—and I include you in this, Bucino—she is worth it. Believe me, you don't know the half of it. There are some high-class whores out there who spend their lives milking their lovers as if they were cows' teats. First one, then another, then back again, until your purse is as sore as your prick from all the pulling. But not Fiammetta Bianchini. No fits of jealousy, no false tears or wheedling from her. She takes what she needs, gives what they want, and makes it her business to keep them happy. I tell you, not every woman who keeps her clothes on is such a lady. She carries her lust with a perfect mask of decency. An honest courtesan, that is what she is. And you are lucky to have her, Bucino. As she is to have you."

He falls back in his chair, exhausted by his own hyperbole.

I am an expert with men in their cups, for I have spent many evenings placating the also-rans while my lady retires to the bedroom and the dawn comes in. It always amazes me how men's characters change when they are *in vino*: how the most timid become like bulls, spitting and raging, or how a scourge of princes ends up licking your hand like a half-blind kitten. But it is only the wine talking, and most of them forget it all the day after.

"Those are fine thoughts, Aretino," I say, refilling his glass. "If you wrote them down, she could use them for her tombstone."

He snorts. "I have already written them, God damn it. Your precious Fiammetta has her entry in the Courtesans' Register, just as I promised. A poet of the flesh, that am I. See—Aretino is a man of his word; my God, he is. As are you—a good man, I've always said it. As is Tiziano. No, not good. Great! Tiziano is a great man! Look at him. That hand can bring alive anything, anything you ask it to. Damn the lute or the pen. Give me his paintbrush any day. You are a great man, Tiziano! Why don't you paint the dwarf? Look at him. There's a face you don't see every day."

But however great he may or may not be, our faithful painter is now happily unconscious.

Outside, the light is growing, and I can hear the sounds of the first boats arriving for the market. I make my way out through the front loggia to the balcony so I can watch the city yawning and scratching its way into life. But while the sky is streaked like raw silk, the top of the stone balcony is the same height as my head, so that to see anything properly I have to clamber halfway up it and hold myself in place with my hands clutched around the edge. Even for a rich dwarf, the world is the wrong size. I flop down again and peer out between the balustrades, and as I do so I spot our gondola drawing up to the dock below. The Saracen throws the rope and secures the boat and stands for a while, waiting. Eventually Treviso clambers out, arranging himself as best he can after his exertions, and moves across the dock to shake his own boatman into life.

Once they are afloat and in the stream, the Saracen helps my lady out of the cabin, and she steps onto the landing bay to watch his boat move away and under the bridge. As it disappears, she turns to look out over the canal and lifts her arms to the sky in a gesture of triumph to greet the day.

"My lady!"

She whirls around and looks for me, catching sight of my hand and half my face through the balustrades. She is somewhat the worse for wear now; her braided headband is a little crooked, her hair is matted in places, and there is a tear in her dress at the shoulder where the gold hems the neckline. But her laugh is like crystal, and in her flushed face I see a house with polished terrazzo floors, light flooding from one end to the other and the sweet smoke of roasting meats curling up around the stairs from the kitchen below. My God, it has been a long time.

"Bucino!"

She waves and beckons to me to join her, and I am just about to turn when I feel Aretino lumbering onto the balcony, leaning over the stone and yelling into the breaking day.

"Aha! Is that Fiammetta Bianchini, Venice's newest great courtesan?"

"Yes, my lord," she says gaily, and sinks into an exaggerated curtsy so her scarlet skirts flood around her like a bloody lake.

"Then come up here and get into bed with me, you whore. It's been a long night, I'm horny as hell, and you owe me that much."

"You are too late, sir," she calls out. "I have a patron now. And he is eager to have me all to himself. For a while at least."

"What? A faithful courtesan? What heresy you babble, woman. Go home and wash your mouth out with the best Venetian soap. What about the demands of France?"

"France is rancid. I leave him for you to handle. Bucino, get yourself down here. I will drop if I don't sleep soon."

I squirm my way out from beside Aretino's bulk and head for the door.

"And the infidel? Aha! Now I have you. You liked him, didn't you?"

If she answers him, I do not hear it as I go down the stairs and out through the water doors onto the dock to join her.

"Traitors!" Aretino's voice whistles above my head. "Come

back here, both of you. You are peasants without souls. Look around you. The greatest city in Paradise is waking up and bringing the world to your doorstep. We'll buy bread from the market, fish from the boats, and drink ourselves stupid into the morning."

"Not tonight, Pietro." She waves her hand up to him as we make our way onto the boat. "Go to bed. We will come and visit when we have our house."

"You'd better! And bring me those engravings to look at, you poxy dwarf."

The traders on the water are watching the performance now, and they whoop and gesture as my lady climbs back into the cabin. The Saracen, who no doubt has seen it all before, offers me his hand as I stumble my way onto the bench close by. I thank him and let the Turk's purse rattle a little on my belt so that he knows his night will be worthwhile too. Inside the cabin, my lady leans her head back against the rumpled cushions and closes her eyes as he steers the gondola smoothly out into the current, weaving us through the rising noise and hustle of a Venetian morning, heading for home.

PART 3

CHAPTER EIGHTEEN

Venice, mid-1530s

On Thursday, my lady takes no visitors, for she is busy about her beauty. She rises at first light, and with the help of her maid, Gabriella, sets about washing her hair. After the first soaping, Gabriella massages her scalp for half an hour with a cedar paste to encourage new growth and then rinses it twice in waters made from boiled vine stock with barley straw and crushed licorice root to bring out the highlights and make it shine. It is grown to her waist again now, and while it has never quite regained its first glorious weight, it is fine enough for those who did not know her then, and the color still runs rich with seams of honey and gold, which light up as it dries, resting like a cloak over the edge of a high chair where she sits with her back to the morning sun. She uses the hours it takes to dry to have Gabriella pluck her hairline so that her forehead is high and clear. Around midmorning La Draga arrives with a series of freshly made ointments, including a special bleaching paste that she herself applies to my lady's face and neck and shoulders. I asked her once about its ingredients, and she told me it includes bean flour, mercury, dove entrails, camphor, and egg white, but in what proportions and with what other refinements I have no idea, since she keeps such information as guarded as any state secret. Whatever is left over from the paste, I keep the pot in my room in case of substitution or theft, for you would be amazed by the espionage of beauty among the courtesan community.

(For a woman with no eyes, La Draga has proved herself a veritable miracle worker in the business of beauty, so that no one—least of all myself—can begrudge her a regular place in our household now.)

When the mask is removed—an hour and half is too short, and two hours too long—my lady's skin is red and sometimes even blotchy, and Gabriella soothes it with cucumber water and warm towels. She spends the early afternoon seeing her dressmaker, practicing the lute, and memorizing some verses. To cleanse her stomach, she drinks only vinegared water prepared by the cook, and before her afternoon sleep she brushes a thicker bleaching paste with rosemary onto her teeth, rubs her gums with mint, and treats her eyes with drops of witch hazel water to moisten and highlight the whites. She is woken at eight, has Gabriella dress and set her hair, and lightly powders her skin, which is now white and smooth as unveined marble, and thus she steps out into the world ready for the night.

In the Arsenale, where no visiting is allowed but about which there are countless stories, there is apparently a great canal bounded by storehouses on either side and manned by hundreds of workers. When a ship is to be launched, it moves slowly along this wet dock, and at every stage through its windows and onto its decks it is fitted out: cordage, mortars, gunpowder, arms, oars, hourglasses, compasses, maps, and provisions, down to its barrels of wine and fresh bread. In this way, within a single working day, from the first Marangona bell to the last, a great Venetian vessel is made ready for the sea. I think of this sometimes while I watch my lady attending to the construction of herself, for while ours is a smaller business, in our way we too fit out a vessel, all of us equally committed and focused on its demands.

As to our house . . . well, it is fine enough. Not on the Grand Canal itself but nearby, in San Polo, to one end of a wide stretch of waterway between Campo San Toma and San Pantalon. Our *piano nobile* is washed by the morning sun, which makes it cooler during summer evenings, when we do a great deal of entertaining, and we have a view over sparkling water with no close neighbors to hook their noses into our business.

Inside, our *portego* is spacious and elegant, its walls covered with the best secondhand tapestries and silk and leather hangings; while in my lady's room, her built-in walnut bed is encased in gold-veined curtains, with linen as white and crisp as a fresh snowdrift. For the first few months, this piece of furniture was the exclusive domain of our soap merchant, in whose company she would also read poetry (unfortunately, most often his own) and run occasional soirees for men of letters and trade where everyone talked literature, art, and money. It was only common sense that, as her reputation grew, she should take on extra customers, for exclusivity always breeds competition, and the business of desire is so fickle that even the best purses go home after a while. When faced with other suitors, Treviso's ardor first grew sharper with jealousy and then became as insecure as his rhyming schemes, so that by the time they parted company, we were already firmly established with other patrons.

As well as Gabriella (a sweet-faced young girl from Torcello, with few airs to match her graces), our household now includes Marcello, our own Saracen boatman, and Mauro, the cook, who reminds me of Baldesar only in the fact that the more he moans the better his food tastes. He and I go daily to the Rialto, which I rank as one of my great pleasures, for in Venice, with respectable women kept indoors, shopping is a trade for men, and these days I am someone in the markets. The early crowds can be fierce, but Mauro's bulk and my purse elevate me above the worst of the crush. The stall owners know us and save us the best cuts or the finest fish, for our kitchen has a reputation that almost rivals my lady's. "Signor Bucino!" I hear their voices calling me. They treat me politely, with an almost exaggerated deference, squatting down in front of me sometimes to point out the shining freshness of a particular fish they have put aside for me. I do not mind their mockery. It is gentle enough, and more palatable than being insulted or ignored.

This fish market is its own Venetian wonder, sitting on the edge of the canal under a high loggia with drains dug under the grilles into the stone floor, so that even in the worst heat they keep the fish watered and cool. I have seen slabs of ocean fish here so thick and scaly-tailed that you can almost trace the line where the fishermen might have sliced off the body of a mermaid at its waist. When the full purses are gone, there are always pickings for the poor, who loiter by the edges ready to grab the innards or discarded heads as they're washed into the water, though they have to fight with the seagulls, which swoop in to land, big as well-fed babies and twice as noisy, their beaks sharp as hammered nails. You can hear their screeching all the way to the San Marco, and I've seen half a dozen senators streaked with bird shit as the gulls let out the remains of yesterday's meal to make room for the next one.

One of those senators will be gracing our casa tonight, and it is his dinner that I am buying now, for he has a passion for roasted fish and meat in rich sauces. He is the jewel in our crown, a colored Crow (for a senator's robes are dark red), as noble as they come; one of the Loredan family, which can trace its ancestry back to the ninth century, as he has told me more than once. He is a member of the Senate, has been on many of the state's most important committees, and until recently was one of the Council of Ten, which is the nearest Venice comes to an inner sanctum of power. He wears these honors heavily. Indeed, he is a fellow of unparalleled pomposity, his jowls as weighty as his business, but he is our chief prize, for he has status and influence, and every good courtesan needs both in her portfolio (not least because, as a state, Venice has the tendency to be prim and censorious, and the better you know those who run it, the more easily you can predict their moods before they have them). He comes every Tuesday and Friday night. We usually entertain him alone, as members of the government are not allowed to fraternize with the citizen class, though this rule, along with every other in this great state, is as bent as the course of its waterways, and my lady much prefers company: "That way he can bore other people and I can be sure to stay awake until I have to go to bed with him. You have no idea, Bucino, how tedious power makes some men."

I leave the cook to haggle and make my way back across the bridge to a tavern near the German Fondaco where they fry the morning fish in a batter so light and fresh that your taste buds confuse the sweet and savory and where the watered malmsey (an acquired taste, but my tooth has grown sweeter with age) is fresh out of barrels shipped from Cyprus. Early on I made it my business here to give tips as large as I am small to the growling proprietor, and now I have a seat of my own at a table near the door with its own bolster cushion, which I retrieve daily from behind the bar. In this way I sit as tall as any man and join in the latest gossip.

This morning the talk is all of an impromptu bridge battle that erupted yesterday on the Ponte dei Pugni, near Campo Santa Margherita, in which the Castellani Arsenale workers inflicted a savage defeat on the Nicolotti fishermen. It is festival time again: the great feast of the Ascension, when Venice celebrates her annual marriage to the sea and for a while the art of street fighting becomes a national sport. When the Turk was still living in the city, he had been as good as his word and sometimes bought a place for me with him on the pontoon to watch such battles (the company of my deformity was evidently more pleasing to him than to my native Italians). But he left for Constantinople more than a year ago, and since then I have not risked the crowds alone.

I glance up from my conversation and, through a gap in the crush, find myself looking straight into the eyes of a man a few tables away: a merchant, well dressed with a new hat, cloak, and nicely turned velvet jacket; and though there is something familiar enough about him, I have no idea who he is. But he, it seems, knows me, for he keeps on staring. A visiting client? Surely not. My memory is near perfect when it comes to business, and I have not taken a purse from him, or heard his moans through the walls of our casa. He stands and carefully makes his way toward me through the crowd.

"We know each other, I think."

The voice is the true man. But my God, he is changed. The dangling curls and cap are gone, and the chin is freshly shaved. Even his walk seems taller. If one did not know, one might think he was a trader from Spain or Greece, for the Greeks have a great community in the city and there is talk that they will get their own church soon enough. Though where this man would worship I can only wonder, for while he is in some ways the very picture of a Christian gentleman, I know him to be a Jew.

"It is Signor Teodoldi, yes?" And one who after all these years still remembers my name. Well, why not? He saw me write it on enough bonds in that darkened little office in the Ghetto where I pawned our jewels a lifetime ago.

A big man standing close to us gives a small grunt, which I ignore.

"Yes, I am he."

"I was not sure at first. You look different."

"Not as different as you," I say bluntly.

"Ah! Indeed. I should introduce myself." He sits and holds out his hand. "My name is Lelio da Modena. Taken after the city I was born in." He hesitates. "Though I was once known as Chaim Colon."

The man is leaning over our table now and gives out a great guffaw, spewing out some venom on the gross corruption of deformity. A few heads turn. But he is marked by the stench of beer and, more important, poverty, which sits ill against the cut of our cloth, and when his taunts get him nowhere, he lunges off into the crowd muttering. We have both suffered worse, and it is a statement of our present status to be the ones who remain at the table.

"So. You are converted?" I say, and he must hear the wonder in my voice.

"Yes. I am converted." His voice is clear and emphatic. "I left the Ghetto three years ago. I am a baptized Christian now."

"And a successful one at that."

"I have been fortunate." He gives a small smile, which feels uncomfortable on him. He always had the air of a too serious man about him, and the change of faith has not made him any lighter. "I was able to use my skills for the cutting and selling of precious stones as a jewel merchant. But you—you also have done well."

"Not bad," I say.

"It is your lady's business?"

"Yes. My lady's business." And I suspect we are both now thinking of certain images in a certain book which once so appalled a Jewish pawnbroker that he could hardly bring himself to talk to its owner, but which might perhaps be more acceptable to a more worldly Christian businessman.

A gong sounds from behind the bar. "Ah, I must go," he says. It is too noisy inside to hear the morning Marangona, and so they must repeat it to make sure the city is ready for work. "I am due at a meeting near the Arsenale. Oh, but this is God's fortune to have found you. I was hoping I might see you again."

"Really?" And I feel again his fury and fear as he pushed the door closed in my face. "I thought you were pleased to be rid of me."

"Well . . . I— It was a long time ago. I was . . ." He is clearly embarrassed. "Look, I must go. But I would like . . . I mean . . . if . . ."

"We live at Casa Trevelli near San Pantalon. Fiammetta Bianchini's house. It is well enough known in the area. I am there most afternoons and evenings."

"Thank you." He is up now and shaking my hand. "I am due to leave Venice in a few days. For the Indies. But if I can come before, I will."

"You will be welcome." I shrug. And why not? We cater to all people. Well, all people except Jews, that is. As far as I know, there is no law in the city against a courtesan entertaining a convert, assuming his purse is big enough, though as I watch him disappear into the throng, I feel somehow disappointed that he of all people should be so changed.

Still, the encounter makes for a good story, and I have honed it perfectly by the time I reach home. My thunder is stolen by the chaos I find there. On the nearby bridge, a crowd is watching as a dozen workmen on a large barge roll up ropes and pieces of cloth while shouting and laughter bounce out over the water from our *piano nobile* above.

I go up the stairs fast (wealth makes for shallower steps,

which are better for smaller legs) and at the corner collide with
La Draga coming down, though as always her ears are sharper
than my eyes, and she grabs the stone banister to protect herself. She stays standing, but her bag flies open in her hand, a
thick glass vial jumping out and hitting the step beneath.

"Ah—I am sorry. I didn't hurt you?"

"No. No . . . I am fine."

I pick up the vial and turn to her. "Here—"

But her hand is already out waiting for it. I might ask her
how she knows I have it, but I will no doubt get some answer
about the sound of glass breaking or not, or the different ways a
man moves with a pot or an empty palm. As it is not Thursday,
I did not expect to find her here, but a busy house has its fair
share of aches and boils and fevers, and a clever courtesan keeps
her servants as healthy as herself. For my part, I am too busy to
cross paths with her often, and when we do meet, we are so mu-
tually civil that if you did not know, you might mistake us for
friends. Underneath, however, the scars inflicted by my suspicion and her retaliation all that time ago still remain, and we
cannot help but be wary of each other. Sometimes I think if I
had the will, I could find a way to heal things, for I am not totally without manners, and these last few years I have charmed
my way into the affections of one or two women infinitely more
appealing than she. But, if I am honest, they were also more stupid, and I think I fear that she would see through me, even with
her eyes closed.

"What's happened? What's going on up there?"

"A gift has arrived. I cannot help you with it. You had best
see it for yourself."

And so I do—the second I enter the *portego*. For no one
with eyes could miss it. It is propped against the wall: a great,
full-length silvered mirror, bigger than anything I have ever
seen before, shining like a starburst in the room, its surface
catching the sun and reflecting the great distance of space and
light flooding in through the loggia opposite. The whole house
is gathered in honor of it: my lady, Gabriella, Marcello; and,
standing, watching their glee, is our glass merchant client, Ves-
pasiano Alberini.

207 IN THE COMPANY OF THE COURTESAN

"Oh, Bucino! Look! Look what my lord Alberini has brought us!" Her face is lit up almost as bright as its surface. "Oh. You should have been here! It took eight men to bring it on the barge from Murano, and when they winched it up from below, each time it faltered, I thought my heart would stop for fear that it would smash. But my lord took charge of everything." And she moves over to him and squeezes his arm, and he laughs at her enthusiasm, for gratitude always brings out the happy child in her. "I wish La Draga had not rushed away so fast. Oh, isn't it the most remarkable thing you have ever seen?"

Indeed it is, and its presence in our house will be all around town by tomorrow, thanks to the drama of its arrival. Alberini is one of our better customers: a substantial merchant, in girth as well as talent, and a man who is abreast of the newest techniques in the foundries almost before the workmen themselves understand their potential. In love my lady says he is like a wild boar, all bristle and bellowing bulk, but hand him a piece of glass, from the most elaborate crystal to the finest ornamented majolica, and his hands are as careful and delicate as an angel's and his voice puts poetry into commerce.

I remember the first time he dined with us. He brought my lady an exquisite crystal wine goblet decorated with her name in the newest diamond-point engraving. "Feed your eyes on this miracle, my friends," he said as he showed it to the guests. "Into this transparent nothingness went sand and pebble and ash and a fire hotter than Hell. It is a testament to the glory of man and a lesson from God: beauty as perfect and fragile as life itself."

And as he said it, he pretended to drop it, so that the whole room sucked in a great breath of fear before he grinned and held it up to the light like a communion chalice. I have watched him repeat the exercise half a dozen times at different gatherings, and I love his sense of theater and his salesmanship. It almost makes me wish I was a priest so I could buy up all the misshapen failures of the workshop and drop them from the pulpit every Sunday to put the fear of death into my flock. No wonder he has made his fortune—there are not many men who can sell philosophy in a glass and yet still know the best wine to pour into it. Luckily for us, over these last few years he has become enamored enough of my lady's body to want to see it reflected every which way in his mirrors, for the business of glass exploits vanity as much as it peddles humility.

"You like it, Bucino?" he says, and his round face is split with a fat grin.

"As always, my lord—you bring us miracles."

"Beauty for beauty. A fair exchange."

"Oh, come, come closer, Bucino—you must see yourself in it." And my lady is beckoning to me. "Really. It is the most amazing sight. Move away, Gabriella, and let Bucino come."

I walk up and stand next to her.

And she is right: it is amazing. The morning sun is rich around us, and there we stand, revealed in our full-length glory: a tall, willowy beauty with a mane of flowing, golden hair and a squat, ugly troll, its fat head reaching barely as high as her breast. I feel my breath catch in my throat. I should have made myself more ready for the sight. God knows, I have done what I can. My clothes are expensively tailored to the proportions of my body, quality shining through the cloth, and my beard— which has many more than the few strands that Aretino once mocked—is combed and perfumed with musk and citrus to go with my kid gloves. Yet in this mirror I am still a shock to myself. For the truth is that in my own head I feel neither as small nor as different as I actually am, so that the sight of myself in any surface—not to mention such a vast, clean expanse of it— is always a greater pain to me than it ought to be.

"Oh, don't scowl so, Bucino. Your face is sweeter without the frown." And she pokes at me. "Isn't it a marvel?"

"A marvel," I say, trying to readjust my features.

"Oh, and look. Just see the way this seam on my skirt bunches to the left. I knew this dress was too bulky at the bottom, but the tailor told me it was only because I was bending to look at it. My God, this invention will make you a fortune, my lord. Not only does our room now seem as large as a palace, but it will change the art of dressmaking forever. We sack our tailor tomorrow, Bucino, you hear me?"

"I think we would do better to pay his bill first."

And we all laugh.

"So," says our benefactor. "I must leave you. The men are needed for another delivery."

"Oh, my lord, surely not so soon." And she pouts most prettily. "I tell you, when you come next, we will set up our table here, right in front of the mirror, so we can watch ourselves as we dine. Say it will be soon."

Her enthusiasm makes him pause. "Well . . . if I finish at the warehouse, I might be able to return later tonight."

She shoots a glance at me, for we both know it is Friday and she is booked out to the Crow.

"Ah, my lord, alas, we are already spoken for," I interject, taking the blame on myself. "But . . . if something should change, I will send you word immediately."

As soon as he is gone, she is again regarding herself critically in the mirror. I start my story of the Jew, but she is only half listening, for the bit of her that is not in thrall to her reflection is busy with her diary. "Oh . . . really? . . . But you must tell me later—I was getting ready when Alberini came, and now I am due at Tiziano's within the hour, and you know how he complains if I miss the light. . . . Gabriella! Tell Marcello to get the boat ready now. I will be there when I have changed my clothes." She turns back to me. "Why don't you come, Bucino? He promises it will be the last sitting. Maybe he would let you see it today."

And she is almost flighty now with good humor. Which is a relief, for in recent weeks she has been rather disgruntled and distracted with me; but then, like most women, my lady lives by the moods of the moon, and over time I have found it is best to ignore what I cannot decipher. The stemming and flowing of such fluids are La Draga's business, not mine.

I shake my head. "I am too busy. I still have the accounts to do." Though the truth is, the mirror has depressed me more than I choose to admit, and I do not care to be seen outside.

"Really, Bucino! You spend as much time with your head in a book as a scholar these days. I am surprised you are not publishing a study of Venice like every second fellow here. My

God, if I have to sit through another evening's talk about the greatness of the Venetian state and constitution, I think I might fall asleep. Oh, I tell you, Loredan and his Crow guests spoke of nothing else last week."

"Then maybe you should hold your soirees in front of the mirror from now on. That will keep their minds on the job at hand."

CHAPTER NINETEEN

Once she is gone I settle myself in my room, which is at the back of the house off the *portego*, and take out my account books. For all my complaining, I love this place. It was built to my specifications, and each thing in it fits me precisely, from the wooden bed, small enough for me to feel not too lonely as I lie alone in it, through the bookshelves in perfect proportion to my height, to the desk and chair constructed so I do not have to use cushions or waste time clambering up and on. Once I am sat here, with my pen in hand, my account books open, and my hourglass in front of me, the sand running free, I am as close as I come these days to satisfaction.

I said once that if we found ourselves living in a house with an abundance of light, I would never complain again. And I swear I do not do so now. It is true that I work harder on our success than I did on our failure. It is also true that my lady and I are no longer as close in triumph as we were in adversity. Of course. Her day is my night, which means that when she sleeps I am mostly at work, and the times when we are in public together we are careful to play mistress and servant rather than comrades. While our clients are less vulgar than some, a trade such as ours is always greedy for the gossip of perversion, and the cohabitation of beauty and beast is safer as a Platonic notion than as an Aretino-type sonnet. Should I choose to feel excluded, which I have done sometimes, for I too have my moods,

I remind myself that the harvest is always the busiest time for the farmer, and there will be space enough for leisure later, when age and fashion make our trade less brisk.

For now, between us, we run a thriving business, as complex and demanding as many others on which the city builds her wealth. With Rome struggling to rebuild herself and Florence a shadow of her former glorious self, Venice has become Europe's great metropolis for travelers: a haven for shoppers, businessmen, and pleasure seekers, all of them eager to sample whatever she has to offer. And high on the list are the charms of her professional women. So much so that there is almost a whiff of the old Rome to her now, and the gossip is that respectable women can barely get into the church on a Sunday these days, such is the crush of new courtesans showing off their wares.

In public, the old doge's face shows all the signs of a man with a permanent bad smell in his nostrils. I daresay disapproval will become state policy before too long—the wheel always turns full circle—but for now sinning is still as profitable as goodness, and so we make hay all year round. The spring months are our busiest time though, for it is then that ships prepare to depart again and the pilgrims gather in readiness for the Holy Land. Once they have glutted themselves on relics (Venice has enough bones to create a small army of semiribbed saints), you would be surprised how many of them give in to an extra sin or two before setting sail on the journey that will absolve them.

As in Rome, I am both the housekeeper and the gatekeeper. I mark down each and every soldo that comes in and goes out, since, when the bedroom door is closed, all kinds of rats can nibble at the kitchen supplies, and we both know of rich whores who died in poverty because of bad housekeeping. In the same way, no one enters or leaves the house without my knowledge. We do not entertain German heretics, for my lady's memory is as long as her hair was once short, and we are careful with passing trade, for while it is sorely tempting to slip foreign visitors in along with the regulars (Aretino's fulsome entry into the Register of Courtesans has brought all manner of rich trade to our door), doing so has its dangers. The pox brought by the French into Florence and Naples forty years ago is now a full-blown plague of the loins, and while you can refuse sick men, it is harder to spot the disease before it breaks the surface. La Draga has drafts and ointments for the lesser brands of itch and heat, and whatever we think of each other, I cannot doubt the efficacy of her remedies. Among her many talents, she is known to be able to rid a woman of a child while it is still in liquid shape in the womb. This is one skill that thus far we have had no need of. For it seems that my lady does not conceive, or at least she never has while I have known her. Had her mother been less ambitious and used her savings to sell her daughter into marriage to a tailor or a shipbuilder, her barrenness would have proved a more defining badge than her beauty. As it is, I think it brings her some sadness now, as there are women in her profession who have a room full of cots by the time they are her age, and while their children will not inherit titles, the city is full of rich men who are fond enough of their bastards to do them favors to help them make their way in life.

It is my job to meet all new customers before they see her and to settle their bills. In this way, I hope to sift out impostors or troublemakers. The worst are the men who use their fists as well as their pricks. Of course, no courtesan earns her living without some punches or bruises. That is a given. There are some men who cannot do it at all unless they have to fight for it a little, while others can be so overwhelmed by the sin that they have to inflict a little punishment as they take the pleasure. But these you can usually spot with their clothes on, for their lust vibrates with anxiety. My concern is with those I cannot read, the men who hold the violence inside them until the door is closed or the first bottle is drunk. I have seen it enough to know that there are a few for whom it is natural, as if they were born preferring the taste of meat over fish, and the devil in their loins is fed less by the act than by the pain they cause and the excitement they get from the causing of it.

In such matters, it's to our advantage that our cook has fists like ham bones and a temperament to go with them, and that

Marcello, the boatman, while he is the gentlest of men, is built like a warrior with a roar like the echo in a cave. In these last few years we have had to use their respective talents only once, and that time my lady was more scared than harmed, for we got to her within seconds of her screams. The man in question ended up in the canal with a broken arm and rib. While I have no doubt he might try it again, he would find it harder to do so in Venice, for though the security police might overlook such offenses (the world is full of women who go to the altar having been forced by their husbands as a last resort in courtship), there is a word-of-mouth register for such offenders among the best-known courtesans in the city.

As to my lady. Well, her moods notwithstanding, she shines bright enough at present, enlivened by fresh blood and gifts. She has been in business now for fourteen years all told, and will be twenty-nine on her next birthday. Which makes her no longer young for her trade—it is rare to find a successful courtesan over thirty who admits to her real age—though she still looks fresh enough for us to keep her age at twenty-two for the new visitors.

In this way we have made up all that we lost in Rome, and while I still fear high tides and yearn sometimes for the coarser energy of the Romans, you could say that we are secure here.

Indeed, you could say we are content.

CHAPTER TWENTY

I am deep into the books when a message comes from our Crow Loredan's man: the great senator is delayed on business about the Sensa and will not be able to make it tonight, which leaves us free to entertain our generous glass merchant after all. I use the news as a reason to close my books. The ordering of numbers has calmed my self-hatred a little, and before I contact Alberini I should inform my lady.

Tiziano's house and studio are to the north across the Grand Canal near Rio di Santa Caterina, and while the walk is brisk, the day is spring sweet and the exercise will do me good.

Tiziano himself, about whom I fear I was a little casual that first evening because I did not know any better, is far and away Venice's most celebrated artist, so famous now that the paint is barely dry on his canvases before they are crated off on boats and mule trains to the courts of half of Europe. For such a great man, I must say he remains refreshingly half peasant. He is as active with his abacus as he is with his brush (he and I share a natural affinity when it comes to ideas for wringing money out of recalcitrant clients), and while I don't doubt he will go down in history for the fineness of his paint, my memories of his house have more to do with the smells from his kitchen, for he and Aretino both love their food, and their cooks often compete to produce the best dishes. Also like Aretino, he has a healthy fondness for women. This is the second time my lady has sat for him. If she has done more than sit, then she has not told me about it, and I have not asked, though when his beloved wife, Cecilia, died a few years ago she may have comforted him then, as I know he grieved sorely.

I cross the Grand Canal at the Rialto. I can almost see Aretino's house from here. He too has prospered. He toyed for a while with going to live at the French court but instead spent a season of Lent in deep and public penance while at the same time dashing off such paeans of praise to his newly adopted city that Doge Gritti was moved to intervene on his behalf, and in this way he was reconciled with both the pope and his old enemy the duke of Mantua. His rise was fast after that, and he is now one of the city's treasures. In public he sports a chain of gold received from the king of France, his letters circulate among the cognoscenti, and Venice is full of people eager to treat him well as a way to keep him from treating them badly.

He and my lady have forged an unexpected friendship over these years. The flame that once burned in them both has faded to the warmth of embers. Success has brought him enough women to fawn and fiddle over him without needing her attention, and, to be honest, I think both of them live so much of their private lives being public that they are grateful for the company of someone who knows them from the inside out and with whom they do not have to perform. When they are not gossiping, they are fond of games of chance, which have become all the rage in Venice now, and sometimes the three of us play together on idle afternoons, turning over painted cards with a dozen different capricious futures written on them. For our part, we have stuck to the bargain and for all these years have kept *The Positions* out of the public domain. With no children in the nursery, it has become our insurance against the bankruptcy of old age.

I skirt the Campo dei Santi Apostoli and head due north through a cobweb of alleys. Wealth gives way to poverty as I move, and I keep my head down now and my purse close to my chest. In contrast to the area around, Tiziano's house, perched on the very edge of the lagoon, is a statement of status, new and rather grand. On a clear day you can see as far as Monte Ante-lao in Cadore from here, which I am sure is why he chose it, for he is a sentimental fellow when it comes to memories of his native town.

His housekeeper opens the door and shows me into the garden to wait, while she tells my mistress that I am here. I sit and massage my legs, for the journey has numbed my thighs. The water is so close here that you can hear the waves slapping against the shoreline. Though Venice will never be Rome to me, there is a certain melancholy beauty to the way she flirts with the sea, like a lovely woman lifting up her decorated skirts—sometimes not far enough—to miss the rising tides. On days like today, when the water is shining and the air is sticky with the scent of jasmine and peach blossom, you can almost imagine you are in Paradise. As sweet as Arcadia. Wasn't that the phrase her mother used with her as a child when she would try to describe the smells of a rich man's garden? It was those same words my lady had used to tempt me onward that first day in Venice, when our future felt as black as her bloodied scalp. As I think this, I am struck with great force by the memory, as if it is only now, here, at this moment, after all this time, that I feel we are truly arrived at where we set out to be. And inside the wonder of the feeling, there is also a sense of terror—yes, terror—that we have risen so far and that there is, therefore, so far to fall.

Her voice, when it comes, makes me jump.

"Bucino! I thought you were tied to your abacus."

I turn to see her dressed in a robe as if she has just risen from her bed. Her hair is long and free down her back. He has especially requested her to wear it in the same style as when they first met. While even I must admit that she is not as fresh as she was then, the braided band of hair and the mischief of tiny curls playing around her forehead still bring out the girl in the woman.

"I was, but a message arrived."

"It had better be important. Tiziano rumbles like thunder when he is interrupted."

"It isn't finished yet? I thought this was the last sitting."

She laughs. "Oh, it will never be finished. At least not to his satisfaction. I will be old before he puts his brush down."

"Well, you look young enough now."

"Really? You think so?" And she twirls around so that her hair flows with her. How she drinks it up, flattery. Feeds on it, grows from it, like a plant moving toward the light, as if she can never get enough. "You do not compliment me so much these days, Bucino."

"I cannot get a word in between all the other voices."

She pouts a little, a device that has more impact on her suitors than on me. But then I know her better, and, unlike them, I have caught her hard at work with her hand mirror, and the look she gives herself there has little enough of flattery to it. Given my time again, I no longer know if I would choose beauty over ugliness. There is too much anxiety in its fragility. "So tell me, what is the message?"

"Loredan is caught up with Sensa business and will not visit tonight after all."

"Oh." She gives a shrug as if it is of no particular import, though I can see she is pleased. "Then perhaps we might send a message to Vittorio Foscari," she says lightly. "I know he would be happy to join me instead."

"I'm sure he would. But we are committed first to Alberini for his generosity."

She groans. "Oh, of course, Alberini." And she wrinkles her nose. "But we told him already we were busy. He would never know. His and Foscari's paths never cross."

Indeed they don't, since one of them works for a living and the other lives off his family. Though I choose not to mention that. "Why don't you give Foscari time to recover?" I say.

She laughs and takes it as a compliment, but that is only half true. He is something of a challenge to me, this Foscari. He is both our newest and our youngest suitor. A Crow by birth, he is as yet still a half-feathered fledgling, but once he takes off his patterned stockings, he is so new to the pleasures of his own prick that he seems to exhaust them both with his ardor and his chatter. Of course, every courtesan needs to be adored some-times, and his worship has made her gay enough. He arrived in the wake of an affair with a gizzard-necked Florentine scholar who huffed and puffed so much that it was hard to tell if he was coming soon or going forever. While I had been careful to nego-tiate payment by the hour, I don't doubt that Foscari's fresh, firm flesh was pleasant enough contrast. Yet this young Crow has proved a disaster when it comes to business, for he does not control his own fortune, exceeds his allowance, and is not smart enough to know how to get himself more.

"You know he still owes us for half a dozen meetings last month."

"Oh, Bucino. You worry too much. He is from one of the best families in the city."

"Which keeps its money for the elder sons rather than him. They paid for his deflowering, not for him to keep a mistress. Business would be better served by a sweet thank-you to Al-berini."

"Really—I don't need you to lecture me on what would be best for business," she mutters irritably. "I think I would prefer to entertain Foscari."

"As you wish. But if he comes, he must pay. Our charity to him is already a matter for gossip in the house, and if we are not careful, it will be around the city that we are giving away what others are charged for. And you know the damage that can cause."

She shrugs. "I have heard no gossip."

"That is because you have the door closed," I say gently. "And I have been snoring louder than usual to cover up the noise."

I smile so that we might find a way to make it up through my quip. But she chooses not to take the olive branch.

"Oh, very well! If you are so insistent, then he had better not come. Even so, I will not entertain Alberini. I shall use the time to rest instead. It is not nothing, you know, sitting here all day like a living statue while Tiziano fusses and fiddles with his brushes."

I look at her for a moment, but she drops her gaze. "Ooh,

this jasmine," she says extravagantly, burying her nose in its blossom. "There is no perfume like it in the world. I have tried to buy this scent on the Rialto a dozen times, but it never lasts longer than a few minutes once it is out of the bottle."

"It is very sweet, yes," I murmur, impressed by how quickly she has moved the subject on, for this is not the first time we have crossed swords over this pup. "Sweet as Arcadia."

And she looks at me and smiles again, as if there is something that she cannot quite remember. "Arcadia? Yes, I suppose it is."

"I don't care how much they're offering, you can't have her, Bucino." Tiziano is at the door. "I was promised the whole day, and I need every minute of it."

"Don't worry, maestro. You are safe enough. I came only to deliver a message."

"Some randy old man wants her tonight, eh? It's a shame— she'll be missing a roasted loin of pork dripping with apple juices. Come, Fiammetta, the light is perfect. I need you back now."

"One moment and I will be there." It is clear that she is relieved to be pulled away. Her smile to me is fast, distracted. "I will see you later, Bucino." The fact that she does not tell me when she will return shows how peeved with me she is over Foscari. She leaves, and he makes to follow her. But it has been a long walk from there to here, and I may not get this chance again for months. "Tiziano?"

He turns.

"Now that I'm here, can I see the painting?"

"No! It isn't finished yet."

"But I thought this was her last sitting."

"It isn't ready," he repeats stubbornly.

"It is only that dwarves have weak hearts." I smile. "I have it on good authority that I could be dead within the year."

He scowls, but I know he likes me well enough, or as much as he likes anyone while he is working. "What has she told you about it?"

"Nothing." I shrug. "Except that holding the pose has given

her a crick in her neck that I have to massage out each evening. Without me, you wouldn't have a model."

"Ah! Very well. But you look and then you go. What you see is not for gossip, understand?"

"Gossip? The only thing I talk to is my account book. Everything else goes on over my head."

His studio is within the house, with a shed next door where he dries his canvases. I follow him upstairs to a room on the *piano nobile* where two great stone-trimmed windows let in a river of light and where the view can take him home sometimes without the journey. The canvas is on a great easel in the middle of the room, and if it is not finished, I cannot see what is left to be done. But then I am something of a blockhead when it comes to art. I have been present at a handful of entertainments where I have heard great men—and the odd show-off courtesan—wax lyrical about Tiziano's "genius" with such verbal flights of fancy that what they describe seems to grow more out of their own imaginations than out of anything I see on the canvas. "Oh! Oh! See how he sanctifies the human body with his art." "In Tiziano's colors God has placed Paradise." "He is not a painter but a miracle." Their flattery is as sticky as honey, and I sometimes think the reason Tiziano favors my lady as a model is that she does not torment him with such prattle and so gives him room to let the brush fly.

As for this, his latest work—well, to minimize the confusion, I will keep the words simple.

The setting is the room itself—in the background you can see part of the window, with a luminous sunset streaking the sky; on the walls are tapestries and in front, two decorated chests, by which two maids, one kneeling, the other standing nearby, are sorting clothes.

But while you see them, they are not where your eye lingers. For in the foreground of the painting, so close that you might almost touch her, is a naked woman. She is lying propped on a pillow on a bed of red floral mattresses covered with rumpled sheets, and at her feet a small dog is snoozing, curled head to toe. Her hair is falling across her shoulders, the nipple on her left breast, firm and pink, stands out against the dark velvet of the curtain behind, and the fingers of her left hand curl over the cleft of her sex. While all this is lovely enough and—as far as I can tell from bits of flesh I already know—a perfect replica of my lady's body, it is familiar even to a dunce like myself, for the pose of Venus reclining has long been a popular one for sophisticated palates.

What is different in this painting, though, is her face. For while every Venus I have ever seen is asleep or gazing out into the distance, modestly ignorant of the fact that she is being observed, this Venus, my lady's Venus, is awake. And not simply awake but staring directly out at the viewer. As for the look in her eyes—well, this is where the simple words break down and I feel a flight of Aretino fancy coming upon me. For her gaze is one of such . . . lassitude, such lazy erotic energy, that it is hard to tell whether she is savoring memories of past pleasures or issuing a more direct invitation for what is to come. Either way, she is honest enough about it. There is not one iota of shame, embarrassment, or coyness in her face. This lady, my lady, is so at ease with herself that however long you stare at her, she keeps on staring back.

"So?"

He is standing impatiently behind me as if he doesn't give a damn what I think but just wants me to say something so I will leave and he can get on with it. What can I tell him? I have spent most of my working life applauding bad poets, laughing at dreadful jokes, lying to second-rate musicians, and flattering stupid rich men who think their arguments are intelligent. One could say that I have grown incapable of telling the truth. I look at it again.

"It is wonderful," I say firmly. "You have created a great Venetian Venus. It would beat that poxy French ambassador on a bet between painting and sculpture any day."

"Tschar!" And the disgust is rich in his throat. In conversations about his genius, Tiziano is always the most silent one.

I sigh. "Oh, look, Tiziano, why bother to ask me? You know I know nothing about art. I am a pimp. A high-class one, certainly, but a pimp nevertheless. You want to know what I see? I see a beautiful courtesan, as luscious as if she were lying here before me. More than that I have no idea."

"Hmm. One more question and then you can go. Do you know what she is thinking?"

I look again. Do I know what is she thinking? Of course I do. She is a courtesan, God damn it. "She is thinking whatever one wants her to be thinking," I say quietly.

He nods. And picks up the brush. It is clear I am dismissed.

My lady comes in and waves to me before moving toward the couch. While I have studied every inch of her body now, I will leave before she takes off her gown.

I get as far as the door. But it keeps on nagging at me.

"There is one other thing."

He turns. "What?"

"It's not her, you know."

"What do you mean?"

"Well, I don't know if you're color-blind, but Fiammetta Bianchini's eyes are emerald green. Not black."

He gives a great laugh, and I see her face light up with a grin.

"Well—you wouldn't want every man who sees her in my studio to come knocking on your door, would you?"

And as she drops her robe, I go out the door.

CHAPTER TWENTY-ONE

I arrive back to find a boat docked at our mooring. For a moment I think it might be the fledgling Foscari, for the canopy is splendid enough and the trouble he is causing has been on my mind as I walk, but Gabriella meets me at the door and announces a stranger who has been sitting in the *portego* for the best part of an hour. "He wouldn't leave a message. He says it is important and that he must speak to you alone."

He is sitting below the mirror, which, now that the light is dying, is become a dark hole in the gloom. I must say I had not expected him so soon. But then men going on long journeys often seek comfort before they leave. He gets up quickly to greet me, which makes him too tall, but it is a nice enough gesture, for believe me, not all of our customers bother. I catch sight of us both in the glowering glass, a bean pole and a runt, but I am prepared for the sight of myself now.

"Signor Lelio, you are welcome. How was your meeting?"

"It went well. The ship is ready. We sail the day after tomorrow. To the Indies."

"The day after tomorrow. So soon? Please—sit down."

He sits. But his limbs stay rigid. His nerves are palpable. If he is here for an appointment, I know already that there is no space for him. But he was good to me once in his way, and it is my job to afford him the same due care as any man with a purse and an appetite. "Is this your first time? To the Indies, I mean?"

"Ah, yes—no. I went east a year ago. Aleppo and Damascus. But to the markets. Not the mountains."

"So, you have not seen the places where the stones come from?"

"No. Not yet." He smiles, for he remembers it all as well as I do. "But this time, God willing, I will."

The room is darker now. Gabriella knocks and comes in with a taper. As she moves around us, a shower of candle flames leaps up and starts to dance in the mirror. "Will you bring us some wine, Gabriella? . . . You will take something to drink?"

"Oh, no, no!" He shakes his head. "I—I mean, I cannot stay. . . ." And his eyes dart nervously.

"Don't worry, Signor Lelio," I say gently as she leaves. "Our business here is as discreet as yours once was."

But he is not placated. "I . . . er . . ." He looks around. "It is a fine house. I did not expect . . ."

"Such wealth?" I smile, and I am back again for a moment in a dingy room as his father puts down the eyeglass from our ruby and in his eyes I see our future draining away. Even now the memory spikes me. "We are lucky. Though everything you see here was once owned by someone else. And no doubt will be again. I think your family would remember our bargaining well enough. How is your father, by the way?"

He hesitates. "He died some years ago."

I want to ask him if it was before or after his conversion, but it feels too cruel a question. While it is not unknown for Jews to take on the Christian faith, the only stories I have heard are of young women star-crossed in love or tempted by a fat dowry from the Church, eager to promote the true faith. For a grown man to leave would be a much greater betrayal of the community. "I am sorry for your loss. Did he settle his argument with the state?"

He shrugs. "The contract was renewed. Only the price changed. But such negotiations are endless."

As is the debate about the Jews. You hear it in the taverns and on the Rialto daily: those who believe that the Devil resides in Jewish loins and that usury pollutes the soul of any Christian who takes their money versus the merchants, for whom pragmatism is a virtue and who need Jewish purses to keep their businesses afloat. I think every Venetian has a bit of both men in him somewhere, though the merchant has the louder voice these days, and as long as Venice lives by her ships, everyone knows that, in some way or other, the Jews will remain. With his father dead, he would have been one of the elders now, responsible for negotiating his community's future.

"Can I ask you something?"

He looks at me, because of course he knows what the question is.

"You want to know what made me convert?" He stares at me for a moment, then drops his eyes. "I—I found Jesus Christ in my heart," he says quietly.

I nod and keep my look grave. I spend my life making money out of sins of the flesh. The odd lie is a small enough business to me. But it seems to worry him more.

"I mean . . . it . . . it is hard . . . to speak about. Always . . . I have always . . . Well, the Ghetto is very small." He shakes his head. "And the world is so big. I think I have always been looking out the window. Even when I was a small child."

"You are lucky," I say mildly. "I could never see that high."

"You should know I am not ashamed of myself," he says, and his voice is firm now. For all his nerves, he has more confidence than that young man with his sad look and eyeglass. "A man must make his way in the world. My business brings money into Venice. I pay my taxes and obey the laws of the state as well as the next man. I am a respectable man."

"I'm sure you are." More so than I will ever be, certainly.

"I have memories . . . of your visits to our shop. You were always most polite to me."

"You were giving me money. It would hardly have done to offend you."

"That consideration did not influence most people." He pauses. "The last time we met . . . I mean, the book you brought me. Did you find someone else to take it?"

"What book?" I say calmly. "There was no book. That was my mistake."

"I see." He smiles. "You do not need to worry. I have told no one about it." There is a silence. "Though I must say I have thought about it sometimes. . . . As I say, the world was very small where I came from."

I wonder how long it will take him to spit it out. I could help him if I wanted. God knows, at first glance *The Positions* would have been surprising to more men than just him. Though once they had seen inside it, they would never be as surprised again. That was its power. Our power. We had had more in common than I had realized, he and I: both of us making our living trading in the forbidden. Sex and usury. How clever of the state to keep itself pure by giving the servicing of sins to those already damned.

"I must tell you, Signor Lelio—my lady is not here at present," I say. "So I cannot introduce you, and I—"

"No, no—you don't understand. I didn't come for her . . . I mean . . . for that." He is up on his feet again now. "I came because . . . because I have something I must tell you. Something that has been weighing on my mind for a long time now. When I saw you this morning, well . . ." He shakes his head and takes a breath. "You see, I know about your jewel. The one that was stolen from you."

Now it is my turn to stare. "The ruby—you know about our ruby?"

"Well, I . . . of course, I cannot be absolutely sure it was yours, but it was the same size and the same cut, perfect, right down to the fire in its center."

"You saw it? When? What happened?"

"Someone came to me. Wanting to pawn it. A woman—"

"Old—ugly, yes?"

"No. No, she was quite young."

"What did she look like?" And just for that second, La Draga's dreamy white face rises up before me. "Did she limp, was she blind?"

"No. No. I remember no limp and she was—I don't know—quite sweet-faced. I mean, her head was covered by a shawl so I could not see much. But—"

"Was she alone?"

"I don't know. I saw only her."

"What happened?"

"She told me the ruby was from a pendant of her mistress. A family jewel. But that her mistress needed the money to pay some private debts for a while. She could not come herself for fear of being recognized abroad, so she had sent her maid in her place."

"Did you take it?"

"It was not our policy to take stolen goods." He pauses. "But it was a beautiful stone. True right through to its heart. Someone would have bought it."

"And paid what for it?"

"Three, maybe three hundred and fifty ducats."

I had been right. A small fortune. The bitterness flows back like bile into my mouth. What could we not have done with that much money then?

"When was this?"

He hesitates. "It was that last afternoon. When you came to see me with the book."

"The last afternoon?"

He sighs. "Yes. After you left, I was about to close the shop so I could attend to your lock when someone rang the bell. It was her."

And I am walking in fogbound streets again, people slipping in and out of the mist like ghosts, the fear of poverty all around me.

"Of course, as soon as I saw it I thought of you. I told her that I would take it but that I needed to check with my father first because the amount was so large. I asked her to come back after I had closed and said I would do the deal then. I was going to tell you when you returned. But then, after she had gone, I opened the book, and it . . . well . . . I mean, I had not seen anything like that before. . . ."

"That is because there has not been anything like it before," I say quietly. "So what happened when she came back?"

"I don't know." He shakes his head. "I closed up the shop before she came. I never saw the stone or her again."

We both sit for a moment in silence, and I find myself wondering if his old faith would have explained the capriciousness of destiny any better than his new one.

"What more can you tell me about her? Do you remember anything else?"

"I'm sorry. . . ." He pauses. "It was a long time ago."

After he leaves, I sit and watch the night come in. I have stopped looking for Meragosa long ago. Instead, I have used our success as a kind of salve for the wound she left in me. In my mind I have decided that she is long dead, have killed her off with the pox or a bout of the plague, the remains of her stolen luxuries no defense against the diseases of sin. But with his story, the pain of her theft now cuts as sharp as a knife again.

Of course, she would never have taken the stone to a pawn merchant herself. She was not that stupid. Even though I had been careful to keep my contacts in the Ghetto secret, she would have known well enough the ones that gave good prices. Instead of going herself, she would have sent someone else. As far as I knew, Meragosa was a woman without a past or a family. In all the time we lived together, she never talked to or about another living soul, save a few of the other crones in the local marketplace. So this must have been an accomplice picked for the moment; a young woman, pretty enough to catch the eye of the Jew she had to spin the story around, who would no doubt have got a small cut for her pains and her lying.

Three hundred and fifty ducats. He was right. It was a long time ago, and as Fate would have it, things had turned out well enough without it. Indeed, you might argue it had been the making of us: the finding of the book, the connection with Aretino, the pact, the evening, our present success. But it doesn't stop the anger when I think about the moment, when I see again her room open and empty and read the horror on my lady's face. If Meragosa were to walk back into our lives now . . .

I cannot wait to tell my lady about it. But she does not return in time for supper. Maybe they are celebrating the end of the painting, or the smell of the pork was too succulent to miss.

Or maybe she needs to show further her displeasure with me. Whatever the reason, by midnight there is still no sign of her, and in the end I retire to bed.

My dreams are full of precious stones falling from my fingers into dank canal water and sinking into stinking mud. I wake suddenly, though it is still dark, and it takes a moment for me to register the sound: a cry of some kind—voices, rising then hushed. Our casa sits near enough to the Grand Canal for revelers to use it as a shortcut home sometimes. My window looks out onto the water with a view of our dock, so I can note the traffic of suitors. I step up on my stool and open the catch. But the dock is clear. Our boat is not even there. My lady must have stayed overnight at Tiziano's.

I am halfway to my bed when the noise comes again. A voice, or voices, definitely. From inside the house. In the early days, before our household was as secure as it is now, my inventory had located a slow leak from the kitchen supplies. The rat that Mauro and I found in the middle of the night was wearing our boatman's uniform and carrying a sack. He left the house by water but without a boat.

I open the door and move out to the landing to trace the sound better.

For a moment there is only silence above and around me. Then I hear it again, quieter than before, almost a murmuring, as if whoever is talking is aware that others will be sleeping nearby. And now I locate it exactly. It comes from my lady's chamber.

But how? If she brought someone home from Tiziano's, where is her transport? Or his? I tread carefully. I know each step and creaking board on the journey between her room and my own. While I have never spied on her, there are moments when the music of passion contains violent notes within it, and with first-time clients especially it is better to be on one's guard. But there is nothing in the voices to alarm me now. What am I thinking as I stand here by the door? That I am helping to save her from herself? No. I don't think that.

I put my fingers carefully over the handle. It is a rule of the house that there is no lock. Safety over privacy once again. If I am wrong, then I will take the consequences. If I am quiet enough, he—whoever he is—might never know.

I turn the handle inch by inch until I feel rather than hear it give. The door opens a fraction, then a fraction more. The crack is enough to give me the view I need, for the bed is placed just to the left, its great carved walnut pillars reaching to the ceiling. For the shy there are curtains that can be pulled all around, for there are always a few men who are looking to return to the safety of the womb, both inside and out. But this man tonight does not need them. He is much too intoxicated by the process of growing up.

The room is lit by two candles, their glow honey, the light they throw dancing into the darkness. Tiziano could not have lit the scene better. The bed is a storm of covers and sheets. My lady is sitting on its edge. He is on his knees at her feet, naked, his arms flung around her waist. The candlelight molds the line of his thighs, his buttocks, and lower back, the skin glistening with sweat, the muscles curved and sinewy, a youthful warrior caught in the fire of perfection. But my lady is not looking at him; she has already had her fill of his perfect beauty. Instead she is folded over him, her body resting on his back, her head down, and her great river of hair splayed over his skin like a cloak. They are utterly still. Flesh on flesh, beauty on beauty. It is a more arresting image than anything Giulio Romano's lascivious pen might conjure up. For this is not the crude excitement of the act. Rather it is its aftermath, the joyful exhaustion that takes over when the body has gorged itself, when lust and hunger are satiated and you are safe, complete, yourself and yet without self at the same time. It is the instant when lovers feel almost as if they have stopped time with their passion. And anyone who is not inside it is cast into the cold wastes of longing.

I close the door silently and go back to my room. I wait, turning the hourglass first one way, then the other. The short stab of pain in my lungs ignites into a slow fire of anger. The scene I have just witnessed may be the closest man comes to

God on earth, but it is not the work of an honest courtesan. The very point of our business is that courtesans are paid to give pleasure and to pretend to receive it. Once that pretense breaks down, the whole edifice crumbles. For then it is almost the money that becomes the sin, rather than the act.

In these few years, we have made up all that we lost in Rome. We are secure here. Indeed, we are content. . . . Which, if you think about it, is a dangerous state in life, for it is always the perfect garden into which the serpent slithers on its way up into the branches of the apple tree.

Now, it seems, there is a snake in our grass.

CHAPTER TWENTY-TWO

But all is not lost yet.

I wait until she rises. We have a ritual, she and I, for the mornings. I leave just after dawn for the market. She wakes late—for hers is a working night—and calls first for Gabriella, who helps her to wash and dress before bringing up the fresh breads and sweet, watered wine, which she drinks while sitting in her chair overlooking the water. Then I join her, and we go together through the day's commitments and anything that I should know about from the evening before. While each and every suitor has his allotted time and requirements, of which I have prior notice, there is the odd occasion when a regular— our Crow in particular—might make a separate arrangement with her or simply stop by on the chance of a favor: for there is a certain frisson to be had from pretending their liaison is one of spontaneous pleasure as much as of regular business. But should that happen, she has a mind like a steel trap when it comes to noting when and for how long, so I will know what to put against their names. That is how it works. She and I in partnership, each and every man treated equally according to his means; for we are both experts at the art of juggling, keeping all the balls moving through the air with equal precision and grace. That she is in trouble with the pup is clear enough for anyone with eyes to see. But she has not become this successful by being reckless. She was trained to have judgment too, and we may yet be saved by her using it.

It is after midday by the time I am summoned. When I enter, she is in the chair with a bowl of white paste and a stand mirror in front of her, applying a mask to her face, though this is not the day for such a treatment.

"Good morning, Bucino." She glances at me, smiling, her voice light, her spirits evidently high despite what I know to be a lack of sleep. "How was the market?"

"I let Mauro go alone. I was late to bed waiting for you."

"Oh, I am sorry. I asked Tiziano to send a message. Did you not get it? He had me sitting for so long that it was easier to stay on and dine. Aretino came. Ah! He was so rude about the painting. You should have heard him. He even accused me of pleasuring myself as I lay there with my hand across me. Imagine! I tell you, he has grown tired of goodness and is back to his old ways. Was it you who told me he is writing scandalous stuff again? I asked him, but he wouldn't talk about it. Still, underneath, I know he approved of the portrait, for he loves almost everything Tiziano does. But you are a more honest judge than any of them. What did you think?"

"I think it is a shame we can't afford to buy it," I say, keeping my tone as light as hers. "We could hang it on the wall opposite the new mirror and charge a sliding scale: one fee for an hour in the company of the real woman, another for the painted one."

She snorts. "Oh, Bucino, don't make me laugh. You know I am not supposed to move my face too much as the paste dries."

"Why so much face care? Or have I got the day wrong?"

She shrugs. "What did you used to say to me? In our business there is never such a thing as too much beauty. See? I listen to everything you tell me."

"Yes," I say. "What time did you get home?"

"Oh, late—it must have been two, three o'clock, I think."

"Marcello brought you back, yes?"

"Uh-huh."

"Where is he now? There was no boat there this morning."

"Er . . . ah, yes. Well, he had waited so long for me, poor thing. I gave him the rest of the night off."

Of course—it would not have done to have him there when

the other boat arrived. I wait. If she is to tell me, it will be now: *Ah, by the way, Bucino—I have a confession to make. Foscari visited me last night. . . . I know you'll be cross, but it was late and my free time, and I am sure he will make it up to us when his allowance comes in.* So easy. But instead she continues to apply the paste, her face disappearing into the china whiteness of a carnival mask. Soon there will no room for any expression.

"Did you sleep well?" I ask, my eyes somewhere else.

"Mmm. You would be surprised how exhausting it is lying propped on a bed staring into the distance for so long."

"I'm sure."

A pause opens and lengthens. We have so much to talk about, she and I. Not just this but the visit of the Jew. She needs to know about the stone and the young woman and how we came within a breath of catching her so many years ago. It is the stuff of our history together. But if she now keeps secrets from me, so will I keep them from her. I feel strange: as if I have walked into a room I just left, only to find the furniture so rearranged that I cannot get my bearings or understand how it could have happened so fast. I find myself thinking back to the garden at Tiziano's yesterday as her gaze slid away from me to the jasmine. Then I see her face in the painting. "Courtesans think whatever you want them to be thinking." That is their job. She, like me, is an expert liar. Even her moaning is fake. Usually. That is how she earns her living. *Our* living.

"Are you all right, Bucino?"

"Me? Why shouldn't I be?"

"I don't know. You seem . . . well . . . so glum these days."

"I am busy. The business takes a lot of time."

"I know. And there is no one who is as good at it as you. But it is worth it? I mean, it goes well enough, yes? You would tell me if it didn't?"

"Yes, it goes well enough."

All around me I hear the rustling. Yet surely if you spot the snake even as it slithers into Paradise, you might prevent it from getting as far as the tree. "Fiammetta." I pause. "I know someone visited last night."

"What?" She lifts her head—the mask is hardened so that the only bit of her that reacts is her eyes. And they are sharp as stone chips.

I take a breath. "I know that Foscari was here."

"How do you know?" And there is panic in her voice. "My God, have you been spying on me?"

"No. No. I slept badly. And then woke to the sound of his boat leaving."

She stares at me as if to check that this is the truth. But I can lie as well as she when it is needed. We did not become partners in this game by accident. She makes an impatient gesture with her hand, for it is clear that now she is exposed, she cannot lie. "It was nothing. I mean, he . . . simply stopped on his way home to give me something."

"A gift. How generous. Did you receive it lying down?"

"Ah! And whose business is it if I did?"

"Mine," I say. "For he owes me money."

"Oh! It is you he owes the money to now. Not me. Well, then I am sorry to disappoint you, but he came only to bring me a poem."

"A poem?"

And she scowls at the feebleness of her own lie.

I shake my head. "What? Did it tell you how much he loves you?"

"Bucino! He is young and in thrall to the drama of it all. You know how it is."

"No, I don't. And even if I did, that is not the point. We have an agreement. If a man comes when he is not booked, you tell me."

"I tried to. Yesterday I said Foscari would like to see me. It was not on anyone else's time. Loredan had canceled. I was free. But you were the one who would have none of it."

"That is not how it was, Fiammetta, and you know it. You refused Alberini, and we agreed that Foscari would not visit because he did not have the money."

"Ah! Then he will pay later. For God's sake. We will hardly become bankrupt without it. What do you want from me, Bucino?" And she is angry now, so that her face is moving despite the mask, small bits of the white paste flaking and falling off. "Do we not have enough for the market? Is there a shortage of clients? Are my breasts sagging or am I drinking too much wine? Do I stint on my time? Does anyone leave here unsatisfied? So—I choose to see one client for an hour or so and do not tell you because you would be ill-tempered about it."

"That is not how it works," I say quietly, but not without anger, for the image of them folded together rubs like a hair shirt on my mind. "You know as well as I do the message you send out when you start giving it away. It is the beginning of the end for your reputation."

"And how will anyone know? Who will tell them? You? Me? Him? Our servants? I think we pay them well enough."

"It doesn't matter who. Gossip is like air. You know that. It is nowhere and everywhere without anyone seeming to move it." I try again to keep my tone steady, but I am not sure I succeed. "He is a customer, Fiammetta. You are a courtesan. Those are the rules we work by. The ones we agreed to together."

"Then maybe we should change them. For I tell you, this is insupportable to me. Rules, accounts, agreements—that is all you talk of these days. We did not work this hard for so long for it all to become so—oh, I don't know—so boring."

"Boring? Really? You find it boring? Wearing the best cloth, eating haunches of roasted meat off silver plates, living in a house where you know it's a new day because you can see the sunlight rather than because your gut aches with yesterday's hunger? Is it so easily forgotten?"

She stares at me, and her eyes close briefly in her whitening face. "You are a good man, Bucino, but some things you don't understand," she says, and her voice is almost sullen.

I have an answer on my tongue but there is a knock at her door. It slides open far enough to show Gabriella's face in the crack.

"What is it?" I hear the anger in my voice. We all hear it.

"I . . . It is just . . . well, La Draga is waiting, my lady. She says she is sorry she could not come earlier, but she was needed elsewhere."

"Ah! . . . Yes," she stammers. "I . . . Let her wait in the *portego*. Tell her I will not be long."

The door closes, and we face each other again.

"Are you ill?"

She shrugs. "A slight case of the itch, that is all." And even her voice sounds different now, caught between the rigor mortis of the mask and her own dishonesty.

A slight case of the itch. Well, in one way it is. Certainly La Draga would have the answer for that. La Draga, whose presence in the house, it seems, is now timed to coincide with what should have been my absence at the market. What treasures might she have for my lady in her bag now? A balm of herbs mixed with holy water perhaps, for her to smear on her lips in readiness for the first kiss? A consecrated host with my lady's name inscribed on it to be dissolved into the beloved one's soup? There is a brisk enough trade in such holy objects around the city these days. While it may turn men's stomachs to hear it, the fact is that most women—and courtesans are the greatest offenders in this—are so in thrall to the business of love that they will use anything, sacred or profane, to capture and hold a man's desire. More often than not, the women laugh it off as more of a beauty aid than magic. They are fooling themselves, of course, for it fast becomes its own addiction: once you believe that a man is bound to you because of spells rather than your natural charms, you become as much enslaved to the potions as he might be to you.

In Rome there were famous courtesans who paid as much to their witchy apothecaries as they did to their dressmakers. Fiammetta Bianchini, however, had never been one of them. She had never needed to be. Not until now—at least as far as I know. But then it seems there is a great deal happening in the house that I do not know.

"So tell me, Fiammetta. What do you think your mother would say of all this?"

"My mother?"

The question takes her by surprise, and I watch her wrestle with it, for in these last few weeks it will not be just my voice that she has blotted from her mind.

"I—I think she would . . . I think she would see what you see, but . . . but . . . I also think she would understand better."

"You do? So tell me."

"Look, it's not what you think, Bucino. I am not stupid. I can see today as well as I could yesterday. And as well as I will tomorrow." Her voice is calmer now, though she still cannot hold my eyes without her own darting away, which, as far as I am concerned, tells a deeper truth than anything the words can say. "But sometimes, just sometimes . . . I need—oh, I don't know . . . some . . . joy. A little sweetness in with all the bloated flesh and belches. And Vittorio Foscari is sweet. He is sweet and young and fresh and, yes, joyful. He does not dribble into his wineglass or fall asleep in his plate, or even on top of my body. He makes me laugh. He makes me feel . . . I don't know . . . like I am a girl again, though God knows I doubt I ever was such a thing. Which is something I think my mother would understand well enough." And there is just a hint of bitterness as she says it. "Oh, how can I explain this to you? The fact is, he is not like the others. He does not treat me as if he owns me. I know, I know . . . you think that is because he does not always pay, but it's not that. When he is with me, he feels almost drunk on the pleasure of life. For him . . . well, for him, I am the most beautiful thing he has ever seen. He did not pick me out of a book, or hear about me through the filthy stories of some other man, or compare me with Julia Lombardino or any of the city's other whores. For him, I am me. Just me. And yes, yes, he loves me for it."

And she is breathless even in the telling of it. God help us.

"Oh, sweet Jesus. If you think that, then you are more a fool than he is, Fiammetta. You are—what?—almost thirty years old. While he is a boy, barely seventeen. You are simply the first."

"That's not true. I am simply the best."

And this time I laugh out loud. "Well, if you are the best,

then why do you need La Draga to help you? Eh? What's she got planned for you today? Spiking the wine with a few incantations? How does it go? 'With this spell I bind your head, your heart and phallus, so that you shall love only me—' "

"How dare you!" She is up now, a great shower of white dust falling like snow around her. "How dare you laugh at me? Ah— now look what you have done. Gabriella!" she calls loudly, turning away from me.

She is still calling as I leave the room.

CHAPTER TWENTY-THREE

I stomp so hard along the corridor and through into the *portego* that my legs hurt. La Draga is waiting in the middle of the room, bag in hand, halfway between the mirror and the loggia. She whirls around almost before I enter, her face lit up with alarm, as if she has heard the fury in my footsteps.

"Who's there?" I watch her hands fly upward in protection. Her eyes are closed today, so that she looks almost like a sleep-walker or some saint at prayer. Ha!

"It's only the egghead housekeeper," I say loudly. "The one who pays the bills but is kept in the dark."

"Bucino? What's happened? What is wrong?"

"You tell me. What are you doing here? This is not your day to visit. Or yesterday either."

"I . . . er, I am come for Fiammetta."

"I know. And I know what ails her too. As do you, I think."

"What d'you mean?"

"I mean she is making a spectacle of herself, cavorting with that mewling pup, and you are helping her."

"Ah!"

"Yes—ah! So what have you got in your bag today for her then?" She moves her head sharply, that fast, instinctive gesture I associate with attack as much as defense. My God, it takes so little to pull us back into the past again. "Some mix of holy wine and menstrual blood to get his heart pounding faster, perhaps?"

"Oh!" And to my surprise, her laugh rings out around the room. "Oh, you compliment me too much, Bucino. If I could change how people felt that easily, I would have slid something into your wine a long time ago."

And despite myself, her answer takes me aback. The fact is, when I rant these days people take notice of me, for I run this house now, and while I may be small, I can be vicious when I need to be. But not her. She has never trembled before me, or if she has, it was always only to give as good as she got.

"So what *are* you doing for her? Because she is sick with it, no doubt of that."

"I know that as well as you. I also know it is a more stubborn illness than many, for it makes the sufferer feel better rather than worse. You do not help, being harsh on her. Perhaps you could let her enjoy a little of the happiness."

"Happiness! My God, it seems everyone is deranged now. This is a courtesan's house. We are here to sell sex to men, not happiness to ourselves. Once she starts to put her pleasure above theirs, it is the beginning of the end. I know this business."

"What makes you think I don't?"

I stare at her. "Well, if you do, then tell her. Stop it now. Before it ruins her. You once said to me that we both had her welfare at heart. Remember? So care for her now. Get her to come to her senses."

"It's not as simple as that. . . ."

"Oh, really? Then God damn you, that's what I say. For you are as much the problem as she."

I turn on my heel and move out of the room, and I can feel her sightless eyes boring into my back and buttocks as I go. No doubt the next time my balls ache I'll be in terror that she has a wax effigy of them in a nutcracker. Money for old rope. I swear that is half the secret with women like her: the more you believe in their power the more it works.

Out on the street I head for the Grand Canal and cross at the Rialto. The day is balmy, glorious; the sky is a bright, fierce blue, as if Tiziano has taken a great paintbrush and dragged it across the horizon. I have no idea where I am going, but I go anyway, walking fast, as if the work of my bandy little legs might outstrip the churning in my head.

Stupid. Fiammetta Bianchini is stupid: like the tavern keeper who gets drunk on his own wine or the gambler throwing the night's winnings away on a hand of cards from a deck he knows is stacked against him.

The city is alive with spring and festival fever. There are people everywhere. I skirt the top of the piazza, noisy with preparations for the great Ascension trade fair—half of Europe will be buying here within the week—and plunge through the tangled branches of streets and canals that run parallel to the great southern docks. I am moving on animal sense now—this is the first route through the city that I ever learned, and I can do it in my sleep. Do it with my eyes closed. Blind. Damn La Draga too.

Stupid. I, Bucino Teodoldi, am stupid: because while I can spot the loss of a gram of sugar in a week's household accounts or work out the discount on a hundred yards of silk before the merchant has done the addition, I have not seen what has been right in front of my eyes. God damn me too.

I pass north of the great convent of San Zaccaria, where the noblest of Venetian families stow barge loads of virgin daughters, unaware of the gossip that its walls have as many holes as a sieve and that it is the nuns themselves who have been easing the bricks out. Men and women. Like bees to honey. Flies to shit. One bite of the apple and the worm is everywhere. Aretino was right. We are damned to lasciviousness. The rest is simply business. Too late now.

Stupid. She is stupid: to have come so far and done so much to risk it all, to throw it away on so little.

With every turn the streets are more crowded. The traffic is going one way and I am going with it, pushed ahead as the pace quickens. I move down another *fondamenta*, this time even narrower than the last, so I have to keep next to the wall to avoid being pushed toward the water. I want to stop and rest, but the crush is such that I have to stay moving, like part of a shoal of fish all darting together upstream.

Stupid. I am stupid: to have been so busy preening myself on our success that I have sat by and let her do it. Well, at least I know what is happening now.

At least I know what is happening now. Even the canal is busy, a mass of gondolas and barges all moving together, so many that their oar strokes are almost synchronized in the tide. Everyone is heading east, toward the Arsenale, where the ship workers and the rope makers and sailmakers live. And the business is mayhem. At one bridge or another, a hundred men will soon be beating one another to a pulp to conquer a square foot of space in the middle. Having lost the battle for the Ponte dei Pugni two days ago, the Nicolotti men are intent on revenge, taking the fight into enemy territory with a flood of loyal Venetians following in their wake, for news of a bridge battle in Venice travels faster than water. Faster than disease. And I am now part of the contagion.

Why not? Madness suits my mood. After all, even La Draga admits that my lady is ill. She has contracted courtesans' disease. God damn it, the symptoms are clear enough now. The laughter I hear from her room on the nights he visits. The impatience through the afternoon of an evening when he is due. An excess of gaiety, a sudden bout of lassitude or bad temper, all with too little time in between. Love: the only other ailment fatal to a courtesan, for while the pox eats the body, it is love that destroys the mind. And for what? Vittorio Foscari! A sap, a colt, a pup barely weaned, still young enough to be in the thrall of a kind of green sickness. I remember when he first arrived, brought by his older brother, like a boy on his first day at school. The fledgling needed help: he had reached the age of seventeen with his nose in books and a gross nervousness of women. My mistress had a reputation for being lovely, honest, and clean. Would she do the decent thing and deflower him? That evening when he arrived, he felt as if he had been taken too soon out of the oven. Pretty enough but soft, unbaked, still warm in the making. Some mothers, I know, keep the youngest ones tied to their skirts, using them as last memories of their own youth. The fear, of course, is that such adoration turns them into womanly men. Well, they were lucky with Foscari. It was clear early on that he was not that way inclined. And that he was a student eager enough to learn from a good teacher.

The crowd is a multitude now. We must be nearing the bridge, for there are so many of us we are hardly moving, with more people feeding in from the smaller alleyways. There is shouting and singing: slogans, war chants composed around the names of famous fighters. If this were not a festival, such a mob would already have been headed off by the city's security forces, for a revenge match so soon after a defeat is bound to end in worse violence. The order of government and the occasional disorder of street life. As with the bilge of prostitution siphoning off excess, the great ship of state thrives on it.

Now the bridge comes into sight ahead, but all I can see is a mass of flailing bodies. The crowd grinds to a halt, for there is nowhere else for the people to go. If I stay where I am, I will see nothing but the man in front of me, and the heat and the crush will overwhelm me. I put my head down and brace my elbows straight out like sharpened sticks. While my arms may be small, they connect at gut level with the softest areas of men's flesh, and I am well practiced in their use. I drive myself through the throng almost to the edge of the water. It is my intention to get onto one of the pontoons that already cover the canal, made from boats and gondolas lashed together and floored with wooden planks as viewing platforms for the richer citizens; merchants, Crows, even some white-frocked clergy and friars. Today's admission will be high because the fight is a wild one and there are small fortunes to be made from betting on the outcome. But the purse in my jacket is mine as well as hers— for Fiammetta Bianchini is not the only one who works for our living. If she is giving it away, then so can I.

That first night he came to us the family paid us a good sum to put on a show: the best wines, conversation, music, supper, bed—all the trimmings. He had never seen anything as lovely as she, and her beauty and power shone in his eyes. I daresay he was lovely enough too when he stepped out of clothes, especially compared to the grizzled old farts who had passed through her bedroom recently. There was laughter, I remember; first from her, sweet, like running water and as cunningly fake as a glass stone, and then from both of them, looser, heartier, more from the stomach than from the throat. I must say, she wooed him very prettily. And in doing so she must have wooed herself. You would be surprised how many courtesans at some point fall in love with the idea of falling in love, to experience the thrill and freshness that they must pretend so many times with other men. It seems to me that the more successful they are, the greater the danger: for, once life is comfortable, there is nothing to fear, nothing to fight for. Which means in turn that there is nothing to look forward to. Which, in a strange way, can make one think more keenly of death and yearn for some way of standing out against it, some hunger for an extravagance of feeling bigger even than death itself.

An extravagance of feeling. It comes in many garbs. Fear, for instance. For anyone afraid of water, the pontoons across the canals hold their own terror, for once you are aboard there is little enough to hold you on, and the canal slaps greedily at the sides. The better purses—of which I am one today—can buy a seat secured by ropes to the floor. Still, my panic is nothing against that of the men on the bridge, for there are no railings at all there, just a sheer drop on either side into dank water. There must be a hundred madmen up there already, with at least as many more crammed onto the ramps, screaming and pushing from behind. Those in the middle have no way forward but by knocking their opponents down and trampling them or throwing them into the canal. The battle is simple: one side has to drive the other backward far enough to take the bridge. Some of them are brandishing weapons, long sticks with sharpened ends, but there is no room to wield them effectively, and most of the men are using their fists. Many are half naked, and a number are bloodied. Every time a man comes off the edge and thrashes into the water a great roar breaks from the crowd and the fighting gets even heavier. The Castellani Arsenale workers are still flushed from their last victory and are on home territory now, so their supporters shout the loudest. But the men attacking, the Nicolotti gang from Dorsoduro, are fishermen off the boats of the Adriatic, experts at keeping their balance on stormy seas while hauling tons of fish flesh from the deep, and today they are fueled by the promise of revenge.

Of course, there are things about him that attracted her. There is an intensity to his innocence. He has a hunger for life, and he is not ashamed of his own passion. Nature has endowed him with a sweetness of disposition that would have made his compliments feel fresher to her, his puppy-dog desire less soiled. As for what takes place between them in bed—well, I have heard too many choruses of moaning from my lady's room to make any judgment based on that alone. But anyone who has been young knows that the great grief of love is that your body feels the most when it knows the least. I see them again, exhausted and entwined in the night silence. My God, what man wouldn't happily give a year of his life to have his stamina and her knowledge welded together? But all fever has exhilaration inside its delirium, and fire consumes more than it warms. In the end there will be only ashes, and her reputation will suffer more than his, for such matches are the stuff of instant gossip and everyone is waiting for the satisfaction of watching a great courtesan impale herself on the sword of her own desire. As for him? Well, he may be sweet now, but he is rich and his head is full of nothing: romantic verses and the bright colors of his own spring. I give him six months until the blossom starts to wilt and he sees life through the same eyes as everyone else: a place where cunning plays better than truth and where my lady is just another commodity that his birth and purse give him access to above others. It is how the world works, and I have seen it all before. So has she. Which is why her fall is so painful now.

In the middle of the bridge, a small space has opened up around two particular combatants, big men stripped and sweating, both fat with muscle and clasped in a wild embrace, their legs knotted together, their torsos swaying toward the water. The spectators are going wild, for these are two perfect specimens and there will be money on the outcome of their coupling. They break apart, panting, then fling themselves together again, searching for a better hold as they stagger step by step closer to the water. A new howl goes up with every lost inch. Their bodies are so close now I can see the welts rising on their flesh from the pummeling they have inflicted on each other. Then, just as it seems as if they are bound to plunge together like a pair of misshapenly joined twins, one of them somehow manages to free a hand and throws a monstrous punch into the other's abdomen, pulling himself away as the man crumples, moaning and toppling, stone heavy, into the water below. His opponent throws up his arms in triumph, and pandemonium breaks out amid the crowd.

The force of the fighter hitting the water sends waves against the pontoon, fierce enough to have us all yelping with the excitement. The crowd is screaming for both the victor and the victim, but when the fallen man comes to the surface, his body is listless in the water. From the Arsenale side of the canal, people start prodding at him with oars. Men have been known to fake unconsciousness at this time, so that when the enemy starts to pull them up they take half a dozen back into the drink with them. I risk my own fear to stand up and watch as they push and poke him toward our boats. A couple of men near me haul him up on the planks and lay him out, but he still isn't moving and his neck falls at a strange angle, exposing a black gouge in one side of his forehead. It makes me think of the man I once saw pulled from a public joust with a lance stuck right through his eye. Or the bodies in bits lying in the streets after the devastation of Rome. On both sides of me, fat purses are changing hands now. Whoever he was, he must have been a champion, because a great moaning chant is rising up from the fishermen, while on the other side of the bridge, the Arsenale fighters are roaring and stomping and waving their arms. The brawl is spreading to the spectators, and people are screaming and starting to push one another, some falling and getting mashed underfoot by the crowd.

On the bridge the scrum has started anew, and with their warrior down, it seems the fishermen are being routed again. There are so many bodies in the water that the pontoon is swaying wildly now. Sweet Jesus, if they ever drained this canal, they would surely find a graveyard amid the pots and pans and leftovers of living. I feel panic rising like vomit in my throat. I have to get off. But I am not the only one. There is an instant crush of Crows and clergy, all pushing to get to dry land. At the same time, the land itself is seething. In the distance I hear the gunfire. On the next bridge, men in civic uniform are pushing their way into the edge of the crowd. It may be a festival, but a riot is a riot, and while the security forces might choose not to risk their lives facing the mob directly, they aren't above maiming or killing where they can as an example to others. But I would take my chances with darting bayonets and shot rather than sink under black water. I hurl myself toward the edge of the boat where a run of planks connects it to the *fondamenta*, but a Crow twice my size is there before me. His bulk throws me, and I feel myself losing my balance.

"Bucino!" I hear a voice calling above the mayhem. "Bucino Teodoldi! Here! Put out your hand!"

And I obey blindly, having no idea where or to whom.

"Buci-i-ino-o-o!"

The cry seems as long as my fall. As I hit the water, I hear the wind of a great bird's wings flapping above me, and I feel the Devil's fingers grabbing at me, pulling me down and around through dark water toward the thick slime, so that I dare not even open my mouth to scream for fear that I will drown in my own terror . . . until I have to breathe.

CHAPTER TWENTY-FOUR

"Bucino?"

The voice comes from a long way away, quiet, filtering through the water, because I must be fathoms deep now, so far down that even the devils have stopped pulling and my body is lying flat and heavy, suspended in some strange, thick current.

"Bucino?"

I take a breath and start to choke. There is water inside me, and I am drowning all over again. I am pulled roughly by my hands till I am sitting upright, and someone is thumping me on the back, and now I cannot stop coughing, for it seems my nose and throat are still underwater, so I have to fight to find the air amid the liquid.

"That's right. Cough the rest of it up. Spit it out, little friend."

I throw up some foul-smelling bile, and the effort of extracting it makes me cry and wheeze at the same time. But at least now I know I am not drowned. I open my eyes, and when I look down I can see that I am lying on a bed, my clothes pulled off me and my barrel chest exposed to the world, pasty and gray like old fish flesh. I am not wet anymore, just cold and heavy. I fall back onto the pillow, and this time when I look up I can make out the face of my Turk, his dark skin made blacker by the cream silk of his turban.

The Turk? My God, then I am dead indeed and gone to

Hell. To the place where the pagans go. The eternal wasteland of the godless.

"Don't worry. You are safe enough now."

"Where am I?"

"You are in my house."

"But you . . . you are gone."

"Gone and come again. Six weeks ago. In time for the Sensa fair. Lucky for you that I am, eh? For I never miss a fight. You, however, are not built to go alone."

"I didn't go alone," I say. "I was dragged by the crowd." The coughing comes again. Only now with it there is a short, stabbing pain in my left ear. "Aaagh."

"I got you out as fast as I could. Though you lashed and thrashed like a great fish. You had taken in a lot of water. We pumped you out and brought you home, but it will make you sick for a while more."

And sure enough, as he finishes his words I throw up again.

"Good," he says, and he is laughing now. "You of all people should know that Venetian water is not for drinking but for pissing in. You are fortunate that liquid is all you swallowed."

I am alert enough now to take in the room, with its closed shutters and the candle on the side. "How long have I been here?"

"A few hours, perhaps more. It was hard to get you here. The city was mad with it all. Don't worry. I am sending a message to your mistress. You are at the same house, yes?"

"Yes . . . but . . ." And the coughing comes again. He waits patiently for me to stop.

"But?"

"Don't send it yet." For if she is told, she will surely come, and I am not ready to see her. I think this is what I think, though perhaps I also want her to wonder a little where I am and why I am not back yet. "She will be worried if she hears. I will be better soon enough."

He studies me for a moment, as if he is not sure, but gets up and pats my hand. "Very well. Maybe you should sleep some more. I will come to you later."

When his servants wake me again, my head still feels full, but my stomach at least is empty. They bring me a thick, sweet drink, made with cloves and cinnamon, and help me up, giving me a robe, one of his long, trailing gowns that I must bunch up in the middle with a sash so that I do not trip as I walk. He laughs at the sight of my clumsiness as they guide me out to sit with him in the inner courtyard.

The air is warm still with a hint of twilight, and the place I find myself in now feels more like I imagine the Orient might be than the city of Venice. In the middle of the courtyard, there is a marble fountain with the water cascading into a series of descending bowls, so that the sound of moving water is everywhere, reverberating like soft music. There are great pots and urns of plants and flowers all around, perfuming the air, and every wall has been tiled so cunningly, each tile with its own intricate pattern, that joined together they make you feel as if you are living in a world of brightly colored foliage and flowers. I have met travelers who say there are palaces in Constantinople where the courtyards smell sweeter than the countryside and where you need never leave the house to feel you are living amid nature. So much beauty, so much green and growing art, yet not one sign, or statue, or image of their God. Alas, they will suffer for it eventually, for the gray wastes of pagan Hell will, I suspect, cause them as much pain as any pit of flames. But I am pleased enough to be with him now, for there is a serenity here after the mayhem of the streets.

"How do you feel?"

"Glad I am not a water rat."

"Hmm. I think there were those who thought you were, or would have watched you drown for the sport of it. They were taking bets on how much water you could swallow. You should take up my offer, Bucino. I am back with a full purse. Why let yourself be ridiculed when you could live in a place where you would be exalted?"

"Alas, how would I understand the compliments?"

"Ah! You will learn fast enough. You think I understood a word of your gummy language before I set foot here? I will teach you on the voyage home."

"Oh, no. Not another boat."

"Ah, it is only Venetian galleys that sink. Turkish vessels rule the sea."

"Yet, strangely, you still boast like a Venetian."

"They learned it from us. That is one of the reasons why I know you would feel at home there."

I smile, and I notice that the movement hurts my ears a little. We have played this game before, he and I. Aretino was right. It seems that men of my stature are prized in the sultan's court, so that along with silks, glass, and jewels, dwarves are high on Abdullah's market list. He has wooed me often enough with stories of Constantinople: how it would be both exotic and familiar to me, with its palaces and gardens and festivals, its library fit for a scholar, plundered from Hungary, and its great statues of Diana and Hercules, booty from Rhodes. It is, of course, the mark of great cities to filch their most treasured possessions from somewhere else: Venice herself is a perfect example, since half the pillars of the basilica and the triumphant snorting horses that grace its front stolen from no less a place than Constantinople itself. Still, for all that his God may be heathen, it seems he comes from a culture where I would be treated as a man of substance rather than a freak. And today of all days, I drink deep on the seduction, for it is not only my body that is shivering.

". . . I tell you, Bucino, such was the abundance of wonder that the sky did not become night for four days from the light of fireworks. They strapped rockets to the backs of the elephants, and they roared and trumpeted as the lights exploded. There were a thousand acrobats on stilts or rope-walking between the obelisks, so many of them in the air that when you looked up it was like a vast spider's web. It was the greatest festival man has ever seen. For there is nothing, nothing, that Venice has that we do not have better or richer."

"Nothing? Then what could you possibly be shopping for this time, Abdullah? Apart from myself?"

"Ah! Well, there are a few odd objects. Trinkets, really. Jewels, glass, fabrics—nothing more."

And he laughs at his own exaggeration. I cannot think of

another city in Christendom where he and I could sit and talk like this. For all that the Venetians and the Turks spit fire and death at each other at sea, neither side lets religion interfere too much when it comes to trade. Two great powers each looking over its shoulder at the other. There are those who say that it is only a matter of time until Portuguese traders and the New World bullion start to bite into Venice's wealth, and that when that happens, the Ottomans will take the oceans from her. But I see no sign of it now; indeed, Doge Gritti's own bastard son lives as a jewel merchant in Constantinople, and thanks to Abdullah Pashna, and as a result of that night at Aretino's, the great sultan Suleiman now has a portrait of himself painted by Venice's greatest living artist, Tiziano having taken the likeness from a medallion. I thought it was rather pompous and lifeless myself when I saw it, but then what do I know about art? His Magnificence was delighted enough that everyone involved, Aretino included, was richly rewarded. As no doubt I would be if I chose to become one of his retinue of court wonders.

I sip at my drink, still rich with spice. But I wish it were hotter, because despite all the wild warmth of the Turk's descriptions, I am cold.

"You know what I think, Bucino? It is not what you might find there that scares you. You are too clever to enjoy the contempt that is shown toward you here, and your appetite is, I think, too big to be afraid of new things. No. I think it is the sadness of who you would leave behind that stops you. I am right, yes?"

I shrug. At this moment I don't even want to see her again, for her selfishness and deceit make me so angry.

"We have a partnership," I say feebly.

"I know that. I have seen it at work. And very fine it is too. Maybe I should take you both. Believe me, it is always the foreign women in his court who are the most venerated. She is not as young as some, but then neither is his favorite, and that one rules like a harridan. Your mistress could make herself a court of her own if she won his soul. The rewards for that for all of us would be great indeed."

"What—you mean living in state in his seraglio?"

He laughs. "You Christian men always say that word with such fear and awe. As if it were the most terrible thing in the world that a man should be given more than one woman. Yet everywhere I go in your 'Christendom,' the cities are full of brothels, where men cannot wait to lie with any number of women other than their wives. I believe you disapprove so much because you envy us."

It is hard to marry one's terror of the Turks with the fact of Abdullah Pashna. The stories—which are legion—curdle the blood: piracy, butchery, the enslavement of whole villages, men with their balls cut off and stuffed into their mouths, children skewered like pieces of roasting meat on sabers. Yet in his company I find a mind as clear as fresh water and sufficient wisdom about life that it seems to me that if he wasn't a heathen he would make an excellent Christian.

How much of who a man is comes from the God he believes in? Did Catholic Spaniards dice fewer fingers off their Roman hostages than German heretics? Will the Jews and the Turks suffer different hells for different heresies? Or will the worst agonies be saved for the Lutherans, who were born into the true faith but then twisted it into another? For years there have been reformers in Venice saying openly that our Church must change. That our appetites are grown into decadence, that salvation can never be for sale, and that, when it comes to the gates of Heaven, the raising of rich buildings is less important than charity toward others who are less fortunate. Yet tell that to the great clerics we entertained in Rome. And what happens if, when you reach the tribunal of Heaven, the God you meet there disagrees? Ah . . . some thoughts are better left unspoken. It is as well that Venice is more tolerant than other cities and that the Inquisition cannot see inside our minds, for if it were otherwise, I am sure I would not be the only one to find myself in the clutches of the magistrates.

I shake my head and find that my ears do not like that movement either. And I know now I am in trouble. "Maybe. Still, somehow I don't think my lady would cope well with being one of many. She has not been trained for such humility."

He laughs. "I think you are right. Also, I think she does not conceive—I am right in that, yes?—which would damage her power terribly. So, I'm afraid you would have to give her up to make your own fortune. And that, I suspect, you cannot, will not, do. A shame, but there you are. Don't worry. I will go to Mantua instead. I hear they are breeding families of dwarves there, for the lady who runs the court has a hankering for them. They will not have your wit or soul, but they will do."

We sit for a while and listen to the sound of the water. I want to think more about what he has said to me, but I can't find the words.

I shiver.

"My friend, I think you should go home. You do not look so well. Come, I will walk with you."

CHAPTER TWENTY-FIVE

He is right. I am not well. It is not far from his house to ours, but the clogged-up feeling in my head affects my balance now, so that it seems as if I am walking on the deck of a moving ship. Still, I will not go by boat. Not for all the gems in the mountains of Asia. Instead we walk: step by slow step. At any other time it would be a fine evening. The light is honeyed as we cross the Rialto, and Tiziano's luscious nudes glow off the side wall of the German Fondaco. He told me once that, until he could afford the company of courtesans, most of what he knew about women's bodies came from the work of his master, Giorgione, whose own fiery, fleshy figures light up the front façade. I daresay it's true enough, for he was much younger then. Though not as young as our damned pup. The evening is warm enough for the Turk to be without an overgarment, but even huddled in a cloak I am shivering, though the worst is my ears, which are humming like the high note of a tuning fork. And every now and then there comes a stab of pain.

I growl it away. I am alive, and I refuse to be felled by something as ordinary as earache, though even as I think it I am terrified of what it might become. I swallow and yawn and use my fingers to massage the flesh under my lobe. In the past these things have sometimes helped. They will again today.

When we reach the door of our casa, he is hesitant to leave me. "You are sure you are all right?"

I nod.

"I can come in with you?"

"No. If you come, people will fuss, and it will disturb the house, and we are busy tonight. I will go to bed. If I sleep, it will be better. Trust me—I know what to do."

He turns to leave.

"Abdullah Pashna. Thank you. I think you may have saved my life."

He nods his head. "Of course I did. I wanted you to be beholden to me. Remember my offer. Look after yourself, my fat little juggler."

I open the door gently. The inner hall is empty, though through the back window of the ground floor I see the water moorings are full, and there is a loud chorus of voices coming from above, with the smell of roasting venison and spices seeping out from the kitchen. I move quietly up the main stairs toward my room. To reach it, while I do not have to brave the *portego*, I must move along the corridor close to it.

The doors are open, and the room is alive with light and sound. The table is filled with seven or eight people, all busy with plates and chatter, so no one notices a small, squat man hovering in the gathering gloom outside. My mistress has her back to me, but in the mirror on the wall opposite, I catch a reflection of her laughing and talking to our client, an elderly man, on her left. I had forgotten that tonight our work started early, at the end of a lecture he was giving to visiting naval luminaries. But the menu is long planned with the wines already chosen, and I would not be worth even my small weight as a majordomo if such a simple entertainment couldn't run without me.

Tonight's company is brought together by our scholar client and best designer, Vettor Fausto, another wrinkled prune of a man whose body is collapsing faster than his desire. Whether he will stay tonight depends on how much he drinks and how lusty he can feel with half a haunch of venison in his gut. Whatever he decides, he doesn't need my help to fail at it. The evening will run itself. I can sleep. And in the morning, when I am recovered, she and I will talk again.

I lock my door after me and crawl onto my bed, too cold and too tired to remove my borrowed clothes. I pull the blanket over me. My head is full and buzzing, and I feel earache, like a stalking cat, at the edge of my consciousness. If I can sleep before it gets me in its grip, the rest may help.

I cannot tell if it is the chill or the pain that wakes me. All I know is that my clothes are soaking as if I have a fever, but the sweat is cold, and though I pull the blanket around me closer, I feel my teeth start to chatter. Inside my head there is a pulse of pain, as if a cord is stretched tight between my ears with someone plucking at it every second, a drumbeat on an open nerve. I try to swallow, but that only makes it come in stronger waves. I try to yawn, but it hurts so much I cannot open my mouth properly. God damn it, the filthy water of Venice has seeped in through my ears and poisoned me.

I am a veteran of head pain. When I was young, it tormented me so frequently that my father told me I must make it my friend. "Welcome it, Bucino, talk to it. Make it your own, for if you fight it you will lose." But though I talked, it would not listen to me, pleasuring itself instead by spiking me so badly that sometimes all I could do was lie and sob. I think he wanted me to have courage so I would prove to him that though my shape was deformed, my spirit at least was unharmed. But you can be only as brave as your body lets you. "It is the way your head grows," he said. "The fault of your deformity. You will not die of it." But I did not believe that then. Now, when I watch the men being pulled through the streets to the gallows howling as their tormentors nip bits out of their flesh with hot tongs, I wonder if their agony is worse than mine, because that is what it felt like to me, that skewering and squeezing of soft pulp with hot pincers. Except that my pain left no marks anyone else could see. Eventually, after hours, sometimes after days, it would lessen and in the end fade away. Each time I would be left dazed and flattened, like a new blossom after a rainstorm. And each time, when I felt it coming again, I would resolve to be braver than before, but by then I was afraid of the idea of the pain as much as the pain itself, and each time I failed. My father and myself.

But he was right. It was about my growing. For years I have not suffered it like this. If I am to cope, I must find some way to dull the horror. We keep a sleeping draft locked in the pantry, one of La Draga's concoctions disguised within the taste of grappa, our secret weapon against the more rowdy customers, for the right dose can turn a bull into a baby softly enough that he never knows he has been felled. What would I give for that oblivion now?

I force myself to sit up and try to imagine that this in itself makes me feel better. I dig out my keys and get as far as the door. But the pain skewers my balance so badly now that the ship is listing dangerously and I have to hold the wall as I move. My lady's door is closed with no telltale snoring, though Fausto is quieter than most, for his aging frame is as thin and frayed as a piece of weathered rope from one of his beloved galleys.

Elsewhere the house is silent. The evening is long finished.

Mauro is asleep in a room off the kitchen, but nothing short of the Second Coming will disturb him. I fumble with the lock and retrieve the jar containing the draft. I have no time to measure but gulp it straight from the bottle, too much rather than too little; no one has died on us yet, and the longer I am unconscious the less I will feel. I am locking the door again when I hear the noise. It comes from the entrance. Near the water doors.

Our scholar leaving? When he could be curled around soft flesh dreaming of potency? I do not think so. If I looked from a window, I doubt I would see any boat arriving now, for it would have dropped its cargo farther along the *fondamenta* and be keeping to the shadows away from our mooring. Our door, of course, would have been locked when the last guest left. Until someone opened it from the inside. Though my brain is singing with pain, I am not stupid with it yet.

I slide a carving knife out from its holding place on the wall and reach the stairs before him. I blow out the candle so that by the time he reaches the bottom I am halfway up, clothed in darkness. My head is in a vise grip now. I want to howl, but it is easier to whimper.

As he puts his foot on the first step, he must hear me, for his breath sucks in quickly. "Who is it? Is someone there? Fiammetta?"

Sweet voice. Sweet boy. I open my mouth and let out a long growl, and it must sound like the dog at the gates of Hell, for he yelps in fear.

"Ah—who is there?"

"Who are *you?* The house is closed."

"Oh! Signor Teodoldi? It is me, Vittorio Foscari. You scared me."

I would scare him more if he saw me, for my face is going crooked with the pain. As for him, I can almost smell the lust and the longing, like soft sweat on his skin. Well, not tonight, pup. Tonight you pay or pleasure yourself.

"You are trespassing, sir. The house is closed."

"No, no. It is all right. Your lady knows. I am invited."

"Ah. You are invited?" I say. "Then I'll just take your purse for what you owe us and you can go on up."

"I, er . . ."

"What—no money?"

"No. I mean—Fiammetta said—"

"It doesn't matter what she said. I am the gatekeeper. And I say, No money, no entrance."

"Look. I don't think—" He takes a step up.

"Haaaaah!" And the sound that breaks from me now is one that is soaked in pain, though it seems only to add to his terror. He is twice my size, and he could take me down easily enough if he wanted, for I am broken already, but it seems my wildness and the darkness have him by the balls. A boy with his head in his books and his tongue now in secret places. He may be a lion in bed, but he is still a lamb at the slaughterhouse. The only fights he has been in are in his imagination, and it is easy to be brave there.

"Vittorio?" Above us, I catch the erratic swoop of candle-light. God damn it, she has heard us. "Where are you?"

He lets out a squeaking noise, and the light appears at the

top of the stairs, its glow falling onto me and bouncing off the steel of the knife.

"My God, Bucino! What is happening? What are you doing?"

"What indeed," I say. "I caught this young puppy trying to swill at your trough without paying." And I may be shouting now, for it is hard to judge my voice over the pounding in my ears.

"How dare you be so vulgar?" she says imperiously, as much for his benefit as for mine, for she is not the only one behaving unprofessionally now. But I hold my ground. She takes a step nearer, and her voice falls. "Bucino, don't do this. You know I asked him to come."

"Ah, well then, so he can. . . ." Below me he makes a move upward, and I yank the knife up sharply. "It's just he'll have to leave his balls with me on the stairs for safekeeping."

"Ah!"

"Oh, God."

And I am not sure who shouts now, he or she, but it is loud enough to wake the household.

"Put down the knife, Bucino. Put it down. Don't worry, Vittorio. He won't hurt you."

"Won't I? He's very pretty, I'll give you that. But it would keep his chin smoother if I took them off him."

She is halfway down to me now. "Why are you doing this?" she whispers fiercely. I shake my head. She must smell me now, for my sweat is like stale fish.

She straightens up. "Vittorio? You had better go. I will see to this."

"Go? But I—I can't leave you with him. He's—he's a madman!"

Ah! That I am. "Ma-a-a-a-ad." For the word is like a howl anyway. My God, but my deformity is on my side now: a midget reeking of sulfur coming out of the darkness to pull sinners down into Hell. You men, beware.

Not her, though. She is not scared. And she does not like his fear either. I can tell. Who wants a lover who doesn't have the courage to risk himself for love?

There are voices downstairs, and more light. There will be

scandal abroad soon enough. Gabriella appears in the hall, wild-eyed and tousled; behind her Marcello; and then Mauro, fists up, ready to pummel some meat, for he enjoys a ruckus more than anyone I know.

"Go, Vittorio," she says again. "I will handle him. Go! . . ."

And go he does.

"Be careful, Vittorio," I call after him. "That churning in your stomach isn't fear, you know. She's poisoning you. Feeding you witchy stuff to make your prick so hard that one day it'll fall off and smash into stone pieces."

But he is gone already. Good riddance. Triumph in the shape of another wave of pain sweeps over me. I feel my balance tilting.

"The rest of you, go back to bed."

"Do you need any help, my lady?" Mauro's voice. Good old ham fist. Loyal to the end.

"No, Mauro. We will be fine. Go to bed. Just leave us alone."

He gives a last growl and then turns and fades away.

She lifts the candle above her. Heaven only knows what she sees in its light.

"In God's name, what is wrong with you, Bucino? Are you ill or just drunk?"

If only she would come nearer now, she would know. She would understand. I open my mouth, but I cannot speak. It takes all my energy to keep the knife in my hand. If there were more light, she could see the damage. Or feel the fever, for where I was an ice block before, now I am a human torch.

Her voice is shaky. "Drunk. And what? Jealous? Is that it? Of what? Him? Me? Our pleasure? Is that what this is about, Bucino? You are jealous because I am happy while you are not?"

And I think for that moment that I am going to pass out, for the world is spinning.

"Oh, my God . . . I am right, yes. This is about you, not me. You are the one who is mad with it. Look at you. When did you last have pleasure, eh, Bucino? When did you last play, or laugh until your sides hurt? When did you last have a woman, for that matter? Success has turned you sour. You live in that room bent over your abacus and your account books like some spider over her filthy eggs. Where is the life in that? My God, La Draga is right. It's you who are the one in need of love potions, not me."

She shakes her head and takes a step upward.

"You think I am the one who is threatening our livelihood, but I tell you, Bucino, you are as changed as I am. You have become an old man. And believe me, that is worse for business than any courtesan becoming a whore."

"It's not me—" I start to speak, but the sound is almost too loud to bear inside my head.

"I don't want to hear it. I have had enough of your fury and your sanctimony. Maybe our time together is ended."

"Ha! Well, if it is, then I'll go gladly." And though every word hurts now, there is something almost satisfying in the pain. "For I am as much wanted as you, you know. I could walk out of here tomorrow with the Turk and have a greater fortune than you will ever see."

"Then why don't you go—and leave me alone."

I make a move toward her, but my legs falter as soon as I start.

"No. Don't come near me!" Her voice is shaking so now that I cannot tell fury from fear. "I don't want anything to do with you. Not now. We'll talk in the morning."

She turns and runs back up the stairs. I would follow her if I could, only I cannot walk now. The knife falls by my side, clattering onto the stairs. Somehow I pull myself up and get to my room. But there is no strength now, even to lock the door.

I am at my desk, counting, the abacus in front of me a set of shining ruby stones. There is a noise at the window, a great commotion. Fear eats at my gut. I take the beads off their string and stick them into my mouth, swallowing them down one by one until I am choking.

Now suddenly I am outside, running along a canal edge, with angry birds wheeling high above me, their cries like screams. I keep close to the wall so they cannot spot me, but everywhere I look I see myself, for the walls, even the ground beneath me, are made of mirrors now. Above me, the bird wind gets stronger. A great flock of seagulls is swooping and squawking in to land, pecking furiously at the carcasses of fish heads and mermaids' tails, which I see now are littered all around. But there is one bird much larger than the rest: a seagull still, but with talons like an eagle's, each claw as big as a pitchfork. He circles above me. I am so scared I cannot breathe, and as he dips toward me, I see his eyes, large and white like communion hosts, wells of scum-covered milk. He swoops, hooking his claws into my ears, the talons reaching deep inside to get purchase, and while I scream in agony, he picks me up by my head and lifts me off the ground.

As we soar into the sky, I look down, and now there is a woman on the street staring up at me, only the bird's eyes have become hers: wide, white circles, scummy and sightless. She is laughing, and the bird is laughing with her. But I am crying, and as the tears drop, each of them turns into a flashing red ruby, and as they hit the water a fish leaps up and snaps at them as we spin out over the ocean, the talons like steel spikes driving into my brain. We are far out to sea when I hear her, my lady, calling to me. . . .

"Bucino. Oh, sweet Jesus, what has happened? Bucino. What it is? Speak to me. Please."

But I cannot see her. Maybe I am dropped already into the ocean, for I cannot breathe properly either. No, I cannot breathe because I am still crying.

"For God's sake, someone get La Draga. Oh, dear Lord. Oh, I'm sorry. How long have you been like this? What happened to you? Oh, I should have known. It's all right. It's all right. I'll help you."

Someone—she—puts arms around me, and I want to tell her that I am sick, that my smell is bad, and that I need another sleeping draft from the kitchen . . . but I cannot stop crying enough to get the words out.

And then the bird sticks its claws farther into my ears.

I do not remember my mother. She died when I was four years old, and I have no image or memory of what she looked like, though my father told me often that she was beautiful, with hair as black and sleek as a velvet cloak and skin so pale that at full moon her face was luminous in the semidarkness. Or at least that was what he said. But then it was his job to find the right words to describe things. That is what secretaries are paid to do. And while there are those who are wedded to the facts and only the facts, my father always had a hankering for poetry. Which is how he wooed my mother. Which is why, when I was born, his world ripped apart at the seams, for there are no sonnets to deformity in any book that I have read, and the only words to describe me, his own son, child of his beloved and beautiful wife, were ones connected with Hell rather than Heaven.

As to my mother's luminosity, well, since I never saw her in the moonlight, I do not know. But memory is not just the pictures that you can keep in your mind's eye. It is also things you know without ever seeing them. So while I cannot tell you what she looked like, I do know how she felt. I know the touch of her skin, the warmth of her hands, and the feeling of her arms around me. For when I was little, I am sure that she lay with me, curled herself around my strange smallness, and held me to her as if I was the most precious and most beautiful thing in the world, so special that she and I could never be separated. And that her warmth helped me with the pain. I know this because, while I do not "remember" it as it happened, the first time I ever slept with a woman, a prostitute in Rome, clean and less ugly than I, I had enough money to pay for the whole night, and while my prick enjoyed being inside her enough to show its excitement and therefore make a man of me, it was the sleeping with her that made me weep like a child. It was winter, and the room where she worked was freezing, or maybe I reminded her of a child she had lost, for she was old enough to be my mother and I was small enough. I remember sometime in the night I woke to the warmth of her breath on my neck. Her arms were around my chest, and her legs were curled under me, like a large spoon lying next to a smaller one. I lay for hours, wrapped inside the deepest comfort, reliving a memory that perhaps I never had of a time when I was loved for, rather than despite, what I am. Then, at first light, I slid out from her arms and left, so that I would not have to suffer the humiliation of her waking distaste.

The pain flows in and out in waves. Sometimes the bird is there with its talons, and I have to beat it off with my hands; sometimes I am alone, beached and helpless. I am awake and asleep. I am freezing in the light. I am burning in the dark. I am dead yet somehow still alive. When I try to open my eyes, I see flashes searing the darkness, and I hear someone crying, a dreadful wailing, which is both in me and an eternity away. "Help me. Oh, God, help me, please."

The answering voice, when it comes, is gentle and cool, as cool as the fingers that rest on my domed head, moist like the chunks they chip off the ice barges in the furnace of summer. "I know how much it hurts, Bucino. I know. But it will not last forever. You will live through it and not always be in such pain. Don't be frightened . . . you are not alone."

After that, there is nothing for a while. Or nothing that I remember. Only, when the fire comes again, this time there is the touch of wet cloth all over my skin. And later, when the cold sets in and chatters my teeth, I am wrapped in blankets, and someone—the same person—now rubs at my hands and feet until they thaw from ice into flesh again. The next thing I know it is night, and I am lying on my side, and one of the gouged holes of my ear is filled with an oily warmth that seeps inside, silky, soothing. I am breathing in a cave inside my head, for that is the only place I can hear anything now. The oil's presumption angers the pain, and the skewering comes again, as bad as ever before, so that I think my eggplant skull must crack down the middle and my brains spew out of my head like those of the men I saw on the streets of Rome that day. But fingers press gently down onto my skin where my neck meets my ears, rubbing around the bone, sending the warmth deeper into my head until slowly, slowly, the pain starts to roll back and fade away. And when it is over, arms come around me and hold me, and I curl up inside them and am safe again, for the bird does not come when I am held.

At some time, I don't know when, the voice comes again, gentle, like a litany, so deep inside that again I think it must be in my own mind. I am in terror at first, for now it speaks of Heaven, as if I am arrived there, describing how our bodies will become like pieces of glass, pure, shining in the sun, moving faster than arrows, but soft enough to merge into and through one another. How, when we open our mouths, the sound will be that of a thousand lutes and we will sing with the intense beauty of it all. Then the voice itself starts to sing, boyish high and sweet, yet clear enough for me to hear it through the howling pain. Only I know it is a woman's voice, for it comes with the warmth of a woman's arms again around me.

I wake. It is night, and for a moment it seems there is no pain. The room is dark, and I see by candlelight my mistress sitting on a chair at the end of the bed. I close my eyes. When I open them again, she has changed and it is La Draga sitting in the same place. She is there the next time too, and I look at her for longer. But the ache begins to flare, and I think I moan a little, because she is staring at me, and I swear that she is seeing me— seeing me—for she seems to smile, and in the gloom I feel a beam of light move from her whitened eye to deep inside my head, her blindness moving through my deafness, and as it reaches me so the ache is dulled before it can take hold.

Yet when I try to thank her, the room has changed and there is darkness again and she is gone. But when I sleep now, I am no longer woken by the pain.

". . . from his deformity?"

"That's what she said. It is the way his ear is made, it seems, so that when water gets in, it cannot get out again, and everything starts to rot inside."

I know I am back, not so much because the pain is gone but because the background roar in my head is absent so that I can hear again, even though their voices are low so as not to wake me.

"My God, the poor bastard, he must have been going mad with it."

"Ah . . . you cannot imagine. You could hear his sobbing all over the house. Those first days were so awful. I was sure he was going to die."

If I had the stamina, I would open my eyes and join in, but as it is, all I can do is lie with my face to the wall and listen. It will do well enough. The sound of my lady's voice has never been sweeter. Even Aretino's growl has music in it.

"So how did she cure him?"

"Sleeping drafts, unctions of special oils in his ears, warm poultices, massaging the bones. She wouldn't leave his side. I never imagined she was so fond, for the two of them bicker more than they talk. But you should have seen her, Pietro: night after night, watching over him, caring for him until the fever broke and the spasms became less severe."

"My God, egghead or not, he's a lucky man. You'd think a deformity like his would put the fear of God into women. Yet you all rally to him. Remember Rome? There were a couple of women there who couldn't get enough of him. It used to amaze me. What is his secret?"

And my lady laughs a little. "Who is asking? Aretino the man or Aretino the scurrilous writer?"

"What? Don't tell me! It is the size of his prick!"

"Oh, shush . . . you will wake him."

"Why not? Now that he is going to live, I'd say hearing this would be a better tonic than anything your kitchen can prepare."

"Shhh."

I hear the swish of her skirts as she moves toward the bed, and even the precision of the sound is a pleasure to me. I do not intend to deceive her, but my eyes are lead shutters, and the ebb and flow of my breathing is natural enough now that the agony is passed. I know she is close by the smell of mint and rosemary mixed on her breath. It must be Thursday. If I did have the energy to open my eyes, her skin would be milk white and her eyes clear and bright. I try to keep my eyelids from flickering and take another breath and let it out. Her scent grows fainter in the air. When their voices come now, they are quieter, farther away, though not so far that I cannot make out the words.

"He is asleep. He looks so peaceful. I have not seen his face so smooth for years."

"You should see yourself, Fiammetta. You look at him almost as a mother looks at a child. It is strange, the two of you. Everybody wonders, you know."

"Wonders what? Oh, Pietro, you of all people don't believe the gossip, do you?"

"Hmm! I told you. He has got a way about him."

"And you have a mind that thrives on such base things."

"Ah, to this sin I plead guilty. So tell me."

"No! You, unlike him, have no loyalty. It's true, isn't it? The rumor that you are penning filth again?"

"Oh, no . . . not filth, *carina*. I would call it more an investigation into the various professions of love."

"Let me guess. In the nunnery and the whorehouse."

"I . . . More or less. But I promise I will never write a word about your beloved dwarf."

"And me? Will you write about me?"

"If I do, no one will recognize you."

"They had better not. If you betray—"

"Sweet lady, I am a slave. To both of you. You know that. We Roman adventurers must stick together."

"Oh, so you are a Roman again. I thought you were become a full-fledged Venetian. You lie as well as they do."

"Oh, that's a little harsh. It's true that when I write about Venice I embroider a little. But this city likes to look good in the mirror. Have you read Contarini's history? Compared with his Venice, Athens would be a failed state."

It's true. It would. And it is to my great wonder that I can think straight about it now without being chewed up by pain. Still, everybody knows that Contarini is as much flattery as truth. Ah! God help me, I am back in the world with things to say, even if there is no energy yet to do the saying.

"Of course the city thrives on praise. Rome was the same. All that marble so the world would be dazzled by the shine. The difference is, the Aretino I knew then was more interested in exposing the dirt underneath. Why don't you spice the flattery with the tartness of truth, Pietro? Or have you really grown so soft on good living?"

Ah, my lady. How I have missed you!

"Hmm. I was young in Rome and didn't mind getting my ass kicked so much and I like Venice better. It works for its living, and its sins are more forgivable. Still, we must be careful. We could be seen as its corruption too, *carina*, and I would be a fool to bring the temple down upon our own heads. No, I will let it be known that my new work is a comment on the old Rome, and thus will I go down in history as a consummate chronicler of life. For when I write about such things—about the dance between men and women—then I do indeed tell it as it is, unvarnished, the whole truth."

"Oh, please! 'Ooh, ooh, put your prick in my ass again, ooh, for I am aflame, and all the pizzles of mules, asses, and oxen would not diminish my lust, even a little.' " And her voice is silly and fluttery with fake desire. "Really, if you think that is the truth about women, Pietro, then you are more addled than your years. You simply write what you think men want to hear. And I warrant a good many of them aren't even thinking of women's bodies as they read it. What was the name of that boy you liked so well at the court in Mantua?"

"Ah, Fiammetta Bianchini! What a mouth you have on you. I should be grateful you have no urge to become a scribe your-self. But who could resist you? I tell you, if I were a marrying man—"

"—you would not marry *me*. God help us both. We would be strung up in San Marco for murder soon enough."

"You are right. It is better this way."

They are both laughing now. There is silence for a moment, yet it feels comfortable enough to me, the silence of old friends. Of which I am one. I am tired now and much in need of water, but I fear to break the spell; while there have been times in the past where my size has allowed me to hear conversations going on above my head, those conversations have never been about myself. What price the fame and riches of a Turkish court com-pared with this?

"Well, since you evidently know so much about these things, tell me about his 'special powers.' "

"First you swear to me that you won't put me in your book."

"I promise that I will never use your name. On my heart."

"You would do better to swear on your prick."

"I must say, Fiammetta, for a woman who has had no sleep for the best part of a week, you are very lively."

"Why not? 'My deformity,' as you call him, is getting better."

"So?"

"Actually, it is simple enough. You are right. He is not like other men. But it is not so much his 'size'—and do not snigger, for I have never seen his prick nor ever will—as you well know, that is not how it is between us. Bucino has a way with women, as you call it, because he enjoys their company. Not just for the pleasure they give but for and of themselves. He is not frightened of us, and he does not need to impress or possess us—and you would be amazed, Pietro, how few men that is true of. All I know is that ever since I first met him at that stupid banker's house where he was pretending to be a jester and failing, I have felt more comfortable with him than with any other man I have ever met. Yes, you included."

Her voice has grown a little louder. She should be careful, or she might wake me.

"So. Does that answer your question?"

"Absolutely. His secret is that he is a woman!"

Their laughter is so infectious now that I struggle to keep my breathing even, not to join in, and my throat is so dry I cannot swallow and I want to cough.

"Shhh . . . our voices will wake him. You may laugh at the idea, but I tell you, for all your skill with words, you will never know what that feels like. Remember that, if you can, next time you put your pen to paper."

And this time when I swallow, as I must or I will choke, I make a noise, though I think it is covered by their laughter.

There is a pause. "You don't think he could have been awake all this time, do you?"

"Ha!" She stops, and they listen some more. But I swear I am silent as the grave now.

I think I hear her move again, though until she speaks I do not know to where.

"Well, if he is," she says, and her voice comes from directly above me now, so close that I feel again her breath on my face, "then I could tell him how much I have missed him. Not just these last few days either, but for the longest while. How without his voice in my ear I have at times fallen prey to melancholy and looked for reassurance in places where the gaining of it could only hurt me more. Ah, you would be surprised, Pietro, the ways in which success can be as painful as failure." I hear the sigh she gives and the breath she takes in after it. "And after I had said all that, I would add that he should hurry back to health, for the latest news is that his troublesome fledgling is due to take wing for Crete next month to be initiated into the family trade, away from the temptations of the city. A migration that will makes us—some of us—sad." She pauses. "Though I think we will survive."

"Ah! Such poetry, Fiammetta, and from the woman who despises whores who compose. Perhaps you could translate it into plain language for me?"

She laughs. "Oh. It is nothing. Just women's chatter. And, since he is an honorary woman, I am sure that even if he *is* listening, he will be modest enough not to let me know he has heard. Isn't that so, Bucino?" And she raises her voice a little.

I take a long breath in, hold it for a second, and slowly, slowly, slowly, let it out again.

CHAPTER TWENTY-SEVEN

The tang of Mauro's spiced sauce over boiled eels. How the room stays still when I stand up in it. The way my ear can distinguish birdsong from the crunch and slap of the water through the thick-eyed glass of my study window. These are the joys of a world where I am no longer in pain. And, most of all, the fact that the household has fallen into palpable disarray in my absence.

Alas, there is no time to celebrate, for my recovery coincides with the busiest of times. This week sees the climax of the Ascension Festival: the ceremony of the Sensa, when the whole government of Venice rides out in a great golden galley into the middle of the lagoon, from where the doge, himself arrayed in gold cloth, hurls a wedding ring into the depths, thus marrying the city to the sea (guess which is the bridegroom and which the obedient bride?) and securing Venice's dominion over the waters for another year. Who could ever believe that Constantinople holds more wonders than Venice?

This ceremonial madness and the great trade fair that accompanies it have the city bursting at the seams, but this year, *this year*, we are doubly blessed. For our black Crow, Loredan, has done penance for his endless pomposity by securing my lady a place on one of the barges that follow the procession, a privilege of such magnitude that the whole house is now awash in dresses and dressmakers, shoes and shoemakers, perfumes and perfumers, and all the paraphernalia of beauty that it takes to put our own small, golden ship to sea.

Marcello and Gabriella are at my constant beck and call, Mauro is so long over a stove that I fear his sweat has become one of his spices (though I do not complain, for since my illness I am fed better than the clients), and as for my lady, well, I do not know if my breathing convinced her of my sleeping or my wakefulness, but there has been no further discussion between us, no baring of souls or asking for forgiveness. Instead we are partners again and are healing ourselves with what we do best, working together and making the house sing with its sense of community.

This is not to say she is without sorrow: her melancholy is evident to anyone who knows her well. The latest news on the pup is that he is due to leave in a few weeks. His visits are less frequent (I do not know about the nights, for since my illness I sleep like the dead), and where possible when he is due I give the servants time off so he and my lady might have a kind of privacy together. We both know that when he leaves, she—and I suspect he too, for such fevers seldom burn so hot without both partners sharing the disease—will feel the separation acutely. But we will deal with that pain when it comes; for now we are reconciled, she and I, with our minds set on her journey to sea and all that it entails.

From all of this creative mayhem, there is only one person missing: La Draga. Since that night when I woke to her presence in the room, she has not visited. When it was clear that I was on my way to recovery, she left a series of oils and drafts with Gabriella for my continued welfare and disappeared into the dawn, and no one has heard from her since. Despite our busyness, the house is not the same without her. At night sometimes when I close my eyes, I can hear her voice as if it were still inside me, and the memory of her care makes me shaky with its intensity. Though my lady would profit from her presence and potions now, I daresay she is too occupied to visit, for when people in this city stop working, they start mating, and those whom she is not helping to marry she may soon be helping to abort. But I know only too well that it is she who saved my life, and wherever she is I have no intention of forgetting my debt to her.

It is the morning of the Sensa, and the whole house and a fair slice of the neighborhood gather to see my lady and me step into our boat, duly decorated for the occasion. Marcello cuts a sleek and clever line through the massing traffic on the Grand Canal to drop us near the edge of the southern docks, from where we must walk to the main landing dock near San Marco.

It is a journey I have done often enough before, when the sun is not yet fully risen and the city is still asleep, and there is always a sense of awe in it. After you have made the long turn out of the Grand Canal and draw parallel with the Doge's Palace, among the first things that you see from the water are the great Pillars of Justice, standing out like high masts through the early mist. And more often than not, as you get closer there is the broken corpse of some offender between them, left hanging as an example to the city. Such is the aching bleakness of this scene that I have come to believe the entrance to Hell will be through those pillars, with us all marching in silent, serried ranks into the steaming mist beyond.

Only now, today, Hell has been turned to Heaven. The Mass is over, and the fleet is boarding. Those same pillars are festooned with streamers, and the scene all around them is like the Second Coming, with the righteous leading the way clothed in God's glory and—more important—Venice's best cloth. There is more gold here than in any altarpiece I have ever seen. Even women are allowed to join this show, and modesty is replaced by fabulous ostentation. The ground around them is a sea of silk and velvet so the sun barely knows where to shine first, caught on miles of golden thread and a thousand neck-laces, rings, chains, and jeweled hair clips.

The golden galley is anchored in the middle of the water, al-ready loaded with its cargo of black and ermine-trimmed Crows and foreign dignitaries, and the spectator barges are fill-ing up fast. To reach the special landing docks, each and every guest must have his or her name on a list. My journey stops here.

My lady turns to me as she moves into the throng. "What

shall I bring you back, Bucino? A mermaid, or another great Crow to boost our account books?"

I shrug. "Maybe you might find something to ease the gap that will be left by your fledgling?"

"Aaah." And I hear the catch in her throat, as if the pain is still lodged somewhere, too raw to digest. "Alas, for that I would need very rich food." She stops and tilts her head away. The noise is rising around us. Soon it will be too late for speech. She turns back to me. "Bucino? The things I said . . . about you that night. I want—"

"No. No, you don't," I say. "We were both demented, and your words were nothing to the cruelty of mine. But it's over now. Lost on the wind. Look at you. I am so proud of you. The most spectacular bird in the flock. Don't let the others peck at you out of envy."

She smiles. "And you—what will you do with the day?"

"Me?" I say. "Oh, I will—" But the push of bodies is already drawing her away, and my reply gets lost in the crowd. I watch as best I can as she moves toward the boats. The women eye each other as they head for their places—they always behave the worst when they are dressed the best—and while there are those intent on cold-shouldering her, it is more because my lady is a stranger than because she looks like a whore. Indeed, if they were all lined up in our *portego* now, there are at least a dozen who would be propositioned before she would, so much have they piled on the white powder and the flouncing style. In contrast, she looks like a noblewoman. The smile that she gives as she turns and waves to me from the loading plank tells me that she knows it too.

I close my eyes so that can I etch the scene on the backs of my lids, and for that second I wish more than anything that I had been born Tiziano Vecellio so I might run home now and re-create it, for the details are already fading. The image of my lady, though, stays clear enough. I wave until I am pushed out of the way, and then I scamper through the crowd out of the madness of the piazza toward San Lorenzo and the north shore.

In my pocket I have directions to the *campo* where La Draga lives, or at least the place where Marcello leaves messages for her when she is needed. For that is my day: I am going to find her. After all these years, it is time we made our peace.

It is my first time on the streets since my illness, and despite my high spirits, my limbs tremble faster, so that I have to rest more often. Still, I am not worried. I am alive and with luck will soon be fitter than I was before, for the fever has stripped away a layer of fat that good living had added to my stomach; every dwarf I have ever known has the appetite of a full-sized man, so that as we grow older, even those without greed are prone to corpulence.

Anyway, what need is there to rush on this of all days? The city is on holiday, and so am I. The streets are quiet here, since the crowds have all drained south to watch the fleet embark, and the scent of garden blossoms is in the air. For a few weeks now, Venice will be glorious, before the summer sun burns everything crisp and putrid again, and I, perhaps, will find time to enjoy it.

"When did you last have pleasure, eh, Bucino? When did you last play, or laugh until your sides hurt? When did you last have a woman, for that matter? Success has turned you sour. You live in that room bent over your abacus and your account books like some spider over her filthy eggs. Where is the life in that?"

I have thought about her words many times since that night. How could I not? When a man thinks he going to die, there is always room to regret the mistakes he has made, the things he has not done. She is right. While my clothes may be as rich as they were in Rome, our success has also been my failure. It is partly that the novelty is gone. She has little need of me to entertain her guests now, and I, in turn, have grown weary of being treated like an imbecile or an exotic by men, most of whom, if their purses were the same size as their brains, would not be eligible for either of our company. Even our cleverest clients do not excite me in the way our salon in Rome once did. In this respect I turned against Venice early. While Rome stewed in her own corruption, she was at least honest enough to enjoy herself openly. Yet here they are so concerned with making the surface shine that all transgression must be tucked away, the sins not even fully enjoyed before they are repented or suppressed. In my experience, such hypocrisy is a breeding ground as much for prurience as for pleasure.

Or perhaps I am fooling myself, plucking reasons from the air to excuse my own misanthropy. For it is true that I am duller than I was. And, yes, more celibate; and while a man does not die of such neglect, neither does he flourish. What can I do? Aretino may envy me my skills, but they are less effective here than they were in Rome. There are, alas, no mischievous matrons with an appetite for novelty in these markets, and the streets are too near the canals for me to stomach the smell of most of the women who work them: relief and pleasure may be the same for most men, but I am a dwarf and too attuned to nuances of humiliation for it to work that way for me. There was a time when my enjoyment of Anfrosina's curves and her capacity for giggling could pull her out of the kitchen and into the bedroom. But the satisfaction gained there seldom lasted beyond the moment, and while there have been a few others along the way, these last years I have grown proud (or maybe shamed) enough to think I could do better. Perhaps the truth is I have become cynical. When one is in the business of slaking male desire, it is hard not to develop a certain contempt for the very appetite one is manipulating.

Whatever the reasons, my loins have grown cold on me. Instead I have lavished my attention on my abacus beads and the richness of Mauro's sauces and have chosen not to think about the warmth of a woman's body. Until, that is, I feel my mother's arms around me again, and find myself crying as much at the comfort as at the pain.

My God, to be beholden to a sightless cripple. Did I come this far for that?

CHAPTER TWENTY-EIGHT

As I make my way across town, I consider what I know of her, this woman who has been in my life for almost a decade yet whom I have chosen to ignore. I know that she came to Venice first as a child, and that her parents died when she was still young. My lady told me once that she had been married, but her husband died early, and since then she has lived alone, which in itself is a thing of some wonder in Venice, for single women of her age are fodder for convents or the casual violence of men. In this her deformity might well have been her aid; that, along with her reputation as a witch, would have most men holding on to their balls rather than flaunting them. There is no doubt she runs a healthy enough business now. I know that ours is not the only casa she visits (a few years ago she disappeared for months on end, returning as quietly as she had gone, with no explanation), but whoever else she tends, like a priest, she keeps other people's confessions to herself. Of course, what she cannot see she cannot tell. Though I have underestimated her talents to my cost in the past. Most recently, it has to be said, to my own shame. I will not do so again.

The place where she lives is to the northeast of the city, between the Rio di Santa Giustina and the convent of La Celestia, an area I know hardly at all. I orient myself by the convent's bell tower, which rises from the rooftops and looks out over the sea (my God, how cold and damp their cells must be in winter).

I cross a canal toward it and move into a mass of alleys and huddled houses. Somewhere in here, there will be a *campo* with a baker's oven and a church and a stone well, an ancient small island joined to all the others, like the one where we first lived and where the old man kept vigil over the water level so long ago.

In the end it is my nose that takes me there, for the smell of roasting pig is always a good compass. The spit is in the middle of the square, the carcass skewered and stuffed, its juices spitting fireworks into the fire beneath. Nearby three men are setting up two barrels of *teriaca*. Like everyone else, they are celebrating, and if I want to find La Draga, I should do so before they start drinking. There are maybe two dozen men and women and a handful of children already gathered, and I am enough of a freak visitor to become instant entertainment, for even a city like Venice has backwaters. I brave a few quips about the roasting of the well-dressed duck that just waddled in and how the perfumes of its beard will do instead of spices before finding myself the most presentable young woman available and bowing low to her in a way that can be seen as cute if I get the flourish right.

The laughter around me is so raucous that I know it has worked, and I have a free bowl of gut rot in my hand before I have time to introduce myself. Why not? We are all guests at the wedding feast of our state, and it is incumbent on us to enjoy ourselves liberally. I gulp it down, and my coughing fit causes another explosion of mirth, so that the girl I have picked has to thump me on the back, egged on by the rest of them. When I come up for air, I note that she is still young enough to be a little shy, and that her lips are reddish and full like the inside flesh of a ripe pomegranate. I smile at her (more beguiling than my weapon grin) and join in with their mockery, taking another, smaller swig and making theater out of the thick burn that it carves down the back of my throat. The girl is staring, wide-eyed, and the woman behind her shoves her sharply in my direction so that she half trips onto me and I have to use all my strength to stop her from falling. As she straightens up, laughing indignantly, I get a glimpse into her mouth and see a run of half-rotted teeth and catch a whiff of decay. And to my shame, my growing excitement drains away.

Maybe Aretino is right and I am more woman than man now, God help me.

The *campo* is filling up fast, and I use the liquor's tongue-loosening capacities to talk to a few others and ask the where-abouts of the healer called La Draga. Everyone knows her, it seems, though there is some disagreement over exactly which house is hers. A woman with a fat scar on her face spits over my shoes at the sound of her name, calling her a whore who heals the rich but lets the poor die. A younger woman disagrees; then a man wades in, and within seconds people are shoving at one another. If I were a general, I'd breakfast my army on *teriaca* be-fore any battle. Just so long as they didn't turn on one another before they reached the enemy. As I make my way out of the square in the direction of her street, I notice that the girl is watching me from the edge of the crowd, though as soon as I catch her eye, she looks hastily away. I move over to her and bow again, and this time I ask her directly for her hand. She is unsure now, like a young colt presented with its first bridle, but in the end she offers it. I turn it over, kiss the palm, and then press a silver ducat into it before folding her fingers back over it gently. I blow her a kiss as I leave, and as I go I see her unfurling her fingers, a look of wonder on her face, and then she smiles and waves to me, and for some reason the sight of her joy makes me want to cry.

La Draga's street is off the *campo* on the edge of a small canal. I approach it from the land. The houses are cramped and half bent over the cobbles, their stonework broken and peeling. In summer you would be able to smell your neighbors' farts, as-suming the other rot hadn't stripped your nostrils first. The smell is bad enough as it is.

Her house, it is generally agreed, is next to the last before the corner. I have lived in places like this, when I first arrived in Rome. I know the gloom that I will find inside. And possibly the squalor. If she is lucky, she will have a room to herself. If she is successful—and I cannot see how she would not be—she may have two. Unless, of course, there is a husband. My God. I have never given it a thought, that she might have married again. She has always been alone in my mind, a woman living off her wits. As I do too.

I knock. And get no answer. Then again, louder. I try the door, but it is locked.

A few seconds later, I hear someone moving behind it.

"Who is it?" Her voice, but rough, suspicious.

"It is Bucino." I pause. "Bucino Teodoldi."

"Bucino?" I hear her surprise. "Are you all right?"

"Yes. Yes. But . . . I . . . I need to speak with you."

"Er . . . I can't see you now."

But I have decided. This is the purpose of my day. "It is important," I hear myself say. "I can wait or come back later."

"Er . . . no . . . no. I—I can come in a little while. Do you know the *campo* nearby?"

"Yes. But it is mad with people."

"Go to the steps by the door of the church. I will meet you there."

I move back to the square. It is fuller already, and the girl has disappeared. I climb the few steps to the wooden door of the church and wait. What is she doing now? Was there someone in there with her? A client perhaps? She must keep all her medicaments somewhere. I imagine a chest full of jars and potions, pestles and mortars for crushing, scales for weighing. It makes me think of that little back room where my solemn Jew measured and bought people's wealth. Or my office full of ledgers and beads. For we are working men and women, all of us: despite the burdens of our race or our deformities, we have found ways to be in the world, dependent on no one, earning our living with a kind of pride. For even I have to admit that there is much skill in her healing, and even in her witchcraft.

I am high enough to spot her as soon as she turns the corner into the *campo*. She is dressed for the festival, a pale blue gown that I think is new—or maybe I have never noticed it before—its skirt full, with lace fringing, and a shawl of the same color over her head. She is carrying a stick, which I have seen her do at other times, and which makes her progress easier, for she can use it to sweep the ground in front of her and assess obstacles faster. People know her enough to move out of her way here anyway, though halfway across a woman comes up to her, and while I cannot hear what is said, it feels from her square stance and the way she blocks the way that it is not a comfortable encounter. I get to my feet in case La Draga needs help (what help could I give?), but it is over almost as soon as it has begun, and soon she is at the steps, her stick sweeping its way upward.

"I am here," I say, and she turns to me with that strange little smile of hers, the smile that she has never seen for herself but that seems to say she knew where I was all along and was simply checking. Her eyes are closed, which she also does sometimes. I think it might be painful for her to keep them open, for I have noticed that when she does she seems never to blink, which is one of the reasons why that dense milk stare is so upsetting when you first see it. I have not given much thought to her welfare before, but then I have a recent experience of suffering against which to match that of others.

The tip of the stick locates my foot, and she lowers herself to the step, next to me. We have never met like this, outside the house. Around us the city is celebrating, meeting, greeting, carousing; it is a day that will have all kinds of consequences.

"How did you find me?" Her voice is soft again now, as I remember it.

"Oh, you are famous around here."

"You are better, yes? To have walked so far."

"Better, yes."

"Though weak still, I think."

"Well . . . Mauro is feeding me well."

She nods. I watch her fingers playing with the top of the stick, and it strikes me that she is as nervous as I am, sitting out here alone with me. How many years have we known each other now? Yet how little do we know.

"I . . . I have come . . . I have come to thank you."

She crooks her head, and the smile becomes puzzled. "I did not do so much. The infection took its course. I only helped hold down the fever."

"No," I say. "I think you did much more than that." I pause "I . . . I would have gone mad with it. The pain."

She nods. "Yes. When it comes inside the head, it is very bad."

Again I think about her eyes. "You said that once before to me. You know about such things?"

"I—I have felt it in other people."

"I used to get pain like that when I was a child."

"It is from the shape of your ear."

"Yes, you told me that too. You have studied such things?"

"A little."

I am staring at her as she talks. Her skin is so pale and smooth, her eyelashes resting like half-moon fringes on her cheeks. My lady tells me that when Tiziano saw her once at our house, he wanted to paint her, for he thinks she has something of the mystic about her. One can see why. The years have hardly aged her at all, and there is a strange light to her face, the way her thoughts and feelings seem to move across it like constantly changing weather. He is right: she would make a fine addition to one of his religious works, and he of all people might be able to capture that inner light, for he seems to see the spirit of a person as clearly as he sees the body. But she is not interested in immortality, or not the kind that he can offer, and when he asked, she would have none of him. I like that about her, though I have not realized it until now.

"How is Fiammetta?" she says after a while.

"She is . . . I don't know what words to use . . . quiet, resigned. You know the pup is leaving? She told you that?"

"Yes. The news of it came when I was there."

"She is sad," I say. "But she will recover?" And while I mean to say it firmly, it comes out as a question.

"If a wound is clean, it matters less if it is deep," she says. "It's when the passion is not shared that gangrene eats its way in."

"Yes." I pause.

Come now, Bucino. If you can survive agony, you can do this.

"I—I am sorry . . . about that day, when I found out about him. I was as much angry with myself as I was with you."

She gives a little shrug, as if she knew that all along and was just waiting for me to realize it too. Only now that I have started, I have to go on.

"You did not need to be so kind to me, you know . . . I mean afterward. God knows, I have not always been kind to you."

"I . . ." And to my surprise she falters a little too now. "It was nothing. You were . . . I mean, the remedies worked for you."

Only now the air suddenly feels strange between us. As if neither of us knows where to step next.

"Your care of me took up a lot of your time," I say, to stem the disquiet I feel. "Yet you did not leave a bill."

"No . . . er . . . I was busy with other things."

"I thought you would come back."

"No. I . . . The city is crowded now. I cannot move around so easily."

"No, no, of course not." Her restlessness is growing, and I am afraid that she is going to leave.

"Well, thank God for you," I say quickly. "For without you I would be dead now."

She frowns. "You must not say that. I did not save your life, only brought down the fever." She repeats quietly, "You should be careful, though; water is not good for you." She starts to stand. "I—I have to go now."

I stand up too, and before I have thought about it, I put out a hand—to help her up, to say good-bye, to get her to stay, for I still have things to say: to apologize for my rudeness, my misjudgments. But she pulls away from the touch almost as I reach her, though more gently than she might have done before, as if she is as unsure of me now as I am of her. I can feel it in the way she moves, in the little laugh she gives, the tilt of her head. What is she thinking now? Surely I cannot be the only one who remembers the way she held me and the soft river of words?

"Well, good-bye then, Bucino," she says, face bright, lips slightly parted on the smile. "Stay well."

"I will. Good-bye."

I watch her move down the steps and make her way back carefully across the side of the square and into her street. I sit for a while staring into the madness of the crowd. Ten, maybe fifteen minutes pass, and then a man sees me and raises his arm and starts to make his way over. But I am not interested in new friends, especially ones made sociable on *teriaca*. I am into the melee before he can reach me. I take the same corner that she did. And the next. I am going to her house again. Will I stand in front of the door and knock once more? I have no idea. I am too busy walking.

But it doesn't happen like that. Because as I turn in to her street, I spot a figure from the back at the end of it. It is she. Same dress, same shawl, though now she has a bag over one shoulder. I watch the sweep and tap of her stick as it moves efficiently in front of her. She gets to the corner and turns. I move after her. When I reach the same place, she is crossing a bridge to the left, and I stop because we are the only ones on the street now and I know how well she sees through her ears. I note where she turns, and when she is gone from view, I follow. Why? Because . . . because today is a holiday and I can do what I wish with my time. Because she saved my life. Because I have never been down these streets before. Because I am curious to know where she is going. Because . . . I follow her because . . .

After a few blocks the air begins to shift around us, and a mist starts to move in, gruel-thin but persistent, pulled off the sea. She, of course, will be unaware of its impact, though I daresay she is acute enough to note the new edge of moisture in the air. I try to imagine what it must be like to be inside her head, to move through continual darkness with only the echoes from walls, stone, and water to delineate her path. She has such confidence. But then these are her local streets, and a city always holds less terror for its natives. I once asked my old man at the well how he had first learned his way around such a mad place. He told me he couldn't remember, for it happened when he was still a child. I listen to people talking sometimes, that great river that is language, with all its undercurrents of grammar and nuance, and I wonder how we all learn so quickly to speak it, given that we begin when we are barely old enough to stand upright. I have no memory of finding it hard. Indeed, I have no memory of it at all. Perhaps it was the same for her. Just as I negotiate a tall world being small, she learned to navigate a sighted world through other senses, "seeing" through hearing or smell or touch. I think of my temporary deafness. What a bizarre couple we would have made then: my eyes and her ears. My waddle, her limp. If we had the time and inclination, we might find our worlds hold many things in common. But for all this time I have been too harsh and proud even to bother.

She is heading north, with the Rio di Santa Giustina somewhere to our left. The closer we get to the shoreline, the heavier the mist. Venice is a capricious mistress when it comes to weather, and I wonder about the fleet now halfway out into the lagoon. Ahead, the dark wall of houses breaks open to expose the thick, gray expanse of the sea. Now, at last, she stops. And turns, one way, then back. On instinct I pull myself into a doorway as if she had eyes—stupid. But it is not me she is hearing, rather the change of sounds that comes with the open water and the absence of buildings. There are voices approaching through the mist, and she moves off, presumably toward them, for her ear is sharper than mine. I quicken my pace to follow. The shoreline is long, the seawall low, and the cobbles are wet, as if a recent tide has flooded them. The mist is at its most dense on the water. Usually from the shore you can see the islands of San Michele and Murano, but there is only gray now.

Ahead is a group of figures: children, people with babies and packages, waiting, as if for a boat. Of course. On this of all days, there will be people moving to and from the islands. Sure enough, there comes the slap of oars, and almost at the same moment a sturdy barge half full, with room for maybe another ten or fifteen people, breaks into view on the near horizon. On land, the group picks up their parcels and children and move closer to the little wooden dock as the boat pulls itself in, tossing its great ropes around the thick wooden piles. La Draga is with them now. God help me. Of course. She too must be going home. What was it the old man said about her once? That she was born on one of the islands but came to the city as a child. No doubt she has family to visit. I stand frozen by the shore.

There are no sides to this great canal of open water, nowhere to be pulled to safety here, while out there in the gloom are birds with wings like the wind and an appetite for small prey. I will not go there again. Not so soon.

The boat is docked now, and there is a stream of people getting off. The shore is sudden chaos, with boxes and bags and shouting. I hear the indignant cluck of chickens, and someone has what looks like a small pig squashed under his arm, for it is squealing louder than any baby; no doubt it senses that, having left the fields, it is destined for the spit. I am lost in the crowd. To the left I hear the thick splashing of the water against the stone, and I know how the pig feels. It is a simple enough choice. If I want to speak to her again, I will have to follow her onto the boat.

I have spent my whole life refusing to be as small as others want me to be. Yet my fear has still let me down. The barge is loading now, the first people jostling and laughing as they push ahead. I am at the end of the line, my feet firmly on dry land. La Draga's bent figure stands six or seven ahead of me.

Let Fate decide. If there is room, I will go and walk on water with her; if not, I will turn around and go home.

There is room.

CHAPTER TWENTY-NINE

I wedge myself in on a side bench, between a spreading old woman and a hefty man. While their smell is bad, their solidity reassures a little. The boat pushes off, and we move into the mist. La Draga is sitting farther to the front, turned away from me, her head held high despite the curve of her spine. The fact that we cannot see where we are going will be of no concern to her, though I know sound travels differently in fog, and she is too alert not to know what is going on around her. The shawl has slipped slightly from her head now, so that I can see a tangle of hair in a long, untidy braid, almost as white as her skin. We have already lost sight of the dock, and my fists are held so tight in my lap that the knuckles are white ridges against my skin. I make myself loosen my fingers and try to breathe. It is not so bad. There are no bird's talons in my ears, and the chickens scrambling in the boxes at my feet are more perturbed than I am. I wonder about my lady, at sea in a very different boat, with the wealth and majesty of Venice all around her, and I hope the more open water of the Lido has chased the mists away so that, when the doge comes to cast the wedding ring into the gray depths, there is enough sun to catch the glint of it before it hits the water.

Even as I think it, the weather seems to clear a little ahead, and to the left a bell tower begins to take shape out of the gloom. I have seen it enough times from the shore to know it as the bell tower of the church on the island of San Michele, a building about which Aretino and his architect friend, Sansovino, are scathing, for they see it as a dull example of the old classical style, though I am more impressed by the miracle of its construction: all that carting of great barge loads of brick and stone and stuff out into the middle of the sea. It takes us maybe fifteen, twenty minutes to reach it, but we do not stop. The only people living here are Franciscan monks, and they have their own boats, to keep them uncontaminated from life outside.

Of course. For a woman who cannot see, it is poetic that the island of her birth should be the one that produces the world's finest mirrors. We are heading now to Murano.

Already the long, thin lump of land is rising up in front of us. I knew the name Murano long before I ever came to Venice. No one who has lived in a house of any substance does not. The word has moved halfway across the world. It is one of the reasons my Turk arrives with such a full purse—the greatest mosques of Constantinople, it seems, are lit by its hanging lamps, and when we packed up my lady's wealth in Rome, it was not mere glass but Murano crystal that we wrapped so carefully in cloth and stored in the bottoms of the trunks so the barbarians would not get their hands on it. Our merchant, Alberini, says there is no other place on earth where they have the ingredients, the knowledge, and the experience to make such quality in such quantity, though I think this is as much politics as craft, for it's common knowledge that if any master glassmaker leaves the island, he is forbidden by law to set up a business anywhere else.

Alberini brought my lady here once, along with a Spanish nobleman whom he wanted to impress with Venetian beauty, both flesh and glass. She came back aglow with stories of furnaces hot as Hell, from where men scooped white-hot globules of glass onto the ends of pipes and blew them into great bubbles of transparent crystal. But the even greater wonder, she said, was the way they played with the glass in its molten state, thick as runny cheese, twirling and cutting and fashioning it into the shapes of a dozen animals or exotic flowers and curling leaves

for the fall of a chandelier. Such miracles a young girl with failing sight would barely have noticed. Though she, like every
woman, would have learned early enough that fire burns and
that out of heat—most especially man's heat—comes creation.

As we move closer, the island grows in size and depth. I
make out stretches of scrubland with buildings and chimneys
all around, though hardly any trees, as the furnaces long ago de-
voured most of them, so that along with the pebbles and
potash, Murano now imports barge loads of wood to stoke the
ever open mouths of flame. The boat follows the coastline and
then cuts into a canal, as in the mother city, its sides a mass of
warehouses with barges lined up at every available mooring
place. Though there is little activity here today, for even the best
of Venice rests on the day when the doge marries the sea.

The first waterway curves into another, and some fine new
palaces rise up on either side. There are Venetian nobles who
have homes here with great ornamental gardens, but it is hardly
the Grand Canal, and however rich my business, I think I
would feel myself a kind of exile if I lived here. The boat is slow-
ing now, and the people are getting restless. The sky is clear, and
the day has heated up. My cushion of an old woman is fidget-
ing, and I grab hold of the side to counteract the tilting. La
Draga is still as a statue, staring straight ahead. We come into
dock, and now at last she moves, her feet if anything steadier
than mine on the shifting surface. The grizzled boatman takes
her hand as she crosses onto the landing bay and smiles at her
as he does so. Maybe he recognizes her from her youth or regular visits. Maybe she can tell a man by the touch of his hand. I
still remember her turning to me that day I ran after her onto
the street, knowing from the way my feet hit the stones who I
was and that I was somehow agitated. It was the first time she
touched me, reading the shape of my great head with her fingers. They were cool then too, I remember, thin stemmed and
delicate despite all the grinding of powders and mixing of
pastes. It gives me a shudder to think about it now, as if I have
already exposed myself too much to her. In the back of the boat,
I pull my cloak over my head and my shoulders so that, if

needed, I might pass for a bent old man rather than a misshapen younger one.

I am curious about where she will go. Maybe some house, once a workshop, now home to an aging grandparent. I imagine an old man, his shelves filled with small glass bottles, for of course a woman of her profession would need a constant source of vials for all her potions. I think he would be a fellow of some intelligence, this grandfather, for she is clever enough under her silence; a glassmaker with an interest in alchemy, perhaps, as the manufacture of glass is its own kind of magic.

But I am mistaken, because she is not heading for home. Instead, to my surprise, she is going to church. The building rises out of a bend in the canal, its back looking out onto the water, an elegant curved apse with light stone arches and brickwork like clever stitching; old Venice rather than new, but I like it more for that. As I come up to it, she is already halfway to the entrance.

Inside, the place is still full of worshipers eager for God's ear. She sits halfway down at the end of a pew, head bent. I place myself a dozen rows behind her. What is she doing here? Prayers for her dead relatives or prayers for herself? What words do witches use when they address God? I think of my lady at confession: "Forgive me, Father, for I have sinned. This last month I have made my living pleasuring twenty men, not one of whom is my husband." A usual enough sin, even if it comes in unusual amounts. But with La Draga it would be different. How to explain the dipping of a consecrated host in menstrual blood to hook a man's lust, or all those semiliquid little bodies washed out from desperate women's wombs? In the mind of any priest, this is God's work done by the Devil. With such stains on the debit sheet of a soul, would the health of a few prostitutes or the saved life of a dwarf mean anything at all?

I drop my eyes and find myself staring at the floor: a lake of stone and marble mosaic triangles, diamonds, and squares constructed into circles that move outward and flow one into the other, like Venice's little islands flowing into a whole. When you look further, you can spot single images: the shape of a peacock with its tail splayed and, nearby, what might be plants or other birds. How many pieces did it take to make such a floor? How many people die every year? How would it be if this was a mosaic of souls: a million beings gone through the flame to make matter molten, in the same way that the furnace breaks down stones into liquid and, if the ingredients are right, purifies them into something clean and clear? Is that what Heaven is? A process of spiritual alchemy in which the body loses its earthly weight and is transformed into the flawless matter of soul?

What were her words that night? That our bodies will be like glass, clear, pure, able to move faster than arrows, but soft and pliable enough to merge into and through one another. And that when we open our mouths, the sound will be that of a thousand lutes and we will sing constantly at the beauty of it all. I hear her voice again, sweet, gentle in my ear. She must have learned her visions here, in a world of transparent strength.

I imagine her under Tiziano's brush, her bent figure uncurling, her eyes opening toward God. Mystic or witch. Healing or hammering. I feel a tension in my chest, as if my lungs will not let me take in enough air. What do I know of such things? I am a courtesan's dwarf, and my business is accommodating men's desires. If I'm truthful, I am no better than she. Yet she helped me. Forgave my anger, warmed me in my ice age, held me through the flame. And I do feel different. More different than I have for years. Without her I would have died, but instead I am aflame with life. So that I want to touch and hear and taste it all again.

Oh, listen to you, Bucino! You're like a lovesick donkey braying in a backyard, tethered to its own fear. From contempt and suspicion you are moved now to cloying adoration. The only alchemy you have gone through is one that thickens the blood and encourages bad poetry.

The voice inside is fierce and snide at the same time. It is one of many that I have grown up with. When you are as ugly as I am, if you cannot find companions on the outside, then you must find some within or you will die of loneliness. But they must be as hard as they are sometimes soft, for everyone needs both to survive. That is why my lady and I have been such fine companions. We were, in our own ways, bred to be alone, to re-sist feeling rather than to fall into it. That was why when she fell to loving the puppy I gave her no quarter. Yet here I am moon-ing over a cripple.

I stare at the back of her head. Then in my mind I turn her around so I can look at her again: the way her limbs do not connect properly as she walks, her smooth face with its milk eyes, the skin so pale it feels as if she has been drained of blood, serene and alarming in equal measures. What is her real name? Elena Crus . . . something? Crusichi? Yes, that is it. Elena Crusichi. Even the sound of it is interesting.

I don't need any voices to tell me what is happening. I know. Of course I know. I am growing to like her. A lot. Or maybe it is truer to say that I am removing the block in my mind that has for so long prevented it. How strange it is when you have known something always, yet at the same time have not known it at all. Like seeing someone every day of her life and yet choos-ing not to notice who she is.

It is a stupid enough story when I think about it. Careless cruelty, to which you would think I would have become inured, even then. But I was young. Well, young in mind. My body was grown, as least as far as it ever would, and it was raging with its own new heat. My father was dead, and I was in the care of his brother in Florence, a notary, well enough known in his trade, though not good enough to be great or great enough to be hum-ble. He took me in because Christian charity said he had to and because I had a better hand and quicker wit than any of his children and he could put me to work doing his copying. But he hated my deformity as a stain on the family, and I hated him back.

I was fifteen when he brought her to the house. She was from Dalmatia, and he had got her from a friend's house to work in the kitchen. She was very small, almost as small as I was, though so thin that I suspect her size was from lack of food rather than birth. But she was also ugly beyond belief. Some-thing had happened to her mouth when she had been pulled out of the womb, and she had a harelip so fierce that it made her look as if she was always sneering, and when she breathed she sounded like a pig. She was instructed to bring me my food at lunchtimes to the study. So that we might become "acquainted." She was angry. I could see that from the start, down deep behind her eyes, though the immediate rebellion, I suspect, had been beaten out of her. I think now she might have been quite smart. But I was not interested in finding out. Two weeks later he offered her to me as a betrothed, with the words "It will not be easy for you to find a wife with your body, Bucino, and you are growing now, and it seems unfair that you should not enjoy the fruits of love like anyone else."

The next week, I left his home and Florence for good. It was the making of me. For though it was hard at first, I found ways to live on the road. Over the next few years, I lost my sensitivity and my virginity. I honed my wits, learned how to pick purses and to juggle, and by the time I reached Rome, where the cruelty is more sophisticated and veiled, I was ready to use my body as my fortune rather than my fate. But the experience left me with a horror of deformity in others. Because I learned something that night when she and I sat at my uncle's table like performing animals, celebrating our informal "betrothal": that it is easier for people to laugh at two than to laugh at one. For when there are two, no one needs to confront you directly, look into your eyes, and read there either the humiliation he has caused you or the challenge that you offer back.

I made a pact with myself that night that I would dissociate myself from others like me. Instead I would live with—and even off—the specialness of my deformity. For in that way I could not be ignored. So of course my lady, when she found me, was the answer to all my prayers. Not because her beauty made me more ugly, though of course it did, but because, in a strange way, it made me stand out as much as she. The world is full of people whom other people forget. But no one forgets my lady. And with the two of us together, they do not forget me either. If I cannot be perfect, then I will be the most perfectly imperfect. For that title I do not choose to compete.

Yet over the years it has left me lonely. Which is why I sit in this church looking at a woman in whose company I might have found wit and intelligence and sustenance, but whom I have chosen to damn simply because she is too like me.

We sit for a long time, heads down, each of us in our separate thoughts. I am so caught in mine that I miss the moment when she silently rises and leaves the pew, and for an instant I panic, thinking I have lost her. I reach the great doors after she has gone through them and move out into sunlight, fierce as a blow, so that it takes a few seconds for my eyes to adjust and to see her making her way down a small side street.

She is moving with a sense of purpose now. Even her walk is more fluid, as if she knows each step. As I am sure she does, for it turns out her destination is close enough. About a hundred yards from the church, there is the beginning of a workshop. A set of buildings with chimneys and warehouses, and to the back some small houses. As I turn the corner she has turned before me, I see her going inside one.

I am lost now. What should I do? Go up and knock on the door and announce myself? "Hello. Is Elena Crusichi here? Yes? Good. You see, I have followed you all this way to tell you that all these years I have misjudged you. And because I think we might have things in common and I want to get to know you better."

She will think the fever made me crazy. At this moment I might agree. It is hot out in the open, and both my head and my legs are dizzy with exhaustion. Barely a week ago I was dying. It is beginning to feel as if I am again. My stomach starts to cramp, and I find myself thinking of the pig on its spit in the *campo* and my saliva starts running. Of course. All I have had since early morning is two glasses of gut rot. What if my weakness is not infatuation but hunger? I shall decide nothing until I have eaten.

I move back onto the streets. The main street—as much as such a thing exists—seems to run parallel to the wharf, and not far away I can see activity, a set of stalls and shops with people gathered. Somewhere someone is cooking something, and the smell draws me on. As I walk into a small half square, the effect is palpable. Dwarves, it would seem, do not visit Murano. A boy with a squashed face and eyes like raisins comes and stands in front of me gaping until I grin at him, and then he bursts into tears. No doubt about it: I should not speak to anyone until I have eaten. I pick an open shop where there are roasted meats and fresh bread, and the owner is too old and gum-eyed to see what a freak he is serving. As the first few mouthfuls hit my stomach, I wonder if I shouldn't abandon the pursuit of women in favor of good food. I must be stuffing my face, because people are still looking. Once the worst of my hunger is sated, I start to exploit the attention. I have taken a handful of bread rolls for the meat, and now I flick two of them high into the air, catching them deftly. Then I take a few more and start them all spinning. Even the boy has stopped crying now and is open-mouthed. I make faces as I juggle, and after a while I pretend to drop one, then catch it again. Three or four people gasp. I think back to Alberini and his party trick with the goblet. Now that I have a full stomach, I am in the mood for some fun. I will make a better impression on La Draga if I arrive feeling appreciated rather than ignored.

A few shops down, a man is selling glass pots and glasses. They are clumsy compared with the stuff I have seen in Venice, full of impurities and bubbles. The best is no doubt exported and the workers must make do with the leftovers. But they are cheap enough for a man with my pocket and free time on his hands after so many years of work, and I buy five of them.

I set myself up by the side of the road, eat the remaining two sausages, and wipe my hands on the grass to get the grease off. Then I take off my hat, pick up the pots, and start to juggle. It is not as easy as the bread, for while they are firmer, their shapes and weights are more variable and therefore unstable, and I have to concentrate hard not to drop them.

By now a small crowd has gathered, and people are starting to applaud. I am enjoying myself. It's a long time since I have had this feeling, mind and body working together. When did I last juggle for an audience? A few performances in the early days of our success in Venice? And before then, that night in Rome. My God, I had felt alive enough then, the excitement that comes with fear sluicing like raw alcohol through my body. And though I am in no danger now, there is a similar edge in me; the heat, the strangeness of the place, the idea of La Draga, and my newfound sense of life.

All I have to do is keep my eyes on the flying glass.

In my defense, I think that if she had come as she usually does, I would have seen her earlier, for somehow I was waiting for her.

It happens like this. I am getting cocky. And, I daresay, a little tired. The crowd is now five or six deep. Someone throws a small coin into my hat, and I give a wink to acknowledge it. It used to be a party trick I had with pretty girls. The move misfires, and I miss the falling pot by a fraction that is also a mile. In my panic to regain control, I make a wild lunge to catch it and only just succeed. A cheer goes up, and I make a face, which makes people laugh as if they think it was all deliberate. So this time I almost miss again, throwing the pots a little to one side so I have to stagger to reach them. And they love that. My staggering takes me closer to the crowd. They make way for me, and soon I am walking as I juggle, the air above me full of turning glass glinting in the sunlight and laughter and applause all around me.

Then suddenly there is a small child in my way, rooted to the spot, eyes out on stalks. The arcing ball moves too far out of my reach and too close to her, and this time I don't get to it in time and it smashes to the ground, right by her feet. I catch the others quickly as they drop and squat down in front of her to survey the damage. She is not hurt. Indeed, she does not seem upset at all. She is very small, at that age when standing is still its own achievement, and her legs are almost as bandy as mine. But it is not her age that sets her apart as much as her looks. She has the palest of pale skins and a crown of wild curls, so fair that they are almost white, while her eyes are like fat, brown almonds, and they are staring at me with an intense concentration but not one iota of fear. I smile with my eyes rather than my mouth and slowly offer one of the remaining glass pots to her, and after she has stared at it a little longer, she puts out a hand to touch it. As she does so, a woman pushes through the crowd frantically, shouting her name. A child on her own and the sound of broken glass. It would have any mother distraught. As she breaks into the little circle where we are now bent together, the child turns and looks up to her.

As do I.

It is strange what one registers in a single instant. In fact, it is possible that, had it gone differently, I might not even have recognized her. The hair is out from its braid and pinned up high on her head, with a few straying curls around her cheeks, and the way she holds herself shows it off to much effect, for her body is somehow released from its painful hunch so that it moves upright, willowy and fluid. She is lovely. That much I re-member, and will until the day I die. But there is no time for me to tell her now because she darts straightway down and scoops the child up in her arms, cradling her deep into her chest, head to head, both faces hidden; then, equally frantic, she starts to push back into the crowd. Only the little girl will have none of it. She has been interrupted at a game, and she wriggles and yells and pulls herself away from her mother's body, so that the woman has no option but to lift her face as well, though so briefly that I am not sure what it is I have seen. The skin is as smooth and white as ever. But the eyes, the eyes are different. Where once there were pools of gray, filmy milk, now they seem livid and active. Immediately she is bent and busy over the child again. But it is too late.

"Elena!"

I say her name loud and clear, and though I have never used it before in her presence, it moves through her like a long shiver, and involuntarily her eyes pull halfway up to meet mine for a split second. I swear she feels the same lurch of panic as I do, though when I think about it, I know that it must be worse for her, because it is her life rather than mine that collapses in that instant. For while her eyes are not good, the outer pale circles red and angry as if there is some irritation or infection present, there are definite and recognizable pupils, sharp and dark at the centers.

La Draga, it seems, is not only an able-bodied young woman with no hunch or spine defect. She can also see.

CHAPTER THIRTY

There is a moment of paralysis, as if the world is stopped still and we are all held rigid inside it. Even the child is quiet. Then, suddenly, all is movement, and she is breaking through and out of the crowd, the babe clasped to her breast, before I have gotten my breath back. My breath or my mind.

Not blind. La Draga is not blind.

The audience is restless now; the interlude is over, and they want more skill or bravura. When nothing happens, they start to drift away. The space opens up around me, and soon I find myself alone, just a few curious souls staring from the sidelines.

La Draga is not blind and she walks tall. She is a fraud, a charlatan, a fake. The words hit like hammer blows all down my spine and ignite a knot of pain. What did she once tell me? That my back pain was because my trunk was heavier than my legs. My God. I had thought her so clever at the time. To know what she couldn't see. Around me the earth is littered with shards of glass from the smashed pot. The sun catches the edges of a few, and they glint and shine like scrubby diamonds in the dust. I pick one up and crush my fist over it. I feel the edge pierce my palm. I like the way it bites into my flesh. La Draga is a fake, God damn her. She can see as well as anyone. She is a fraud. We have been deceived. I open my fist on a fragment of glass smeared with blood. I hold it up and watch the sun play with it. Not so much a diamond now as a ruby. Colored glass. The thoughts fall heavily, like flat stones into water, each one causing a larger ripple.

Colored glass. Of course. There is a shop off the Rialto that sells only the cream of Murano glass. It has a sailing ship in the window, a miniature Venetian round galley, so perfect in every detail that there are even lines of rigging between the masts, teased and stretched out from small globules of glass. Everything in the shop is glass pretending to be something else. Many are more expensive than the real thing, like the bunch of red grapes so real-looking they seem to have the sheen of the sun on them. Trinkets for rich people. But they do offer one thing cheaper to bring in the crowds: a basket of fake jewels, bright and busy, crude when you know the real thing, of course, for it is impossible to fake the inner dazzle of diamond, though the colored stones are more convincing, the rubies and the emeralds. Indeed, there is a rumor that if you know where to go and are willing to pay more . . .

Suffice it to say I had not seen these stones when I took our bulging purse to the pawnbroker all those years ago.

La Draga is a child of Murano. She more than anyone would understand the power of glass. This young woman, who is not blind and does not limp. Like the pale, sweet-faced young woman who offered the ruby to our Jew, walked straight off the street and looked him directly in the eye as she told him a sob story about her mistress's plight with our stolen gem.

My back still skewers me, but my mind is working again. I am in our old house by the canal that morning, the squint-eyed bat across the water, and La Draga sitting on my lady's bed. It was a familiar enough pose in those days when our furniture was so scarce and she was mixing ointments and creams from the pots all around her, her hands everywhere. Including, no doubt, when no one is looking, between the slats of the mattress to find a purse containing a dark, rich ruby whose quality you would recognize instantly if you knew your jewels and which, if you knew the right pair of hands in the right workshop to take it to, could be faked at least well enough to fool its owners.

Now I am moving too. As fast as my throbbing little legs

will take me, across the street and along the wharf toward the dock, where I can see a boat taking on passengers ready to return to the mainland. La Draga will not be one of them. Whatever she decides now, she must leave the child before she can come back, so I will get there before her. What I will do there I do not know yet, but get there I will.

They are pulling away from the mooring by the time I reach the dock, and my heart is pounding so fiercely and my legs hurt so much that I cannot even summon up the energy to be afraid of the water. As we plow through open sea toward the city, I sit transfixed, writing a short treatise on the life and times of a fraud in my head.

La Draga. I watch her walking down the street, her head crooked to one side, one leg dragging behind the other because her back has a twist in it. I low easy! I would not waddle if I didn't have to, but I have watched enough men try to ape me, and if they took the time to study harder, they might convince, for it is just a question of practice. And God knows, the city has enough cripples to learn from.

But what point is there to a crooked spine on its own? It cannot help to cure disease or seem to give you second sight. But being blind when you can see all along . . . now that is indeed a clever way to go. The first time she saw my lady, her hands flew like soft bird wings over her stubble head, and, without being told, she could trace the cut exactly from her scalp to her forehead. Just as she knew what kind of dwarf I was, without asking. Or that Aretino had a mangled right hand and a scar on his neck. I watch his eyes go wide with wonder at her wisdom. Knowing things that no blind person could ever know.

If an apothecary sees a wound and cures it, he is a good doctor. If a blind girl senses the same thing and then it heals, she is a miracle worker. And once you are a miracle worker, the rest is easy. What you cannot cure by your medicines you can cure by faith. He loves me, he loves me not. Well, no one can be sure of that. But if he was nicer to you after a potion, then who is there to thank but the potion maker? Thank God for La Draga. She gets the men by the balls and ties them to women's heartstrings.

Where would Venice be without her? Maybe that is what she did to me. Slipped me a potion along with my cure . . .

As for the rest, the bigger fish . . . well, she just has to wait and watch and take her chance. Like at our house. If there are valuables to be had, then the last person you suspect is the one who cannot see them. Does she always have an inside accomplice? Probably. It was easy enough with Meragosa. The old whore hated us anyway. Who knows? They had probably already cheated Fiammetta's mother out of the last of her wealth as she lay rotting in bed. La Draga had told my lady that she never met her mother, but what is one lie amid so many? By the time La Draga came to us, Meragosa couldn't wait to get out. This way they both got what they wanted. The proceeds of a fat ruby, while one took the sting and the other remained to go on milking the cow. Repeat that through a city where most people have a servant they neither like nor trust and where the feelings are heartily reciprocated and you have a tidy little business. My only question now is practical. How? How does someone who can see make her eyes so blind?

The boat docks on the northern shore, and I clamber off immediately. The golden galley will not return until late afternoon, and then there will be an evening of processions and banquets. It is, of course, forbidden that someone like my lady should find herself as a guest at one of these, but she will be there nevertheless. With her absent, who can I go to, who can I tell? I retrace my footsteps from the dock. Now that the mist is gone, it doesn't take long to find her street. I stand in front of La Draga's house. Whatever she keeps in there is important enough to warrant a fat lock fixed to the door. Though I have led a disreputable life, housebreaking is not one of my talents. I do, however, have others.

The houses back onto the canal, where there will almost certainly be windows too small for a man but large enough for an able dwarf. If I could find a way to negotiate the water . . . I reach the *sotto portego* and move down it. My nose curls as the smell rises, and as I get to the end I understand why. The canal is there, all right, but there is nothing in it. Like the one near the Arsenale where I once drank myself stupid after we had been robbed of our future, it has been drained: dammed two bridges down with thick wooden pylons and the water pumped away to reveal a mass of evil sludge reaching three-quarters of the way up to the level of the walkway. It must connect straight to the Rio di Santa Giustina and the sea, for the northern tides slide powerfully in here and often silt up the smaller arteries, making it impossible for heavy cargo to travel, so that after a while they must be dredged. This is a route for the barges from Murano, and while it is a poor district that might otherwise be left to rot, Venice lets nothing stop trade.

For today, though, the city's obsession is my savior, because along the edge where the silt meets the walls, they have sunk temporary walkways so the men can haul themselves in and move in the wheelbarrows. All I have to do is clamber along it to reach the level of her first-floor windows. The other houses are deserted; even the oldest of bats will be out celebrating, which means there is no one to spy on me, no one to see how inch by inch I feel my way along, my hands against the wall, my back to the drop. How far down would the mud go? Deeper than a dwarf? To drown in the sewage of Venice. The trick is to not think about it. My God, how scared does she get? I wonder. A woman who spends her whole life faking and stealing. Or does it become easier the more people you fool?

The window, when I reach it, is glass, but crude fat eyes of it in a rickety frame and with a rusted catch, and it gives with little enough work. I push it open, hoist myself up, and push myself through. The drop on the other side is farther than the pull up, and I misjudge it and go sprawling. But though I was always too clumsy to make it past the second layer of the human pyramid, I still learned how to fall well enough, and I recover quickly.

I get my bearings. There is little enough to see. The space is small and frugal: a bed and chest, locked. I move into another, equally small room. But this one is different: this is almost an apothecary shop. Everywhere I look there are makeshift shelves stacked with glass vials and pots like the ones on Murano, a line of herbs and powders—I recognize sage, fennel, tartar, ground peppers, and what looks like flour. She could beat Mauro at his own game, though the ingredients grow more sinister with the liquids and solids. There is no mistaking the dirtied-gold tint of urine and the splashy black-red of blood. There is a box with eggs, all shapes and sizes, a jar containing the pulp of some animal organ preserved in brine, and a pot of what looks like congealed fat. Underneath the shelves I find magnets, with a few preserved dogs' paws and pieces of rolled parchment decorated with words: OMEGA ALPHA. La Draga, it seems, is not just a witch of the womb. She is dabbling in astrology too. Last year Venice's Holy Office flogged and exiled an ex-priest who sold luck along with forgiveness and claimed to be able to predict the outcome of votes in the government. Though he lived in a slum, they found a bulging sack of ducats under his floorboards, for even pretending to manipulate the future is a profitable business.

I take a poker from the fireplace and move back into the bedroom. The chest is old and easy enough to pry open. Why not? I want her to know that she has been found out, to feel the sense of violation, just as she has violated others. The lid lifts to reveal layers of clothing—old dresses, slips, shawls, petticoats—and as soon as my fingers touch them, the scent of her wraps itself around me, the individual smell of her flesh and something sweeter, the leftovers of some homemade perfume perhaps, and it skewers me in my stomach. I swallow back the feeling and keep on digging. What am I looking for? A cache of fake jewels, a sack of coins, stolen treasures from other people's houses?

If there is booty, she doesn't keep it here. Or not the kind I am looking for. Toward the bottom, wrapped in a shawl, I come across a small notebook, its seams broken and pages adrift. When I open it, I can barely believe what I see. Each and every page is full: line after line of small writing, punctuated by diagrams and figures, crude, annotated drawings of parts of the body. That she is this literate is unexpected enough. What is more remarkable is that she is writing in some kind of code, the letters jumbled and interspersed with numbers and signs. These are secrets, all right, but none that I can fathom. All I know for sure is that it is some register: dates and people, ailments and remedies.

My God, she may be a fraud in some ways, but not in all.

As I push it back, my fingers connect with something else, deep in the corner. I pull out a small wooden box, and as soon as I open it I know I have found it, though what exactly I cannot tell. The inside lid is a mirror, best quality, fine, clear, and below, cradled in black cloth, sit two curved, misty-white glass circles, small enough to catch a single drop of rain or dew.

They look so fragile I am almost afraid to touch them. I put the top of my index finger onto my tongue, then press it gently into the convex curve. The little glass shape sticks to my tip, and I lift it carefully, the box beneath in case it should fall. It is so fine, so thin, that it is hard to know how it could have been fashioned. Just as it is hard to know how anyone could make a glass stone glow almost as fiercely as a ruby. I see my face in the mirror with the tiny dish in front of me, and I know that what I am holding on the tip of my finger is her blindness. But how? How would this fit? Directly over her eye? No. That is crazy.

But only half crazy. Everyone knows glass helps eyesight. The workshops of Murano have saved an army of scholars and illustrators from a miserable old age by making curved lenses that magnify the page. Our old shipbuilding client uses a pair himself, with leather and metal frames that he fixes behind his ears so he can get the glass close to the eye. The closer the better. But this—this is something quite different. This she would have to put somehow inside her eye. And if she did that, what would happen? Would she see the world larger or just mistily, to make her eyes look white? And how could she bear it? It would be torture, to have something resting over your very eyeball. And it was. You could tell that from the irritation it had caused, the redness I had noticed in that single glimpse. I think back to all the times I have seen her. The fact is, she was not always milk blind. There were odd times, like today, when her eyes were simply closed, or hovering half open with no eyeball showing. God knows, you need to see that mad whiteness only once or twice to be convinced. Maybe she uses them only sometimes, precisely because they hurt so much. Of course, I hurt sometimes, and I have learned to bear it. People deal with all kinds of suffering. Walk through the market any day and you will see old men moving like yelping crabs, they have so much pain in their joints. There is always a pain worse than the one you have.

Yet to subject yourself to it deliberately would take the most extraordinary act of will. Maybe if the prize is big enough . . . I slip the glass back into the box and close it up, then sit for a moment against the bed, trying to imagine how it would be for her. But the thought undermines me and her smell envelops me again, so that it is harder to resist now, for with the memory of pain comes the pleasure of comfort, the feel of her arms around me, the whispering in my ears, the singing and the soothing.

But why? Why on earth should she bother to look after me so tenderly if she is only a thief and a fraud? Why, indeed, did she ever bother to come back to us? It is years since the ruby, and she has taken nothing else since. Though we are only one of her clients, we hardly make her fortune: pots of bleaching paste, cures for a few itches and fevers, and maybe a love potion or two, which she knows I will not pay for. Yet she has been loyal to us and, for all my bad temper, spent days and nights at my bedside, saving my spirit as well as my life.

And for what? She didn't even ask for payment, left before my lady could offer her anything. When she was holding me in her arms, did her fingers ever sneak under my mattress, just in case? She would have been disappointed. I am cleverer now and have found a safer form of concealment. For this time it is hidden by not being hidden at all. Petrarch's love sonnets sit on my bookshelves with three or four dozen books looking just like it. There is no one in the house who can read anyway, and if a servant should get as far as picking it off the shelf—in itself impossible, since my door stays locked when I am not in the room and only my lady has a key—they would never be able to break the code.

As for our crippled, blind healer, well, of course it has never occurred to me . . .

But it is occurring now, and the panic of it slices open my gut. Oh, sweet Jesus. No—surely not. I try to make my mind slow down. Step by step. So now there is someone in our house who can read. A thief who has indeed had access to my room, most important, when I am not there. I see myself lying in bed, felled by the fever, unconscious, her sitting through long nights watching over me, her back at right angles to the bookshelf. And this thief is clever enough that, should she find a book with a lock on it, not only would she know instantly that it was something of value but she might even be able to decipher the code.

The fact is I have no idea if the book is still on my shelves. Though I am careful enough with every item of inventory, the last time I looked was—what?—ten days, maybe two weeks ago, before I was ill. In the time since my recovery, well, I have been too busy and even—oh, how fine is this?—too happy and preoccupied with my new sense of life to bother to check. Though surely, surely, I would have noticed if . . .

No. It isn't possible. She couldn't have done it.

Of course it is. Of course she could. Anyone as determined as she could do anything. God damn it, I have been cured of one malady only to fall ill with another. To be coddled and caressed so I could be swindled. Who is the blind one now? It explains everything. Why she was so nervous with me in the *campo*. Why she left so early that last morning without asking for payment. Why she has not been back since. Of course, why take that risk when she already had something infinitely more valuable in her hands? Without the book, we are nothing. While what we earn may seem rich from the outside, it barely covers the style we have to present to the world in order to go on earning it, and as my lady's beauty fades, so will our income. Once the walls are stripped and the gifts are pawned, the rent will run out and we will find ourselves in the underworld again;

for God knows, there are no charities for old whores, however powerful the men they once seduced. We did not work this hard for this long to contemplate such horrors.

A locked chest. It might seem like the place to keep your secrets. But then things are never what they seem. I move back into the other room, and this time I put the poker to more effect. But it's not there. Not behind any of the bottles or the jars, not under the boxes, not in the fireplace, or in the stove, or up the chimney, or in the stuffing of her straw mattress.

My own destruction tires me. I sit on the bed, staring at the floor, for a second thinking back to the church with its tiny mosaic pieces, like souls forged into patterns for God. Good stone to be buried under. I see the floorboards again. I move the bed and then the chest to check the lines where they meet. It isn't hard to find when you know what you are looking for. I use the poker to lever up the planks that have obviously been levered before, and a deep, dark hole greets me. I stick my hands down, but my squat arm isn't long enough to reach the bottom. I lay myself long across the floor and try again. At my fullest stretch, the tops of my fingers come upon something. The rough material of some kind of sack. I hook on to it and start to lift. Ah! It is heavy enough. I move it carefully, carefully, until it clears the hole, then I scramble up and tear at the string around the neck, and when it gives I empty the contents onto the bed.

But there is no book here. Instead there is only a shower of little bones—animal leftovers, no doubt, for grinding into powder. More witches' trimmings. I am about to turn away when something makes me look at them more closely. I pick up what is evidently some kind of tiny leg. I know about legs. And arms. In Rome my first employer was a man who was fascinated by dwarves and had a collection of their bones in his house. I think he was waiting for me to die so he could add me to his collection. He showed them to me once, to explain how my deformity worked; how while the bones of my trunk had developed normally, my arms and legs had stayed child-short. While the bones I am holding are far too small and fragile to be from dwarves or even those of the smallest children, one thing is clear. They do not come from animals. And if they are not children's, that means there is only one kind of human left. These are bones from the bodies of babies; newborn, maybe even smaller.

What was the word about her on the streets? That she can help a pregnant woman if the child is still in a liquid state. Well, I daresay not all of them were still liquid. Maybe this was her price. That after she had helped dispel them she took them away with her. My mind goes back to another story: of the young girl new to Venice who disappeared, only to be found under the Pillars of Justice collecting the ashes of burned criminals. I had dismissed it as tittle-tattle then, for gossip grows with the number of mouths it passes between. But now I see it differently.

We are not the only ones, it seems, who have something precious to steal.

I clamber back out, the bag in my hand. The light is going fast now, and the walkway and the canal are already gloomy. My feet hit the boards with a thud. Somewhere near my ankle an angry yowl cuts into the silence, and a scrawny cat jumps out of the gloom in a spasm of fear, arched and spitting. In my panic I miss my footing and feel myself slipping backward. I grab upward for an iron mooring embedded in the wall, but I am too heavy to hold myself properly and I have to let go of the sack. The cat streaks past me, and the sack slides under its flung paws. I have my balance now, and I make a lunge for it, but I am too late, and I hear it hit the mud beneath with a thick slap. Frantic, I shimmy myself to the edge, only to watch as the black sludge sucks it down.

There is nothing I can do. I do not have the bones. But I still have the knowledge of them. That will have to do. I crawl back along the planks, but the commotion has stirred someone and I hear the sound of a shutter opening somewhere across the canal and a woman's voice starts to shriek. God knows what she must think she is seeing in the gathering gloom, but I do not stop to find out. I pull myself to the end and down onto the bridge, where I am too small for her to see, and then I start running toward home.

CHAPTER THIRTY-ONE

It takes me a long time. While the crowds have thinned in the darkness, the city is rough-edged with people too drunk to care where they are going or whom they trample upon to get there. Some have already tipped from merriment into maudlin, and a few single me out as a desperate confidant, one twisted soul confessing his disability to another. Because I cannot afford to get knifed or pulped now, I am cute when I have to be and rude when they are too drunk to follow. And all the time I am thinking about what is to come.

My lady is still out when I get home, and the rest of the casa is locked and dark. The servants have been given the day off, and even if they choose not to celebrate, it is not their duty to wait on or up for anyone. My thighs are so weak that my legs tremble as I climb the stairs. My fingers can barely manipulate the key into the lock of my room. Inside, I move too fast, and the candle flickers and almost gutters out. I have to pace myself to the bookshelves. It was on the middle shelf, nine books in, amid a run of volumes with similarly colored leather bindings. Another book, irrelevant to those who cannot read, ordinary enough to those who can. My God, what will I do if I find it now, safe, in place? How much less of a villain does she become if she is only an old thief? Maybe even reformed now . . .

But the book is not there.

Our fortune is gone.

But where? Where? Surely she cannot have passed it on yet.

She may be an expert on jewels, but she would need specialist contacts to move something like this, and even if she went for an easy sell, Venice is on holiday and the printers and book-shops have been closed for days. Which can only mean that she took it with her to Murano. In that bag she was carrying after she met me. Of course! Now it all makes sense. The way she was so nervous with me in the square. What? Was I truly stu-pid enough to think it might have been affection? What she re-ally had on her mind was the fear that I already suspected her soothing fingers to be those of a thief. God knows, the minute she finished with me, she was out of the house again, the bag on her back. She must have worried that I had followed her be-cause I knew about the book.

Well, when she walks into her house, she will understand soon enough that I do. So much for my newfound sense of life and companionship.

I must eventually fall asleep, for the next thing I know Gabriella is shaking me.

"Signor Bucino? Are you all right?"

It is morning, and on the table is a tray with food and drink. Mauro is still solicitous for my welfare, and I must look gray with yesterday's exertions.

"Bucino?"

But I am up now, the rest of my life pressing like a thunder sky down upon me. "What time is it? Where is she? The mis-tress? Is she back?"

"It's early. Mauro wants to know if you will go to the market with him. The mistress is home. She came in a few hours ago, in Lord Loredan's boat. She looked very fine, though her dress was rather spoiled from all the festivities." Gabriella giggles, for she has a spirit to her that still finds our sins great sport.

"And now?"

"Oh, now she is asleep."

Not for long.

When I wake her, she has barely slept, and in the instant before she senses my anxiety, her mind is still filled with the marvels she has lived through: a sea aflame with gold and wealth, a day rich with compliment and the confidence that comes from being inside unassailable power. If this were any other morning, we might sit together and revel in it, for we have worked all our lives for such a moment, and the fall from grace will be unbearable. So I take it slowly, holding back on the book, saving the worst until last. I begin with the first betrayal: the great ruby and her blind eyes. Even this is hard enough for her to believe.

"No, no. Not La Draga. It can't have been—"

"I know how it sounds. But if you had seen her with the child, if you had seen her eyes and the foul glass coverings . . . I never understood how Meragosa had the skill or the connections or the money to buy such a fine fake jewel alone—for it would have cost something—or the opportunity to make the switch. But if they were in it together . . . La Draga had all those things. And the Jew's description of the woman who came to him selling it fits her perfectly."

"How long have you known that, Bucino? I mean about the Jew?"

"Only a few weeks."

"Why didn't you tell me?"

"I—I was going to tell you, but you were busy . . . with Foscari, and we were arguing . . . and—well, it didn't mean anything then."

"You still should have told me." She shakes her head. "But . . . even if it was her, why has she stayed with us all this time? Why? She's never taken anything else—and God knows there are enough things of value in this house now."

"I know—but—"

"She's been more than a friend to us. Both of us. Sweet Jesus, she saved your life, Bucino. I saw her with you. You don't know what she did. How she cared." She stops. "What? What is it?"

"Fiammetta, listen to me. There is more."

I have her attention now. Oh, God, how I wish it could end here. Because for all the horror, there is something about this moment: I sitting on the end of her bed, she nest-ripe still from sleep, lying back against the pillows. It is how it used to be between us, in the old days, when I would come to her in the morning to discuss the entertainment of the night before: the character of each client, his potential, his drawbacks. Our partnership was so sweet then, before success and the trappings of formality overcame it. But there is no going back now: even the past is littered with deceit and betrayal.

"More? What more?" I watch her brace herself. "Tell me."

So I do. After a while I can't look at her, for retelling is reliving when something hurts as much as this. Even before I take the poker to the room in search of the book, she is groaning.

"Oh my God, no."

"It's all right. It's all right," I interject. "The fact that I couldn't find it doesn't mean it is sold already." Which one of us am I trying to reassure? "I think—"

"No!"

"I think she's taken it to Murano. I think it was in the bag she was carrying when I followed her, and if we—"

"No, Bucino. No!" And now she is across the bed, grabbing at my hands frantically. "Stop! Listen to me."

"What?"

"She—she doesn't have it. La Draga doesn't have the book."

"What? What do you mean?"

"She didn't take it."

"But how—"

"Because I have it. I took it."

And of course I hear. She says the words loudly enough. Of course I hear them. "What?" But it still takes time.

"I took it—oh, my God, oh, sweet Jesus, I took it. The day you got ill. The day you stomped out after our row and didn't come back until the night. I was so angry with you. Your . . . arrogance, your righteousness. I took the key and went into the room and went through the bookshelves and found it and took it."

"You!"

Her words spread like a bloodstain across the sheets between us. The book is not stolen. We were robbed and betrayed once. But now I find we have betrayed each other. La Draga took our jewel, but my lady took our fortune. I am the one groaning now.

"Bucino. It's not what you think—I wasn't taking it for myself." She is breathless now. She stops, hesitates. "I . . . I took it to show Vittorio."

"*Vittorio!*" His name spews out of me like vomit. "You took it for Vittorio!" And now my voice is a howl, that of an animal cornered and skewered in the night. My God, here I am drowning in deceit, my world pulled down around my head, and still he pokes his puppy snout through the rubble to mock me.

"I know. I know . . . I know we said we would never do that. And it's all right. Because he didn't see it. Are you listening to me, Bucino? I took it, but in the end I never showed it to him. Because that was the night when you wouldn't let him in. Remember?"

Oh yes, I remember. How could I not, for already I am back there again, caught in the fire of my mad pain and her fury?

"Bucino." In contrast, her own voice is soft now. Almost tender. "Bucino. Look at me. Please. If it hadn't been for your illness, I would have put it back. I would have put it back and you would never have known. Because it's over. What happened between him and me is past. Your illness brought me to my senses. You know that, yes?" She stops. "I never intended to hurt you. But at the time . . . oh, sweet Jesus . . . how do I say it? At the time, well, it had never happened to me before. Ah! Look— you know this . . . you know how it has been for me. How it has always been. How I have spent my whole life being with men who wanted it more than I did. That's what we've lived on— men's lust. Since I was fourteen years old I've watched men drowning in it, driven mad with it, furious for it, even unmanned because of it. And I have never come close to knowing it myself. I mean . . . maybe once with Pietro when I was young I felt something, but it was my heart rather than my body and my mother had him out of the house the minute she spotted it, and the feeling got lost in my anger toward him. And after him there was just an army of others in between."

She stops and swallows. I look up at her now and feel the tears rising.

"You were right. He was a boy, *is* a boy. He knows nothing. Oh, God, Bucino, but there was something in him. Some flame in his desire that lit up something in me. Ah . . . I cannot explain it. . . . Even the words are . . . what? . . . stained with overuse. But I felt it. Oh, God, how I felt it! That fever from which no one wants to be well. I think now maybe he was my punishment. To feel it once. So that for the rest of my life I will know what I am missing when I never feel it again."

She is crying now, but she is angry with herself as well and keeps pushing the tears away with her hands.

"Anyway . . . anyway . . . the important thing is he never saw it and the book is safe. Of course I would have put it back. Only that same night you were ill. And after that . . . well, after that there was no time. I didn't think about it anymore."

The room goes quiet. She is waiting for me to speak, but I don't know what to say. While a part of me is reassured, another part is wild still, only in another way. For while I am looking at her, I am also seeing La Draga: her pearly skin, her slender, willowy body, her newly seeing eyes. La Draga. The woman who betrayed us so long ago but who did not, I know now, steal the book. The woman who saved my life. The woman whose life I have now destroyed in turn.

Here we sit, God help us: a courtesan and her pimp, eaten up by feelings for others that they should not have. She is right. Of all the diseases in the world, this surely is the one that hurts most sweetly.

CHAPTER THIRTY-TWO

She recovers faster than I do. Or maybe she is simply thinking my thoughts too.

"You—you said that there was a child? That when you saw La Draga on Murano she had a child?"

"Yes . . . a child."

"Was it her child?"

I nod.

"How did you know?"

How did I know? The shock of white curls? The translucent skin? Or the way that it stared at me, stubborn already in its sense of self, as curious as it ought to have been afraid? Or the way she burst into the crowd to save it from possible danger, the way their bodies came together in that instant, the way mothers hold their children, whoever they are, however strange or deformed they may look . . . ?

I tell it again, seeing it more clearly this time, and my lady listens intently. I know what she is thinking. That she will never have those feelings. And she wants to have them. Oh, how much she wants to. . . . I have seen it before, the way women yearn more for a child when they have fallen in love. It is part of the disease, like the ague that goes with the fever. Maybe the real lover's prick goes deep enough to ignite some longing in the womb. Maybe it is the promise of a future, something left over once the passion is spent.

The future. Hers and ours. What of that?

"So, Bucino, what do we do now? She will know that it was you, yes? Who was in her house?"

"Yes."

"How much damage did you do?"

I shake my head. "Enough."

There is still one thing left to tell. I watch the small white bones tumble out of the sack and disappear into the liquid mud again.

"Ha! But she won't know that's what's happened to them. So—what? She will think *we* have them now?"

"Yes. I think she might."

"In which case she will be scared of us. Of what we might do with them now we know she is a thief. And we do know that, don't we? I mean, God knows, I don't want to believe it of her, so we need to be sure."

I think about it. "Yes, I am sure. I think that along with Meragosa, she took our ruby and sold it."

"But then why did she come back and help us?"

I shake my head. "I don't know."

"And all this time—what? She has pretended to be blind to convince us—and others—of her powers?"

"Yes."

"So she is a fraud?"

"Yes . . . No . . ." I see the tiny writing in her book again, the pages of notes and diagrams and all those rows and rows of bottles and jars. "I—I think she has a talent to heal. I think over the years she has studied and worked out remedies and that what she doesn't know she experiments with."

"And the bones? She uses them too?"

"I don't know. You're the one she played the witch with. What potions did she give you to snare the pup's—I mean, Foscari's—heart?"

"Oh, no, no, you're wrong. It wasn't like that. She helped me, yes. But it was only ordinary things: pledges, incantations, a few throws of the beans to see into the future; there was no blood or consecrated hosts, as you said." Her voice sounds almost sad now. "She didn't need those kinds of things. She . . . well, she saw things—oh, God, it is obvious now because she was looking at us the whole time, of course she saw—but not just physical things. She also seemed to understand people's minds."

My lady is right. She did. So what of my mind? What did she understand of that? But I will not ask the question. It is too late now.

"I tell you, she saw a lot, Bucino. You know what she said about you once? That you are a man who should forget what is wrong with him and celebrate what is right. For—and these were her exact words—there is much to enjoy." Despite herself, she laughs. "I used to think how brave she was: that in her own life she had overcome much worse than you and yet was so strong with it."

There is a silence. I feel her gaze upon me.

"And now you have thought about her too, haven't you? You have been in her house. You read her notebooks and discovered her secrets. You've watched her, seen her with a child, enough to be certain that it is hers. Oh, it seems to me you know a great deal about her, Bucino."

Does she see it in my eyes? Is there something in my voice when I talk about her? How does one read the symptoms in oneself?

"Is that why you followed her? Because all this time you've suspected something?"

I don't know what to say. "I . . . No." I look down. "I—I went to thank her. For saving my life. And because . . . because I wanted . . . to know more about who she is."

"Oh, Bucino." She looks at me gently for a while, but whatever more she sees—and I know it is there to be seen—she lets it be. It makes me ashamed, for she is more generous with me than I ever was with her.

All that day we wait, though neither of us, I think, really knows what we are waiting for. For her to come to us to ask forgiveness? To plead for her bones back? Or maybe she is waiting for

us to come to her and make our own demands. The price of a
ruby for a bag of bones. But nothing happens. Outside, the city
goes slowly back to work. A Genoese merchant in town for the
fair and leaving the next day arrives at our casa on the chance
that my lady might dine with him tonight, for he has read some
new poetry about her in the Register of Courtesans. But when
she turns him down (or rather I do) on the excuse of a prior en-
gagement, he looks almost relieved and, I daresay, goes home to
bed. The city has been celebrating for a long time now, and
everyone, it seems, is tired.

We both sleep early and the next morning we both know we
have to go to her. My lady veils herself, and Marcello takes us,
for over the years it is he who has ferried messages to the baker's
shop in the *campo* whenever we need her. He drops us at the
quayside a few bridges up from the damming of the canal and
settles down to wait.

Though it is past the first work bell, the streets are still sluggish. A man pushes past us, swearing to himself as he goes. It is
as if the city has a communal sore head after the celebrations.
This is not the time to get into disagreements, for tempers will
flare easily. On the bridge leading to the back of her house, a
sullen mule is pulling a cart with barrels filled with black slop.
Both my lady and I are dressed modestly enough, but I can feel
her nervous next to me. It is a while since she has walked the
poorer parts of town, and her elegance and my size will in-
evitably draw attention to us.

In the dank canal, the dredging has begun. Half a dozen
men are up to their waists in the middle of the silt, black as
demons, shoveling up evil clods of sludge with cloths tied
around their mouths to save them from the stench that the digging unleashes. It will go on for weeks, this process. A couple of
them look up as we pass, and one yells something. Now that the
city is running out of volunteers to man its galleys, it has taken
to using criminals instead: there are some jobs that even hunger
will not sell. We cross quickly and make our way into her alley.
I count the doors to reach hers, though I know it well enough.
There is no outside lock on now, but if she is in, it will be bolted

from behind, as it was when I first came. So I am unnerved when it pushes open at my touch.

My lady glances fast at me, and we move in together. The gloom dulls our sight, so our first working sense is smell. The air is pungent with strong herbs and the high sourness of decaying animal matter. This is the room of her remedies, and my poker, mixed with my panic, sent a few flying off the shelves. What option did I have? When something cannot be reached easily, you pull at it as best you can, and the book could have been anywhere. But here, everywhere we step, our feet crunch glass and stick on thick puddles of liquid, and as our eyes accustom themselves to the light, I take in a room in a state infinitely worse than I left it. Vanilla mixed with rooster hearts, rosemary soaked in urine. I never caused this much destruction. Every single pot and vial is off the shelf, smashed into bits on the floor. Chairs and a small table are axed, the stove is pulled apart, even the fireplace has been emptied, with ashes and soot flung all around.

Beside me I register her shock. "I didn't do this," I say quickly. "This—this wasn't me."

The door that leads to her bedroom is smashed open, one hinge lying loose. From the threshold we can already see that the bed is in pieces, the floor like a barn with straw and matting everywhere. And the chest . . . well, even with it empty, I could not have lifted it. But someone could. Did. Axed it into bits and shredded every bit of clothing in it. Whoever came after me was not interested in finding anything they might have lost. Nevertheless, they took something away with them. I look everywhere, but I cannot find them: either the notebook or the wooden box. And I know right away the depth of the trouble. I move back hurriedly into the other room.

"Jesus, which devil's ass did you spring from?"

The man is blocking the outer door from the street, another at his shoulder. Big and caked black, both of them, devils pulled out of the slime.

My lady recovers before I do. "I . . . We are looking for Elena Crusichi."

"Why?"

"Because my dwarf suffers from his gut and Elena was due to visit him this morning." Her voice is as clear as glass. She may have come out of a Venetian slum, but she has risen to live in the *piano nobile* of a great casa.

"And what does she give you for that, squat fart?"

He is staring at me. Was he in the *campo* yesterday? If so, he might recognize me. I play the idiot and start to groan and whimper, rolling my hands over my gut.

"Oh, he has no idea. Alas, he is a simpleton," my lady cuts in impatiently. "Where is she?"

"She is taken."

"Taken? By whom?"

"By the security forces."

"When? Why?"

"This morning, early. For murder and witchcraft."

"Oh, but that's absurd. She is known by everyone as a healer."

"Not to people around here she isn't. There are women lining up to swear she was stiffing the Devil."

Yes, and I bet I know which ones would head the line. If Venice were built like any other city, I swear its gossip would be less poisonous. My lady feels the mood well enough too and is making ready for us to leave. "Well, it seems we must go and find help elsewhere."

"Before you 'run' away . . ." He takes a step closer, and even in this stink of medicines, he reeks of the canal. "It's my job to take down details of anyone who visits her. For evidence."

I groan again and move my legs tight together. "My lady!"

She glances at me. "You must hold on as best you can, Antonio. I must say, sir, for a church officer you have a strange smell."

"And for a rich lady you are a long way away from home," he says, and the smile is not one of charity.

"Madam!" I yelp.

She moves into her purse and brings out a silver coin. Then, seeing the man behind, another. It is more than he would earn digging out a dozen canals, and more than he ever dreamed the scam would get him. I read that in his eyes. Indeed, it is so much it might even make him greedy. So I let out a great fart, just in case he should harbor any thought of a double cross.

"Aagh! You disgusting monkey. Get out of here, both of you."

He moves aside, and she sweeps past them like a ship under sail with me as her rolling dinghy.

I limp down the street as best I can while still being in the throes of manufactured gut rot. We make our way toward the boat via the *campo* to avoid the canal, and as we do I glance in the direction of the bakery. Two young women are coming out: one is the girl to whom I gave the silver ducat. My God, how long ago was that? She waves and is across to greet me before I can get any farther.

"Hello, sweet little man." She giggles first at me and then at my lady, for her presence makes me even more a man of substance. "How are you?"

"Well," I say. "I am well."

"You haven't come to see La Draga again?"

"Er, no."

"That's good. For she's been taken. As a witch."

"A witch? Why, what happened?"

"The men digging out the canal found some bones stuck in the mud outside her house."

And I know it, of course, because it is what I have been fearing as I acted my way along the street.

"They say the bones came from babies. Ones that she pulled from the womb. They say the Devil has been visiting her. The woman across the canal saw him two nights ago, climbing out of her window in the shape of a great dog. When they heard that, they took her away."

CHAPTER THIRTY-THREE

"You are right. It would be madness."

"Oh, then you tell him. I swear, he won't listen to me."

"What? Do you want your balls cut off and fed to the pigs, Bucino? They may have been underused recently, but it's as well to keep them on your person for the future."

I take a breath, for I am tired of hearing my voice say the same thing. "I am not out to risk my balls. All I'm saying is, if they know I was the dog, then they cannot accuse her of sleeping with the Devil."

"The Devil, no, but you are still a deformity consorting with a witch."

"There was no consorting, for God's sake. She was not even there."

"I know that. You know that. But why should anyone believe it when the alternative is so much more juicy?"

"And what about the bones? Your confession can't help with the bones." My lady's voice is more worried than angry now, for, like me, she is caught between the need to save our skins and the desire to help La Draga.

"On their own, the bones don't mean anything," I say firmly, for I have spent hours thinking myself into the mind of the church inquisitors, acting the advocate on her behalf. "Canals throw up bits of old corpses every time they are dredged. Everybody in Venice knows that. Any woman living there for the last hundred years could have washed an early baby away in the mud."

"No, that will not do. Anyone 'could,' yes. But the fact is that there was a witch living there who did. Fiammetta is right, Bucino. If you continue to think like this, it will undo you. Your conscience—which I must say is a new and wondrous thing to behold—has made you stupid. We live not on truth, man, but on the power of gossip and malice, as you well know."

We are sitting in the beautiful loggia of our *portego*, which looks out over the water. The Sensa is a week over. The city is proud and busy, its dominion over the waters secure for another year and its coffers stuffed with the coins of a thousand visitors. All is well with the world. And no one wants to hear bad news. In fact, when the business is witchcraft, theft, and prostitution, there are few enough men anywhere to whom one can go for advice.

Yet for all his hunger for fame and riches, Aretino has an appetite for the underbelly as well as the surface, and though he pretends hardness, he is not without compassion.

"But I thought that in Venice . . . I mean, you are forever telling us the Church is not as bad here as other places. . . ."

"Nor is it. Not as vicious, or as corrupt. Because it is more independent of Rome—the government makes sure of that. Listen, if this were somewhere else, they'd probably be piling up the faggots between the pillars now: God knows, there are places where they burn witches as freely as candles. Even so, these are queasy times for Venice when it comes to heresy. For both Church and state. Or are you two too busy sinning with good Catholics to have noticed? I seem to recall you don't take men of heretical faith as clients, so maybe you don't know what is happening in Germany."

"You mean Münster." My lady, though she spends more time on her face these days, still sees what is in front of her eyes.

"Münster! Yes. And a line of other cities going up in the flames of heresy and revolution."

He is right. Though Münster is the one that has them trembling. The freshest horror is always the best, and the story of Münster is as fresh as they come, newly arrived with the German merchants over the spring passes of the Alps. The fact is that the heretics, men *and* women, who took Münster were so mad for their new God that they defied not only the Church but also every rule and custom of government. Having butchered those who ran the town, they declared their own Republic of God, in which there was no wealth, no privately owned property, no kings or rulers over others, indeed, no laws at all. We had sat in this very room, my lady and I, and joked about the fact that a world of Münsters would have us out of business soon enough, since there is no marriage either and therefore no sin.

But a poor man's Heaven is a rich man's vision of Hell, and when the German princes finally starved and blasted them into submission, they matched savagery for savagery, ripping the flesh off the preachers and sticking their carcasses up in cages around the spires of the cathedral so that their slow rotting would act as a lesson to others.

"What? You don't really think the Crows fear that kind of revolution could come here, do you?"

"No! This Anabaptist nonsense is more for rabid scholars and paupers. Venice is far too comfortable to need to fear heresy, especially because the Lutherans show such a talent for trade. But for that very reason, the city must also still be seen to be pure in its faith. Hence this latest decree against blasphemy and curses, which we all know is as much about their nervousness over vice as it is about the promotion of the true faith. It's unlucky timing for your healer, for she may get caught in its undertow. Fiammetta is right. Even if you told them the truth—that you were there because you thought she stole your ruby from you six years ago—that still makes her a thief and you a courtesan's dwarf consorting with a woman accused of child murder and witchcraft with a house full of stinking unctions and a book of spells written in code. It wouldn't save her, and it could very well damn you all."

"So what will they do?"

"Look, my specialty is the life of whores, not witches. I don't know what they will do. They will put her on trial—"

"Will they hurt her?"

"God's blood, man, of course they'll hurt her. They hurt everyone who hurts the state, you know that. What—are you soft in the head as well as in the groin now, Bucino?"

"Don't mock him, Pietro." My lady is quiet now that she has got her way. "La Draga saved his life. You know that. And though it seems she stole from us, she has also been good to us for a long time."

"Hmm. Well, I know what it is like to nearly die. Still, you would do better to let her go. Or make your representation from behind the court rather than in front of it. If you have someone in your bed who can influence justice, Fiammetta, give him a particularly good time and then ask for a favor. But if you stick your head above the parapet, don't blame me if it gets blown off."

It is dark. Aretino is gone, and my lady is at work in bed, lying next to our old shipman, helping him to huff and puff his way to a kind of leaky pleasure. Loredan, our influential Crow, is due to dine with us in a few days' time. La Draga is neither dead nor condemned yet, and there is nothing we can do but wait. And while there is not enough wine in the world to take away the horror of what may be to come, there is enough in my stomach right now to dull the panic for a while.

The night is warm, and I am sitting outside watching black boats glide through black water, their lamps like guiding fireflies in the night. There is chatter and laughter carried on the air. Aretino sees it well enough: Germany may be aflame, but Venice is far too comfortable for revolution. It never fails to perplex me, this city: the way it believes its own propaganda. In Rome, men said all kinds of things about civic greatness, but privately—even publicly sometimes—they could always acknowledge the smell of rot. Not here. Here we live in the greatest state in Christendom; powerful, rich, peaceful, just, and inviolate, the virgin city that no enemy can penetrate, which is strange enough considering that men come here from all over the world with the express intent of penetrating wherever and whatever they can, virgin or not.

Of course it is myth. If Heaven were on earth, why would men need to die to get there? And yet . . . and yet . . . in some ways it is also true, which is the most perplexing thing of all.

There's a book that is argued over in educated circles nowadays. By a Florentine named Niccolò Machiavelli, a man who was thrown out of government and subjected to the *strappado* and who used his exile to write a treatise about the art of governing, which he sees as based less on Christian ideals than on pragmatism. For him, the most successful rulers control by force and fear rather than consent. When I read it first, I found it fine enough, for men, I think, are much as he describes them, more susceptible to punishment than to kindness. Still—for all that my natural disposition is that of the cynic, I do not think that is how Venice works. Of course men are frightened of power (God knows, at this moment we are terrified of it ourselves—but I will not think of that now), but it's not just fear that keeps this state intact. Once again, Aretino is right. Venice is too comfortable for revolution. And not just for those who rule it either. Even poverty here, it seems, is more bearable than in other places. Yes, there are often more beggars than can be sustained, but while those who come from outside the city are subject to exile after a good whipping, if you are born here and sit on church steps with your hand out, as long as you stay in your own parish, no one will cut it off, and you will be given alms enough to exist, if not to live. And while you may be hungry, there is always another festival to look forward to, to be caught up in its ceremony and splendor, to have the chance to exploit its drunken charity. It would not be enough for me, but then I live on my wits, not the stumps of my arms or legs.

For the rest, the professionals who follow trades or risk their lives on business—well, each and every one of them has a confraternity that looks after its own. Pay your dues and the confraternity will pay you back: help with your daughter's dowry, support you if you lose your job, even cough up for your funeral if you can't and supply mourners to swell the procession. So what if you cannot be part of government? At least you have enough independence not to feel ruled and enough money to enjoy it. Every cog in this wheel of state is well oiled and maintained, so that as long as the ships keep coming in and the money keeps flowing, who would want to live anywhere else?

Who—except the criminals? And yet even here, even with its reputation for severity and violence in justice—thieves and frauds flayed and losing their limbs between the Pillars of Justice, traitors and heretics flung into the deep—it is not without some understanding of clemency. Aretino is right about this too. In all the years I have been here, while I have seen enough murderers strung up and left to twitch, I have never smelled witch flesh on a pyre. Though I daresay the bones of small souls snuffed out before birth will qualify fast enough as murder at a time when the world has grown so afraid of slandering God.

The wine bottle is empty now, and I am too blurred to fetch another. But not so blurred that I cannot still tell black from white, hopelessness from hope. We cannot help her without hurting ourselves. Worse: even by hurting ourselves we cannot help her. I have spun it every which way, like juggling plates on the stick, and they all crash to the ground. If the Devil as a dog at her window turned out to be a dwarf with a talent for housebreaking, it would make no difference: she would still go down for the bones and the book and the dogs' paws and the astrological signs and the gossip that will grow now like fungus—the young girl who cured fits with the ashes of a sodomite, the woman who washes wombs free from unwanted babies, the witch who binds men's pricks with holy water and incantations. God knows, I believed some of it myself. God knows, some of it is true. Venice, after all, is the mistress of the market: if someone wants something enough, then someone else will make money from providing it, be it silk, sin, or witchcraft. A woman buys a new dress to attract a lover, only to find herself pregnant with his baby while she is still a virgin or her husband is away on business. What can she do? Some flush out early babies in blood naturally and we call it God's will. For others, desperate for such a release, La Draga is a substitute. The result is the same. No baby. How much worse is her intervention than the acts of the men and women who practice the sin of sodomy in marriage to avoid conception? I think it is less the act than what we call it.

Similarly, when we are afflicted and there is no remedy, the Church tells us that suffering is good: the will of God again. Yet which one among us would not stop the pain if we could? Drink this cup of herbs and blood and you will feel better. Is the Devil in the herbs, the blood, or the woman who prepares them? As for the business of love and obsession: well, since any man with a head on his shoulders knows it to be a disease that infects the mind as well as the body, a clever poet can be as dangerous as a witch when it comes to spreading or attacking the affliction. So La Draga is a witch. I am a pimp. My lady is a prostitute. We are all guilty. The difference is that she is exposed for it. For which I am to blame. But my sacrifice will do nothing, only incriminate my lady as well as myself. Once a courtesan is publicly arraigned, even on the whisper of witchcraft, her bed becomes as contaminated as her reputation.

And were it not for my lady? If the sacrifice was only mine? Would I do it then? Try to help this thief and fraud? This liar? This woman who held me in her arms and saved my life? Even if I could not save hers in return, at least she would know that I had tried, that it was never my intention to have her so damned.

So would I do it? I cannot answer that. For I do not know. All I do know is that every time I think of her my stomach fills with bile, but whether it is for her betrayal or her suffering I cannot tell, for the panics of them both have somehow become interwoven in me.

And this confusion, I swear, has nothing to do with the wine.

CHAPTER THIRTY-FOUR

The days pass slowly. Men come and go, but our Crow sends messages that he is delayed on government business. Gabriella, who grows seemingly more innocent the longer she serves in a house of sin, is sent out with Marcello to the office of the church prison to inquire after her cousin, a young woman from the Celestia district who was taken by the church officers ten days before. The news she brings tells us mostly what we already knew. A woman, Elena Crusichi, has been arraigned for witchcraft, with depositions from the Church and witnesses, and she is to be brought to trial when the evidence is ready. She has been moved from the local district prison to the central one, beneath the Doge's Palace, and is being held there at the expense of the state, which means that she will slowly starve— Venice is as canny as anywhere else when it comes to questions of money and justice. Food will be allowed in from outside from relatives, but only if it is shown not to contain anything that might help her in her spells or Devil worship.

If we cannot free her, we can at least keep her well fed. From now on, Mauro will be cooking for a prison as well as a whore-house.

He is already under pressure. Tonight, at last, Lord Loredan is to visit, and since it is well known that his juices flow as freely from his palate as from his prick, Mauro has the job of producing the first climax, to which end he is now clucking away in the kitchen, as loud as the capon that, roasted with orange and cinnamon sauce, will make up one of the dishes. After that, assuming our lordship can still locate his prick under all the food in his belly, it will be up to my lady.

Though La Draga's fate has affected us all—even Gabriella has lost something of her sparkle—my lady has subdued her anxiety to her will, throwing herself into business and the task of making herself irresistible again. In this way, while she cannot keep her lover, she might yet save her friend. She is as much in charge of the household as I am now, and her energy almost gives me hope. She has spent the whole day in her own kitchen with pastes and perfumes, creams and tweezers. Her skin is swan-white and smooth as silk, her breasts push out like rising full moons from a dark velvet sunset, and her smell is jasmine with a hint of musk rose underneath. Most men would give her anything she asked just to have the pleasure of watching her unlace her bodice. But Loredan is a man born to privilege, someone who expects rather than enjoys perfection, and he has been known to come and leave without a single compliment passing his lips (though he is not so stingy with his purse).

The fact is, apart from his ability to pay on time, I know little about our great Crow, or what he does when he is ruling Venice. All I know are the harsh little cries he makes when in the throes of his pleasure: staccato bursts that I have come to liken to the sharp cawing of his namesake bird. Some of our regulars bring their worries and triumphs with them (when business is good, Alberini offers miracles of reflection or transparency; when it is bad or a shipment arrives broken and the bill is on him to replace it, he growls and complains as if my lady were his wife rather than his paramour). But Loredan leaves the affairs of state in the chambers of the Doge's Palace: while he is happy to talk of Venice as an ideal, the facts he keeps to himself. As a member of one of the greater families, those who in effect rule the rulers, he is, I don't doubt, both a diligent servant of the state, serving where he is elected, and a politician who uses his family influence to bribe or buy the votes he needs to get himself exactly where he wants to be. While he is no longer at the very heart of the matter—his place on the great Council of Ten expired a few months ago—there is no one he does not know, and if there is a scandal to be revealed or concealed, he will surely have intelligence of it. As to his capacity for sympathy— well, he has been known to be generous with what is in his power to give, such as an invitation to the Sensa. But this . . . God only knows what he can or will do.

Though we too will know soon enough.

He comes usually at twilight and leaves in the early hours. But tonight he is late, so that she and I are as nervous as caged dogs by the time he arrives. I sit in my room while she entertains, a book on my lap but no words going into my head. Sometime after midnight I hear the boat push off, the call of his boatman as he moves into the main channel. I wait for her to come out. Finally I go to her. She is sitting looking out onto the water, her hair a great storm around her shoulders in the way I remember it from that catastrophic night in Rome when she screwed the enemy to save our lives. Soldiers and bureaucrats. Always the toughest of clients. She turns, and I can almost read their encounter in her eyes.

"There was nothing I could say, Bucino. He knew about it all already."

"How? What does that mean?"

"I don't know, except that it is being talked about. In the government. That much is clear. The trial starts next week, before church officials and a representative of the state court."

"What else did he say?"

"Ooh—that the laws on blasphemy and cursing are there to protect the state against the spread of disorder and heresy. And that the murder of babies, in or out of the womb, is a serious offense. My God, and that was after I had serviced him! I swear his head is back in the council chamber before his seed is dry on the sheets." She laughs bitterly. "And I am supposed to be good at my job."

"It's not your fault. He was always a cold fish. We celebrated his status, not his amiability. What did you tell him?"

"That she had healed my neighbor's child and that I had offered to intercede for her. I don't know if he believed me. I didn't tell it very well." She laughs again. "For six years I have been his way of relaxing after the rigors of government. He has never seen me cry before, and I don't think he knew quite what to do with it."

She stops, and we both know the tears are still close by. She is not used to failing with men, my lady, and in different ways she has experienced more of it in these past few weeks than in many years. But now is not the time for her to be felled.

She shakes her head impatiently. "He said he would do what he could. And as far as that goes, I think he will. Aretino is right, Bucino. There is a palpable nervousness in the air. He was distracted all evening, even before I took him to bed. When I asked him why he was so busy and delayed, he said it was for-eign business, and when I tried to find out more, he closed up like a clam again. But when Fausto was here the other night, he told me that the Turks are harassing Venetian ships again and that no one wants to admit to the losses."

La Serenissima. The tension underneath the serenity.

So what do we do now? We don't need to ask the question, for the answer is clear to both of us. We must wait and see.

CHAPTER THIRTY-FIVE

Marcello and I take the food daily, docking the boat at the edge of the wharf to the left of the Pillars of Justice and making our way across the *piazzetta* to the side entrance of the prison. I have come to appreciate a certain symmetry in the architecture of justice and punishment that I hadn't noticed until now: not just the fact that the scaffold is constructed in full view of the Doge's Palace but that the palace which houses those who make the law also incarcerates those who break it. Though in this, as in everything else, there is a hierarchy. With enough money, you can buy tenure in one of the cells whose grilles look out onto the *piazzetta* itself, from where you will enjoy fresh air and a view of the pillars, which with money and good counsel you will not end up between. I swear there are beggars who would swap homes with these inhabitants, for along with eating their own food, they even get to entertain friends and relatives. On more than one occasion I've seen noblemen charged with fraud, or some such, playing cards or in conversation with young-bloods or even the occasional well-dressed lady.

Those with less influence and no money are buried in the danker cells under the floors, and while they may not hear the agonies of the men and women who are strung up outside, no doubt we cannot hear theirs either. I still remember my old well historian telling me how when they burned a notorious gang of sodomites—which was the greatest crime, for some of them were nobles and their association smacked of insurgence against the government—they garroted the Crows before the fire hit them but left the poorer, prettier boys with whom they had played to do the screaming.

At the prison entrance, we give the food to the jailer and—on Aretino's advice (his low-life connections are impeccable)—slip a coin half under the pot to make sure it gets to her. I have asked a dozen times if I might see her to be assured that she is being fed, but my jiggling charm gets me nowhere and the answer is always the same: those accused of heresy are confined alone and allowed to see no one.

Our days grow darker as the summer sun lifts higher in the sky.

Two mornings ago my lady's young lover left on a round galley bound for Cyprus. He spent a last night with her before he went. I shook his hand when he came in and asked his forgiveness for my bad behavior. He seemed almost embarrassed—for all her experience, he is still only a pup—but it was important to me that we made our peace. What passed between them I have no idea, except that the sounds which came from her room that night were as much about pain as about passion and the next day she did not emerge until the sun was already down. I, who would do anything to ease her sorrow, was useless. I know she was missing La Draga dreadfully. As a man who has lived so long with women, I have learned that there are times when they are the only ones who can help one another.

I miss La Draga too. Not just for the moment, but for all the moments before when I chose not to recognize her.

The trial, once it has begun, takes place behind closed doors in one of the council chambers of the palace. For the first few days I stand outside the entrance to see if I can spot the witnesses arriving, sustained by the fantasy that if I recognize the woman who accosted La Draga in the square I could show her how much damage a devil with dog's teeth might do to a liar. But the palace swallows hundreds of people daily—the governors and the governed—and one angry old woman looks much like another.

After a while gossip starts to spring like so many leaks from an old pipe: that one of her accusers had lost a baby in her eighth month and later found rusty nails and extracted teeth under her pillow, a sure sign of witchcraft. Yet La Draga admits nothing, and her defense—a quiet, clear logic—has at times caused offense to those adjudicating. Also, that to test her veracity, she has been subjected to the torture of the rope, though it would seem it has not changed her testimony.

I, who am not much of a praying man—I have never quite understood if I am talking to God or to myself—have grown into the habit of addressing Loredan instead. His strangled croaks of pleasure echo in the night with monotonous regularity as my lady saves her greatest ingenuity for the one who has the influence. I think the longing left in her for the pup she now feeds into Loredan. He must feel it, because she is incandescent with beauty and tenderness, and despite his seeming implacability, he is not a cruel man. I know he has registered the anxiety of the household; even professionals cannot pretend joy when there is so much sorrow. It was he who, when the rumors of trial began to circulate, went out of his way to assure my lady that the court's treatment of La Draga was moderate given the temper of the times and that the rope was used only sparingly.

A few days ago while he was at dinner, I helped serve and engaged him in conversation about reform of the Church and Contarini's history of the state, and we talked about the emphasis of charity over devotion and the role of purity in just government. I doubt he was fooled by my passion when it came to the power of clemency within justice, but I think he enjoyed the discussion, for his arguments shone through well enough.

It would be easier if we were ruled by fools; then at least we would expect nothing. I don't think I have ever been so afraid.

On the afternoon of the sixth day, I am returning home from delivering the food when I spot a well-dressed boat docked at our entrance. There are no suitors booked until evening, and my lady would not entertain newcomers without my vetting

them first. As I cross in through the water doors, I hear footsteps coming down the stairs, and the figure of the Turk
emerges in front of me, turban tall, in rich, flowing robes.

We have not seen each other since that day he saved me
from drowning and the bird's talons sank themselves into my
ears. My God—how many aeons ago was that?

"Ah, Bucino Teodoldi. I had hoped I might see you before I
go." And his smile is broad. "I was . . . visiting your lady."

"You were?"

He laughs. "Don't worry. I am not to be put in your precious
account book. We had business to discuss. I had wanted to
come before to ask after your health, but . . . there have been
other things demanding my attention. Tell me, how are you?"

"Alive."

"In body, yes, but not, I think, so much in spirit."

"I—I am burdened by a certain worry, that is all," I say.

"Ah. Such is the way of the times. I am come partly to say
good-bye. I have been recalled to the court. The relations between our two great states have grown sour again, and while we
are not yet at war, it is clear I will not be welcome here much
longer." There is a pause. "I shall miss teaching you my language." And he pauses again, no doubt to give me more time to
change my mind. "But I think perhaps you make the right
choice. While Venice may not appreciate you, there are those
who are fond enough." He holds out his hand to me. "Take care
of yourself, my little friend. I have enjoyed your company."

"And I yours." I take his hand, and as I do so I see an image
of a city filled with elephants and fountains, peacocks, mosaics,
and tightrope walkers, and I wonder for a flickering instant
what the great Constantinople might have offered me. But it is
only an instant; it passes.

Upstairs, my lady is in the *portego* in deep conversation with
Gabriella. But she stops as she sees me and dismisses the maid.

On her way out, Gabriella's eyes do not meet mine. My gut
squeezes with panic.

"What is it? What has happened?"

"Bucino, come." My lady holds out her hand to me, smiling.

Her eyes are bright, but she is an expert at faking enthusiasm when she feels none and I am too eaten up by nerves to know the difference anymore between wild hope and despair. "You look tired. Do your legs hurt? Sit down with me."

"My legs are fine." On the table I notice the rich red leather binding of Petrarch, the silver lock twirled into place. "Why is the book here? Has something happened? Tell me."

"I—I have heard from Loredan. It—it seems he can get us access to visit her in prison. Only it involves money, a payment, a kind of bribe. . . ."

A bribe. Of course. The lubricant that oils every position and principle in this pure state. You are baying at the moon, Gasparo Contarini—for this city is already sold to the Devil.

"How much?"

She opens a small drawer in the desk and slides a purse across the surface to me. I pick it up, I who can tell the shape and the weight of a ducat through material better than most men. It is not a small amount.

"Where did you get it?"

"It doesn't matter."

My eyes fall back to the book.

"It's not what you think," she says hurriedly. "I haven't jeopardized our future. I haven't sold the book." She pauses. "Merely . . . extracted a few pages."

"What?"

"I—I have removed two of the prints, and the sonnets to go with them."

"For whom?"

But of course I already know.

"My God, you sold them to the Turk. How—"

"Listen to me, Bucino. It made sense. I know how we live hand-to-mouth, and this was too great an amount for us to raise alone. If I had tried to sell the whole book, there would have been no time to find the right bidder for the right price and the city would have been alive with gossip. But then I heard the Turk was leaving, and I went to visit him. The sultan's appetite for novelty is famous, and since he has more women than I have men, I thought he'd enjoy the company of a few lascivious Romans. This way we keep the bulk of the book intact and raise the money we need. Your Turk was most generous."

"But why didn't you tell me about it? We should have discussed it."

"Because . . ." She stops. "Because you would have seen it as too great a risk for our future and said no."

Is she right? The old Bucino would have refused, certainly. As to what this new one might have done, I have no idea, for she has done it for me.

"Aretino? Does he know?"

"Abdullah Pashna was his idea. He says by rights he owns only one of the engravings anyway. For without us they wouldn't exist at all."

Ah, my Turk is right. There are those here who are fond enough of me.

"I doubt your mother would approve," I say quietly.

She shrugs. "My mother died alone of the pox. That's what putting business above the heart did for her. You are lucky. Abdullah would have given a lot more for you, you know. But, as we are partners, I told him you were not for sale."

"Oh, thank God for you, Fiammetta Bianchini." I laugh.

"Bucino"—she puts her hand over mine—"I am sorry . . . but there is something else you must know."

What? Had I expected that they would let her walk free? Disregard the bones, forget the book, forgive the amulets and potions, the signs and incantations, block their ears to the poison of Devil gossip? The fact is that La Draga was guilty before the law long before she was arraigned in any courtroom. I am not so stupid or so love struck that I didn't know that. But then so are a thousand others, equally guilty, and how many of those go on to die in their own beds? There is not a state in Christendom where justice isn't a commodity as salable as a shipment of silk or a woman's virginity. You just have to know the price and the people to pay it to. Not a state in Christendom.

Except, it seems, for Venice.

Our great Crow says he did what he could. That is what he

told my lady, and that is what she believes. She says he did not need to tell her ahead of the verdict being announced, but he wanted to warn us. There have, it seems, been "discussions" about this case; while the potions and divinations on their own might have been seen as misguided faith, the bones have condemned her. They and the fact that she consorted openly with prostitutes and courtesans. Though in all of this it is only rumor, for she would give no facts and no names. It is, as Aretino said, a question of timing as much as guilt. With instability building abroad, the state must feel unassailable at home. All these things have conspired to make the verdict harsh but inevitable. The verdict and the sentence.

"But he can and will intercede here, Bucino. That he absolutely promised me. She will not burn, do you hear me? She will not burn, and neither will she suffer unduly."

Not suffer unduly. And for this, it appears, we must be grateful. God damn the complacency of his mercy, the foul righteousness of his justice. It is as well La Draga is not freed, or I would have a potion from her that would have his prick drop off the next time he tried to use it. I am so angry that my head hurts. But for now, when he comes, I must simper and smile and thank him for his boundless generosity, for the fact is, without his intercession, we will never get ourselves through the prison bars.

Yet in the end, it is not we who go.

The next evening, just before dusk, I clamber ahead of my lady onto the boat, the purse hidden deep in my doublet, and put out my hand to help her on, as is my wont, so the world can see how much I am her servant. But she smiles and shakes her head.

"I cannot come with you, Bucino. The intercession that Loredan has arranged allows for only one visitor. And however much we pay them, there will be some gossip. For that reason it cannot be me. No—" She stops my protest at the same instant it leaves my mouth. "This is not a matter for discussion. It is already decided. You are the one who is expected at the gate. I will wait here for you. Go now."

CHAPTER THIRTY-SIX

He is a different man from the one to whom I have delivered her food each day. This one smirks when he sees me—no doubt there are a million jokes to be made about a dwarf visiting a witch—but it seems that not all men who do foul jobs are made foul by them, and whatever his thoughts, he keeps them to himself. He lets me into a small courtyard, where another man meets me and takes me through a door down one, then a second, then a third set of stairs. The little light that was left in the day is snuffed as we descend. This far below ground it is perpetual night. Here a third jailer is waiting, this one built like a barrel and smelling as foul as his prisoners, though as much from stale beer as from the stench of his own body. He looks at me as if I am a cockroach until the purse is on the table. He empties it and stacks the coins into three separate piles. Three jailers, three piles. He counts them again, then looks up at me, sneering. "Where's the rest?"

There was a time when men his size frightened me, as much for the bluntness of their brains as for the force of their fists. But now I don't care. Now I just think of them as pieces of meat with mouths attached. God take their souls, if he can find them.

"Up your ass," I say, grinning.

He growls at me for a moment, as if he might flatten my head against the wall, then he starts to laugh and moves over and slaps me on the shoulder as if I were his long-lost brother, and suddenly he is as sweet as tooth rot, offering me wine and insisting on bringing extra candles and a stool with us as he takes me to the cell, so I will not have to sit on the floor.

I follow him down the black corridor. We pass maybe a dozen chambers, each the size of a pigpen, the smoky light of his two candle lamps throwing up the occasional figure curled on the floor or in the corner, but no faces, and I am suddenly more scared of my own footsteps than I could ever be of his belligerence. The dark, the smell, the dankness. My God, why should anyone be afraid of dying if this is what passes for life? He has to count the cells to be sure he has reached the right one, and he puts down the candles as he opens the lock.

I walk inside. At first I think there is no one here. Then, in the gloom, I make out a small figure sitting on a pallet at the back of the cell, her body facing the wall. She—What shall I call her now? For she is no longer La Draga in my mind. She, Elena, does not look up or move in any way as I come in. I glance at the jailer, and he shrugs, dumping the stool and one of the candle lamps next to me and clanging the door behind him. The keys chatter loudly in the lock.

I move in front of her, adjusting the candle so that I can make out her face. Her eyes are in a terrible state; that much I can see from the start. They are swollen; one is almost closed, and the other is twitching and full of puss, and she blinks it constantly.

"Elena?"

No response.

"Elena. Can you see me? I'm here. Right in front of you."

She puts her head to one side and frowns a little. "Ha! Is that the Devil or a dog?"

And because we were never familiar enough to laugh together, I am scared for an instant that this might be madness rather than humor.

"Neither. It is me, Bucino." I take a breath. "Remember?"

She makes a small noise. "Then you had better wear white from now on and make sure you walk upright or you could be mistaken for both."

I cannot help but laugh, but then nerves take men in different ways. From somewhere close, the next cell, I hear a thud, then the voice of a woman, moaning.

"Are you . . . I . . . How are you?"

Her face is half sneer, half smile. Each and every one of its gestures I have seen a thousand times before, and yet something closes in my throat to watch them now. "I am a witch, you know. Yet I can't free myself by flying out of the window."

"I . . . There is no window in here," I say gently.

She makes an impatient little noise with her tongue. "I know that, Bucino. So how did you get in?"

"Money. Fiammetta interceded through her great Crow, and we paid money to the guards."

"Ah."

"We would have paid money to the court also, I mean, to try to stop it, only—"

"—only they would have none of it. It is all right. I know. They were most proud of their sternness."

"Yet people say you were as clever as they."

She shrugs. "She swore it was the Devil's dog coming from my window when everyone knew she could barely see past the ends of her own fingers. In the court, when I asked her, she couldn't tell the judge from the statue next to him."

She makes a crooked little smile at the memory of it. The light is better now, or my eyes better adjusted. Her face is grimy with dirt. Except for the rivulet of tears that leaks out from one of her eyes. I want so much to lift up my hand and wipe it clear. I watch as she tries to twitch the pain away.

"You have been getting the food we send, yes?"

She nods, though it doesn't look if she has eaten much of it.

"Did they tell you it was from us? We have done everything we could for you."

"They said I had 'a benefactor.'" She pronounces the last word as if it was almost a libation. "'A benefactor for a malefactor.' Then they said 'good for bad,' because they didn't think I'd understand it. They thought my notebook was written by the Devil until I told them the code. They read some of it in court—it was a remedy for constipation. Perhaps I should have charged them for it."

"I doubt it would have helped. Shit builds up again fast in some people."

She smiles at my crudeness. "How is she? Is Foscari gone?"

"Yes," I say. "She is . . . she is lost without you."

"I don't think so." She blinks fast a number of times again. "She still has you."

I watch another spasm of pain cross her face. I take a breath. "What of your eyes, Elena? What's happened to them?"

"It's an infection; it comes from the glass. I have had it for many years. There is a remedy I use, a liquid to soothe it. Without it . . . well, you'll be pleased to know that I see almost nothing now."

"Oh, no," I say. "No. It gives me no pleasure at all."

From the next cell the thudding comes again, and then the moaning, louder this time. Then, from somewhere else, a voice yells out abuse, a chorus of madness.

She lifts her head to the sound. "Faustina? Don't be frightened. You are safe. Lie down, try to sleep." And her voice is soft, like the one that spoke of glass souls to a dwarf drowning in pain. She turns back to me. "She bangs her head against the walls. She says it makes the thoughts go away."

The moans turn to a whimper, then stop. We sit for a moment, listening to the silence.

"I—I have brought you something."

"What?"

"Put your hand out."

As she does I see the bloodied marks left by the ropes on her wrists and lower arms.

"They are Mauro's sugared cakes. Each one has special syrup inside it, to help you."

"Who made up the dose?" And her head tilts upward in that way I know so well.

"You did. It's your recipe. From the one we mixed with grappa. Mauro made a syrup paste from it. He's tested them. One will dull pain and make you sleepy, two will drug you enough to . . . to rise above it."

She holds the parcel in the palm of her hand. "I . . . I think I will try a little now. But only half of one. Mauro's sauces were always rich for me."

I take one from her and break off a part—more than a half—and feed it to her slowly, mouthful by mouthful. She chews it carefully, and I see her smile slightly at its sweetness.

"They hurt you?" I put a finger onto the weal on her arm.

She looks down at it, as if somehow the arm belonged to someone else. "I've seen worse in others." She grunts. "It stopped me thinking about my eyes for a while."

"Oh, God, oh, Christ, I am sorry," I say, and once it starts, it comes out in a great river of anguish. "So sorry . . . I didn't inform on you, you must know that. . . . This is never what . . . I mean, I did break into your house, yes. After I saw you that day on Murano . . . I—I opened your chest, and I found the book and the glass circles. But I put them back, and I didn't show them or talk about them to anyone. As for the bones, well, I didn't—I mean . . . they were in my hand, and the sack fell as I was trying to move. . . . This was never meant to happen. . . ."

She is sitting very still now, in that way only she can, so much so that in the end it is her quietness which stops my chattering.

"Elena?"

"Don't talk about it anymore, Bucino. There is nothing to say. The glass is broken and the liquid is spilled. It's not important anymore." Her voice is quiet, no anxiety, no emotion at all, though it is too soon for the drug to be working. "The woman across the canal had been angry with me for a long time. I tried to help her with a baby that died in the womb. When I couldn't save it, she decided I'd killed it. She was shouting it loudly enough everywhere she went—it was only a matter of time before someone heard."

"What about the bones?" I say after a while. "Where did they come from?"

She says nothing. Now, in the set of her lips, for the first time I see an echo of the old La Draga, the one I used to fear, the one whose silence spoke of secrets and hidden powers. If she resisted the rope, she will surely resist me. Maybe they came from her? Or maybe, like a priest, she is keeping other people's secrets? God knows there are women enough in this city hiding swelling bellies under their skirts to save their reputations. And babies die as they are squeezed and spat out of the womb every day.

"You must have known they would condemn you for it?"

She shakes her head a little, and her face softens. "I never could tell the future, you know. I just threw the beans and told people what they wanted to hear. Easy money. As for the past, well, nobody can change that. Oh, you could charge a lot if you could do that. . . ." She falters. "Then I could have given you your ruby back. My grandfather said it was the best copy he ever made."

We sit for a moment without speaking. No doubt we are both remembering.

"Still, I was worried that you would notice before you took it to the Jew."

"Hah . . . Well, I didn't. You grandfather was right. It was a most superior fake."

"But you knew it was me, yes? Afterward, when you found out?"

I see us again, her sitting on the bed, frozen like an animal, me with my lips close to her ear. I remember the texture of her skin, the dark circles around her eyes, the way her lips trembled slightly. "Yes, I knew it was you." But the fact that I was right gives me no satisfaction now. "Was it your idea?"

She hesitates. "If you mean have I always been a thief, no."

"Why then?"

"Meragosa and I decided on it together."

"That's not what I meant."

"Why? I want to say it was because she found out about me. About my eyes and what I was doing, and, knowing it, she made me steal the stone." She stops. "But that's not how it was. We did it together because we could and because at the time— well, at the time I needed the money."

"So did you steal from her mother too?"

"No, no! I didn't. I never did that." And she is suddenly very agitated. "I knew nothing about her mother. Meragosa never came to me for help—and I could have helped, there were things I could have given to soothe the suffering. I told that to Fiammetta, and you must believe me. I knew nothing about her illness or death."

"It's all right, it's all right. I do believe you." I put my hand on hers to steady her, and for a while it rests there in silence. "I know you are not cruel."

"Oh, but I would have been to *you* if I could have, Bucino." And her voice has some of the old La Draga spirit in it now. "I was angry with you at the beginning. That much I do admit. Those first months I worked so hard for her—for both of you. But you never trusted me, never. As soon as her hair was grown, you would have had me out of your lives. Meragosa saw that as well as I did. We'd never have been good enough for the two of you. That was what she said."

Too late for lies now. Especially to myself. For all her foulness, Meragosa was right. We had come as a partnership, my lady and I. And I had been determined that no one would join us. Even those whom we needed most.

"If that's what you felt, why did you come back? You knew I suspected, yet you came and helped us again. My God, I was so impressed by you then."

She doesn't say anything. In the silence, the moaning returns. Now that I know what is happening, the force of the thud against the stone is almost worse than the cry that comes after it. Once, twice, then again and again.

"Faustina?" She moves her hand to locate the rest of the cake, then stands and shuffles her way to the bars. I get up to try to help. "Faustina. Can you hear me? Put your hand through the bars. Are you there?"

After a while in the gloom I see a long, thin arm stretch itself out, like the limb of some dismembered supplicant. Elena pushes the cake into the palm and closes the fingers over it. "Eat it. It is sweet, and it will make you sleep."

Now, as she moves back toward the bed, she puts her hand on my shoulder for support. I can't tell if it is weakness or the potion working.

"Your size makes you a good walking stick, Bucino. I often

wanted to lean on you when my back was hurting from pretending to be so bowed. But even when I stopped being angry
with you, I was too afraid of your grumpiness."

I watch as the smile moves over her face. She has always
teased me, right from the beginning. Yet there had also been an
edge to it, and in her as in me it was not only anger; it was as if
she was afraid of something in herself. See—I have always
known what she is feeling: anger, mischief, fear, guilt, triumph.
I have seen and read every emotion as it moved across her face.
Just as she must have done with mine. My God, how could we
have mistaken so much?

We sit together on the pallet now, though there is barely
enough straw in it to tell it from the floor, and she leans back
against the wall.

"I still don't understand. You stayed with us and helped us.
And you never took anything else," I say after a while.

"No . . ." She stops. "Though you have a rude fortune inside
your silver lock."

"What?"

"One-five-two-six."

"My God. When did you find it?"

"When do you think? When was I ever allowed into your
special chamber?"

"You broke the code?"

"I've always been good at things like that." She pauses. "Does
she use them for her men?"

"No. It is an investment. We will sell it to pay for our old
age."

"Then I hope you get a fat sum. When you get old, you'll
have to be careful with your joints, Bucino. They'll grow stiff
faster than most men's."

And her concern curdles my insides again. "Did you always
know so much about dwarves?"

"A little. I learned more after I met you."

"I wish . . . I wish I had taken more time to learn about you."

She shakes her head. "We haven't time for that now." She
puts out a hand, and it connects with the top of my head. "It's

not really an eggplant, you know," she says. "I only said it to get you angry that first time when you asked me how blind I was. Remember? Oh, you were always so eager to fight with me. . . ." And now, suddenly, I feel a shakiness in her. "I don't . . ."

"Shush." I bring my hand up and put it over hers again, then pick it up, holding it carefully between both of my own. I stroke her skin, running my finger gently along the wrist where they have applied the rope. "You're right. We don't need to talk about the past." Her fingers helped me so much. Made the ocean tides of pain drain away. I would give anything to do the same for her now.

"I think . . . I think I'm tired. Maybe I will lie down for a while."

I help her as she stretches out, and as I do the smell of her, sweet and sour, is like heady perfume all around me. I watch a long shiver pass across her form. "Are you cold?"

"A little. Will you lie with me? You must be tired too."

"I—I . . . Yes, yes I will."

I try so hard to be careful, arranging myself so I do not disturb her, but as soon as my body comes into contact with hers, I feel myself start to grow hard. My God, they say men get erections when they drop the trap on the scaffold. Did Adam have more control over his own body before the apple? I think if God wanted us to behave better, he should have helped us more. I draw away quickly so she will not feel me.

We lie that way for a moment, then, gently, I move my arm across and over her body. She takes my hand and holds it in hers.

Her voice, when it comes next, is sleepy, blurred with the power of the draft. "I'm afraid I was never good at such things, Bucino. I only ever did it a few times, and I never grew to like it." She lets out a long breath. "Still, I would not take it back. For her sake."

So at last I understand it all. Now, when it is too late. "Oh, I think you have little enough to regret," I say, and I squeeze her hand gently. "Believe me, I have seen enough of it by now to know it is more a thing of the body than a thing of the soul. You have done more for people in your life by taking away their pain than by giving them pleasure."

"You think so?" And I daresay, if she were not so tired, she might tell me more, for it is a conversation long overdue. But I can feel her slipping away. I pull her closer to me and hold her, feeling the rhythm of our breathing, rising, falling, until her body goes slack against mine. She sleeps. As does the sad Faustina in the cell next door. And, while it is not my intention, for I want to remember every second of this night, it seems that I sleep too.

Dawn does not penetrate underground stone, and the candle has long ago sputtered out. So it is noise that wakes me: his thumping footsteps and the angry clank of the keys. I sit up because I do not want to be found like this, but I cannot extract myself properly, for she has hold of my hand still and even in her sleep does not let it go.

He is at the door, his candle poking into our intimacy. "Time's up. I'm out of here, and if you don't go now you'll be underground for the rest of your life."

"Elena. Elena?"

I feel her moving beside me.

"Had a good time, eh?" He lifts the lamp above him so that it throws light on us both. "Well, everyone deserves a last fuck. Especially if they pay for it."

She is sitting up now, though her eyes are so caked and closed that I'm not sure she can see me at all.

"Elena," I whisper. "I have to go. I'm sorry. Listen to me. Remember the cakes. One for the pain and two . . . two or three for before they take you. . . . It will help. You can remember that, yes?"

"Hey! Get yourself out, quick now." Now that the money has run out, I am a cockroach again.

Only now it is I who cannot let go of her hand.

"It is all right, Bucino. It's all right." And she withdraws it gently herself. "We are not fighting anymore. You can go now."

I get up and walk stiff-legged through the half-open gate. I see the jailer's smirk. And at that moment I want to kill him, throw myself at him, sink my fangs into his neck, and watch the blood spurt.

"Bucino?"

Her voice calls me back.

"I . . . There is something I have to tell you. Her name . . . her name is Fiammetta." She stops for a second, as if it is all too much of an effort. "And I came back because I missed you. Both of you. And because I wanted to be part of it."

The door slams behind me, and she turns her face to the wall again.

CHAPTER THIRTY-SEVEN

I spend the night of her execution propped in my chair in the loggia, high enough to see the water, the rooftops low enough to catch the first gray before sunrise. Time moves slowly. I do not sleep, and I do not think. Or if I do, I cannot remember what or about whom. I am up in anticipation long before the moment. The hour before the dawn always has an edge to it. The hour of the last wager, the hour of the final intimacies of the night, the hour of prayer before the matins bell.

The house is silent as I move down the stairs to the bottom and out onto the wooden dock. The current slaps carelessly against the sides of our gondola, and I edge myself to the very end of the wood, until the canal is beneath me. Dawn is in the air now, if not yet in the sky. I can feel it, like a great winch, pulling the sun slowly up to its breaking point above the horizon. I look down into the water. I am still frightened of it. Even though I know it is perhaps no deeper than the height of a room, it still feels fathomless to me. I am right to be scared. I have been inside it now. I know that drowning will be the most awful death in the world.

But Elena Crusichi will not drown. She will hear the hollow slap of the water against the wood as they row her out into the middle of the wide Orfano Canal. And though Mauro's fruit will have made her drowsy, she will feel the panic rising. But she will never feel herself sucked down into the black depths. Because as she sits there, next to the priest, with her hands tied in front of her, waiting, without warning the man behind her will slip a rope over her head and around her neck, and, with two or three hard, fast twists, choke first the breath and then the life out of her. Of course garroting is not nothing. As with every form of death, there are degrees of proficiency: it can be long or short, a bloody semidecapitation or a sudden, intense throttling. It all depends on the skill and experience of the executioner. And we have been promised the very best. She will gasp and retch for breath, and the struggle will be sharp and over soon enough.

Only her body will go down into the deep. Elena Crusichi will already be gone.

That is what Mauro's rich sauces, my lady's pleading and her open legs, have done for us. There was no last-minute pardon. Loredan did not lie to us. He did what he could, but he said it himself: at another time, perhaps; but an inflammatory crime in an inflammatory moment calls for a stern response. There will be no gloating, no spectacle. The point is not cruelty but stability. Venice the peaceful demands Venice the just.

As for what comes next, well, as I stand here, I am comforted by a memory—my God, it is so sharp, down through so many years—of a poem that Aretino read to me once in Rome, when he and I were both new to my lady's house and he would come into the kitchen to practice his vernacular wit among the servants. Oh, he was outrageous then; pretty, almost like a girl, clever, strutting, willing to fly into the face of the sun, and I was young and angry enough with my deformity to want to fly with him, to find the idea of rebellion against the Church and even God intoxicating. I remember his voice, so caustic and strong.

From summer to winter the rich
Are in Paradise, and the poor are in Hell.
And the blind fools who await the dove
With fasting and absolutions and Our Fathers
Serve only to fatten the orchard
For friars for their cloisters.

"So, Bucino! If that is true, which of us should be afraid of death now? Those who have it all already or the ones who go without? Imagine it. How would it be if the end was not Heaven or Hell but just an absence of life? My God, I swear that would be Heaven enough for most of us."

I am sure he confessed such heretical notions long ago, for he writes with a certain beauty about God now, and it is not, I think, just to keep him in the good books of the state. Revolution is a young man's fantasy; there is so much of life ahead in which to change your mind. Yet I am no longer young, and I still think of that poem, still wonder about the man who wrote it, if his absence of life proved also an absence of suffering.

The air is warm and gauzy. In front of me the sky is stained with pinks and mauves, mad colors, too wild for the moment— just like the morning when I set out from my lady's house in Rome to try to find the cardinal. So many died then. Thousands of them . . . like broken fragments in the mosaic floor.

The struggle will have stopped. The deed will be done. She will be one of those now.

And what of us? What are we now?

"Bucino?"

I don't hear the door opening, so her voice, though quiet enough, runs like a knife through me.

She is in her robe, her hair long and untidy down her back. Of course she has not slept either, simply kept her own vigil. She is carrying a pottery drinking cup. "Mauro made this for you: warmed malmsey."

"He is up?"

"They are all up. I don't think anyone has slept."

I take a sip. It is sweet and warm. Not like the water at all. After a while she puts her hand on my shoulder. I hear someone crying from inside. Gabriella. There is a lot to cry for. She will have no one to soothe the stabbing pains she gets during her cycle of the moon anymore.

"It's done," I say.

"Yes, it's done. Come in now and we will sleep a little."

But it seems it is not done. Not quite over yet.

I sleep, though for how long I have no idea, because, when

the frantic knocking wakes me, it feels as if it is still dawn. Somehow I get myself to the door and open it to see Gabriella's amazed, excited face. Oh, God, oh, God, what if they have pardoned her? What if we are saved?

"You have to come, Bucino. She's downstairs on the dock. Mauro saw her when he went out to throw away the rubbish. We don't know what to do. My lady is there, but you have to come."

My legs are bowed with tiredness, and they almost trip me as I rush, I am so bandy. I move to the *portego* loggia first, for at least I can see from there. My lady is standing almost directly beneath me on the dock, still, almost frozen. In front of her is a small child. She has a cloud of white hair, with the rising sun ablaze behind her. And at her feet sits a small, bulging bag.

I fall down the stairs and out through the water doors. My lady throws her hand behind her to stop me from going any farther. I halt. The child glances up, then down again.

My lady's voice is richest silk. "—tired to have come so far so early. Who brought you? Did you see the sun come up over the sea?"

But the child says nothing. Just stands and blinks in the light.

"You must be hungry. We have fresh bread and sweet jams inside."

Still nothing. Her mother pretended to be blind; now her daughter is as adept at faking deafness. It is a shrewd test, to be so good at keeping one's own counsel. And a skill one cannot learn early enough. I move around my lady's skirts carefully until I am in front of her.

She is smaller than I, and in the last weeks her legs have grown sturdier. I daresay she is using their new firmness now to back up her will. My God, she has enough of her mother in her to hound me to my grave. Oh, the pain of it, to see her again. But also the utter, utter joy. Her eyes flick to me, hold there for a whole, unblinking, solemn second, then move away again. At least she has acknowledged I am here.

My lady rests her hand on my shoulder. "I'll go and fetch us some food."

I nod. "And bring the engraved goblet out too," I say quietly. "The one that Alberini brought you as a first gift."

Her footsteps move inside.

I study this imp in front of me. There is griminess around the edges of her mouth, as if she has recently eaten something sticky, and there is a smudge on her forehead. Maybe she slept against the dirty wood on the boat and woke up with it. Under the halo of wild, white curls, her cheeks are fat, as if they have great bubbles caught inside them, and her mouth is pouting full. My God, she is lovely. I can see her on the ceiling of a room in a palace, wings too small for her chubby body, her truculence transformed into mischief, as she holds aloft our Lady's train while they propel themselves toward Heaven. Tiziano could use her to charm a flood of ducats out of his tightfisted mother superiors. But is it innocence he would capture here? I am not so sure. Certainly there is strength. And suspicion. I warrant something of her mother's intelligence too.

Of course she would have known better than anyone that there would be no children in this house unless someone gave us one, and how much it would be loved and cared for if someone did. An old great-grandparent and a mother at the bottom of the sea. The last will and testament of Elena Crusichi. And I understand that this is how it will be for me: how every time I look at her I will taste one in the other. Now and for as long as I live. That is the nature of my punishment.

My punishment, but also our saving.

My lady is so nervous with excitement that she almost drops the glass. The bread is warm in a basket, half a dozen small balls of it. I hold one out to her, for its smell would tempt Saint John the Baptist out of the wilderness. She wants it, I can tell. She won't give in, though. But this time there is slight movement of the head.

I put down the basket and pick up four or five more rolls. They are almost too soft for it, but I try anyway: juggling a few of them in the air until the aroma of fresh baking is all around us. She is watching now, and there is excitement in her face.

I let one drop. It falls close to her foot. I catch the rest, then pick it up and solemnly hold it out to her. Her hand comes out, and she takes it. For a second it looks as if she will just hold it, but then in one swift move it goes into her mouth, all in one bite.

"Look," I say as she chews. "I have something else for you." I lift my hand to take the goblet from my lady. "See? This here on the side, the writing? Isn't it clever? Does your grandfather do things like this?"

She nods slightly.

"It's for you. He left it here with us. Do you see? Look. Look at the letters. Here is your name. F-i-a-m-m-e-t-t-a."

Behind me, I hear my lady's sharp intake of breath.

The child looks eagerly to see where I'm pointing. Though she is too young to decipher letters, she knows her name well enough.

"It's for you. To drink out of while you are here. You can hold it if you want. Though you must be careful, for it will break easily. But then I think you know that already about glass."

She nods and holds out her hands for it, cupping it between her palms carefully as if it were a living thing that she is holding, and staring at the letters. And already I think I see a flash in her eyes that makes me know she will be reading them soon enough. She looks at the goblet for a long time, then hands it back to me.

"So, shall we go in?"

I pick up her bag, and she follows us into the house.

AUTHOR'S NOTE

The Venice of this novel is deeply rooted in research. While its main characters, Fiammetta Bianchini and Bucino Teodoldi, are born of my imagination, the city (like Rome before the sack) was famous for her courtesans, and a few such women were known to have kept dwarves, along with parrots, dogs, and other "exotics."

Some of the other players in the novel are real. The painter Tiziano Vecellio (Titian as he is better known) and the writer Pietro Aretino both lived in Venice at this time, as did the architect Jacopo Sansovino, who was responsible for many of the city's most beautiful High Renaissance buildings, though his most famous commissions were just beginning during the years in which this book is set.

During his long and stellar career, Titian painted a number of nudes, in particular a portrait of woman lying on a bed with a small sleeping dog and two maids in the background. The setting of the work was a room in his own house, and the canvas seems to have been in his studio in the mid-1530s. It ended up in Urbino in 1538, purchased by the duchy of Urbino's heir apparent of the time. Hence its present title, *The Venus of Urbino*. While art historians differ on the meaning of the painting, it seems likely that the model Titian used was a Venetian courtesan. The work hangs now in the Uffizi gallery in Florence.

Pietro Aretino is less well known outside his native land. He was nicknamed the Scourge of Princes, and his letters and satires earned him as many enemies as friends. He was known for his relationships with courtesans and was remarkable in that he penned both religious works and pornography, in particular "The Illustrious Sonnets," written in support of his friends Giulio Romano and Marcantonio Raimondi to complement their series of sixteen drawing-engravings known as *The Posti* or *The Modi*, which caused a huge scandal in Roman society in the mid-1520s. There is no extant copy of the original engravings, though a few fragments are held in the British Museum. Aretino's verses were republished alongside more crude woodblock copies of the originals, and from the mid–sixteenth century onward they were (and are still) highly sought after by collectors of erotic memorabilia. Two of the sixteen drawings and the accompanying sonnets, however, have been lost entirely. Aretino later went on to write *The Ragionamenti*, another largely pornographic tract including a section on the training of a courtesan, published in the 1530s. A few years after his death in 1556, the Counter-Reformation produced the Index of Prohibited Books. Aretino's work was high on the list.

With regard to the Jewish Ghetto in Venice, it is known that one Asher Meshullam, the son of a leader of the Jewish community, converted to Christianity in the mid-1530s. Because I could discover very little about him, I chose to give my convert a different name, and no doubt a different experience.

Which brings me to La Draga . . . A woman called Elena Crusichi, more popularly known as La Draga, is actually mentioned in court records of the time. She had a reputation as a healer and was partially disabled, with failing eyesight. I was entranced by the fragments of her story that are available and also by her name, but I have taken considerable fictional liberties with her character and her fate, for the real La Draga appears to have survived into old age, despite brushes with the authorities. Venice, in fact, behaved better than many states when it came to accusations of witchcraft, and there are no existing records of public burnings. However, criminals who embarrassed the state with either their crimes or the timing of them, were known to be dispatched more quietly at night by drowning in the Orfano Canal.

Also in the spirit of confession, I should add that, while a Register of Courtesans (a somewhat satirical tract with comments about the prowess and charges of such women) did indeed exist in Venice, I have predated its existence by a few years.

This is the extent of my conscious manipulation of history. Other mistakes, for which I apologize here, are due to the fact that extensive research and a deep love of the period cannot, alas, turn a fiction writer into a historian.

ACKNOWLEDGMENTS

I could not have written this novel without the inspirational support of many people.

For his scholarship and his invigorating conversation, I am greatly indebted to the Renaissance historian Lauro Martines. Also to my former art teacher Berenice Goodwin, and to Sheila Hale, Titian's latest biographer: each contributed her sharp eye and love of Venice, which saved me from many of my own mistakes. Tom Shakespeare helped me create Bucino as a living, breathing character. Gillian Slovo, Eileen Quinn, Michael Cristofer, and Janessa Laskin all proved to be stalwart companions on my journey. In Venice, Estela Welldon offered me the most perfect place to write, and in London, the staff of the British Library and the Warburg Institute made my research as painless as it could be.

I am indebted to everyone at Little, Brown, U.K., and Random House, U.S., for their powerful encouragement and support, and most especially to my agent, Clare Alexander, and longtime editor and friend Lennie Goodings.

Special mention must go to my teenage daughters, Zoe and Georgia, who endured endless spontaneous lessons on Venetian history, Renaissance Catholicism, and the sexual politics of the time with remarkable good humor and only the occasional hint of exasperation. And who, as the going got rough, devotedly fed their mother dinner when—because of the excitement of the story—she forgot to feed them.

But most of all, my love and gratitude go to Tez Bentley, who accompanied me intellectually on this rich, sometimes intimidating journey into the past, and whose acuity, sensitivity, and vision helped me to be more ambitious than I would otherwise have dared.

BIBLIOGRAPHY

Aretino, Pietro. *The Ragionamenti*. Odyssey Press, 1970.

————. *School of Whoredom*. Foreword by Paul Bailey. Hesperus Press, 2003.

————. *The Letters of Pietro Aretino*. Translated by George Bull. Penguin, 1976.

Beecher, Donald, and Massimo Ciavolella, editors. *Eros and Anteros: The Medical Traditions of Love in the Renaissance*. Imprint Ottawa: Dovehouse Editions, 1992.

Bradford, Sarah. *Lucrezia Borgia*. Penguin Viking, 2004.

Calimani, Richard. *The Ghetto of Venice*. Oscar Montadori Press, 1995.

Camporesi, Piero. *Bread of Dreams*. University of Chicago Press, 1989.

Castiglione. *Book of the Courtier*. Penguin Classics, 1967.

Cellini, Benvenuto. *Benvenuto Cellini's Autobiography*. Penguin, 1999.

Chambers, David, and Brian Pullan, editors. *Venice: A Documentary History 1450–1630*. Blackwell Press, 1992.

Crouzet-Pavan, Elizabeth. *Venice Triumphant*. Johns Hopkins University Press.

D'Arogona, Tulia. *Dialogue on the Infinitive of Love*. University of Chicago Press, 1997.

Davis, Robert. *Ship Builders of the Arsenale*. Johns Hopkins University Press, 1991.

————. *The War of Fists*. Oxford University Press, 1994.

————, and Garry Marvin. *Venice: The Tourist Maze*. Berkeley: University of California Press, 2004.

Elsenbichler, Konrad, editor. *The Premodern Teenager*. Toronto, Centre for Reformation and Renaissance Studies, 2002.

Ferraro, Joanne. *Marriage Wars in Late Renaissance Venice*. Oxford University Press, 2001.

Fortini Brown, Patricia. *Private Lives in Renaissance Venice*. Yale University Press, 2004.

———. *Narrative Painting in the Age of Carpaccio*. Yale University Press, 1998.

Goffen, Rona. *Franciscans in Venice*. Yale University Press.

Guicciardini, Luigi. *The Sack of Rome*. Italica Press, 1993.

Hollingsworth, Mary. *The Cardinal's Hat*. Profile Books, 2002.

Hook, Judith. *The Sack of Rome*. Palgrave Macmillan, 2004.

Hope, Charles. *Titian*. Chaucer Press, 2003.

Howard, Deborah. *The Architectural History of Venice*. Yale University Press, 2002.

Lane, Frederic. *Venice: A Maritime Republic*. Johns Hopkins University Press, 1973.

Lavin, Mary. *The Virgins of Venice*. Penguin, 2004.

Lawner, Lynne. *I Modi, Erotic Album of Sixteenth Century*. Northwestern University Press, 1988.

Martines, Lauro. *Strong Words*. Johns Hopkins University Press, 2001.

Masson, Georgina. *Courtesans of Rome*. St. Martin's Press, 1976.

McCray, W. Patrick. *Glass Making*. Ashgate Press, 1999.

Molmenti, Pompeo. *Venice Private Life*.

Morris, Jan. *Venice*. Faber and Faber, 1993.

Muir, Edward. *Civic Ritual in Renaissance Venice*. Princeton University Press, 1981.

Norwich, John Julius. *A History of Venice*. Penguin.

Pullan, Brian. *Rich and Poor in Renaissance Venice*. Blackwell Press, 1971.

Riddle, John M. *Contraception and Abortion from the Ancient World to the Renaissance*. Harvard University Press, 1992.

Rodgers, J., and R. M. Ward. *The Turks*.

Roissaude, Jacques. *Mediaeval Prostitution*. Barnes and Noble, 1997.

Rosenthal, Margaret F. *The Honest Courtesan*. University of Chicago Press, 1992.

Ruggiero, Guido. *Binding Passions*. Oxford University Press, 1996.

———. *Boundaries of Eros*. Oxford University Press, 1989.

Talvacchia, Bette. *Taking Positions*. Princeton University Press, 2001.

Teitzan-Conrat. *Dwarfs and Jesters in Art.* The Phaidon Press, 1957.

Toso, Gianfranco. *Murano: A History of Glass.* Arsenale Editrice, 2000.

Turner, J. G. *Schooling Sex.* Oxford University Press, 2003.

———, editor. *Sexuality and Gender in Early Medieval Europe.*

Zorzi, Alvise. *La vita quotidiana a Venezia nel secolo di Tiziano.* Rizzoli, 1990.

SARAH DUNANT is the author of the international bestseller *The Birth of Venus*, which has received major acclaim on both sides of the Atlantic. Her earlier novels include three Hannah Wolfe crime novels, as well as *Snow Storms in a Hot Climate*, *Transgressions*, and *Mapping the Edge*, all three of which are available as Random House Trade Paperbacks. She has two daughters and lives in London and Florence.

FAVONIVS.

P

FRICVS

A

FR. AFRICVS.

M

MERCVRIVS PRECETERIS HVIC FAVSTE EMPORIIS ILLVSTRO

VENETIE
M.D